THE BLACK ROCKS OF MORWENSTOW

By John Wilcox

The War of the Dragon Lady

Fire Across the Veldt

Bayonets Along the Border

Treachery in Tibet

Pirates – Starboard Side!
(a short story)

Dust Clouds of War

Starshine

The Black Rocks of Morwenstow

a&b

The Black Rocks of Morwenstow

John Wilcox

Allison & Busby Limited
12 Fitzroy Mews
London W1T 6DW
allisonandbusby.com

First published in Great Britain by Allison & Busby in 2016.

A CIP catalogue record for this book is available from
the British Library.

First Edition

ISBN 978-0-7490-1729-3

Typeset in 11/18.2 pt Sabon by
Allison & Busby Ltd.

The paper used for this Allison & Busby publication
has been produced from trees that have been legally sourced
from well-managed and credibly certified forests.

Printed and bound by
CPI Group (UK) Ltd, Croydon, CR0 4YY

Many years ago I was encouraged to write and taught how to do so by Judy Lamb.

This novel, then, is dedicated to her – wherever she may be now – with love and thanks

CHAPTER ONE

Key West, USA. Midsummer 1842

Joshua Weyland felt vaguely uncomfortable as he walked along the shoreline of this most southerly port in the United States of America. It was a sensation that was unfamiliar to him, for in the latter part of his twenty-five years he had trodden with confidence the docksides of most of the major ports of the world, from Shanghai to Singapore, Marseilles to Montevideo.

It was not that he looked out of place. He was a sailor in a sailor's environment and he looked the part: wide-bottomed canvas trousers held up by a broad leather belt from which a sheathed knife hung at its back; a faded canvas shirt, worn open at the neck; his weather-beaten countenance topped by a battered straw hat, tipped well back, so that sun-bleached curls peeped from under its brim, brown eyes set in open, regular features. Ordinary enough in this seafaring town. Only the folded copy of the *The Times* of

London thrust under his arm struck a discordant note.

Why, then, this sense of unease? Certainly, the humidity that seemed to cling to the merchants' warehouses fringing the sidewalk was unfamiliar. So, too, was the vista offered by the waters of the Gulf of Mexico. Out to sea the ocean presented, on this side of the island, a broad panorama of tropical blue or green. Nearer the shore, however, where the water was shallower, it merged into a sullen brown.

Further out, unseen from land, Josh knew that there were many islands of limestone outcrops, of which Key West itself was the largest. They seemed harmless, dotted here and there over the horizon, even looking picturesque in the daytime, like basking whales. Beyond them, however, he knew there lurked the greater danger of the half-submerged coral reefs, one of which had torn the bottom out of his ship as though it had been made of paper.

Perhaps it was this memory that made him feel insecure. He shook his head and walked on. He was thirsty and looking for an inn, a tavern where he could sit quietly and read his four-week-old copy of *The Times*, a luxury he had picked up in the shipping agent's office in the town. News from home was hard to get and the last letter he had had from Mary had been received in Cape Town, some six weeks ago.

Ah. Mary! He smiled as he conjured up her round, apple-cheeked face, her brown eyes sparkling as they walked on the cliffs near her home above Dover. The smile disappeared quickly as the thought of Dover, the nearest point in England to the Continent of Europe, reminded him that it was also the gateway to the cholera epidemic that had swept through the country. She had survived it, but it had taken her father, the vicar, and her two brothers. Did it still linger in the country? Perhaps *The Times* would tell him. His stride lengthened. He must find a bar – and he needed a drink, anyway.

A sign carrying an anchor and hanging low over a window that had been salt-spray washed by scores of hurricanes beckoned and he pushed the door open and entered. The bar was crowded and noisy and a fug of tobacco smoke enfolded him. The bottom of the counter was lined by a row of spittoons and he leant into a small space between the drinkers.

The barman raised an eyebrow interrogatively.

'Whisky and a beer,' said Josh.

'Rye, bourbon or Scotch?'

'Er . . . Scotch, thank you.'

Josh cursed himself for adding the pleasantry. Americans, he knew, never said please or thank you. He took the drinks, threw coins onto the counter and looked for somewhere to sit.

A small bench behind a table was vacant and he sat at it and took a sip of the whisky followed by a draught of the beer – 'starting a fire and putting it out' his father had called it. Then he opened his newspaper.

England seemed to be in a state of turmoil, with the nailers of the Black Country rioting, the army putting down demonstrations against turnpike tolls in Carmarthen and riots against the Corn Laws in Lancashire. And good Lord! The government has introduced income tax for the first time in peacetime – seven pence on the pound for incomes over £150! Ah well, at least that wouldn't affect him. That was far beyond what he could earn as second mate on a merchant ship.

He turned the page, squinting in the poor light to scan the small print. No sign, as far as he could see, of further cholera outbreaks.

Thank God! He hoped that Mary had continued to escape the dreaded scourge, escaped it so that he could hurry home now and they could be wed . . .

'You're a Limey, ain't yer?'

He looked up. The man standing, swaying slightly on the other side of the table, was huge, looking almost as wide as he was tall. Dressed in rough, well-worn sailing clothes, his face, carrying a six-day beard, was scowling.

Josh sighed. 'Well,' he said, 'I'm English, if that's what you mean.'

'Same thing. Bastards, all of you. Burnt down the White House, you did.'

'Oh come on. That was thirty years ago.'

'Well, we Yanks don't forget them things.' He put huge hands down on the table and leant forward. Josh could have put a match to the whisky fumes. 'An' I'll tell you somethin' else.'

Josh knew better than to argue. He didn't want to stoke the fire. He looked around. The bar, previously a hubbub of raised voices, had gone strangely quiet. Every face was now turned to him, most of them grinning. The barman, himself the size of a stevedore in the new steamships, was leaning across his counter, a half smile on his face. Josh gulped, he was about to receive a public beating. He decided to make one more conciliatory effort.

'Look,' he said. 'I don't see why you've picked on me. I'm English, yes, but I'm a sailor, just like you.'

'Are yer.' The big man straightened up. 'What's yer ship, then, sonny?'

'The barquentine, *Jenny Lee*. She foundered on the Washerwoman Reef three days ago. We were lucky to be rescued.'

'Oh no, you weren't, you lyin' bastard. We all know what 'appened there. Your ship was 'companied all the way from the Bahamas by a wreckin' ship from there an' was standin' by when your skipper deliberately ran his ship onto the reef, to get 'is share o' the insurance money. You was all rescued nice and neat, together with yer cargo. It was well planned.'

A chorus of approval rose from the crowd.

'What's more,' the big man leant across the table and prodded a huge finger into Josh's chest. 'That little arrangement, matey, stopped us wreckers 'ere in Key West from doin' an honest piece o' salvaging. If there's one thing we can't stand, it's English bastards from the Bahamas takin' our work from us.'

The howl of agreement was even louder now.

'Look,' said Josh, 'my skipper and his first mate are being investigated by a tribunal as we speak. If there's been wrongdoing it will come out in a court of law and they will be punished.'

'An' my aunt is the President of the USA. You're goin' to be punished 'ere an' now.' He seized Josh's shirt and pulled him towards him, raising his fist as he did so.

Josh Weyland, however, had not sailed the Seven Seas without fighting his way out of more than one barroom brawl and he acted instinctively now. Instead of pulling away from the big man's embrace he leant towards him, drew back his head and crashed his forehead into his assailant's nose. Then he pushed the table hard towards the sailor and crashed the edge down onto his toes.

Blood gushed from the nose and the man howled as the table crashed down. Josh skipped aside, ducked under a wild swing and then delivered two punches, from left and right fists, into the man's ample paunch.

11

Josh knew enough about fighting not to let an advantage slip away. As the crowd now, it seemed, roared him on, he rained punches, hard blows, into the big man's face, splitting open an eyebrow. Inevitably, however, it could not be all one-way traffic and the sailor swung a backhanded blow that sent Josh flying. For a moment, he stood gasping, his back to the wall.

This encouraged his assailant, who, spitting blood, lurched forward and swung his right fist in a great arc. Too great, in fact, for Josh was able easily to duck underneath it and sink two more heavy blows into the sailor's stomach. The shouts from the crowd now were undoubtedly those of applause, in appreciation of a man who knew how to handle himself in a fight.

This was true, however, of the sailor, too. For him, there were no rules in this sort of conflict. Blood streaming down his face and gasping for breath, he fumbled behind him and produced the knife that every sailor carried hanging in the small of his back, ready to cut away rigging that threatened the safety of his craft or himself.

'I'll carve yer eyes out, you Limey bastard,' he cried, advancing warily, the knife held back as he extended his other hand to judge his thrust.

'Oh no you won't.' The barman's voice rang out firmly as he swung a large belaying pin onto the big man's wrist, sending the knife spinning away. Then he hit the man firmly at the back of the head, so that he stumbled, dazed, onto the floor.

'You know the rules of the 'ouse,' the barman bent over and spoke loudly. 'Fists is fine. Knives is crime. Now get out of 'ere, Louis, before I call the militia. Get out, and don't come back until you've learnt some sense. Oh, and don't lurk around the corner waiting fer this lad to come out, cos he's got a knife too and the way he was goin' he could probably cut you up before you got near him.'

The barman looked around. 'All right, lads, the fun is over. Get on with yer drinkin' now.' As Louis slowly got to his feet, the barman gave him a half-friendly kick up the bottom to send him on his way.

'Now, son,' he said. 'Yer drink's bin spilt. You're due another on the 'ouse. Go on. Put the table up again an' I'll bring yer a beer and a Scotch.'

'Well, thank you. But I can pay.'

'Do as you're told. Sit down. I don't want any more fights 'ere. Things get broken an' they never get paid for.'

Josh realised that he was shaking, breathless and his knuckles hurt like hell. He licked his lips and regained his precious copy of *The Times*. The crowd, it seemed, had lost interest and the hum of conversation rose again as the barman deposited the Scotch and the beer on the table, drew up a stool and sat down.

Looking at him now, Josh realised that the man had a kindly, if gnarled, face that had probably seen many a watch at sea, with twinkling eyes and grizzled grey hair. His accent, though, was puzzling: difficult to pin down – certainly not southern states American – and yet vaguely familiar.

'What's yer name, son?'

'Joshua Weyland.'

'Ah yes. Second mate of the *Jenny*, eh?' He extended a hand. 'Albert Wilson from Liverpool, although they call me Al around here. Yes, a Limey, like you.'

Of course, that accent retained strong traces of the English north-west. Josh raised his eyebrows. 'Good Lord, what are you doing here?'

'Making more money from this place than I ever did from Yankee whalin' ships off Nantucket, I can tell you. Now,' he leant forward, 'not much goes on in little old Key West that I don't hear about in my bar. All that stuff that Louis was talkin' was the truth, from what I hear. Is that right?'

Josh frowned. 'I honestly don't know. It's true that our skipper seemed to pick up the wrecking ship in Nassau and she sailed with us until we hit that reef in the darkness. But, if there was some sort of wrecking deal, I know nothing about it. All I want to do now is to get home. Look,' he leant forward, 'I don't really understand this wrecking business. From where I come from, wrecking is really about luring a ship onto rocks and then plundering the cargo. But it seems it's different here.'

'It certainly is.' Wilson turned around and gestured to the woman – his wife? – who had taken command of the bar. 'The usual, Bessie,' he cried. 'I'll take it here. No, wrecking is a respectable, accepted trade here. It's even licensed by the State of Florida. You can't go to the aid of a ship in trouble to get her off the reef and take off crew and cargo unless you've got a licence from the State Government.'

'Louis and people like him,' he gestured to the crowd, 'and that's most of them in here, they earn their living, waiting for a ship to hit the reef, then they race out to be the first to offer help to the grounded skipper to save crew and cargo and claim salvage.'

He shook his head. 'It's a rough game, sailing usually in filthy weather in fast schooners and then working like pigs on the reefs to unload the ships and then get 'em off the coral. Oh yes, we lose quite a few lads here in Key West in this game. You could say that this town is the centre of the wrecking business.'

14

Josh nodded his head and then frowned. 'But how do the schooner captains know when a ship has hit a reef? Visibility will be terrible in a storm, won't it?'

Al's eyes lit up. 'Well, if you walk around Key West you'll see quite a few high wooden towers. Probably the highest of them is right in the centre of town at Mallory Square. The wreckers with telescopes man them during daylight hours and as soon as a ship in trouble is seen the call will go out "wreck ashore" and then the fun begins. There is a scramble to put to sea and the first boat to reach the wreck is called "the wrecking master". That skipper then has control of the wreck and him an' his crew usually gets the biggest cut.'

'What about the crew of the wrecked ship and passengers, if they have any?'

'Well, by federal law the wreckers are obliged to try to save crews and passengers as well as the ship itself. In fact, the law says that they are only allowed to remove enough cargo to float the wrecked ship free at the next high tide, unless of course it is totally wrecked.'

Al's brown face broke into a sea of wrinkles. 'Obviously, when the matter goes to court there are a lot of questions to be answered. But the judge usually sorts it out amicably enough, though there can be lots of fuss.'

Josh nodded. 'Is there any question of ships being lured onto the reefs by disreputable wreckers?'

'No. Maybe that used to happen years ago, but not now. The wreckers play fair and will warn a skipper if he is likely to be heading for a reef.'

Josh rubbed his sore knuckles and took a pull from his beer. 'But are there enough shipwrecks to keep these men in business?'

15

'Oh bless you, yes. These are some of the most dangerous waters in the world. First time here?'

'Yes.'

'Even so, you will probably know that the Florida Keys lie in a one-hundred-and-fifty-mile semicircle along the northern and western edges of the Straits of Florida, guarding the entrance, so to speak, of the Gulf of Mexico. Key West is to the Gulf of Mexico what Gibraltar is to the Mediterranean. It commands the outlet of all trade from Jamaica, the Caribbean, the Bay of Honduras and the Gulf.'

Wilson sat back proprietarily. 'We've got a wonderful harbour here in Key West. Incidentally, d'you know how this place got its name?'

'I've always presumed because it was the most western of the islands.'

'That's true, but it's not the reason. No.' Al was warming to his tale now. 'The Spaniards were the first here, of course, and it was then an Indian burial ground, so the dons found scores of bones. Accordingly, they called it "Cayo Hueso", Bone Island. When the British took over in the seventeen hundreds the name sounded to them like "Key West". And so it has remained, thanks to us Limeys.'

Josh grinned. 'Old what's-his-name, Louis, didn't seem to give us credit for it.'

'Oh, he's a bit of a drunkard but all right when you get to know him. Now – I was telling you about this harbour.'

'So you were.'

'It's deep enough to take the largest ships and it's protected on all sides from the weather, except from the south-west and bad stuff doesn't often come from there, so sailing ships can enter the harbour in any wind. But, by gum, the weather can be foul. We've

16

got the Gulf Stream current, goin' at a rate of knots, unpredictable countercurrents, calms in summer, hurricanes in the autumn – what they call the fall here – and gales in the winter. And all of this swirling around God knows how many reefs just above and below the surface, with teeth sharper 'n sharks.

'Why,' he leant forward, 'this year we've been having shipwrecks at the rate of one a week.' He seemed almost to be boasting of the dangers of his adopted home.

'Blimey! So wrecking is quite a profitable business here?'

'Profitable and almost the only trade, except for merchanting, of course. And most of the merchants around here own the wrecking schooners.'

A silence fell between them, broken eventually by Wilson. 'You'll see now why old Louis cut up rough a minute or two ago. First of all, these chaps are all sailors and bloody good ones. They would never deliberately wreck a ship, which the word is what your skipper did. And they are very protective of their trade here. The Bahamians used to come and try and pinch it. But our lads roughed 'em up and they don't try it much now.'

Wilson screwed up his eyes. 'Have you got involved in this tribunal?'

'No, and I don't want to be. I know nothing about any plan to deliberately drive the ship on to the reef. I wasn't on watch when it happened. The first I knew was the crash when we hit the rocks. It threw me out of my bunk.'

'Did your skipper try and get her off?'

'Not that I remember. There wasn't much he could do, I guess. He just signalled for help from the Bahamian ship nearby.'

17

'Hmm.' Wilson let his gaze wander around the room. 'Sounds fishy to me, son. What are your plans now, then?'

Josh gave a sad smile. 'Try and find a ship that can take me home and then get the hell out of here. I've been away for nearly two years, sailing round the China Seas and other parts of the East. I've got a fiancée that's been waiting for me for all that time and I don't want to be drawn into hanging on here and giving evidence at this damned tribunal.'

'Got any money to pay for your passage?'

'Well, I managed to get my wages out of the *Jenny Lee*'s agent here so I have some money, but I want to hang onto it to pay for the wedding and to find a place for Mary when I'm away after we're married. Would you know of a ship in port that needs a second mate?'

'Got your ticket?'

'Oh yes, I'm qualified.'

'Well . . .' Wilson drew out the word and rubbed a hand over his chin. 'There is a brig in the harbour that's due to sail for Bristol, Gloucester or somewhere like that the day after tomorrow and I hear she's short-handed. But I doubt if you'll get a second mate's berth. She only runs to about ten hands in all.'

'That doesn't matter. I'll ship as a deckhand if I can get a berth.'

'Right. She's called *The Lucy* and she's alongside the main jetty here. Just walk down the dockside until you come to her.' He frowned. 'Don't know much about the skipper – a Yankee called Lucas – but I hear he's a bit of a queer bird. Know anything about the Bristol Channel? I remember it can be a real bitch when a nor'westerly blows.'

'I'm from Somerset, so I know it quite well.'

'Good. That should help you. Now I've got to get back to the bar, or Bessie will start giving pints away to good-lookin' sailors.' He extended a hand. 'Good luck to you, lad. Remember me to good old England.'

'Let me buy you a drink before I go.'

'Better not. It doesn't do to get a woozy head in this bar. No. Off you go now. Go find *The Lucy*. Oh, and keep a weather eye peeled for that mad bugger Louis. He likes to carry a grudge.'

'I will. Thanks, Al – particularly for what you did back there.'

Carefully folding *The Times* and slipping it into his trouser pocket, Josh made for the door and, once outside, drew in the sea air thankfully. Humid or not, it was better than the fug of the bar.

The Lucy was not difficult to find. She was secured alongside the quay and she sat virtually motionless, for there was no swell inside the harbour. Josh walked away a little and, from a doorway, carefully studied the brig.

She carried four square sails on each of her two masts, although now, of course, they were furled and lashed rather slackly, Josh noted, to the yards. An immensely long bowsprit pointed upward from the prow above a figurehead fixed beneath it. The ship was rigged to carry a fore and aft triangular sail between the masts and a furled jib and staysail on stays from the foremast to the bowsprit and a gaff-rigged spanker on the main boom down aft. Viewed in profile, *The Lucy*'s lines were elegant, with a sharply raked bow and an overhanging stern from which a jolly boat hung from davits. She had been painted with a fashionable white strip along her length just under the gunwale, giving her the touch of an old frigate from Nelson's time. But Josh noted that the strip needed repainting and there was a slight air of neglect about the ship overall. The anchor and what could be seen of the chain cable was well rusted and the ropes by which she was held against the dockside were frayed. What was it that Al had said about the skipper – 'he was a bit of a queer bird . . . ?' A lax one, too, by the look of it.

Josh left the protection of the doorway and approached the gangway. He noted a man on deck, wearing the peaked, if battered, cap of an officer. 'Permission to come on board, sir,' he called.

The reply was not welcoming. 'What's yer business?'

'I understand you're short-handed. I'd like to sail with you.'

The mate walked across to the head of the gangway and stared across at Josh. 'Last ship?' he asked laconically.

'The *Jenny Lee*, out of London. Last port Cape Town. She struck a reef here three days ago.'

'You've signed off from her?'

'Aye, sir. I have my papers. I've got a second mate's ticket, too.'

The mate looked skywards. 'Ah, we're not looking for officers, sailor. There's not room for another mate. It's just me and the skipper.'

'But don't you need another watchkeeper?'

That seemed to have struck home, for sailing ships usually had three watches with an officer of sorts in charge of each. The master stayed aloof from such duties. 'Wait there,' said the mate. 'I'll find the captain.'

He returned within three minutes. 'Come on board and follow me,' he said.

The two made their way aft. 'Where are you bound?' asked Josh.

'Gloucester.'

'What are you carrying?'

The mate gave him a sharp look as if to say 'Mind your own business' but thought better of it. 'Cotton,' he said. 'Millions o' bales of the bloody stuff.'

The master's cabin was small but well lit with a stern window looking out over the hanging jolly boat. Josh detected a smell of whisky pervading the interior. Captain Lucas had obviously been lying on his bunk because his breeches were undone and his shirt open and hanging over his belt. He had not shaved between the luxurious sideburns that hung over his jowls and his eyes, which eyed Josh incuriously, were sunken. Unsteadily, he walked towards a chair stationed behind a crowded desk and sat in it heavily. He made no gesture for Josh to take the chair facing him.

'All right, Mr Mitchell,' he said to the mate. 'Get back to your work.'

The mate knuckled his forehead and left the cabin.

'So, you were on the *Jenny Lee*?' Captain Lucas spoke in the flat, nasal tones of the north-eastern states of America.

'That's right, Captain. I sailed as second mate on the passage from Canton.'

'Aren't you goin' to be called as witness in this damned enquiry that's being held?'

He unstoppered a wide-based ship's decanter that stood on his desk and poured himself a tumblerful. Josh smelt whisky again, but he was not asked to join the captain.

'I have received no summons,' he said. 'I am just anxious to get out of here to get back to England. I have been away from home for nearly two years now. I am due to be married when we reach land.'

Lucas looked up, a half-smile on his lips. 'I wouldn't hurry if I was you, sonny. Marriage ain't exactly what it's made out to be.'

'That may be well so, sir, but I am anxious to see my girl again.'

'Huh. Right. How long have you been at sea and what ships have you sailed in?'

'Went to sea when I was twelve as cabin boy on a big East Indiaman. I'm twenty-five now. Served as a deckhand in a variety of ships: barquantines, topsail schooners, brigs – brigs mainly. Just like *The Lucy*. Studied for my tickets and have made second mate so far. I mean to be a master.'

Lucas took a long draught of the whisky and wiped his mouth with a grimy hand. 'Do you, now. Don't be in too much of a hurry. You might regret what you wished for. Well, I'll take you on. Have you sailed the Bristol Channel?'

'Many times, sir. I was born in Somerset.'

'Ah, that might just come in handy. You'll ship as a deckhand with a deckhand's pay.' He leant forward. 'But in view of your experience, I'll make you watchkeeper and, if you prove yourself worth it, I'll give you another two pounds on top at the end of the voyage. Agreed?'

'Agreed, sir.'

'Right.' From among the mess of papers on his desk he drew forward a large daybook. 'What's your name?'

'Weyland. Joshua.'

'Very well, Sign here.'

Josh did so.

'Welcome aboard, Joshua Weyland. Now, go and get your gear and stow it in the fo'castle. Then report to the mate. If we get a decent offshore wind, we'll sail at dawn. There's not much tide to worry about here.'

'Thank you, Captain.'

There was a spring in Josh's step as he made his way back to the office of the *Jenny*'s agent where he had been allowed to stow his canvas bag safely for two nights, while he slept in a dosshouse near the dockside. Saving money until he got home was ever-present in his mind. Picking up his belongings and returning the copy of *The Times*, he walked on to his miserable so-called lodgings and collected the small washbag that he had left there and turned back to *The Lucy*. He was on his way home at last!

It was his heavy kitbag, in fact, which saved him. Walking down a backstreet on his way to the dockside – a dark street so narrow that he could almost touch the sides with outstretched arms – he stumbled over a cobblestone, just as a knife hurtled over his arched back and buried itself, quivering into a doorway.

Instinctively, Josh picked up his bag to provide some sort of defence as he whirled round. He just had time to see Louis rushing at him, a second knife in his hand. Josh threw the bag at the feet of the big man, causing him to trip and sprawl on the wet cobbles.

Immediately, Josh leapt upon him and thrust his own knife just under Louis's ear. 'Now, listen,' he hissed. 'If you move, I'm going to slit your throat from ear to ear. Understand?'

The man nodded, still gasping for breath.

'Good. Now keep listening. If I so much as catch sight of you again in this town I will kill you, as sure as God made little apples. Now, just to say goodbye to you and to stop you following me, I'm going to give you a little parting present. Just remember that Limeys can fight too, you great hulking brute.'

Turning quickly, Josh thrust the knife deeply into the calf of the big sailor. Louis's howl was loud enough to fetch the US militia from its new guardhouse, so Josh jumped to his feet, swung his bag onto his shoulder and hurried away.

Once he had crossed *The Lucy*'s gangplank he allowed himself to feel safe and pushed his way, nodding, past the hands working on the deck until he reached the fo'c'sle, the crew's quarters in the bow. Like all fo'c'sles it was dingy, dark and smelling of perspiration, damp and tobacco, but to Josh it felt like sanctuary. Breathing heavily, he made a pillow of his kitbag at the end of what was an unoccupied bunk, laid down his head upon it and closed his eyes for a moment to regain his breath.

Then he sprang up, pulled out his belongings from the bag, changed into working clothes – old shirt, leggings, overalls and a woollen hat – and threw the rest of the bag's contents into the wooden locker under his straw mattress. He saw with relief that there was a small hinge and padlock on the locker, with a key in the lock. Carefully he placed an oilskin bag, containing his second mate's ticket, his letters from Mary and his savings of thirty guineas in gold coins, underneath his clothes at the bottom of the locker and locked it.

Then, with a huge sense of relief, he turned out on deck to report to the mate. He was not sorry to leave Key West behind him. He was at sea again, where, despite the wrecking of the *Jenny Lee*, at least he felt secure and at home.

CHAPTER TWO

Well before the sun rose, the crew of the *The Lucy* answered the cry of 'All hands on deck to make sail' and both watches (there were only two for this voyage, it seemed) swarmed up into the rigging to set the royals and the topgallants so that, when the early morning offshore wind arrived to please Captain Lucas, the canvas bulged obligingly and the vessel eased away from her berth with hardly a ripple.

Lucas may not have been the most demanding of skippers or Mitchell the most houseproud of mates, but they seemed to know their business, for they took *The Lucy* unerringly between the coral reefs and half-islands that studded the surface of the sea off Key West.

As the brig began to heel to the wind, Josh watched with interest as she passed several of what he presumed to be wrecking schooners, returning to harbour. They seemed comparatively flimsy craft, with little freeboard, so indicating that they would be wet boats in a seaway, and carrying plenty of fore-'n-aft canvas. All of them were making good headway, creating creaming bow waves and leaving straight wakes astern of them.

He wondered how vessels with such little freeboard would be able to stow the cargoes they salvaged from the stricken ships they serviced. They would surely have to make many trips to the wrecks.

Josh shook his head. What a strange business, with so-called 'wreckers' being licensed to do their scavenging work! When he was growing up in Burnham-on-Sea, Somerset, he had heard stories from the past of how the wild men of the North Cornish coast would set up lights on the cliffs to offer false hope of safe anchorages to storm-swept ships coming in from the Atlantic. Their skippers, expecting protected harbours, would instead be lured onto the rocks of that forbidding coastline. But that, he knew, was long ago. It wouldn't happen now.

Or would it? He seemed to remember, before he set sail for the East, reading a reference from a Constabulary Force Commission report that spoke of men onshore 'using every endeavour to bring a ship into danger rather than help her', so that she could be wrecked and plundered.

It was true that he knew of no cases of wrecks being caused by false lights onshore. But then the Cornish coast, both north and south, was thinly populated and poorly policed and it would be no surprise therefore if such cases were never, or rarely, brought to court. There was, of course, a law against the practice, which offered death as the penalty for such transgressions. Yet why should such a law be put onto the Statute Book for a crime that was never committed?

Smuggling was a different matter, which, despite the efforts of the newly established coastguard, flourished throughout Devon and

Cornwall and, indeed, on most of the coasts of Britain. Certainly in the south-west it was regarded as a right, a respectable source of income for the people of the peninsula. As, of course, was wrecking – their word for salvaging and making off with the cargoes and sometimes the very structure of the ships that were tossed onto their cruel coasts. He had heard that many houses in Cornish villages near the coast had been constructed of timber broken off the wrecks.

A wry grin crept across Josh's lips as, high aloft, he shuffled along the mainsail yard, his boots swaying on the 'horse' – the safety footrope hung under the yards – to cast off the lashings and let the slack mainsail fall. How many different interpretations there were of the word wrecker! But he had had enough of the whole murky business and he was glad to leave behind him in the Florida Keys his own experience of the practice.

The wind was fair and before long they were completely clear of the Gulf of Mexico and its encircling Keys and the skipper ordered a course to the north-east to take them across the Atlantic to their next landfall at the tip of Cornwall.

Josh was glad to feel the fresh, keen air of the ocean on his cheeks and to see the smudge of land that was the mainland of Florida sink below the horizon. Whenever sailing with a new ship he was glad to get away from land so that, if the weather turned dangerous, they would have plenty of sea room. Autumn was the season for hurricanes in the Caribbean, he knew, and it was best to test *The Lucy*'s seaworthiness out in the open sea when and if they were caught in these vicious storms.

That afternoon he took his first trick on the wheel. He was less than pleased at the ship's response to the small adjustments he made to keep her on course. She seemed sluggish and unresponsive, compared to the *Jenny Lee*, perhaps because the keel of his new ship was coated with barnacles. Another example of the poor maintenance operated by Captain Lucas?

Down below, he met the men of his watch for the first time. They were the usual mixture of nationalities to be found in a ship far from its base: Englishmen, of course, but also an American from Boston, a Lascar and a large, genial Dane from Copenhagen. He took to the Scandinavian right away and afterwards they sat together on deck as *The Lucy* heeled slightly to the gentle wind and the stars began to twinkle as they peeped down at them from between the sails.

The Dane, Jorgen Grumm, looked at his watchkeeper with interest. He saw a fresh-faced, brown-eyed young man in what appeared to be the peak of physical condition: about five feet ten inches tall, broad shoulders, no beer-drinker's belly, but a muscular stomach and slim hips.

Equally, Josh considered the Dane. He was built like a Viking, well over six feet tall, with the bluest of eyes, and legs and arms that took him over the rigging with ease and grace.

'Have you sailed with this skipper and mate before, Jorgen?' he asked.

The Dane puffed on his pipe and nodded. 'Oh *ja*. I joined ship at Oslo, made the passage to London and then to here.'

'Are they good sailors, would you say?'

The Dane shot him a quick look from under his bushy eyebrows. 'Why you ask that?' he said. 'You got good reason to ask, eh?'

'No, well, not exactly. It's just that the ship doesn't look as though it's as well maintained or even sailed as well as it should be.' He pointed upwards. 'Look at that mains'l. I would say that the trim is not set to get the best out of her. What do you think?'

'I tink you are right,' he nodded again. 'I saw it earlier. These officers are – what do you say in English – a bit sloppy, I tink.'

'Did you have any weather coming over?'

'No. Sea very calm.'

'So the skipper and mate weren't exactly put under any strain?'

'No. But they do nothing wrong, as far as I can tell. I tell you one ting, though.' He lowered his voice. 'The skipper, he drinks. Whisky, I tink.'

'Yes, I smelt it. Well, let's hope that the Atlantic is kind and that the south-westerly that's normal in the Bristol Channel doesn't veer to a nor'westerly and blow into a gale. There's not much room to manoeuvre a sailing ship just south of Lundy Island.'

'Ah *ja*. I hope, too. Perhaps we both swim home, eh?' They both laughed.

The Atlantic was, in fact, kind to them until they entered the Doldrums, that strange patch of water in mid ocean where the wind deserted sailing ships, so that vessels seem to wallow, like flies caught in aspic, with no forward movement and where the same patches of seaweed would keep them company for days at a time. So it was now. The ship was dressed in lightweight, fine-weather sails to catch the faintest of breezes, but they hung, flapping plaintively from the yards as though they too were depressed at losing their sense of purpose.

Not that it was a time of relaxation for the crew. They were kept busy continually, bracing the yards round and trimming the sails to capture the merest hint of a breeze that might mature into a wind, a proper wind. There was still time, however, for Josh to take out his precious cache of Mary's letters and reread them all. Not that she was, he had to reflect ruefully, the most colourful of correspondents. She wrote, in her schoolgirl, rounded hand, of the daily chores she undertook in the vicarage to help her mother, now so painfully bereaved: of milking the two cows that they possessed, of regularly cleaning the church and of looking after the domestic needs of the young, unmarried clergyman who had replaced Mary's father in the parish. She and her mother had been allowed to stay on at the vicarage, in fact, in exchange for undertaking these tasks.

At first, when Mary wrote of the young man's arrival from the east London parish where he had served as curate, Josh had developed strong feelings of jealousy towards him. These gradually died down, however, as the tone of Mary's news about her life in Kent changed little. It seemed that the young man had slipped into the family's life without causing even a ripple of change or resentment.

The Reverend Charles Osborne, in fact, sounded as innocuous as he was, well, boring: a man of the cloth, completely dedicated to his calling and the caring of his flock. From Mary's infrequent references to him in her latest letters it seemed as though the clergyman had no interests or desires outside his vocation. No cause for jealousy any more.

No. Mary had stayed true to him, of that he was sure. She was anxious to be married and to have children. And she always ended her letters declaring her love for him, although she now regularly expressed the hope that, after his return, he would settle down in a seafaring job that did not take him so far away and for such long periods.

They had met, in fact, when he had shipped as a hand on the cross-Channel packets that allowed him to lodge with the vicar and his wife and children near Dover most nights. It was his desire to widen his experience and to gain promotion that had prompted him to serve in 'blue water' ships. While he was lodging at the vicarage, however, he worked hard to be useful: drawing water, chopping wood and even milking the cows, efforts which he redoubled after the cholera had taken the men of the family.

Josh had fallen in love with Mary almost immediately. At first she did not reciprocate, shaking away his hand as he tried to twine his fingers around hers as they walked on the clifftop above Dover. Gradually, however, she came around and, although she allowed no fondling – a discipline which frustrated Josh, for Mary had a more-than-ample bosom and a swan-like neck – she was happy to be kissed and hugged when they lay on the edge of a cornfield.

He proposed to her shortly after her father and brothers had died and was accepted shyly by Mary, although, of course, she insisted that any union had to be blessed by her mother. Mrs Jackson, however, was not happy to see her only child betrothed to a penniless deckhand, despite her fondness for Josh.

'Give it two years, Joshua,' she said. 'You are young. Go away if you must but show me that you can prosper in your profession and provide a good home for my Mary. Then you can wed.'

So, for the first time, Josh had taken sailoring seriously. While serving on long-haul ships to Africa and the Far East, he had studied assiduously and won his tickets as third and then second mate. On landing, he intended now to submit his application for the next examination so that he could qualify as a first mate and then find a ship that traded in coastal waters off Europe. Then Mrs Jackson could not possibly withhold her consent and he and Mary could marry and – he tingled at the prospect – make children.

A cry from the masthead ended his reverie and he tucked the letters back into their oilskin packet. A sharp crack like a pistol shot sounded as the mains'l split in two as a sudden gust of wind – real wind – hit it hard.

Josh filled his lungs to shout orders, then thought better of it. That blast of wind, he knew, was the forerunner of a heavy squall and the lookout on the masthead was pointing to the western horizon where blue-black storm clouds were gathering. He must fetch the mate or the captain from their cabins.

But the mate, at least, had heard the sound of the torn mains'l and burst from his cabin, buttoning up his jacket.

'All hands on deck to shorten sail,' he bellowed. 'Watch on deck furl the royals NOW. Weyland, get your watch to put two reefs in the topgallants. Quickly, before we lose all the bloody sails.'

Josh scrambled up the ratlines and, looking to the west, saw the squall bearing down on them, causing the once placid surface of the ocean to spring up angrily as the heavy raindrops thundered down. Reaching the topgallant yard, he edged his bare feet along the horses and began pulling up the buntlines into a loose reef, which he tucked under his arm, while he hung onto the yard with his other arm – 'one hand for the ship, the other for yourself' was the motto to be followed in a storm. He began trying to grab the reef lines, the ties that hung down from the sail, so that he could make a proper reef. He felt the horses tighten under his feet and realised that Jorgen had joined him, so he edged further out along the yard to make room for him. Within a minute, they had subdued the flapping sail and reefed it.

The rigging was now crawling with sailors as most of the square sails were reefed and the ship, which had heeled over dangerously as the full force of the squall had hit her, was now racing ahead at a more acceptable angle, the helmsman on duty happy to bring her to the bearing that would take them home.

Looking down, Josh could see the mate, standing four-square to the wind, with a great smile breaking his normally melancholy features.

But . . . where was the captain?

Josh could see no sign of him as he heard the mate call to bring the crew back down to the deck. He presumed that the task of changing sails would commence, as soon as this squall abated. Surely the captain would have noticed the heeling of the deck and would make his appearance? Yet his cabin door remained closed.

Josh looked across to catch Jorgen's eye. The Dane grinned broadly and made a drinking motion with his hand. Josh smiled back but he felt less than happy.

The North Atlantic in September could be a treacherous place. As they funnelled down into the Bristol Channel, the brig would need a cool head in command to take her up past that Cornish coast, with its rocks reaching out like sharp, black fingers into the sea. He recalled that the cliffs that ran from Bude up to Hartland Point were called 'The Wrecker's Coast'.

He also recalled a ditty that had stuck in his brain since he had first sailed those waters as a child:

From Padstow Point to Lundy Light
Is a watery grave by day and night.

He shuddered involuntarily.

The skipper never did put in an appearance on that day, as all hands were put to bending on the heavy canvas sails. Josh eventually plucked up courage to talk to the mate about it.

'Mr Mitchell,' he asked. 'Has the captain been ill?'

The mate's great eyebrows came down like a hedgerow. 'Not that I know of. What business is it of yours, anyway, Weyland?'

'Well, sir, I know the waters we are going to be sailing in once we round the Lizard and they are not easy, particularly if we hit bad weather. The distance between Lundy Island and Hartland Point, for instance, is only ten miles and I know from experience that the light on Lundy can't easily be seen once visibility gets bad. I—'

He was cut short. 'That will be enough from you. Get back to your work. When the skipper and I want your help we will ask for it. Get up to the fore t'gallants and stay there 'til I call you down.'

'But—'

'Up that mast, damn you.'

Captain Lucas, in fact, ventured out on deck when they were nearing landfall. The weather was fine and it was the sort of day that made Josh glad that he was a sailor: the wind strong enough to keep *The Lucy* bowling along at some eight or nine knots, the sky a clear blue, the sun sparkling on the water and the ocean itself bluish green with a gentle swell that seemed to have been born off Newfoundland.

The skipper looked wizened and hunched and his face, in stark contrast to those of his crew, a sickly yellow. He cast a quizzical eye up the rigging to the sails and, presumably liking what he saw, he coughed, turned and went back to his cabin.

'Another liddle tipple, I tink,' said Jorgen.

'Well, I just hope the weather doesn't turn on us.'

They were interrupted by a cry of 'Land ho!' from the masthead.

'Is it Cornwall, then?' asked Jorgen.

'No. More likely the southern coast of Ireland, because the course we have been set will have taken us in a wide sweep, a sort of curve, across the Atlantic.'

'Ah, you know navigation. I wish I did. Will we put in somewhere, d'you tink, before we reach this Gloucester place?'

'Not if we are to sail up the Bristol Channel, which we must. There are no real harbours on that Cornish north coast until we reach Bristol and, if I was the skipper, I would want to make up the time we lost in the Doldrums. So straight up to Gloucester, I would say.'

He sniffed the keen breeze. 'Weather seems fine, anyway. We should make the most of it.'

And so they did. *The Lucy* had stood well out to sea approaching the British Isles, giving the coast of Cornwall a wide berth so that Lucas resisted the temptation to put in at Penzance or St Ives, setting a course to take her north-east up the centre of the Bristol Channel.

'Good,' said Josh to Jorgen, as they smoked a pipe together before turning in. 'The wind's from the south-east, so he should keep her slightly to the north to give us plenty of room south of Lundy. Let's hope the wind stays.'

But it did not.

Josh awoke well before his watch was due on deck. He realised that the wind had come up and, by the feel of the ship, had now backed from the north-west. Ah, hell! Just what he had feared! He laboured to pull on his oilskins, for he could hear the rain beating down on deck, and was dressed before he heard Mitchell cry: 'All hands on deck to shorten sail.'

Quickly, he fumbled in his locker for the little waterproof bag that contained all his worldly treasures. He tied it firmly to his belt under his oilskins and groped his way towards the hatchway. His worst fears were realised as he gained the deck. The night was black but not so dark that he could not see that the sea had turned into a maelstrom of short-pitched waves, their tops white and sending spume away in horizontal sheets. The wind was howling between the masts like the voices of a thousand demented souls and he became concerned for the safety of the sails, despite them being heavy storm-proof.

'Don't stand and gape,' howled Mitchell. 'Get up aloft and put a reef in the topsails.'

Josh caught a glimpse of the skipper, a small figure standing by the helmsman, huddled under oilskins, before he hauled himself up the ratlines, gripping tightly against the force of the wind. He realised that the order to shorten sail had been belated; a good seaman would have reacted as soon as the wind had shifted. Now, there was precious little time as the wind bulged the sails out and the ship heeled over strongly to starboard. He stole a glimpse to the south-east. No sign of land yet, thank God, although he could see little, anyway.

Josh had experienced typhoons in the China Sea and caught the edge of a hurricane when leaving the Bahamas, but they were nothing like as frightening as this. It was no mere squall but a real nor'westerly, coming out of the northern Atlantic and screaming on its way towards the Bay of Biscay. What made it worse was that Josh had no idea how far they had been able to sail up from the Atlantic into the Channel towards Bristol – and, of course, how near they now were to the fearful north-Cornish coast.

With the strong figure of Jorgen at his side, he was able to reef the topsail. As best he could sense from near the masthead, the helmsman down below was trying to bring the brig round towards the north. As he watched, the diminutive figure of the captain joined the man at the wheel and together they wrestled against the forces of wind and sea.

It seemed to make no difference but Josh could not stay to watch for he and Jorgen must now slip down to the topsail yard to double-reef that straining sail, which fought them like a mad thing, water guttering from the ends to be whisked away by the rampaging wind.

Would the skipper order all sails to be reefed, so that they would ride out the storm under bare poles? Of course not! That might be a rational thing to do, given the strength of the wind, if they were miles from land in mid Atlantic. But it would be madness with the Cornish coast so near, for they would need sails to harness some of the wind's force and take them past the dangerous headland ahead. Josh remembered, too, that the sea hereabouts narrowed down to the Lundy Tidal Stream, a strong current that rushed up the Channel from the Atlantic. If it took *The Lucy* in its grip, then it might carry them through that so-narrow gap between the island and Hartland Point. Or, of course, it could push them to the south-east and negate all efforts by the helmsmen to bring the head around and gain some precious sea room away from the coast . . .

The ship was now heeling over so that the tip of her main yards dipped into the sea and the mate had detailed a man to nail down the hold hatches and put extra lashings on the boats and water butts: a sure sign that the conditions were demanding the most extreme measures.

Josh's seaman's brain pondered what else could be done. A sea anchor, perhaps – a makeshift raft-like structure that could be streamed astern of the ship to bring her head round? No. The rush of wind and water taking the vessel towards the south-east was too strong to be influenced by such a device; indeed, it would be more likely to accentuate *The Lucy*'s leeward drift.

Shielding his eyes from the wind, Josh peered to the north-east, hoping to catch a glimpse, at least, of Lundy's Light. Nothing. Except . . . what was that flash? Something had lit up the underside of the black clouds. Yes, there it was again, the Lundy Light. But it was coming from much further west than he expected. That meant that they were almost level with the most dangerous part of the Channel, where the sea room was limited and the cliffs of the Cornish coast were towering and broken only by a small beach or two – no anchorages!

His musing was broken by a cry from the captain, who was pointing to the south-east. Josh followed the captain's outstretched arm and, yes, there, briefly, flashed a light; perhaps a lantern, perhaps the riding light of a ship at anchor. As he tried to focus his gaze, he realised that the intermittent light must be coming from the north-Cornish coast, but too high to be a ship's light. This glow must be coming from halfway up a cliff face. Perhaps the light from a cottage or . . . wreckers?

Then he heard the captain scream orders and he and the helmsman pulled at the wheel so that *The Lucy*'s bow swung joyfully round, giving up the thankless fight against current and wind to run before the wind and head straight for that light and the dark cliffs that were now beginning to loom out of the darkness.

'No!' Josh screamed. He slid down the rigging, making his wet fingers burn, and ran towards the two men at the helm. 'No, Captain. That's no ship. There's no anchorage there.'

'Damn your eyes, don't you tell me what to do. Get back aloft.'

'You can't head that way, Captain. I know this coast. You are about level with a place called Morwenstow. There's no haven there.

Only cliffs and a shingle beach at the foot, which you will never reach past the rocks. They'll tear the bottom out of your ship. Turn the wheel, man.'

'Mr Mitchell.' The captain's face seemed weirdly yellow in the darkness. 'Put this man in irons. Or lash him to the mast. Get him out of my sight.'

The mate spun Josh round and pulled him away. 'You can't interfere with the captain,' he shouted. 'You could end up in jail.'

'And we will surely all end up drowned if that fool takes the ship straight into the cliffs. Stop him, Mr Mitchell. That light is not showing an anchorage because there isn't any. I know this coast.'

A scream from aloft interrupted them. 'Breakers ahead. Straight ahead.'

The two men peered past the bowsprit and glimpsed a sight that made them catch their breath. The ship was sailing – almost surfing with the wind behind her – straight towards a dark mass that stretched up much, much higher than the masthead. There was no flickering light now, only the towering cliff face and the roar of the sea breaking onto the rocks at its foot.

Josh caught a glimpse of the captain and the helmsman frantically working the wheel to swing the ship's head around, when the brig crashed onto the rocks with a force that tossed them onto the deck. *The Lucy* struck and stayed fast, the waves immediately breaking across the deck so that it was impossible to stand.

'Up to the masthead,' shouted Captain Lucas, crawling as best he could across the deck. They were the last words he uttered, for a wave picked him up and tossed him over the side, as though he was matchwood.

Josh made it to the ratlines and hauled himself aloft, the mate close behind him. The two men joined Jorgen at the crosstrees, hanging on for dear life as the foremast swung with each wave that crashed onto the stricken hull. They watched as first the water casks and then the longboat were swept overboard.

'We go in a minute,' shouted Jorgen. 'And we don't live in this sea, I tink. Bloody fool captain.'

Instinctively, Josh groped under his oilskins to feel his waterproof bag still firmly tied to his belt. Thank God for that, he thought.

All he could see about them now was white-crested breakers broken by black, glistening rocks stretching to the foot of the cliffs. But were those men he could see on some sort of beach ahead? He shook the spray from his eyes. Nothing. It must have been an illusion.

'How long before the mast goes, Mr Mitchell?' he asked of the mate. But the man only shook his head mutely.

Josh had no idea how long the three of them clung to the yard, but he was aware that he had never been so terrified in all his life as the men swayed sickeningly with each wave that crashed into *The Lucy*. The driving rain made it difficult to make out much of whatever beach existed beyond the jagged rocks that pinioned the ship. Josh stared at the black wall that faced and rose above them to a seemingly giddy height. Clearly it offered no succour, for no vegetation could be glimpsed on its vertical face, just barren, gleaming, black rock.

Suddenly, the mainmast went over with a crash taking the remnants of the sails with it. Josh could see no other sign of the crew and could only presume that they had perished. He turned his head and met the gaze of Jorgen. Of the mate there was now no sign.

'I don't see Copenhagen again, I tink, Josh,' said the Dane. 'I tink—'

He did not finish his sentence for, with a creak and a groan, the foremast split at its base and the two men were hurled into the sea.

Josh was a good swimmer but this was no sea to tolerate swimming. He felt himself whirled around and then surged forward so that he slammed into a rock. He gulped in air until the undertow pulled him back and down underwater again so that all he could see was blackness broken by bubbles. He thanked his Maker for the fact that he was not wearing his heavy sea boots, for they would surely have now dragged him down. As it was, he surged forward again with the surf and was thrown onto a rock once more. This time he felt a deep pain as his leg crashed against the sharp edge. The pain was excruciating but the edge saved him, giving him something angular to grasp so that he was able somehow to pull himself up onto a flat surface away from the sea that plucked at him.

He lay there gasping from pain and the lack of breath. A tug at his feet made him realise that he was far from safe so he inched his way forward, further onto the rock and away from the surf. Was the rock jutting out of the bottom of the cliff face? If so, he might be safe. He lifted his head to see ahead but the spray and the blackness defeated him.

Expecting death and desperately trying to summon up Mary's face, he lay his cheek down onto the wet surface until, with a sigh, he lost consciousness.

CHAPTER THREE

He came to, slowly, his consciousness trying to come to terms with the pain that jolted up his leg every time the platform on which he was resting lurched. He turned his head. He was lying on a bed of straw on some sort of open donkey cart and he could see that dawn was turning the dark sky into a miserable grey. His injured leg was bound in some sort of way but it hurt damnably every time the cart bumped into a pothole.

Ahead, he could see the hunched back of the driver: a slim youth or young man by the look of him. He called out: 'Where am I?'

'I'm taking thee to a doctor. Lie still.'

'How the hell can I lie still when this damned cart is lurching all over the track?'

'That is no reason for thee to use such bad language.'

'Aaargh.' He bit his lip. 'You would swear if your leg felt like mine.'

'No I would not. I was taught never to swear.'

The driver turned his head to utter the rebuke and Josh realised that the he was a she. He was being driven by a young girl, whose long hair was being blown behind her, stretching inland away from the still storm-swept cliffs.

'Oh. I beg your pardon, er . . . miss.'

'That's better. I am trying my best to control this donkey but he is bad enough when the sun shines. Now he is slithering all over the place. But I am sorry if it hurts thee. Not long now, though.'

'Where are you taking me?'

'To the house of my father, who is a doctor. We live at Hartland Quay.'

Josh lay silent for a while, gritting his teeth against the pain. Then, 'Where are the others?' he asked.

'What others?'

'The rest of the crew of my ship.'

Now it was her turn to be silent for a moment or two. 'I think they have all drowned,' she said eventually. 'I am sorry. Nobody could live in that sea pounding on those rocks. Thou were lucky.'

'Ah. All . . . all gone?'

'Aye. I am afeared so.'

'There was no big sailor – a Dane – saved? He was my friend.'

'Nay.'

'Haah! That drunken, stupid captain . . .'

'Why so stupid? Most ships would founder on this coast, in that storm. It was the worst we've had for many a year.'

'He thought he saw a light on the coast and put the ship towards what he thought was a harbour. I warned him against it, but—' He groaned again, as the cart jolted.

She remained silent.

43

'What could that light have been? I thought I saw men on the shingle when we hit the rocks.'

'Ah, they must have been the Preventers.'

'The Preventers?'

'Aye. The Revenue men.'

'Why would they—?' His head jolted as the cart slipped into what seemed like a cavern in the track and his skull crashed back onto the floor of the vehicle, the straw doing little to soften the blow. The stars above seemed to come down to dance before his eyes as once again he slipped into unconsciousness.

It was the pain again that brought him back. He was being lifted roughly out of the cart and carried into a house, the door of which was open, shedding welcome light. 'Aaargh,' he moaned.

'I should be able to put you out of that pain, once we get you inside.' The voice was deeply masculine and came from a large man, framed in the doorway, who was supporting himself upon a wooden crutch. 'Take him into the surgery,' he ordered.

Josh was laid onto a couch and a cloth that smelt very strange was pressed against his nostrils and, once again, he knew oblivion.

He had no idea how long he had been unconscious when he awoke to find himself lying in a darkened room on clean white sheets, his head resting on a deep pillow. That head, however, was throbbing and his tongue felt like a lump of blotting paper wedged into a mouth that seemed to have been scraped out with sand.

He blinked and, turning his head, looked hopefully towards a bedside table that in a fairy story would have housed a glass of water. It did not.

Feeling his right leg under the bedclothes, he realised that it was clad with splints bound tightly on either side of the shin bone. Tentatively, he attempted to move it. Immediately, a shaft of pain travelled upwards.

He bit his lip to stop himself from crying out again.

He looked around him carefully. The room was low-ceilinged with overhead beams he felt he could reach upwards and touch. He did not try. The two windows were partly curtained but between the fabric he could just see a patch of sky above a row of houses. The sky was blue, so the storm must have receded. The room was papered with a floral pattern and there was a dresser facing him at the bottom of the bed, containing a jug, a washbowl and – yes! – a carafe of water with a glass by its side.

Josh struggled to sit upright but the jarring pain returned to his leg and he subsided onto the pillow with a sigh. Who the hell would have put a carafe of water so tantalisingly out of reach? Was there a bell he could ring? No. Should he cry for help? Yes!

'Hello.' His voice sounded little more than a whimper. He tried again, this time louder. And from somewhere below he heard footsteps.

He lay back, trying not to appear helpless. 'Hello,' he tried again.

'Yes, yes, I'm coming.' He recognised the voice. It was that of the young girl who had driven the donkey cart. She pushed open the door and, with it half open, paused theatrically, poking her head around the edge.

'Thou called, my lord?' she asked with a mock frown.

'Yes . . . er . . . sorry to disturb you, but could I have some of that water, do you think? My mouth is fearful dry.'

She nodded. 'Yes, I expect it was the ether,' she said, and bustled into the room. She spoke with the soft burr of the south-west.

He raised his head a little to see her better. This was the first opportunity he had had to look at the girl and he observed her carefully. She was quite tall – perhaps five foot eight inches or so – and very slim, with a waist he felt he could clasp with one hand. Her brown hair, which had been blown out behind her like a flag pennant on the night of the storm, was now strewn across her shoulders, giving the impression that she never disciplined it into a bun or some other fashionable constriction. She was dressed in a rather drab woollen dress but large golden hoops dangled from each earlobe. As she turned and approached him, he realised that her face was well structured, with large black eyes and high cheekbones that looked as if they might cut any hand that wandered randomly to touch them. Her skin was that of a peasant girl, browned by sun and wind.

'Let me help thee,' she said. Putting down the glass, she put one hand behind his shoulders and lifted them forward, the easier for him to drink. He gulped the water down, as though trying to extinguish a fire within his throat.

'Be careful now,' she said. 'Thou mustn't wet the bedclothes.'

Josh wiped his lips with the back of his hand and gave her a smile. 'Oh thank you. I needed that.'

She smiled back, revealing an even set of small, white teeth. 'Lie back,' she said. 'I think thou must be still very weak.'

'No. I am feeling much better, although the leg pains me still.'

'I fear it will, for a little while yet. Though we have bound it.'

He lifted an eyebrow. 'We?'

'Aye. My father and me. I always help him with the surgery.'

'Hmm. You seem to do everything here. What is your name, child?'

'I am not a child. I am eighteen now, thank thee very much, Mr Weyland.'

Josh's jaw dropped. 'How do you know my name?'

She turned to the bedside table and drew open the drawer, lifting his small weatherproof bag. 'I have thy belongings here. They seem to have survived the wreck and your swim, which is right amazin' I would say.' She lifted the bag even higher. 'Your thirty guineas is still safe and sound and so are your letters from fat Mary Jackson.'

'What! She is not fat and how do you know her name?'

'Because I read her letters, that's why. And of course she's fat.' She sniffed and tossed her head. 'She sounds fat and she writes very borin' letters, I must say.'

Josh struggled to sit upright. 'You have no right to read her letters, nor to say rude things about her. We are betrothed. She is my fiancée.'

'So it seems. But if thou hast been away sailin' for two years or more I'm amazed she still wants to marry you – if she does, that is.' She sniffed again. 'It seems to me, from her last couple of letters, that she was gettin' a touch tired of all this waitin'.'

'That's just not true. You have no right to . . . what did you say your name was?'

'I didn't. But it is Rowena Acland, although,' she paused and gave a frown, 'it isn't really. The Acland bit is right an' fair, but I was christened Emma.'

'Emma is a fine name. Why have you changed it?'

'Oh,' she tossed her head again. 'It is a very dull, common name. Like Mary. I hate it. If anyone wants to talk to me now, they have to say Rowena. That's a fine,' she hesitated for a moment, 'a fine, romantic name. A proper name.'

Josh could not resist smiling. 'Does your father call you that?'

'Er, no. But this is his house, so he can call me what he likes.'

'Very well. Thank you, Rowena, for fetching me back from the rocks and for looking after me, although not for reading my correspondence. Now, tell me. How long have I been here?'

'Oh, it is a full day and a half now.' Her voice dropped a little. 'Look, Mr Weyland, I am right sorry that thou lost thy friends on the ship. We have found a couple of bodies but the rocks will have caught the others deep down and they will be gobbets now . . .'

'Gobbets?'

'Aye. That's what the folk around here call the human remains that are eventually washed up long after a wreck. They are always torn to pieces, by the rocks. It is not nice, not nice at all.'

Josh blew out his cheeks. 'It doesn't sound it.' He lay for a moment with his head turned away on the pillow, thinking of Jorgen, the Dane, and the other men from his watch. When he turned his head back, she had quietly drawn a chair to the bedside and was looking at him, a small tear at the corner of each eye.

'Thank you again, Rowena.' He reached out a hand and took one of hers in it. It was small, very brown and she seized his and gripped it tightly. They sat for a moment, hand in hand, before he gently disengaged himself.

'Tell me, lass. Who pulled me off that rock? It could not have been you, surely?'

'Oh no. I am strong, but not that strong. It was two of Captain Cunningham's men.'

'Captain Cunningham?'

'Yes, he commands the Preventers on this stretch of the coast.'

She gave a shy smile and looked down. 'I think he is sweet on me.'

Josh grinned. 'And I don't blame him. And are you sweet on him?'

'Oh no.' If she had been standing she would have flounced. 'He is *far* too old for me. As well as . . . oh, never mind that.'

'Of course. Of course.' He adjusted his features so as not to smile. 'But tell me, Rowena. What were the Preventers doing on that tiny beach at night in the middle of a storm like that?'

She looked away. 'Oh, I expect the news that a ship was in trouble came to them – they are based here, in Hartland, thou knowest – and they rode quickly to where the ship was likely to be thrown ashore.'

'Yes, I thought I saw them on the beach when I was in the water. But there was a light. My captain swore it was a ship's masthead light and headed *The Lucy* for her, thinking there was a safe anchorage. I *know* that there was a light, for I saw it from high up on the foremast. What could it have been?'

Rowena tossed her head. 'Oh, I know nothing of that.' She stood. 'They must have stayed to do the wreckin', I expect. Now, I must be goin'. Canst thou eat something? Thou must be starvin'.'

'Well, yes. Now you mention it, I realise that I am quite hungry.'

'Very well. It is some time afore luncheon, but I will bring thee somthin' to fill thy tummy afore we eat properly. Now, thou must excuse me . . .'

Josh lifted his hand. 'One more thing, Rowena – no, three more things.'

'What might they be?'

'Firstly, you must call me Josh. Everyone does.'

The smile came back. 'Very well, Josh.'

'And secondly, I must ask you. Why do you address me in that old-fashioned way, using thee and thou instead of you. I should think that it must be fifty years or more since folk spoke like that in England – even down here in remote Cornwall or Devon.'

For the first time, Rowena looked embarrassed. She studied the floor, then: ''Tis a bad habit I have gotten into, I fear. You see,' she gave him a half-smiling look from beneath her eyelashes, 'there is not much to do down here. As you say, we are remote. In fact, we are just over the border in Devon, from Cornwall, and there cannot be more than fifty people – if that and barring the Preventers – livin' around here within twenty square mile or so.'

'So . . . ?'

'So I . . . I . . . I read.'

'That is capital. What do you read?'

'The works of Miss Austen and others but, lately, I have been goin' through all the books that Sir Walter Scott has written. All those wonderful things about knights in armour and very fine ladies. I seem to have lived in his world now for so long that I have picked up the language, so to speak. But I do concede,' she smiled broadly now, 'Sir Joshua, that it is rather silly and fanciful and I shall try and give it up now that thou . . . you are here. Certainly, it will be a right relief to my father.'

'He has never minded?'

'Oh no. You see, my mother died in childbirth and I am his only child. He has brought me up himself and I have to confess he indulges me.' She gave a tiny laugh that sounded to Josh like birdsong. 'You know,' she continued earnestly, 'he was a sailor too before he took up medicine.'

'Really? How unusual. I seem to remember that he was leaning on a crutch when I arrived here. How did he sustain that injury?'

'A shipwreck. Like you. Only there was no surgeon near him then to set his leg. Thou . . . you were luckier than him, I think. He and the captain – Captain Cunningham, that is – were injured in the same wreck. They were shipmates, you see, in those days. Father broke his leg and the captain lost his hand – caught in the rocks. Now he has to wear a horrible hook.'

'Indeed? How awful. Now, I must not keep you.'

'You had three more things. What might be the last?'

Josh frowned. 'Yes. You said something about the Customs men staying to do the wrecking. What does that mean?'

'Oh, the wreckin'? That's what people hereabouts call the pullin' in of salvage – you know, the cargoes – from ships that have gone aground. Everybody does it. It has always gone on on this coast. Folk here consider it their rights. It's what the sea gives them. And the Preventers are not above joining in. 'Tis not illegal in any way.'

Josh nodded his head slowly. 'I see. So *The Lucy*'s cargo will all have been salvaged by now and, presumably, spread around the local population?'

'Aye, though I understand that you were carryin' bales of cotton and they won't be of much use to folk, after they've been thoroughly dowsed in seawater and torn about on the rocks. Now, I must go.'

'Of course. Thank you, Rowena.'

He watched her as she turned and walked towards the door. She moved with an easy grace that belied her appearance as a country girl and, at the door, she turned and flashed him a warm smile before tripping down the stairs.

Josh lay back and put a hand to his forehead. So much to consider! First of all there was this strange girl. Eccentric – how dare she read Mary's letters and then have no shame in admitting it! – but fascinating, too: at times like an urchin, at others a coquettish young woman. Damned attractive, too. Which meant that she was dangerous. He shook his head.

Then there was the matter of the light that flashed in the storm. Rowena – Emma? – had not answered his questions about it. What's more, he had now gained another definition of 'wrecking' to add to his childhood memories of the deliberate luring of ships onto the rocks. At Key West there was the remarkable practice of waiting for vessels to go aground and then racing to offer assistance – and all licensed by the state, too! Now, here in North Cornwall (or was he now in Devon?) it seemed to refer to something akin to beach scavenging. It was all very confusing.

Josh stared hard at the ceiling. He had yet to meet his benefactor, the ex-sailor who now practised as a doctor and surgeon. Tentatively, he sought to move his right leg. The pain responded, although perhaps it was less intense now.

He frowned. Was the man qualified? But then this was such a wild and remote part of England that it probably didn't matter. In any case, he was completely in his hands. What a strange and mysterious corner of England it was that fate had thrown him into now!

He must have dozed off because he became startlingly awake as Rowena pushed open his door and bustled in, carrying a tray.

''Tis only two hours afore we take our midday meal,' she said, putting down the tray, 'so I have only given you bread and cheese.' She bent to put her arms around his shoulders before gently easing him up the bed and slapping an extra pillow behind his head. Josh could not help wondering whether, in the act, she had deliberately buried his head between her breasts. They were small but firm and he enjoyed the experience.

'Mind you,' she said, ''tis best Devon cheese and very fine, local butter.'

'Thank you. Are we in Devon, here, then?'

'Aye, just over the border from Cornwall. In fact, the boundary runs through Morwenstow, where you were shipwrecked, some ten miles away.'

He began munching and Rowena showed no signs of leaving. 'Tell me,' he said, 'are there many shipwrecks at Morwenstow, or here, in Hartland, for that matter?'

'Yes, indeed. 'Tis such a terrible coast when the nor'westerly blows. There have been at least three wrecks so far this year on this stretch.'

'What about the crews? Did they survive?'

She looked away. 'I can't be rememberin' that.' Suddenly her mood changed and she became restive. 'Now, I'm sorry, but I have work to do. I shall bring you luncheon in due course.'

'Of course, Rowena. Thank you. I am sorry to be a burden.'

At the doorway, she shook her head. 'You are not a burden, Joshua Weyland.' She seemed to blush, although it may have been a trick of the light. 'It is good to have thee – you – after such an ordeal you have gone through. We didn't think that anyone would survive, so . . .' Her voice trailed away and she turned abruptly and descended the stairs.

Sometime in the mid afternoon, Doctor Acland came to visit his patient. He was, indeed, a big man with wide shoulders, a considerable paunch and large hands – more those of a sailor than a surgeon. The nautical link was emphasised by the small, seemingly golden, earring that hung from his left earlobe. His hair was snow white and he boasted mutton chop whiskers and a trimmed beard that seemed to bring into contrast his red face, where broken veins betrayed signs of good living. For movement within the house, he had replaced his crutch with a stout stick.

'I am glad to see you looking considerably better, young man,' the doctor boomed, putting a hand to Josh's forehead. 'How does the leg feel?'

'Thank you, sir. I am grateful for your attention. The leg seems to have stopped throbbing and only hurts when I attempt to move it.'

'Well don't move it, then.' The tone had a touch of asperity, indicating that this was a man who was used to being obeyed. 'I will inspect the wound in a moment but it is better for you to stay in bed for the next two days. It will heal itself, but only if you don't put undue strain on it. Then you can leave your bed and we will get you into an old wheelchair outside, if the weather remains clement. I am a great believer, Weyland, in fresh air as an aid in treating any malady.'

'Quite so, sir. Rowena . . . er . . . Emma tells me that you once were a seafaring man yourself.'

'Ah. She talks too much, I fear. Now let us remove the dressing and splints and take a look at that leg. EMMA!' His voice seemed to shake the house's foundations. 'Come here. I need you.'

The girl arrived and together she and her father untied the bandages holding the splints to the leg and gingerly removed the dressing that covered the wound. Josh winced.

'Hmmm.' Acland adjusted spectacles to look more carefully. 'Luckily it is not a break, as you would think. But the wound is quite deep and I have administered iodine to prevent infection. Thankfully there seems to be no more bleeding and I have stitched the skin to close the wound. There is a dressing over all, which we will need to change regularly. No, you were lucky and your strong constitution should help the leg to heal. We must now let nature take its course.'

'Thank you, Doctor. But I cannot impose on you. Is there a hospital, perhaps, somewhere near where I could stay while the leg heals? I have money, although not a lot . . .'

'Good Lord, no sir! You would need to go to Exeter for proper hospital treatment and the journey would be arduous. It would shake the leg and upset all the good work I have done. No, you shall stay here until you can walk properly. And there is no question of payment, thank you. Emma here can look after you. She is a good nurse and we don't want for money.'

He smiled at his daughter, who looked sheepishly at the floor, before flashing a quick look of gratification at Joshua. She obviously welcomed the new chore she had acquired.

'You are very kind, Doctor.'

'It is my calling, sir. I am here to heal the sick. Now, try and get some sleep and we will try and get you into a wheelchair in the morning, if you feel up to it. Now, Emma. I leave you to change the dressing, administer a little more iodine and replace the splints. Wash your hands first, of course. You can do all that, can't you?'

'Of course, Father. I have done it before.'

'Very well. Now sleep, Weyland, when Emma is done with you.'

'Thank you, sir.'

Rowena rose, shut the door behind her father and returned to her patient. A small pink tongue – how fascinating, thought Josh – poked between her lips as she set about her work.

'So you are a nurse, too, Rowena. You truly do seem to do

everything in this house: cooking, driving the donkey cart, devouring the latest novels and looking after sick patients. My goodness!'

She replaced her frown of concentration with a smile. 'Well, there is no one else here to help Father. We do have a woman who comes in from the village on top of the cliff to help with the cleaning, so . . .'

'What? So Hartland is not here?'

'No. This is called Hartland Quay and is but a hamlet, down here virtually at the foot of the cliffs. It exists as a very small port and a place for lime smeltin' for minin'. The main village is some mile and a half away up at the top.'

'Ah.' Josh thought quickly. How to discover if Acland was a trained physician and surgeon without causing offence? He coughed. 'So your father has trained you in basic medicine, then?'

'Oh, I wouldn't say that. I am merely a nurse, really.'

'And, surely, an assistant when surgery needs to be done?'

'Well, yes. I suppose so.'

Josh took a deep breath. 'It is most unusual to find an ex-seaman practising as a doctor. Did he . . . er . . . qualify comparatively recently, after he swallowed the anchor, as we seamen say?'

'No. He was comparatively young when he was at sea . . .'

'In the Royal Navy?'

'No, on a merchant ship like yours. He was an officer, of course. But he became interested in medicine after his injury.' She looked up, a pin clenched between her teeth. 'He studied at one of the great London hospitals and qualified quite quickly. You see,' she nodded solemnly, 'my father is a very intelligent and clever man. There are so many things he can do. But he chose to come down here to serve this remote community. And,' her eyes danced and she smiled, 'it was here he met my mother.'

'Ah,' Josh returned the smile. 'A love match, of course.'

'Oh yes, though, of course, I never knew her. But I visit her grave regularly.'

'Of course. Tell me, where was your father injured? Where was he shipwrecked?'

She shook her head. 'At Bude. He doesn't seem to want to talk about it, so I don't press him.' Quickly she replaced the splints and tied them together with new bandages. Then she patted her work and smiled. 'There you are, Sir Joshua, all clean and tidy and ready to go into your wheelchair when you are better.'

Josh frowned as a quick pang rose from the wound – more of discomfort than actual pain. 'Thank you, Rowena,' he said. 'Now, I mustn't keep you. I know you have much to do.'

'Yes.' She frowned and stood still for a moment, as though uncertain of her next move. Then she moved forward, bent her head and planted a quick kiss on his forehead, before swiftly moving through the doorway and skipping down the stairs.

Josh smiled and touched the drop of moisture that she had planted above his left eye. What a fascinating creature! He felt desire begin to grow within him as he recalled her wide eyes, as she bent down to plant the kiss. Then the frown returned as he realised that he had not thought about Mary at all since he had arrived in this strange house. Guilt consumed him. Before he had sailed he had scrawled a quick message to her to say that he had shipped aboard *The Lucy*. What if she had read in some journal that the ship had been wrecked? She could think him dead. He must write to her immediately. Damn, that meant recalling Rowena!

Softly he called, then, when there was no reply, he lifted his voice. 'Rowena.'

'Yes, I am coming, Josh.'

He could tell that she was running up the stairs. 'Are you in pain?' she cried as she entered the room.

Josh felt suitably ashamed. 'No, no. Sorry. But I have just realised – I should have asked you before – is it possible to have pen, ink and some notepaper, so that I can write a letter?'

Immediately, Rowena's expression changed. Hands on hips she said, 'You want to write to fat Mary, I suppose?'

Josh winced. 'Oh, please, Rowena, don't call her that. Let me repeat that she is not fat and it is most disrespectful of you to refer to her so. And yes, I must write to her. She will know by now that I sailed here on *The Lucy*. It would be terrible if she read about the shipwreck in a newspaper and thought that I had drowned. You must see that I have to write to her right away.'

Rowena's face was now a picture of misery. She nodded gloomily. 'Yes, I suppose so. I shall bring you writing materials. After all, I have nothing else to do . . .'

'I am sorry to . . .' but the girl had disappeared through the door and was clumping loudly down the stairway, in great contrast to the light steps with which she had descended a few moments before.

Josh penned his letter with great care, telling Mary all that had befallen him. However, he made no mention of Rowena. Somehow, it seemed unseemly to put her forward as though she was an important member of the household. She was, after all, just a young girl, who was helping her father. That was all there was to it. Was that not so?

He handed the letter to Rowena when she brought him his supper.

'I hate to add to your labours, Rowena,' he said, 'but could I ask you to post this letter for me as soon as possible?'

'Very well.' She scanned the address. 'Ah, she lives in Dover, then, does she? Quite a long way away from here, then.' She seemed pleased by the discovery. 'Yes, I will post it tomorrow. It means going up the hill to the village.'

'Oh, I am sorry to impose on you.'

She shook her head, so that her hair floated up from her shoulders. 'No. No. It is no trouble.'

Josh cleared his throat. 'Now, Rowena,' he began awkwardly, 'You won't open the envelope to read—'

She stamped her foot. 'Of course not. I only read the others because . . . because they had been smudged by the seawater and I wanted to make sure you would be able to read them.' There were tears in her eyes.

He extended a hand. 'Oh, I am sorry, Rowena. Now, please don't be upset. And thank you for the supper. It looks delicious. Did you cook it?'

'Yes.' She forced a smile. 'And I vow I am a better cook than your Mary.'

He sampled a little of the roast chicken, desperately anxious to make amends. 'Oh, undoubtedly. Delicious. Thank you again. Why don't you stay and talk awhile while I eat? If you have time, that is.'

Her smile broadened. 'No, I cannot. I must serve my father. Enjoy the chicken. They roam freely here, so they are usually good.'

She approached as though to kiss him, then changed her mind and left – skipping lightly down the stairs once again.

Joshua took a little more of the chicken. It really was good. He shook his head in mock exasperation, but there was a smile on his face.

That night he woke and lay, his head turning on the pillow, as he searched his brain to reveal why his sleep had been disturbed. Then he realised. It was the light on the cliff face that he had seen from the masthead shortly before the ship hit the rocks. It was only a glimpse and it never reappeared. But Captain Lucas had seen it too and it was the reason why he had changed course. The light burnt in his subconscious and it was as though the thought of it had caused him to wake. *He had seen it!* He could not have imagined it.

Could it have been . . . what was the term used in the olden days? Ah, yes. Could it have been a 'false light' – a lantern held aloft to lure the ship onto the rocks of Morwenstow, a light held by modern-day wreckers?

The thought disturbed him. This part of northern Cornwall was a barren, savage place, judging by its coastline. Were the people who lived here similarly heartless? Not fishermen, of course, for seamen in this modern age would surely not tempt other seafarers to their destruction. And hadn't whoever had been on the shore that night saved his life by pulling him off that rock? But what of the miners, the 'tinners', who lived in these parts and followed such a miserable, low-paid occupation? They would have no such scruples.

He lay in the darkness staring sightlessly at the ceiling. He vowed that, when he could leave his bed, he would begin the task of trying to solve the mystery of the light that flashed in the storm.

CHAPTER FOUR

The thought lay with him as he lay fretfully in his bed for the next two days. The following morning broke brightly, with sunlight streaming through his windows. His leg caused only a dull ache now and Joshua decided that the time had come to attempt to be self-sufficient and rise from the bed. He failed. He could slip his good leg to the floor and just about stand but the wounded one could bear no weight and he was forced to hop to the washstand, clinging to whatever piece of furniture was near. Rowena found him swaying precariously on one leg as he tried to wash.

'Joshua Weyland,' she cried, 'get back into that bed immediately. Put your arm around my shoulder. Now lean on me and hop. That's it.'

He collapsed onto the bed, grimacing.

'Don't do that again. Lie here until I bring your breakfast. Now, don't move.'

Eventually, she helped him to dress and wash and, with the aid of one of Dr Acland's crutches, he was able to move to the head of the staircase and somehow navigate his descent. The house was dark and, he noticed, furnished with an eclectic variety of chairs, tables and side pieces, none of them matching and some of them wearing a nautical air. Salvage from shipwrecks, perhaps? What was more impressive, however, was the collection of porcelain and paintings carefully placed on show on walls and tables in the drawing room.

Outside, the air was cool but refreshing, with the unmistakable tang of the sea making his eyes blink. A wheeled, basketwork chair was waiting, its long, tiller-like handle allowing him to steer the single wheel at its front. Reluctantly, he lurched onto the seat and Rowena took her place to push him from the rear.

'Where would Your Grace wish to go?' she asked, far too loudly for his comfort.

'Good God,' he exclaimed. 'This thing is for elderly folk. I would prefer to hobble on my crutch.' He made to get out but she pushed him down.

'Father says you must put no strain on your leg so you must stay sitting. Now. Where would you like to go?'

Josh looked about him. They were in a narrow street, with a row of terraced houses between them and the sea and the cliff face rising behind another, facing terrace. The doctor's house formed part of the terrace, which seemed to back on to the cliff and at this point rose less sheer. It was distinguished by second- and third-floor windows, which jutted out from the lower floor, dormer-style. It was by far the most distinguished house in the street, but Josh could not help but wonder why the doctor had chosen to live in this tiny hamlet at the foot of the cliff, with so few people to form his patient catchment area.

'This is Hartland Quay,' he said, 'so there must be a harbour of sorts. Can we see it?'

'Aye, but it is only a tiny place, really just a cove, though small craft do come in and out, because there is a smelting works there.' She began to push him. ''Tis just the end of the street here, down the slope.'

He turned his head. 'Will you be able to push me back up?'

She showed her teeth in a grin that lit up her suntanned face. 'I am much stronger than I look, Josh Weyland. You will see.'

The street ended abruptly onto a small, rocky plateau that jutted out from the bottom of the cliff. The quay had been built out of local stone and curved around to the right from the bottom of the street, offering protection from the sea, which beat unrelentingly on its wall. As a harbour, it was indeed tiny, but its existence was explained by several squat, smoke-stained buildings sitting on a level patch of rock that projected from the base of the cliff and the beginning of the harbour wall.

'What are they?' called Josh above the crashing of the waves on the wall.

'Lime kilns. They are used to turn limestone into what they call slaked lime. The stone is brought from Wales by those little boats,' she nodded to where two single-masted sailing smacks huddled together behind the protection of the wall, 'and the lime is used by farmers and masons hereabouts.'

Josh's jaw dropped. 'How on earth do the smacks get in and out of the harbour? There's hardly room to swing a cat at the entrance, getting round the end of the quay between the rocks. And impossible, I would think, with any sort of sea running.'

'Oh, it's quite a palaver. Look,' she pointed. 'There's a boat comin' in now. You'll see.'

Indeed, the little harbour was buzzing with activity. As Josh watched, a dinghy was rowing out to meet the smack, which seemed to be running under full sail straight into the rocks that jutted out in long runes from either side of the harbour entrance. A line attached to a ring on the top of the wall was unravelling from behind the dinghy.

'What the hell . . . ?' muttered Josh.

Suddenly, the smack dropped its mainsail and rounded up into the wind as the dinghy ran alongside. In a swift, well-practised movement, the end of the line was transferred from the dinghy to the smack and made fast. As it became tight, it acted to spring the smack around, pulling her stern about and slowing her headway, so that she was pulled around the end of the pier. Another dinghy had meanwhile rowed out and thrown a mooring line to the sailboat. At this point the vessel's remaining sail was taken down and she was hauled under the lee of the quay and moored on each bow and quarter so that she nestled snugly against the inside of the massive wall. The whole operation had taken less than three minutes.

'Good Lord!' exclaimed Josh. 'There's seamanship for you.'

'Aye.' Rowena's eyes were gleaming. 'They do it all the time.'

The man in the lead dinghy, who had rowed his boat up onto the shingle, now looked up and waved. 'Mornin' Rowena,' he called.

Rowena raised her hand and gave a desultory answering wave and then turned her back.

'A friend of yours?' enquired Josh.

'Not really. Just an acquaintance.' She spoke quickly. 'Have you seen enough?'

'Well, yes. I suppose so. Are you sure you can push me back up this hill?'

She gave no reply but bent her back and swung the chair round quickly. They rattled over the cobblestones so quickly that Josh was forced to cling to the sides of the bath chair. 'Steady, child, or you'll have me over,' he cried.

'I'm not a child, Joshua. I've told you afore. I'm eighteen and I can run up this hill faster'n this, if you like.'

'I do not like, Rowena. I can see how strong you are, thank you very much, and I am most impressed.'

Rowena, having made her point, stopped outside the house to get her breath back and Josh realised that the doctor and his daughter lived next door to an inn, whose sign swung in the sea breeze. Further along, the buildings ended abruptly and the path curved upwards to begin the long, steep climb to the top of the cliff. Halfway along the climb, on another patch of rocky level ground, a building stood on its own, its dark stonework and few windows giving it a brooding appearance.

'What is that?' asked Josh.

'That is the Preventers' barracks. That's where they and the captain live.'

'The Revenue men who pulled me off the rock?'

'Aye.' She paused for a moment. 'They are a rough lot.'

'Well, rough or not. I owe them my life. Do you think you could push me up there so that I could call and express my gratitude?'

'Aye. But it is very steep and you must help me by pushing the wheels with your hands. Forget the steering.'

'Yes, of course. I should have thought of that.'

It was indeed steep and it was all the two of them could do to make the basket chair mount the hill, particularly as Josh had to let the steering tiller swing freely, so causing the chair to career across the path. As they neared a large studded door, which formed the entrance to the building, it was pushed open and a tall, broad-shouldered man strode through it to meet them.

'Good mornin', Emma,' he said, his voice so low it was almost a growl. 'I see you've brought your patient. Come inside and take tea.'

'Well, I don't rightly think we should, Cap'n. Mr Weyland has much to do but he wanted to say thank ye to your men for savin' him from the sea that night.' It was clear that Rowena was less than comfortable in the presence of the captain and Josh regarded him carefully.

He wore what seemed to be a faded sailor's uniform of blue and white and a curved cutlass hung from his belt. His face was weathered a dark brown and his eyes were as black as Rowena's. Hatless, his hair hung in ringlets and he had a long, jagged scar across his cheek. But the most notable feature of his appearance was the curved hook, which took the place of his missing left hand. Yet the overall appearance was not menacing; more jaunty and even dashing.

Josh immediately averted his gaze from the hook. 'That is right, Cap'n,' he said, smiling up at the big man. 'I'd very much like to shake the hands of the men who rescued me. And,' he shot a quick look up at Rowena, 'if my nurse will allow it, I think we have time for a quick cup of tea, if that would not inconvenience you.'

The captain smiled, revealing large, tombstone teeth. 'No inconvenience at all, young man.' He extended his good hand. 'Jack Cunningham at your service.'

'Josh Weyland.' They shook hands. Was Rowena scowling? It seemed so.

The three entered the barracks, the chair swaying over the rough cobblestones. 'Tea for three, Brown,' Cunningham called brusquely to a man holding a musket in the doorway. 'Move yerself, man. Serve it in my cabin.'

'Aye aye, sir.'

'Can you get out of that chair, Weyland?' asked the captain. 'We'll not get you inside while you stay in it. Entrance is too narrow.' He smiled at Rowena. 'We don't pursue comfort much in the barracks, I'm afraid.'

Josh nodded. 'I think so, sir. I've got one of the doctor's crutches and I am learning to hobble with it. Lead on and Rowena . . . er . . . Emma will help me.'

After some difficulty, with Rowena clutching him tightly – in fact, he felt with some embarrassment, almost proprietarily – they reached a room lit only by one small window set high on the seaward side of the building. A flight of wooden steps led up to a small platform arranged by the window and bearing a large telescope, set on three legs and trained so that its long barrel pointed out to sea. The furniture reminded Josh of that in the doctor's house – very masculine and redolent of the sea. High up on the walls, Josh recognised bound copies of Lloyd's Register of Shipping resting on a shelf that encircled the room.

'I'm afraid you won't see the lads who hauled you ashore,' said Cunningham, gesturing them to sit in two rather overstuffed leather armchairs. 'They are out on patrol. So you must call again if you wish to thank them. But please do so. You would be most welcome.'

'Thank you, I will. Tell me, Captain . . .'

'Call me Jack.'

'Thank you. Tell me, Jack,' Josh paused for a moment to pick his words carefully. 'I have been away at sea for so long. What actually do the Preventers do? What do they prevent, in fact?'

'Smuggling. That's our main work.'

Josh smiled. 'Yet I thought that that was almost a national sport in this part of the West Country, with both gentry and ordinary folk involved in it.'

Cunningham scowled. 'Well, that may be so, but it is illegal. Smuggling cheats the government of this country of a very considerable amount of revenue. Income tax has now been reintroduced for the first time since the Napoleonic War and them that pays it now would pay far less if we could catch them that smuggles.'

Brown entered the room carrying a tray laden with a large brown teapot, three mugs and buttered bread cut thickly. 'No cakes, Captain,' he said. 'This is all I could find.'

'Oh, that is absolutely fine,' Rowena cut in quickly. 'We can't stay long, Cap'n Jack, and, anyway, we don't expect frills in the Revenue's barracks.'

Cunningham gave her an affectionate smile. 'You'll get plenty of frills, girl, when you agree to marry me.'

Rowena blushed. 'You know very well that's not goin' to happen, Jack, thank you very much. I don't want to marry and settle down here.'

The man's black eyebrows settled down in what appeared to be a straight line above his eyes. 'Well you damned well ought to, young lady,' he said curtly. 'It's not right that a young woman stays single for too long. Apart from anything else, it upsets the unmarried menfolk.' He shot a quick glance at Josh. 'And the married ones as well, for that matter.' But he softened the harshness of the expression with a quick smile and went on:

'But I was talkin' about smuggling, or "fair trade" as it's called around here. Do you know that between 1780 and 1783 as much as two million pounds worth of tea and thirteen million pounds of brandy were smuggled into these islands?'

'Good Lord!'

'Aye. And it got worse, of course, during our war against the French when heavy taxes were levied on luxury goods comin' in to raise money for the British Navy and Army. If we hadn't had income from that source, now, we would never have defeated old Boney.'

Josh switched his gaze to Rowena, but she was frowning and looking at the telescope up above her, seemingly paying no attention to the conversation. 'So is there much smuggling going on around here, Jack?' he asked.

'Enough to keep us busy.'

'I would have thought that this coast would have been too far away from the continent of Europe to offer safe landings for smugglers. The southern coast of Cornwall and Devon, facing France as it does, would surely be a far more attractive target for smugglers?'

'Well, yes, of course it is and the Preventers on the English Channel coast are just as busy as us, if not more so. But that doesn't mean we don't get attempted landings here, and often.'

'Would the French smugglers come all the way round Land's End, then, to make drops here?'

'Sometimes. But it's not them that's the real problem. It's the transatlantic ships that come up the Channel to Bristol from America and the Caribbean that like to earn a guinea or two by dropping off their fine stuff here to smuggling boats that come out to meet them.'

'How do you prevent it, if it is so prevalent?'

'Three ways. We have fast-sailing cutters who intercept skippers out at sea who are suspected of runnin' in goods – these can outsail most of the ships they are after. Mind you, the devils hide away the contraband with great cunning: under cargoes of fish and even coal.'

'And rock for smelting?'

The captain frowned again and levelled a cool gaze at him. 'Not really,' he said, 'there's no excise duty applied to that sort of cargo.'

'How do you operate in other ways on this coast?'

'Men along the cliffs – that's us and devilish hard work it is. Smugglers are usually good seamen and, in this part of the world in particular, they will land their stuff in tiny coves and breaks in the cliffs, which are damned difficult to approach by land or sea. And they will often sneak in during a storm when the weather is too foul for us to be out of doors.'

Josh's mind swiftly flashed back to the skilled seamanship demonstrated by the sailors bringing in the smacks to the harbour at Hartland Quay, but Cunningham was continuing.

'Lastly, our third arm, so to speak, are mounted dragoons, who can pursue the smugglers inland if they escape us.' The black eyebrows shot up. 'But tell me, young Josh, why are you so interested in smuggling along this coastline?'

Josh took a gulp of his tea. Recalling the taste from his days in Far Eastern waters he suspected it was made from the best China leaves, a somewhat surprising discovery to be made in a Revenue barracks. 'Oh, don't worry, Captain, I am not planning to take up smuggling. I am just interested in how folk make their living here.

70

As I understand it, the price of tin has fallen and it seems to me that the land hereabouts is a bit windswept to provide good farming. But I may be wrong.'

'Yes, well, wrecking is the other source of income to the folk of the coast. Although that, o' course, comes in kind – bits of the ship and so on – and can't be relied on and depends on the weather.'

'Are you supposed to stop it?'

'We do if we can, but folks are damned quick now at plunderin' a wreck, and often the ship has been stripped to its bones by the time we get there.'

'Hmmm.' Josh followed Rowena's gaze up to the window. 'But you were quickly on the scene when *The Lucy* foundered. I saw you on the beach as we came thundering in. And,' he smiled, 'I'm damned glad that you were for you saved my life.'

Cunningham shifted in his chair and carefully folded a piece of bread and butter before replying. 'Well, we had seen you comin' up the Channel just before the storm broke and I was fairly sure you would run into trouble. You were sailin' far too close inshore.'

'I fear you're right. We had a drunkard for a captain. Why, he even saw a light glowing on the cliff face that he thought indicated a safe anchorage, even though I told him there was no such place on this coast.'

'Oh?' Cunningham drained his cup and put it down on the table. 'More tea, Emma?' he asked.

'No, thank you.' She stood. 'We must be goin'. Father will be wonderin' where we have got to.'

Cunningham rose. 'Well, I'm glad you both stopped by. Call in any time, Josh.' He held out his hand.

Josh seized his crutch and struggled to his feet. 'Just one more word, about that light, Jack. There was a light just above the beach. I saw it myself.'

'Really?'

Rowena broke in quickly. 'We must go. Come on, Josh.'

The captain shook his head. 'There was no light on or about that beach during the storm, Josh. I was there. You can take my word for it.'

Josh slowly nodded. 'Of course I will, Jack. Thank you for the tea. Best China, by the taste of it.'

'No. Indian rubbish. We can't afford good tea here, lad.'

Further smiles were exchanged and then Josh struggled through the door and out onto the path. 'Let me walk for a moment or two, if I can, Rowena,' said Josh. 'I want to be as mobile as I can as quickly as possible. You go on with the chair. I'll come behind. I'm sure I can manage.'

Rowena tossed back her head. 'You will do nothing of the kind. You could fall and ruin all the good work Father did on that leg. And, anyway, I can't push this damned contraption on my own without someone steerin' it.'

'Oh, very well. But can we just go out on this flat piece of rock and get the sea air and talk for a bit?'

'Of course. Back in the chair now.'

She pushed him down the hill, not without difficulty, for the chair had no brake and Rowena had to lean back and ease it down the hill to save it careering away. Eventually, they reached the rocky outcrop, which provided a good view of the coastline and even, on this fine morning, a fine perspective of Lundy Island.

'The captain seems very fond of you, Rowena,' said Jack, pretending to study the horizon.

She tossed her head again. 'Well, he shouldn't be, because I give him no encouragement, I tell you.' She frowned. 'He thinks that just because he is my father's friend that he can take liberties. Well, he shouldn't.'

'Ah yes, of course, he was a shipmate of your father.'

'Aye, it was many years ago, o'course, when they were both young men. They were the only two to be rescued from the wreck.'

'What was their ship and where did she founder?'

'She was a brig – a bit like yours, I think – named the *Evershot,* and she hit the rocks off Bude, south of here.'

'Hmm.' They sat silently for a time. Josh gazed around at the few stunted bushes and low trees, their tops scythed off horizontally by the cruel wind from the sea, and the brambles and gorse that fought gamely to thrust upwards from cracks in the rocks. Overhead, crows were a'cawing and, higher up, two buzzards circled lazily. Yet he saw little and noted less, for his mind was elsewhere.

'Did you say *Evershot*?'

'Yes.'

'Although I must have been very young, I seem to remember reading something about it. Didn't the Bude lifeboat try to come out to the ship?'

'Yes, but the sea was too high and she couldn't get near to the brig.'

'Do you recall the Line that owned the brig?'

'Oh aye. It was the Blue Cross Line, a Scottish company. Father hated them.'

'Why was that?'

'He said their ships were death traps. They was not properly looked after in terms of maintainin' the shrouds and the caulkin' and all that sort of thing. He said that there was so many barnacles on the hull that she was difficult to steer.'

Joshua nodded slowly. 'That is a bit familiar. *The Lucy* – my ship – was owned by the Blue Cross Line and she was not kept up to scratch either.'

They both fell silent again until Rowena said, 'Josh, do you mind if we go in now? This wind has sharpened and I'm gettin' a bit cold.'

'Oh, I am sorry. Of course, let's go back to the house.'

Josh hoped to seize an opportunity to speak with the doctor but it seemed that he had been called away and had ridden up to Stoke, the village about half a mile inland back from the clifftop, where he was warden of the fine old church there. The two of them ate lunch together in the dark dining room. Rowena attempted to make conversation but Josh was too busy with his thoughts to be sociable.

Eventually, he smiled and said, 'Do you think it would be possible for you to take a little time off from your labours, say the day after tomorrow, and take me in the donkey cart to Morwenstow?'

She nodded. 'I think so. Father likes to ride his mare to make his calls so I think he could spare us the donkey and the cart. But why d'you want to go to Morwenstow? There's hardly anythin' there but for the church an' the new vicarage, which the Rev. Hawker has just finished building there, down towards the sea.'

'Oh, I would just like to see if there is anything left of *The Lucy* and also see where I was thrown up by the sea onto that rock. I don't suppose you have heard if they have found any more bodies?'

'No. Afraid not. It can be months afore the gobbets get washed free of the rocks down below and are cast ashore.'

Josh shuddered. 'Gobbets. I hate that word, but I suppose it is descriptive.'

'Them remains are not nice to see, Josh.'

Josh realised that the efforts of the morning had taken toll of his energy and so he retired to his bed that afternoon to rest and, later, the doctor took supper in his own room so that, once again, there was no chance for conversation with him. Was he, wondered Josh, deliberately avoiding meeting his patient, who had been, so unexpectedly, thrown into his care?

The doctor, however, made no objection to Josh and Rowena's excursion to Morwenstow in two days' time, not least because it enabled him to ask his daughter to deliver a letter, concerning church business, to that village's vicar, the Rev. Robert Hawker.

Again, it was a fine morning and Josh felt much more comfortable sitting alongside Rowena in the donkey cart than in the basket chair for the rest had certainly eased his leg. The two chatted as they rode along the clifftop between white thistle-tops and over moorland trimmed by occasional drystone walls. Rowena pointed out the white sea compass flowers dotted amongst the heather and warned Josh about walking along the moor at this time of the year because of the adders that lay coiled catching the last of the year's sunshine.

It became clear that she was well versed in the history of this part of northern Cornwall and, glad to be back in the medieval world of Walter Scott, she burbled happily about its past. The church and the village of Morwenstow itself, she explained, were named after the lady Morwenna, the daughter of a Welsh king in the ninth century.

She related how the girl grew up so learned that King Ethelwulf, King of Saxon England, asked her father to allow the girl to travel to England to be tutor to his daughters.

'And she did so well in this calling,' continued Rowena, 'that the English king said that she could have whatever she wanted . . .'

'What did she ask for?' demanded Josh, intrigued, despite his scepticism.

'"Oh sire," cried Morwenna to the King, "there is a stately headland in far Cornwall, called Henna Cliff, or the Raven's Crag, that cries out for a font and altar to be built there." And the King said, it shall be so. And the church was built and named after Morwenna, who by this time had become a saint, so that many pilgrims have come here to worship in her name.'

Rowena's eyes were now alight with fervour, or perhaps just the thrill of telling a good story. Joshua didn't care, because he could not but admire the blush on her cheek and the way she laughed with it all. No wonder, he reflected, that Jack the Captain of the Preventers desired her – and probably all of the village's young men too.

As though to underline the thought, a young man approached them now and Josh recognised the young sailor in the dinghy who had hailed Rowena on the previous day.

'Good day, Rowena,' he called, pulling off his knitted cap. He was a handsome fellow, roughly of Josh's height and build, although he was probably a year or two younger. His complexion was tanned with sun and wind, and he walked with the slightly rolling gait of a sailor. 'And good day to you, too, sir,' he said with a half bow – perhaps a little mockingly? – to them both.

Rowena sighed and reluctantly pulled the donkey to a halt. 'This is Tom Pengelly,' she said. She indicated Josh, 'Josh Weyland.' She spoke curtly.

'Ah, Mr Weyland. You had a lucky escape from the wreck of *The Lucy*, I hear.'

'I did indeed, Tom. But you must call me Josh. I am a mere sailor, a man of the sea, like you.'

'Not quite, sir, for I understand you are a second mate. I do not aspire to those heights. I am just a rower of "hobblers" . . .'

'What are they, then?'

'That is what the people here call the dinghies that go out to help the smacks round the end of the harbour wall and in to anchor,' Rowena interrupted. 'Now, Mr Pengelly, you must not detain us. Mr Weyland here has urgent work to do in Morwenstow.'

'Ah, forgive me. Be careful as you go, Rowena, the clifftop beyond has crumbled at its edge.'

Rowena clucked at the donkey and shook the reins. 'I am as well aware as you of the dangers of the cliff path here, thank you, Tom Pengelly. Good day to you.'

After they had left the young man behind, looking after them, his cap still in his hand, Joshua said: 'Rowena, you spoke very sharply to that young man. You were almost rude to him. And I don't have urgent business in Morwenstow, as you know.'

'Humph. If I had let him he would have kept us gossiping all day. Everyone in Hartland wants to know about you. And anyway, you do have business of a sort in Morwenstow.'

'Yes, well I suppose I do.' Josh shrugged and smiled inwardly. Tom Pengelly was clearly another of Rowena's admirers in Hartland, but her sense of possession of him was becoming rather irritating. He wished he could hear from Mary . . .

After perhaps an hour and a half they turned off the cliff road and followed a path, little more than a sheep's track, down towards where it opened out onto a small, flat common, containing a small group of dwellings, most of them huddled around a weather-ravaged farmhouse and a ramshackle inn.

'This is Morwenstow,' said Rowena. 'I told you there was not much here for you to see.'

Josh looked about him keenly. Immediately ahead, the ground ended abruptly to reveal the sea stretching out to Lundy, now distantly to the right of them. On their right, a path hung over with ash trees and thorns, wound its way down the hill, disappearing into a cleft in the clifftop.

'Can we get down there in the cart?' asked Josh.

'Only as far as the vicarage, where I have to go anyway to deliver Father's letter. After that there is a track of a sort, which is quite steep and we could not take the cart down it. It leads down to a little shingle beach and the terrible rocks that wrecked *The Lucy*. I doubt if you could get down there, Josh.'

He nodded. 'But that's just where I want to go, or at least halfway down. I am getting much better now walking with this crutch. I'll be all right. Take the cart down to the vicarage and I'll get out there and walk to the beginning of the track and wait for you there.'

Rowena frowned. 'I don't like this, Josh,' she said. 'I don't like this at all. What if you slipped? You could be killed.'

'Well, let me see for myself. I am determined to look at that rock where I lay. Come on, girl, I promise I won't go on down if it looks too dangerous.'

Shaking her head, Rowena turned the donkey down through the lane, which now appeared to be like a green tunnel. After a hundred yards, it bent to the left and became even more steep, but the donkey pulled back in the traces and retarded their descent until they met an open gateway, which allowed them a view, immediately below them, of a fine new house.

''Tis the vicarage,' said Rowena. 'The Reverend Hawker had it built as soon as he came here.'

Josh grunted. 'Well, the living must have been well endowed. That house would grace an earl or archbishop.'

'They say his wife had money – and that virtually all of it was spent on the building of it. But he is a good man and the house is gifted to the parish. He supports the poor and has built a school in the parish for the children, all at his own cost. He is also a bit, what shall I say, peculiar.'

'In what way?'

'He has built himself a little hideaway out on the cliff where he can look out to sea and write poetry. It is also said,' her voice dropped away, 'he smokes opium there.'

'Goodness me!' Josh spoke in assumed shock. 'Whatever next!'

'Now don't you mock me, Josh Weyland. We are simple folk around here and not accustomed to the weird things you have seen in your travels round the world. We don't take kindly to them.'

Josh bent his head. 'I'm sorry, Rowena. I didn't mean to sound patronising.' He looked up at the sky. 'But I think we should get on. That could be a storm cloud coming up from the west and I wouldn't want to be caught on the cliff.'

'Very well. We can go a little further in the cart and then we must get down.'

The donkey picked his way round another steep bend in the track and they halted at the edge of a lawn, which led to the house. It was indeed an imposing building. Built of local stone, it had five distinctive chimneys, each different in design, and copies, explained Rowena, of the various church towers of the parishes where the vicar had worked before coming to Morwenstow. It stood end on to the north-west and so shouldered the prevailing wind and weather, secure in a V-shaped cleft in the cliff, alongside a stream which plunged down to the sea.

It seemed a remote, if beautiful, outpost of civilisation in this wild and cruel landscape and Josh wondered what kind of poetry its occupant created. He had an indication when Rowena returned to join him where he waited by a wicker gate leading onto a field.

'The vicar's not in,' she said, 'so I have left Father's letter. But I have been able to memorise the words, which I knew he had carved into a stone above the doorway. Now,' she paused for a moment, 'yes, I have them. Listen:

A house, a glebe, a pound a day,
A pleasant place to watch and pray!
Be true to church, be kind to poor,
Oh minister, for evermore.'

'Hmm.' Josh nodded. 'I am not sure about the poetry but he sounds quite a character. But, do help me along here. I want to get on. It looks as though there is a way down over there.'

As Josh hobbled slowly over the tufted grass, Rowena tightly gripping his arm, he could see that the defile was sharply marled by the division between the rich green of the sloping farmland and the black line where the gorse grew untrammelled and the rocks began, like the stubble on a sailor's chin. To their left, on the other side of the cleft, the grey-black stone of the cliff fell almost vertically, revealing, at its foot, a small beach of grey shingle.

They were now inching their way down a steeply falling track, which followed the stream on its journey to the sea. As they rounded a twist in the stream's course, they reached a small plateau where they could rest for a moment and from which they could look down onto the black, foam-shrouded rocks of Morwenstow, which reached out into the ocean.

There, piniomed between two of the jagged fingers of rock, lay what was left of *The Lucy*. She was now little more than a wooden skeleton, her ribs and keel shuddering as each wave hit them, but her proud bowsprit still pointing up to the heavens.

'Ah,' muttered Rowena, 'the wreckers have been at her. Look, Josh, look. And that's the rock where you lay. Look . . .'

But Josh was gazing down at their feet, where a hole in the turf showed where something had been thrust into the ground. And the hole itself was surrounded by what appeared to be a circle of grey ash.

Josh spoke slowly. 'I've found what I came for. This is where they put the brazier into the ground and this is where the ash fell from it. So there *was* a light. I knew it! Now I must find out who planted it,' his voice dropped, 'and why.'

CHAPTER FIVE

They drove back to Hartland Quay in comparative silence. Rowena seemed sullen, petulant perhaps that Josh had shown far more interest in a hole in the ground than in the rock on which he had nearly perished. She did, however, confirm that she had not arrived at the site of the shipwreck until Josh had been taken, still unconscious, to the path at the top of the cliff, and had seen nothing of the actual rescue, nor, for that matter, of the Preventers who, it seemed, had been down below on the beach.

For his part, Josh was lost in thought for most of the journey. He had found one answer to the puzzle of the light. It had definitely existed and, seemingly, it was that that had lured Lucas onto the rocks. But was the luring deliberately carried out by someone on the cliff face? Who would have lit the brazier in the face of the storm and kept it blazing during that fierce tempest? Was there some innocent reason for its existence – a boundary light to help shepherds and other farm workers keep their animals away from the cliff edge, for instance? Possible, maybe, but unlikely.

If there was, then, a malevolent reason for the light, why was he allowed to survive the fury of the storm and be rescued to tell the story? Was smuggling – so prevalent in this corner of England – somehow behind it all?

He studied Rowena as she skilfully persuaded the donkey away from the cliff edge. She had set her jaw firmly in that determined way he had come to recognise when she felt uncomfortable with the conversation. He relied on her to be his means of transport and, indeed, his confidante. But looking at her now, her cheeks glowing from the sea air and her long hair blowing in the wind, as it did on the night of the storm, he recalled her reluctance to talk about wrecking, even about the shipwreck of her father and Cunningham.

He shook his head. Perhaps he had been away from England for too long. Certainly, this piece of his homeland seemed strange and even menacing. And when was he going to hear from Mary?

For once Doctor Acland was in evidence when they reached the house. In fact, he seemed to be waiting for them, for he had left the door to the sitting room ajar so that he could see the front entrance. He seemed concerned.

He rose and, leaning on his stick, shuffled towards them. 'I shouldn't have let you go, Weyland,' he said. 'No man with a leg bound in splints and walking with a crutch should have gone anywhere near that blasted clifftop at Morwenstow. Damn it. It is four hundred feet from top to the sea. Emma should not have taken you there.'

'We did not go to the highest point, Father. Nor did we go down to the sea edge.'

Josh nodded. 'No, sir. Row—Emma was very caring of me. We only went about halfway down the little track to the beach. But I found what I was looking for and—'

The doctor looked at him sharply, his face lined from a fierce frown. 'And what, pray, was that?' he demanded.

'If we could sit down together for a moment or two, I would like to tell you and to ask your advice about it.'

'Well,' the doctor half turned away. 'I have work to do.'

'I appreciate that, Doctor, but what we found at Morwenstow worries me and I think that maybe you could throw some light on the matter.'

Acland sighed. 'Oh, very well. But I must return to my study. If you want to talk you must join me there.' He shot Josh another gaze from under lowered brows. 'It's on the third floor at the top of the house and quite a climb. It is difficult for me to make it and could be dangerous for you with that crutch and your leg in splints. Perhaps we should talk at another time, eh?'

Rowena responded quickly. 'I could help him, Father.'

'No, child. Why don't you make some tea – and bring us some of those scones you made yesterday, eh?'

Josh frowned. Was the old man trying to evade him once again? 'Well, sir,' he said. 'I think I can manage the stairs if there is a handrail and I really would value a few minutes of your time this afternoon, if you could indulge me . . .'

'Oh, very well. But take care. I do not wish to operate on you again.'

In fact, the stairway was not difficult to climb at all for Josh was able to use his free hand to pull himself up with the help of the handrail. The doctor, surprisingly, went on ahead, trusting that his patient could, indeed, look after himself.

The study was a surprise. It was a large room and Josh guessed that it ran completely across the top of the house. But it was spartanly furnished: a desk, two chairs and a chaise longue. The walls, however, were completely lined with books; on one side they appeared to be musty tomes and Josh presumed that they were medical publications. But two walls carried serried ranks of Lloyd's Register of Shipping – books instantly recognisable to Josh.

The fourth wall was completely dominated by a large telescope. It seemed exactly the same as that in Cunningham's cabin: standing on three telescopic legs and directed to look out of the large window. By the look of it, it was positioned so that the viewer could focus over the top of the terraced houses opposite and scan the ocean beyond.

Josh exclaimed at the sight.

'What?' the doctor swung round, seemingly in some alarm. 'What's the matter, boy?'

'Oh, I am sorry, Doctor. But this seems to be almost exactly the same as Captain Cunningham's cabin in the Preventers' barracks. He, too, has rows of Lloyd's Register and a powerful telescope, mounted in much the same way as yours.'

'Ah, so you've been there, have you?' He growled so that Josh could hardly hear him. 'We have much the same interests.' He gestured to one of the two chairs. 'Sit down. Now what can I do for you?'

Josh took a deep breath and related all that he knew about the shipwreck: the sudden appearance of the light, Lucas's ignoring of

Josh's warning, the figures glimpsed on the beach and the discovery that day of the hole halfway up the cliff path and the ashes surrounding it.

'Don't you see, sir. It was obviously the site of a brazier specially erected on a spot where it could be glimpsed from the sea, even though the visibility was poor. Why should a light be there? It was many yards from the nearest habitation, which I presume was the Reverend Hawker's vicarage, so that it could not have been a lantern.'

Acland interjected quickly. 'How do you know that? The light could have been that of a lantern carried by a shepherd worried about the safety of his flock on the clifftop and in that storm.'

'I doubt it, sir. I looked around me carefully when we drove there today. I could see no evidence of farm livestock anywhere near the cliff edge. And, anyway, the turf is moorland growth on the clifftop, not at all suitable for animal grazing. It certainly looked to me as though no livestock would be allowed to venture near such a dangerous drop, in any case.'

'Humph.' Acland looked quickly around the room, as though seeking inspiration. 'Those ashes could have been there for some time. People sometimes come down from Hartland itself, or even Stoke, to light a fire and picnic.'

'I suppose that is true. But that hole in the ground was rectangular, as though a post had been hammered into the turf. And it all seemed to fit. Why would anyone deliberately lure *The Lucy* onto the rocks? I thought all of that business of "false lights" ended years ago.'

'And so it did. No one here – certainly none of the seafaring folk – would commit that murderous act now.' He paused for a moment. 'Unless, perhaps . . .' His voice tailed away.

'Yes. Did you have someone in mind?'

'I don't know. It could have been the tinners – you know, the tin miners who work on this coast, although some way away towards the south. The price of tin is low, now, I understand, and many of the poor beggars are near to starving. They don't share our comradeship of the sea.' He held up a hand. 'It is just a possibility and I have no evidence at all to support the notion. I still maintain that, if there was a light, it would have been there without murderous intent. Have you consulted Cunningham about it all?'

'Yes. He states firmly that he was there that night and saw no light.'

'Well, there you are, then. That must be conclusive, young man. I feel that you must let this matter drop.' He lowered his voice. 'This is, indeed, a rather primitive part of our country and I don't think the local populace would take kindly to you going around making accusations. It could, in fact, be a dangerous thing to do.' Then, as an afterthought he asked: 'Did you tell the Reverend Hawker about this business?'

'No, sir. He was out when Emma called.'

'Well, if you do see him, it would be best not to mention the matter. He is a man of great worth but, ah, what shall I say, of rather eccentric habits. It would not do to disturb him, you see.'

Josh did not see, but decided not to argue. It was clear that this was as far as Doctor Acland could go. Indeed, it seemed as though he had issued a warning to deter Josh from further investigations.

'Very well, sir. I shall let the matter drop. But I am concerned about staying as your guest here without paying my way. I have a little money and would be happy to pay you, say, five shillings a week, while I stay here to recompense you for the cost of feeding and watering me.'

The doctor raised a hand, almost in relief, sensed Josh. 'Certainly not, my boy. You are most welcome to stay here until you have completely recovered. As I have already said, we do not need money here. And,' he allowed a rare smile to cross his countenance, 'I rather suspect that Emma is enjoying looking after you.'

As though on cue, the door opened and Rowena appeared, flushing slightly and carrying a tray with teapot, cups and a plate of scones. Had she been listening at the door? wondered Josh. He made a mental resolve to find an excuse to ask Rowena to take him down the coastline south to where the tinners lived and worked. Perhaps there might just be a clue there. He certainly was not going to give up his investigations. He owed it to Jorgen Grumm, if no one else.

On returning to his room, however, he decided to let the matter drop for the moment. It seemed he might have provoked some resentment within the village and he did not wish to exacerbate the matter. And, in any case, he was anxious to increase his daily exercise in an attempt to heal the damaged leg. He might, he pondered sourly, have need of greater mobility in the days to come.

So it was that he declined further offers of rides in the donkey cart with Rowena. This, of course, earned her displeasure and she retaliated by doing her best to ignore him for the next few days. As a result, Joshua took to venturing out with the crutch by himself, either up the cliff path towards Morwenstow or hobbling down to the harbour to admire, once again, the excellent seamanship of the men of the smacks and the dinghies.

It was on the second day that, as he inched his way upwards

towards the Preventers' barracks, he first became conscious of a horseman, right on the clifftop and therefore silhouetted against the sky, who seemed to be observing him. He was there again the following day and on the next. He was too far away for the rider to be recognised but he seemed gently to urge his mount forward to walk in parallel with Joshua as he stumbled along. Josh thought that he saw light reflected from the lens of a telescope levelled at him, but he could not be sure.

He shrugged his shoulders. If he was being spied upon there was very little he could do about it, so there was no point in being concerned.

Some four days after his conversation with Acland, however, something occurred which did concern him. He was hobbling along in mid morning down the sleepy street, now glistening from a night-time shower, towards the harbour again. Suddenly, it seemed as if his crutch was kicked from behind and he would have fallen badly had it not been for strong arms that held him.

He turned and looked into the smiling face of Tom Pengelly, who was gripping him tightly.

'Agh!' Josh winced with pain as his injured leg thudded back onto the cobblestones. 'Did you kick my crutch away then?'

'Certainly not, Mr Mate.' The young man's grin seemed to widen. 'Your crutch slipped on the cobblestones and I jumped forward and was able to save you from falling. You should thank me, not accuse me.'

Josh nodded his head slowly. 'Yes, well then. Thank you, Tom. I could have damaged my leg again, it seems, had it not been for you.'

'Well, Mr Weyland.' The grin had disappeared now. 'You really must be more careful, you know. Walking about on one leg, so to speak, you could easily slip over the clifftop. And that would be the last anyone would hear of you. I do urge you to take care.'

Josh's eyes narrowed. The meaning was clear. This was a warning and a threat. 'Very well, Tom,' he said. 'I shall be very, very careful in future. Thank you, but I can manage now, I think.'

Pengelly raised a languid forefinger to the brow of his straw hat, nodded and walked away down to the harbour. Josh decided not to follow him, and instead, turned and walked back the way he had come. Then, on impulse, he turned into the inn next to the Acland house.

It was his first visit to the hostelry and he looked around him with interest. Although the weather was mild, logs were burning on an open fireplace and the bar top was brightly polished, with pewter pots hanging in a row above the counter. Barrels lined the wall behind the bar counter and flags of shipping lines hung from the ceiling. He noted the blue star on a white background of the Blue Cross Line. There seemed to be no customers and, indeed, no bartender either, so the room was empty.

He fumbled in his pocket for coins and rapped the counter with a penny.

Immediately, an elderly man appeared, wearing a leather apron and beaming from a round face that featured the blue, bulbous nose and bright, shining cheeks of a publican.

'Good day, good day,' he chortled. Then he noticed the crutch. 'Ah, you must be the sailor the boys pulled off the rocks down at Morwenstow. My word, sir, you had a lucky escape an' that's the truth.'

Josh held out his hand. 'I am indeed, landlord. Joshua Weyland.'

The innkeeper grabbed the extended hand and shook it enthusiastically. 'Jacob Millbury,' he said. 'Welcome to The Unicorn. I wondered if you might pop in, like. The doctor next door used to come in regular, but we ain't seen much of him for some time now. I 'ope he is well?'

'Apart from his leg, which I believe still gives him some inconvenience, he seems well, thank you. I would like a pot of your best beer if I may, please, and do join me, if you have the time.'

Millbury reached up and brought down two pint-sized pewter pots. 'That's very kind of you, sir. I don't mind if I do. That will be six pennies, please.'

Josh handed over the coins and took an exploratory sip. It was sour and dark and he could taste the hops. It was the first English beer he had tasted for more than two years. It was welcome. But his mind raced. He must be careful how he handled this conversation – not least having just been warned to keep his nose out of the comings and goings of Hartland Quay. He smacked his lips.

'Very good, Mr Millbury. Best I've tasted for many a month.'

'Brew it myself, out the back there. People do say as it's the best beer in Devon – or Cornwall.' He took a draught which seemed to half empty the pot.

'You mentioned my escape from the wreck a minute ago. D'you know, I still don't know who pulled me off that rock and took me to the top where Ro . . . Emma was waiting. I was unconscious and was never able to thank them. Do you know who it was? Presumably one of the Preventers. I would like to shake their hands.'

'Oh no. It was not the Preventers. T'was young Tom Pengelly

and one of his mates from the harbour. From what I've 'eard, they actually crept out on the rock 'alf into the sea to pull you off. Then the two of 'em carried you up the cliff face. Quite a performance, by all accounts. Don't know the other lad's name but Tom will tell you. Young Emma knows 'em all.'

The last sentence was said with a smirk, which raised Josh's ire. But he took another pull at his beer while he absorbed what had been said. Pengelly, then, the man who had just kicked away his crutch and warned him about prying into other men's business – it was he who had saved his life, for certainly, unconscious, he could not have resisted the pull of the surf much longer. He could well imagine the dangers inherent in crawling out onto the slippery surface of the rock and then carrying him away from the crashing waves.

He sighed. Rowena must have known that Pengelly was there that night. Why did she not introduce him as his saviour, when they met on the Morwenstow road that day?

He took refuge in his pint pot to hide his puzzlement. What other secrets would this strange village throw up?

But Millbury was continuing. He leant across the bar conspiratorially.

'I expect you knows about young Emma?' he asked with a leer.

'Well, I don't know much about her, apart from the fact that she is the doctor's daughter.'

'Well, she's that, all right. But the gravestone where the poor lass goes to pray for 'er mother, ain't that of 'er mother at all.' He pulled away from the bar and waited for Josh's reaction. He was not to be disappointed.

'What! But is that gravestone not that of the doctor's late wife, then?'

The publican threw back his head in silent glee. 'Oh, it's that all right, sir. But she wasn't Emma's mother, yer see. Oh no, she wasn't her mother.'

'So,' began Josh slowly, 'who was her mother, then? And is the doctor not her father?'

The barman put a finger alongside his nose. 'Oh 'e's 'er father, all right. But 'er mother was a young gypsy lass who was a real looker.' He wiped his lips with the back of his hand. 'The doctor couldn't resist 'er and I don't blame 'im. His wife was very ill at the time, so 'e didn't 'ave what you might call much comfort at 'ome. No wonder he strayed a bit. In fact, 'is wife died just before Emma was born.'

'What became of Emma's mother, then – the gypsy lady, that is?'

'She died in childbirth, so the poor old doctor lost two loved ones within a few days. His wife is buried in the churchyard at Stoke Church, up on the top. But, the doctor drew a line at 'aving 'is two ladies in the same place, so to speak. So 'e arranged with old Rev. Hawker down at Morwenstow to bury 'er in his churchyard. 'E's a free-thinkin' sort of bloke and 'appily agreed.'

'So Emma doesn't know about her real mother – about her existence, that is, and where she lies now?'

'Course she doesn't. Doctor couldn't bring 'imself to reveal 'is shame, so to speak.'

Josh frowned. Was this just tittle-tattle? It all seemed rather far-fetched. 'This was some time ago, obviously,' he said. 'Were you here then, or did you pick up the story later?'

Millbury threw back his head at the obvious charge that he might be retelling old folk tales. 'Oh no. I was 'ere then, keepin' the pub, like. I knew because the doctor asked me – on the quiet, so to speak – to arrange for flowers to be sent down to Morwenstow. I was 'appy to be of service an' to keep silent about it all.'

Well, you're not keeping silent about it now, thought Joshua. But he pressed on, hoping to take advantage of the publican's loquacity. 'Thank you . . . Most interesting. I presume very few people know the story in the village?'

'Oh no. I doesn't tell anyone of it now, really.' The man had the shame to look embarrassed. 'I only tells you of it because you're livin' there now, see.'

Josh put down his pint. 'Would you put a half in there please, landlord, and have another pint yourself.'

'Ah, that's very kind of you, sir. I don't mind if I do.'

He filled up the pots.

'I understand that the wreck of my ship was only one of many on this stretch of the coast,' said Josh innocently.

'Oh, bless you, yes. When the weather's bad – from the north-west that would be – we seem to get one every two or three days, it seems.'

Josh pulled on his half pint. 'Really? I'm not from round here, of course, but I did hear rumours about false lights; of ships being lured onto the rocks by wreckers. Does that still happen?'

Millbury's face immediately froze and Josh realised that he had gone too far.

'Course not. That 'appened – if it 'appened at all – many years ago. An' it's an 'angin' offence now. I don't know where you picked that up.'

'Oh, it was part of the mythology of the coast, I suppose. Old stories, of course. Nothing to do with me, anyhow.' He quickly finished his beer. 'Well, thank you, Mr Millbury. I've enjoyed our chat and the beer. I must get back for Emma will be scolding me for being late for lunch. Goodbye to you.'

'Good day to you, sir.' But there was a certain coldness in the publican's voice. Josh kicked himself for pushing the questioning too far, but there was nothing he could do about it now. He tucked his crutch into his armpit and swung himself through the door of the inn, his mind running.

So that was where Rowena got her dark beauty and vivacity from. She was a Romany! He frowned. How tragic, though, that she prayed at the grave of a woman who was not her mother, while the real parent languished ten miles away, probably in an unmarked grave. Perhaps the Rev Hawker could . . . no! He must not blunder into this sad episode. There were enough secrets in this hamlet as it was. He must not get involved. He tried to summon a picture of Mary's round, smiling face. Why oh why had she not responded to his letter? There would have been time to do so. He resolved to send her a second letter.

At the luncheon table, he studied Rowena's face anew. Her acquired name certainly now fitted into her maternal background. Those high cheekbones, long, wild hair and black eyes were all redolent of the Romany race and her strange impetuosity fitted into the pattern. She was undoubtedly beautiful and he wondered if her suitors – the ill-assorted pair of Pengelly and Cunningham among them – had ever acquired even the merest sniff of the story of her birth. The Preventers' captain had been, after all, shipmates with Acland and, presumably, stayed friends with him throughout Rowena's young life.

The thought of Cunningham made him wish to walk unaided up

to the Preventers' barracks and accept the captain's invitation to meet the men who had allegedly pulled him off the rock. Would they be 'out on patrol' again? If so, that would add veracity to the publican's story.

'Where are you goin', Josh?' cried Rowena as he hobbled through the door.

'Oh, I thought I would just get some fresh air. Might perhaps see if I can walk up as far as the Preventers' place. It would be good exercise.'

'You don't want to walk up that steep path on your own, Josh. I'll come with you. Let me get my wrap.'

'No. No. I must try and walk by myself. And I know you will have plenty to do back here.'

She pulled a face but retreated to the kitchen. Josh swung out onto the street and made for the turning that led up the cliff face. He was pleased that he was acquiring a confident rhythm in walking now, even though the ascent was gruelling and he was forced to gulp air into his lungs.

Instinctively, he looked up to the skyline above him. Was he being watched again? But no rider appeared. He bent his head and concentrated on the climb.

As he neared the iron-studded door he heard the clash of steel from within. It was as though a battle was being fought beyond it. He picked up a giant ring, which hung from its face and thumped it on the door.

It was Cunningham himself who opened it: but a Cunningham with a cutlass in his hand. The scar on his cheek stood out blackly from a face red from effort.

'Why, it's young Josh,' he cried, a warm smile lighting his countenance. 'Do come in.' He nodded to where a surly-faced man in a bedraggled uniform of sorts stood, panting for breath and leaning on a cutlass. 'I've just been exercising Hawkins here in the noble art of fighting with a cutlass. Come in, come in and provide us with an audience.'

'Oh, I would not wish to stop your training, Captain,' said Josh, eyeing the curved blade that shone in the afternoon sun. 'I just wondered if your men who saved me from the sea were here today so that I could thank them personally.'

'Ah, alas no. You've missed them once more. They are patrolling again. Pity. But come in, anyway. Can you handle a sword, Weyland?'

'Well, I once had a lesson from a marine captain in Canton, who said he would make a man of me, but I fear I wasn't much of a swordsman.'

'Here, now. Try your hand with me. Hawkins, hand your weapon over to Mr Weyland.'

Josh blew out his cheeks. 'Oh no, sir. I am just not mobile enough to match you, what with my leg in splints and all . . .'

'Ah we won't go at it that hard, Josh. Let me try and teach you how to handle a naval cutlass. As a sailor you ought to know. Now, stand over there and wedge your back into the wall so that you don't overbalance and I will show you some of the basic moves and the responses to them.' He smiled, teeth flashing white against his dark features. 'You never know these days when you might need to display that kind of skill. Here, come now. Take the cutlass. Go about your duties, Hawkins.'

Reluctantly, Josh accepted the weapon and lurched across to the wall, where he laid down his crutch and braced himself against the stonework behind him. He took a deep breath. Was this some form of trial of strength he was being put to, or was Cunningham genuinely about to impart some knowledge?

'Now,' said the captain. 'The first thing to remember about the cutlass is that it has a point as well as an edge.' He held up the blade and fingered its end. 'Because this thing is heavy and is curved, first-time users want to swing it so,' he brought it down in a fearsome diagonal slash, a few inches from Josh's nose. Josh steeled himself not to flinch.

'So much time and effort is wasted that way. The thing to do is to thrust with it, so.' He immediately bent his knee in classic fencing style and thrust forward incredibly quickly, so that the point of the blade hit the brickwork behind Josh's ear with a crunch as the brick splintered.

Josh gulped.

'So, two basic attacking moves. Now I will show you how to counter them. Stay with your back to the wall, but lift your blade to bring it down on my shoulder, as though you are going to split me in two. Go on, man, swing it down at me.' He lowered his own weapon and thrust his head forward provocatively.

Josh did as he was told, half fearing he would cause some terrible injury for Cunningham was close to him. But before he could bring down the blade, the captain's point was at his throat.

'See?' said his tutor. 'When the blade is lifted in that crude fashion, it gives you time – if you use the point – to take advantage of the opening provided and thrust forward. Now you try it. Thrust as I swing my sword backwards for the downward lunge. Go on. You won't hurt me, I promise you that.'

Half-heartedly, Josh did as he was told and, indeed, he was quick enough to beat the downward swing of his opponent and he could have caused serious injury had not Cunningham moved his head aside at the last moment.

'Good,' cried the captain. 'That was good. Now let's try it again.'

And so this strange gavotte danced by the two men – one fixed against the wall and with the bottom of his splints on his injured leg now thrust into the gravel at his feet to give him some sort of stability, the other moving backwards and forwards with the grace of a bullfighter, the hook on his left hand held incongruously high behind him – continued for several minutes.

Cunningham showed Josh how to deflect the thrust of his sword by using his own weapon to slide down the attacker's blade and, with a last minute twist of the wrist, deflect it away. Because of his immobility, Josh could not assume the classic posture of the duellist, as demonstrated by the Preventer, but the quickness of his eye and the strength of his forearm did much to compensate and, after ten minutes, he was almost holding his own against a man who, it became clear, was an expert swordsman.

'My word, Weyland.' Cunningham lowered his sword and then brought the hilt up to his chin in salute. 'You've done well. You could become a good swordsman if you kept at it. I salute you!'

Josh wiped the sweat from his forehead, threw the cutlass to the ground and picked up his crutch. 'Well, thank you for the lesson . . . er . . . Jack. But I think I will leave the fighting to you chaps. It's a mite too dangerous for me.'

'Well done, anyway. Now come into my cabin and let's have a brandy and soda.'

'Thank you, sir, but it's a little too early for me. But I would welcome a cup of your tea.'

'Very well.' The captain led the way inside and bellowed. 'Brown. Tea for two and brandy and soda for me. Quickly now.'

Once inside the room – it was always 'my cabin' to the captain – Josh looked around him again with interest. 'Do tell me, Jack,' he asked. 'Why do you have so many copies of the Lloyd's Register on your shelves? I notice that Doctor Acland has as many, if not more. What is your interest?'

'Well, I can't answer for the doctor, but mine is a professional interest. I like to know as much as I can about the comings and goings up the Channel and I tend to keep the back copies for reference.'

'Smuggling?'

'Aye. You can never know too much about shipping movements in this game. The more you know about legitimate movements of our ships, the more you can be aware of strange vessels that poke in and out of our coves and tiny harbours on this coast. Here, take your tea.'

Josh frowned. He decided not to press the point. He sipped his tea gratefully and decided to try another tack.

'The two chaps who rescued me. I seem to always miss them, so I would be grateful if you could give me their names so that I could write a brief note of thanks to them. It's a bit difficult for me to keep climbing this damned hill to the barracks, but Emma can deliver the notes for me.'

For a moment the captain frowned. Was there uncertainty now in his expression? Then he recovered. 'Of course,' he said. 'They were Tom . . . er . . . Gardner and George Smith. If Emma brings me the notes I will see that the fellows get them. Mind you,' he smiled, 'I'm not sure that they can read. We don't require literacy as a qualification for becoming a Preventer, you know.'

Ah, the names! Josh smiled to himself. Obviously a fabrication. But what a strange man was the captain! He certainly seemed to have some kind of affection for Josh. The schooling in swordsmanship seemed a genuine attempt to help the injured man have some kind of defence if attacked. But why, oh why, should he *be* attacked? What kind of community was it that he had blundered into? He drained his cup and staggered to his feet.

'Thank you, Captain, for the lesson and the tea. I must be going. It takes me a month of Sundays to get up and down these hills and I shall catch a scolding from Ro—Emma if I am late.'

'Of course. I will see you out.' At the door in the high walls he held out his hand. 'Call in anytime, Josh. But do be careful.' His face was now deadly serious. 'You are so vulnerable walking alone with a crutch on this terrain.'

Josh nodded slowly. Another warning! 'Oh, I will, Jack. Yes, I will. I must buy me a cutlass.' He grinned but the grin was not returned and the great door was slammed behind him.

If at the back of his mind he was concerned about a possible attack, he thought nothing of danger as he took a brief constitutional before supper on the following day with dusk approaching under dark clouds. He was standing in the semi-darkness on the little plateau just outside the hamlet looking out to sea when something made him look behind.

Two men were approaching. They were heavily wrapped, although the approaching darkness was not bringing a particular drop in temperature. Their heavy topcoats made it difficult to see, from their garments, what sort of men they were, but they had hats pulled well over their eyes and scarves covering the lower part of their faces. Ominously, they carried heavy sticks and they walked towards him with a sense of purpose.

Josh looked around him quickly. There was no one else in sight. This was a time when the people of the Hartland street gossiped on their doorsteps but the road was deserted. He lifted his gaze to the high clifftop and there he was, the solitary horseman. Well, whoever he was, friend or foe, he was too far away to intervene. Josh's eyes fastened on to a flat slab of rock that rose vertically from the cliff face and stood out from the gorse growing around it. At least it would protect his back. Reaching far forwards with his crutch he hopped and skipped towards it until he was able to flatten his back against it, rather as he had the day before when facing Cunningham – except that, this time, he had no cutlass.

What he did have, however, was the sailor's knife that hung from his belt under his jacket. The two men had stopped, perhaps ten paces away from him, while they eyed him up and down.

'What do you want?' asked Josh. 'I have no money with me.'

Then he produced his knife. It was a sizable weapon, the blade perhaps seven or eight inches long, and it shone in the faded light. 'But I do have this and I know how to use it. Come along, then,' he cried, presenting the tip of the blade towards them. 'Come and have your throats cut.'

For the first time the two betrayed some uncertainty, then the taller of the two sprang forward, his stick raised high above his head. Immediately, Josh braced himself against the wall and pushed his crutch forwards, so that the tip caught the man squarely in the midriff, winding him. Quickly, Josh swung the crutch around and hit the other assailant across the cheekbone, causing him to cry out.

They both hung back and Josh realised that this would be the moment of truth. He could not defend himself against the two of them if they attacked at the same time. The crutch was no longer of much use to him so he threw it aside, twisted the bottom end of his splints into the turf to gain stability, transferred the knife from left to right hand and waited.

They did attack together, the taller one catching him a severe blow across the left shoulder, forcing him to cry out. But his stick struck the rock behind Josh's head, breaking it off, and causing the man to unbalance. It gave Josh just enough time to slash the tip of his knife into his forearm, causing him to squeal in pain. Josh twisted the man around and hurled him against his companion who seemed uncertain how to tackle this cripple with a knife. Josh struck again with his blade cutting deeply across the cheek of the first attacker who fell to the ground, blood spurting from his fingers as he clutched at the wound.

The second assailant hesitated and then sprang forward, his cudgel lifted on high. Before he could bring it down, however, Josh thrust forward, in approved Cunningham fencing style, his left hand balancing himself against the stone slab behind him. The man averted his head just in time to avoid having the knife penetrate his cheek. Then he pulled away, cursing.

It was enough. The second man pulled the first to his feet and pushed him away. He cried something indecipherable, grabbed him by the collar and led him towards the path, looking behind him at Josh with startled eyes, as though fearing that he would pursue them.

His breast heaving, Josh shouted after them, 'Tell whoever sent you that anyone who attacks me from now on will die. I can kill if I have to.' He looked up to the top of the cliff but darkness had descended and he could not tell if the horseman remained there.

'Josh, Josh, what has happened?' Rowena was racing up the hill towards him, her hair flowing behind her. 'Oh my God! Are you hurt?'

She saw the blood on the turf, let out a shriek and threw her arms around him and clutched him so tightly that Josh, without his crutch, nearly fell to the ground. Roughly, he pushed her away, anxious to regain his breath.

'Now, now, Rowena. Don't make a fuss. I've just had a crack across the shoulder, that's all. But my pride has certainly been dented.'

'Who? What? What happened? Tell me.'

He bent and retrieved his crutch. 'I was standing, admiring the sunset, when these thugs attacked me. I told them I had no money but they came on. I think they were determined to give me a good beating.'

'The swines! Did you glimpse their faces?'

'No, and I probably wouldn't recognise them if I did see them. One thing is clear, though. There will be a man somewhere near with two very nasty cuts on his arm and face and another with a bruised cheek. I don't suppose they will come to your father for treatment, but if they do you must let me know. I have a score to settle.'

'But Josh, why would they attack you?'

He sighed. 'I suppose I am asking too many questions. Rowena, it seems that this is a village with much to hide. Come on. Help me down the hill; I could do with a taste of your father's brandy – for medicinal purposes only, of course.'

Together they made their way down the hill towards the house, on whose doorstep the doctor had now appeared.

'What's this?' he shouted. 'You've been hurt. Come inside and let me look at that shoulder. What on earth is happening around here now? Come in, come in. Whatever next!'

'Doctor,' said Josh, 'would you happen to have a glass of brandy I could taste? I feel in need of some restoration.'

'Of course, of course, my dear fellow. Emma go on and open the dressing box. Quickly now.'

Chapter Six

Once inside, while Rowena fussed with dressings, iodine and bandages, the doctor went to his desk and from a wide-bottomed ship's decanter poured a glass of amber-coloured liquid, then, as an afterthought, another, which he held aloft.

'This is an 1805 French cognac,' he said, holding the glass up to the light. 'Distilled in the year of Trafalgar, although I can't say how it got here during the French wars. I think you will find it to your liking. Now, see if you can divest yourself of that coat, sit down and take a sip. Then tell me what happened.'

The brandy took Josh's breath away but he could tell that it had a maturity and depth of taste that he had never experienced before. He winced and took another sip.

'My word, Doctor,' he spluttered. 'Where did you get that? It is delicious.'

The doctor had the grace to look a little embarrassed. 'Yes, well,' he muttered, 'good cognac is an indulgence of mine.'

'It certainly is, Father.' Rowena was frowning down at him. 'As a man of medicine you drink too much of it.'

'Umph! As a man of medicine, I have great respect for its remedial qualities. Now, keep still, young man, and let me look at that shoulder.'

He ran his finger along Josh's exposed clavicle, dabbed away with iodine where the skin had been broken and then directed Rowena as she fixed a dressing and bandage to the shoulder – not the easiest part of the anatomy to which to apply a dressing.

'Good. Nothing is broken. Now, tell me what happened. I want to know everything.' The doctor spoke with a degree of emphasis that almost bordered on vehemence.

Josh told his story. At the end Rowena jumped in.

'Father, he was *so* brave. There were two of them and he was alone and he couldn't move properly but he fought them off. And all he had was a knife.'

Acland grunted. 'Well, he certainly knew how to use it. I doubt if I shall be seeing these ruffians in my surgery asking for treatment, but I shall put the word out. Now, Weyland, why on earth should they attack you? We don't have footpads in this village.'

Josh frowned. 'I really don't know, sir. I have done no one here any harm at all. I have . . . perhaps . . . well I have been asking people about the wreck of my ship and about that light I saw . . .'

'You saw no light, young man.'

'I am afraid, Doctor, that I must insist. I know what I saw and I saw the evidence. It seems to be that people here have something to hide and they do not like a stranger prying into these events. It's all to do with wrecking, I suppose.'

The room fell silent. Then the doctor rose and refilled the two glasses from the brandy decanter.

'Father, may I . . . ?' began Rowena.

'You may not. Go and get yourself a glass of lemonade.'

Rowena stamped out of the room. The silence continued until broken by the doctor. 'Weyland,' he began.

'Sir?'

The doctor levelled a stern gaze at him from under corrugated brows. 'Can I trust you with my daughter, eh? Can I?'

'What? Trust me? Of course, sir. I am engaged to be married to a clergyman's daughter in Kent. I have come home to marry her and will do so as soon as I can travel.'

'Ah. I see. That is good news. Yes, indeed. Well we shall get you away as soon as we can. In the meantime . . .' He let the word hang in the air.

'In the meantime, sir?'

'Yes. Now listen. I think you must have disturbed people in this little hamlet; there seems no doubt about that. I think it would be wise if you stayed away from here for, say a couple of nights, at least.'

'I see. Where would I go?'

'I think Bude. Emma must go with you to take care of you . . .'

'Oh, I think I can take care of myself now, sir.'

'Yes. You probably can. But I don't want you gallivanting about on those crutches. One slip could undo all my good work. Now, if you give me your word of honour that you will treat Emma with respect, I suggest that she should come with you. You have expressed an interest in the tinners, I understand. Well, there are no mines near here but they very much exist further down the coast. I suggest you go with Emma in the donkey cart. There is an excellent inn at Bude where you can stay for a couple of nights. I know the proprietor there and you can use that as your base.'

The doctor looked over his shoulder to ensure that Rowena was not near. 'Now, I have your word that you will respect my daughter as an inexperienced young woman and I am prepared to trust you. But, Emma . . .'

He let the word hang again. 'Weyland, you must have noticed that she is a . . . what shall I say . . . strong-willed young woman. I love her with all my heart but I do worry about her and the romantic notions that she carries . . .'

Josh's mind raced to conjure up a picture of the beautiful young Romany that must have conquered the doctor's heart eighteen years ago.

'You see, she will almost certainly fall in love with you and beseech you to take her away from . . . from . . .' he gestured, 'this dull life in Hartland Quay. She has a romantic disposition but I do not want her hurt in any way. I don't like this air of violence that you seem to have introduced to us here . . .'

'But Doctor . . .'

'Well, this may not be your fault, but there are persons here, clearly, who wish you harm. Go with Emma to The Dolphin in Bude – I shall give you a note to the owner – and stay away for, say, three days. Ask your questions amongst the tinners, by all means, but let things settle down here, while I make my own enquiries. Do you agree, sir?'

'Of course, sir. I presume we could leave tomorrow?'

'Yes. Go at first light. And for goodness' sake, be careful how you employ that knife of yours.'

'Very well, sir.'

Rowena burst into the room carrying a glass of lemonade. 'I am sure that this tastes much better than your horrible brandy, Papa, but I think I should be allowed to taste it and judge for myself. After all, I am eighteen now.'

Acland shot a meaningful glance to Joshua. 'Now,' he said, 'I am going to my bedroom to rest for an hour. Before you prepare the evening meal, Emma – and there will be no cognac for you – Mr Weyland has something to say to you. Then you must get back to the kitchen and get to work.'

They set off next morning as first light was just beginning to bring out the colours of the landscape. The doctor came to the door in his dressing gown to see them leave. 'Remember, Emma,' he called as they pulled away, 'behave yourself.'

'Of course, Papa.' She waved and whisked the donkey's rump with the end of her whip. She tried to disguise her delight at being allowed to leave with Joshua but she failed. Instead, she bobbed up and down beside him, clucking at the donkey and shooting grins at Joshua.

'Oh do sit still, girl,' he reproached. 'You will have the poor old donkey pull us over the edge on the clifftop.'

'Oh no, I won't. But don't you think it *such fun*, Josh, driving through the countryside on this lovely clifftop on such a fine morning?'

Josh turned his head and looked up to his left where the skyline marched along with them, some two hundred yards above. Yes, there he was. The mysterious figure on horseback, his apparel and appearance too indistinct to give a clue to his identity but, as before, he sat on his mount, with shoulders hunched, his horse keeping pace with them but slowly falling behind, his head turned their way.

'Rowena,' said Josh. 'Look up to your left. Who is that man on horseback? I have seen him several times. He seems to be keeping track of me, somehow.'

She turned and then tossed her head. 'Oh, that's Jack Cunningham,' she said, matter-of-factly. 'He likes to ride his horse along the top of the cliff and keep an eye on what is going on in the district. I think he thinks he owns the place but he doesn't, of course. Father is of much more importance in Hartland than that old man.'

Joshua lifted his eyebrows. 'He's not that old, surely?'

'Oh yes. He is *very* old. He must be at least forty.'

'Good Lord, girl. Forty is not old. He is just middle-aged. He must be far younger than your father, though.'

'Yes, I suppose so. But he doesn't interest me. Now,' she put her free hand on his knee. 'I have brought some food with us so that we can have a picnic, Josh.' She gurgled with glee. 'Won't that be fun, now?'

Josh sighed. 'Of course, Rowena. What fun!' He shifted his buttocks on the hard seat and put his hand behind him to check that his knife was in its sheath. He could not but help feeling that the two of them, riding along this little used path halfway down the cliff face, were vulnerable to another attack from whatever malevolent power seemed to pursue him. He fingered his bruised shoulder and grinned involuntarily. Well, this time, he would have Rowena to defend him! He looked at her with affection.

There was a little wind off the sea to stream her hair and she had tied it behind her head with a red ribbon. Her face glowed with health and happiness and he was forced to admit that she was beautiful. What a wonderful catch for someone!

The thought turned his mind towards Mary. Still no letter from her and he had written to her, what was it? At least a week ago. He frowned and turned towards the smiling figure at his side.

'Rowena,' he said. 'Are you sure you posted that letter to Mary?'

Her smile diminished a fraction but her eyes still danced. 'No, dear Joshua,' she said. She felt under her cloak and produced the envelope, now somewhat creased and with the flap tattered and stuck down with tape. She held it up, almost as a trophy. 'I thought it would go quicker if we posted it from Bude. A much bigger town, of course, with a better postal service.'

'What? You thought nothing of the kind. You swore to me that you had posted it. And – look – it has been opened and the flap stuck down with paper tape. Did you open it and read it?'

The girl's face flushed. 'Yes, of course, I did. But I didn't alter any of it. I just wanted to see if you mentioned me in it.'

Josh shook his head. 'You had no right to do that, my girl. Of course I did not mention you. There was no reason why I should. Rowena, you are incorrigible.'

She hung her head and did her best to look crestfallen. 'Josh. Why didn't you mention me?' Then more shyly. 'Do I mean nothing to you?'

'That is not the point. Of course I am fond of you and grateful to you for looking after me. But – and I don't know how many times I have to repeat this – I am engaged to be married to someone else. And I intend to keep my vows to her.'

A thundercloud descended onto Rowena's face. One tear glistened in the corner of her eye and then rolled down her cheek. Her head fell forward and she spoke in little more than a whisper. 'But, Josh. I love you. I really do. I would make a much better wife for you than this fat Mary.'

'Do not call her that. There can be no question of that. I intend to marry Mary Jackson and that is that. Now, there can be no more question of love, Rowena. We must be together now for at least two days. I promised your father that I would respect your . . . your . . . innocence and you told him that you would behave yourself. Now let's get on and say no more about it. But give me that letter. I will make sure that it is posted.'

They rode together in silence, broken only by an occasional sob from Rowena. But, eventually, her sunny disposition, the beauty of the day with an early autumn sun casting a warm glow, and the sound of two skylarks singing their way to the heavens from the field next to the track, banished her gloom.

'You are quite right, Joshua,' she said, eventually. 'I am sorry I did not post the letter – although I brought it today to make sure it went from Bude. And I had no right to read it. Now,' she turned to him, her teeth gleaming in a face-splitting smile, 'let us be friends and enjoy our outing.'

He seized her hand. 'Good girl. Let us do just that.' He was silent for a moment while he thought. Then: 'I still wonder why Cunningham seems to have been watching me almost since my arrival. Do you think he is behind the attack on me?'

She shook her head decidedly. 'No. He would not do that. As captain of the Preventers he virtually represents the law here. Anyway, when we met him, I was sure that he had taken a liking to you. He even tried to teach you to fence, did he not?'

'He did, indeed. Oh, Rowena. I don't know what to think. This is a very strange part of England. I do not understand it at all.'

She patted his knee. 'You will become used to it and its strange ways the longer you stay. And I shall be looking after you all the time. You will not be attacked again, I vouch for it.'

'Ah, what better guarantee of safety could there be than having you at my side . . .' He laughed.

She looked at him sharply. 'Are you making fun of me, Josh? I don't like that.'

He sucked in his breath. 'Oh, certainly not, my dear. Certainly not.'

They jogged along in silence for a while, Josh looking out at sea and studying the various white sails that marked the progress of ships up the Bristol Channel. The sea was a lustrous dark blue, marked only occasionally by the occasional white flick of a wave top. It seemed impossible that this passage of water could have turned so recently into a screaming, raging, ship-breaking sea.

He held up his hand. 'We have to pass Morwenstow on the way south to Bude, don't we?'

She nodded.

'Good. Then let us pay a call on the Reverend Hawker. He sounds a fascinating character and I would love to talk to him.'

She shook her head. 'He is likely to be out, making his rounds of the parish . . .'Tis a big territory he must cover . . .'

'Let us call, anyway.'

Rowena frowned but did not argue further and, within the hour, they were turning down that steep path from the cluster of dwellings on the heath, down towards the Hawker vicarage and its nearby church and graveyard, nestling by the stream in a cleft in the cliff side.

'Can we stop by the church? I would like to look at the churchyard.'

They descended and Josh looked around him keenly. There were some freshly dug graves. 'They are what was left of your shipmates,' explained Rowena. 'The Reverend always buries in his churchyard whatever remains from shipwrecks here. He makes no charge on the parish funds for that. He considers it his duty. He is a good man. Later he will put up a cross or even perhaps a stone to commemorate the men who died.'

'Yes, he sounds a good man.' But Joshua was not, for once, interested in what had become of the mortal remains of his shipmates. He was looking for another, single grave. He found it in a corner of the graveyard, under a yew tree. It looked freshly tended, for flowers had been laid on its surface. A simple gravestone stood at its head, stating: 'Josephine Mulrooney 1806–1824. She gave her life to produce life.'

He turned his head to look at Rowena. 'Poor girl,' he said, 'she was only eighteen when she died. What does that dedication mean, I wonder?'

'Oh, I suppose she must have died in childbirth. Like my mother did. Shall we call at the house now?'

He looked at her keenly. She expressed no obvious sadness and obviously had no idea that this was the grave of her real mother. 'Yes, of course. You go on ahead and knock on the door. I can manage on my own.'

She skipped away and, after a brief consultation on the doorstep, turned back to him. 'Mrs Hawker says that the Reverend is on the clifftop, in his special hideaway. She thinks he is writing poetry. Do you still want to disturb him?'

'Oh dear. Would he mind, do you think?'

'I don't know, but he is an even-tempered man. I know where his little cave is. But you must hold onto me. It can be dangerous for it is right on the cliff edge. Hold my hand tightly, now, Joshua.'

There followed a brief and, for Josh, awkward, scramble across the gorse high above the sea, where, down below, the wreckage of *The Lucy* lay, still caught between the black rocks, looking like the vertebrae of some giant leviathan. He gripped Rowena's hand tightly as he limped along. Only a slightly worn piece of grass, winding suddenly and almost vertically down the cliff face, showed where the Reverend Hawker took refuge. It proved to be a hidden and deep indentation in the rock, the sides of which had been roughly lined with timber and fronted with a two-piece door, the top half of which had been left open so the occupant could look out at the seascape.

The Vicar of Morwenstow was, indeed, in residence as Rowena handed Josh down to the flat piece of rock that afforded an entrance. She wrinkled her nose. 'Opium,' she whispered. The moist, sweet smell met them as they stood, a trifle uncertainly, at the entrance.

'May we disturb you, Reverend?' called Rowena.

'Ah, Emma. You never disturb me. Come on in, if you can find room.'

There was, indeed, little space to spare in the domed interior. Hawker had constructed a simple bench against the walls of his tiny retreat and there was just room for them to sit down beside him. He was a large, stout man, dressed comfortably, if untheologically, in an old fisherman's sweater and wrinkled sea boots that came up to his thighs. His kind, open face, unfashionably bore no heavy whiskers and he was smoking a long clay pipe from the bowl of which soft, white smoke emerged from time to time as he drew on it.

He waved away the smoke and eased along the bench to make room for them. 'You are most welcome, Emma,' he said. 'And,' he looked down at Josh's crutch, 'I think I know who you are, young man. Joshua Weyland, is it not?' He extended a hand, which Josh grasped.

'It is, indeed, Reverend,' said Josh, thrusting out his crutch so that it touched the other side of the little cavern. 'And I do apologise if we are interrupting some great work of literary conception.'

The clergyman threw back his head and laughed heartily. 'Oh, I wish that were so. Most of the time I just sit here, you know, occasionally working on a piece of very second-rate poetry or, even worse, a third-rate sermon. Or, most of the time, smoking this old pipe and looking out at God's glorious creation of this wonderful ocean.'

He gestured towards where the sea glinted in deepest blue through the half open wooden door. 'Oh,' Hawker waved away the smoke, 'I do hope you don't mind this indulgence of mine. Some people do, you know.'

'Not at all, sir. I sometimes indulged when I was in China.'

'Well, did you now? It shows your open mind and good judgement. There is nothing that soothes the mind more than a little opium. Would you care to share a pipe now?'

Josh shook his head. 'Thank you, sir, but no. We are on our way to Bude.'

'In fact,' Rowena interrupted hurriedly, 'we do not wish to interrupt you, Reverend. We merely wished to pay our respects to you as we were passing your door. And, of course, to convey to you my father's warmest regards. But we must be on our way.'

Joshua frowned. 'Well, sir, we certainly do not wish to interrupt your contemplation here. But, I would be most grateful if you could spare me a moment or two to give me your views on something that concerns me deeply.'

'Oh, Joshua!' Rowena stamped her foot in frustration.

'Well, of course.' The vicar drew on his pipe then carefully laid it to one side. 'How can I help you?'

Josh took a deep breath and then, slowly and carefully explained his experience of being wrecked at Morwenstow, his memories of the light that lured *The Lucy* onto the rocks, of his turbulent moments in the surf before he was thrown onto the rock and then his rescue by two men. He then related how Rowena and he had discovered the hole in the ground, halfway up the cliff face, and the ring of ash, which revealed where the brazier had stood in the storm.

'Before I go on, Reverend,' said Josh, 'I understand that you have worked to bring in what is left of my shipmates and to give them a Christian burial. As the last survivor of *The Lucy*, may I express my thanks to you for that. You are certainly doing the work of the Lord here.'

The vicar nodded slowly. 'Well, thank you for that Joshua – may I call you that?'

'Of course, sir.'

'Yes. As you know, only too well, this is a terrible coast and many ships founder on it. Before I came here, it was the common usage of the coast to dig, just above the high-water line, a pit on the shore and therein to cast, without inquest or religious rite, the carcasses of shipwrecked men. This was a terrible thing, for which one of us would not wish to "rest as our brethren did"? Now, however, I make it my business to see that these poor unfortunates – such as your shipmates, Joshua – are laid to rest in what I hope is peaceful and certainly hallowed ground.'

'Indeed, sir. Perhaps I could ask you . . .' But the vicar had the biblical bit between his teeth.

'One man,' he continued, 'who, like you, Joshua, was rescued from these very cruel rocks, quoted to my congregation the words from the Good Book, so very appropriate for a wrecked seaman. I quote: "But there the glorious Lord will be unto us a place of broad rivers and streams; wherein shall go no galley with oars, neither shall gallant ship pass thereby. For the Lord is our judge, the Lord is our law-giver, the Lord is our king, he will save us".' Hawker frowned and shook his head. 'Dash it, I cannot remember more, but you will get the appropriate gist for a seaman, Joshua.'

'Of course, sir. Of course. Could I just ask you, however—'

'We really must be going, Joshua, if we are to reach Bude before nightfall.' Rowena was nodding towards him, meaningfully.

'Yes, indeed, we must, Reverend.' Josh took a deep breath. 'But I would like to ask your advice on something that has been puzzling me, before we leave you.'

'Of course. Pray continue.'

Ignoring Rowena's frown, Josh returned to the story of the light and then he recounted the attack on him. 'I am concerned, sir,' he said, 'that because I am trying to discover the true meaning of that light on the cliff side in the storm, I have unleashed some distress amongst people in Hartland Quay, and perhaps even here, that I am trying to reveal wrongdoing. I feel, undoubtedly, that this part of the coast – perhaps even including your parish – has something to hide and is trying to prevent me revealing it.'

A silence fell on the little redoubt and Hawker picked up his pipe, puffed to rekindle the flame, and then replaced it on the bench.

'If you are saying, Joshua,' he spoke slowly, 'that there are wreckers here, in the old-fashioned sense of the word, in that there are people here who would deliberately lure ships onto the rocks, then I would argue that you are wrong. That is a wicked thing to do, which, indeed, now carries a capital punishment.'

'Well,' interrupted Josh, 'why should there be a crime now carrying a hanging on it, if no such crime exists?'

'Ah, I can see that you are a good debater, young man. Just let me say that I know my parishioners and I am sure that there is no one amongst them who would be guilty of such a heinous crime. They live close to the sea, after all, and would never deliberately consign seamen to the deep.'

'Well that may be so, Reverend, but, if you don't mind me correcting you, your parishioners are landsmen, mainly farmers, working up here high above the cliff and the ocean, who would not necessarily have a respect for the calling of the sea – the respect that fishermen, for instance, would have.'

Josh realised that his cause might not best be served by scoring debating points off the clergyman, so he hurried on. 'But, of course, sir, I defer to your knowledge of your flock here. May I ask you, though, if you were present at the wreck of *The Lucy?*'

'I suppose the answer to that must be rather evasive: yes and no. As you know, the storm in all its severity rose quickly in the middle of the night and, like most people around here, I was fast asleep. I was aroused by Captain Cunningham, who knocked on my door and told me that a ship was being driven onto the rocks and that it was likely I would have to make ready to receive the bodies of those members of the crew who were most unlikely to survive the shipwreck.'

Josh looked puzzled.

'Yes, you see I have made it a rule that those poor souls should have their mortal remains treated with dignity. So I have prepared one of the outhouses here as a kind of chapel to receive them until they can be committed to the Lord's keeping with full ceremony. Alas, with this weather so unusually clement, we have been forced to bring the bodies – or what is left of them – to put them into God's good earth, temporarily, to be followed with a proper committal later when we have retrieved them all. But, to get back to the events of that night, I hurriedly dressed; I called on the men who help me in this way to prepare the chapel accordingly. As a result, I did not witness the actual striking of the vessel on the rocks below.'

Nodding, Josh asked, 'So you did not see my rescue from the rock and my being carried up to the clifftop?'

'No, Joshua, I did not.'

'And did you see a brazier burning brightly, halfway down the cliff path?'

The vicar took a long, indulgent pull on his pipe and slowly nodded. 'Oh yes,' he said, 'I saw that all right.'

Joshua felt his jaw drop and heard Rowena sigh. He had not expected such a sanguine acceptance of this key point of his story. 'You saw it, you say?'

'Yes, of course.'

'But is this not evidence of the deployment of "the false light" tactic to lure the ship onto the rocks?'

'No, it is not, my boy. Now,' Hawker settled himself onto the unyielding bench, as though to begin a long story. 'What I am about to tell you should not leave this, ah, cabin – although, indeed, the facts are known to virtually everyone on this part of the coast, although rarely spoken about. Do I have your word?'

Joshua paused for a moment, for he felt uneasy at giving this kind of undertaking without knowing what was to come. Then, 'Yes, Reverend. You have my word.'

'Good, I need no such undertaking from Emma, for she will be well aware, I am sure, of what I am about to tell you.'

Josh shot a quick and surprised glance to the girl, but she was looking hard at the floor of the cave, although her face bore a heightened colour. What had she been keeping a secret during their time together? But the clergyman was continuing.

'That fire, that brazier, was burning as a signal all right, but not to *The Lucy*. It was as a notification to smugglers that they could not make a landing that night, not only because the storm would not allow them to do so but also because the Preventers were in the vicinity. The brazier would have been lit before the storm hit the coast and would have been flickering and spluttering in the rain when your captain and you saw it, and would have been extinguished quickly afterwards, I would have thought, by the storm itself.'

Joshua nodded slowly. 'So smugglers lit the signal, not wreckers?'

'Indeed, so, my boy. Now, before you ask your next question about my role in all of this, let me tell you that what I have just related is supposition on my part, but based upon what I know about smuggling here.' He shook his head. 'I do know that this is a signal used to call off a landing. I do not approve of breaking the law, of course, and therefore I oppose smuggling and, indeed, have preached against it. I play no part in it myself and do not benefit from it, but, living here as I do amongst my parishioners, I well know that it is practised by virtually everyone here – if not as active smugglers themselves, bringing in the contraband to our coves from ships out at sea, then as beneficiaries in purchasing the expensive goods that come in cheaply this way.'

Joshua, who felt now he could taste once again the doctor's fine French cognac, stared once more at Rowena but the girl still had her gaze fixed firmly on the floor. He understood now her reluctance to let him talk to the vicar. Her father, with his taste for fine European porcelain as well as vintage brandy, must himself be a prime supporter of the smuggling ring. And his own naive enquiries about wrecking must have been taken as a threat to unveil the existence of the practice in this part of Cornwall–Devon.

But the vicar was continuing. 'Smuggling here, Joshua, is deeply rooted. Why, when I arrived here I was told that the folks on the coast for a long ways north and south of here would teach their children to say in their prayers at night times, "God bless Father n' Mother, an' zend a ship to shore afore mornin'."' Hawker's chuckle briefly lifted a sense of oppression that had descended upon the little cabin.

Frowning now, Joshua broke the silence. 'But Reverend,' he said, 'when I asked Captain Cunningham if he had seen the light, he swore that he had not. If his presence with his men that night was a belated attempt to apprehend the smugglers, as was his duty, why should he not explain that to me – and, indeed, give me the reason for the light?'

The vicar shrugged and once again picked up his pipe. 'That is not for me to say, my son, perhaps he had motives of his own. But you will see that the recent attack on you was an attempt, I would say, to warn you off, so to speak. Ah, these are evildoings, whichever way you look at them, Joshua, all prompted by men's greed.' He sighed. 'Smuggling, you see, is thought here to be a man's right to exercise his ingenuity to outwit wicked politicians in London who are taking his money unfairly via taxes. Even men of good virtue benefit from it.'

The vicar might well have directed that last remark at Rowena but, instead, he puffed his pipe and looked out to sea. He seemed now to be immersed in his own thoughts and Josh recognised the sedative effects of the opium and determined to make the most of the vicar's honest openness while the opportunity existed. He had one last point to check.

'Do you know the men who carried me up the cliff face, Reverend?'

Hawker nodded. 'I know one of them, Thomas Pengelly, for he lives here in Morwenstow, at the top in the cottage of his widowed mother who died some time ago. The other man I know not, but I understand he also was a seaman, though from Hartland Quay. Young Pengelly is a very fine sailor. I once sailed with him. I understand that he acts often as a pilot for ships sailing up the Channel and approaching Bristol.'

Josh nodded. He disregarded this last piece of information, however, for he knew that piloting was a highly specialised occupation and that pilot cutters operated out of Bristol, often racing each other to be first to pick up a piloting assignment from a big ship at the end of its trans-Atlantic passage. There would be no role in that fiercely competitive environment for a 'part-time' pilot from a tiny harbour at Hartland. But he let it go.

'I am grateful to both of those men for saving me from that rock,' he said. 'But I can't help wondering what they were doing here at Morwenstow in the middle of a terrible storm.'

'Oh,' the parson waved his pipe, 'people hereabouts will gather on the clifftop if there is the prospect of a ship going aground. They will want to save lives, of course.'

Or to be early on the scene to indulge in profitable wrecking, thought Josh, but he did not put the thought into words. Instead, he struggled to his feet. 'Mr Hawker,' he said, 'you have given me much to think about and I am most grateful. Perhaps you could send word to the quay when you have fixed a date for the final committal of my shipmates. I would like to attend if I may.'

'Of course, my dear fellow. I must wait a little longer for it can be weeks before the sea gives up its dead here. But as soon as we decide on the date to complete their passage to the next and happier world, I will send word to you, if you are still here. Now,' he took Emma's hand, 'give my warmest regards to your father. Tell him he must make an effort soon to ride here to share lunch with us – and you would be most welcome too, my dear.'

'Thank you, Reverend.'

Rowena and Joshua made their way back to the donkey cart –

a silent, introspective Rowena for once. Josh also made no attempt at conversation for his mind was in turmoil. It seemed clear that Cunningham and his men had gathered at Morwenstow on the night of the storm because they had picked up intelligence of a smuggling landing operation in the little hidden cove at the foot of the cliffs, an operation that the storm, and probably their presence, had aborted.

Who, then, was at the centre of the smuggling ring and who had determined to protect it by employing the thugs who had attacked him? And what was the role of Pengelly? That staged saving of Josh from slipping on the cobblestones near the harbour, was that, too, a warning? Wasn't Pengelly known to be a fine sailor – and it would take a fine sailor to make a smuggling landing on that patch of shingle at the foot of the steepling cliffs of Morwenstow. Did that creepy, gossipy publican, Jacob Millbury, have a role in this? And, he shook his head at this thought, where did Doctor Acland fit into this complex pattern? After all, Rowena had said that he was the senior figure of the little community. A man of fine taste for opulent furnishing and great French brandy! Acland had said that he should get away from Hartland while he 'would make some enquiries', and he had sent his daughter to ensure that he did, in fact, leave.

The two settled into the donkey cart, still in silence, until Josh said, 'Rowena, why on earth did you not tell me about the role of the brazier and why would your father deny its existence?'

She turned a face towards him that was drained of colour now and put a hand on his arm. 'Oh, Josh, we all know about smuggling here. It is part of our heritage and we do not think it wrong. But everyone is sworn to secrecy because it is an offence and there would hardly be anyone in families along this coast who would not go to jail if these secrets were revealed. That is why I tried to discourage you from asking all your questions. I knew it could lead to harm for you.'

'Who, then, is trying to warn me off? Who is at the head of this smuggling ring? Do you know?'

She shook her head. 'No, I don't Josh. It is all kept so secret. Nobody will talk.'

'Well, the reverend did, up to a point. Do you think he knows?'

'No, I don't. He is outside of it all. I am sure of that. In view of what you have learnt today, do you still want to visit the tinners? Do you think they could still be involved?' She was frowning, hanging on his reply, for it was clear she did not want to turn back to Hartland.

Josh looked up at the sky. 'Yes, I don't feel I am anywhere near the bottom of this business and I can't help feeling that the men who are working in the mines – and, so poorly paid, or so it seems – might have some role to play in this miserable affair. So let's keep moving. We don't want to be on this road after dark.'

Rowena smiled with relief, tossed the reins, flicked the whip but only lightly – she was a gentle horsewoman – and they resumed their journey. At Joshua's insistence they ate their lunch as they rode and Rowena's usual equable state of mind returned as they jogged along in the sunshine. Once, she quickly leant across and kissed him on the cheek and, when Josh pushed her away, she grinned and put out her tongue to him.

The sun was setting beneath dark clouds on the horizon as they arrived at The Dolphin, a new, handsome inn a little way from the harbour. Joshua asked for two rooms and presented a letter from the doctor to the receptionist, who bowed, asked them to wait and took it away. A large, red-faced man with grey mutton chop whiskers appeared and immediately made a fuss of them.

'Please give my regards to your father, my dear,' he said. 'And you, sir, are most welcome. The doctor has enclosed ample funds for a two-night stay here, including breakfast and dinner, so there will be no worry about payment. Joseph here will take you to your rooms. I hope you enjoy your stay.'

Their rooms were side by side, looking down on the little canal that trickled down in front of the hotel into the sea on their left. There was an interconnecting door, which Josh firmly locked, and the two arrived promptly for dinner in the dining room at six-thirty.

Josh could not help but feel ridiculously uncomfortable, sitting tête-à-tête with this beautiful young woman, who had, of course, dressed for dinner in what he assumed must be her best dress of fine silk. She had applied a little powder and rouge and played the part of a young wife, studying the other diners with care and sipping very slowly at the glass of white wine that Josh had reluctantly conceded to her.

They chatted animatedly enough, however, over the meal – mainly with Rowena explaining how she had been sent away to boarding school in Exeter, which she had hated, and of how she wished to follow her father into the medical profession if she could persuade him to allow her to be trained. Josh found himself enjoying her company and finding it extremely difficult now to conjure up the image of Mary, while sitting opposite such an animated and attractive companion.

She offered him a demure cheek to kiss at the doors to their rooms and waved him goodnight. He was not at all surprised, however, an hour later to hear the handle of their connecting door turn.

'Go away and go to sleep, Rowena,' he called.

'Oh let me in, just for a minute, Josh,' she whispered plaintively.

'Certainly not.'

'But I have something to tell you. Let me in, just for a moment, please.'

'No. Tell me in the morning. Now, goodnight Rowena.'

He heard her turn away, deliberately dragging her heels, and a creaking of springs as she flounced onto her mattress. He shook his head and grinned before burying his head in his pillow.

Chapter Seven

A brief conversation with the hotel's proprietor in the morning gave Josh the location for the nearest tin mine, near to Bude, together with the name of its owner and manager. It was inland a couple of miles south of the town and it did not take them long to find it, for the great winding wheel and engine, which took the miners down to the bowels of the earth, could be seen prominently rising from the moorland long before they approached the buildings.

'I know a bit about this mining business,' said Rowena proudly as they approached. 'I learnt about it at school in Exeter.'

'Really? Tell me about it, then. It's quite a traditional industry hereabouts, isn't it?'

'Oh yes. Father used to say that a mine was a hole in the ground with a Cornishman at the bottom.' She shot him her quick, all-embracing smile. 'Mining here, Josh, goes back to almost 2,000 BC and—'

'What?'

'Oh yes. We used to export tin, more or less just scraped from the ground in those days, to the Romans. They had open pits then. Now they go really deep, and mining for other stuff, like copper, began in this century. It's all grown with the steam-pumping engine, and tin and copper ore is mined even in the old mines now.'

Josh nodded. 'I am impressed,' he said. 'Have you ever been down a mine?'

'Oh no. Papa would never let me go. And the tinners, as they are called, are skilled men but I think Father thought that they were a rough lot and I should be somehow . . .' she sought for words '. . . somehow defiled by contact with them.' She threw back her head. 'What nonsense!'

'What do you know about present conditions, Rowena?'

'Well, as best as I understand it, the tinners have always been up and down in terms of earnings, depending upon the price for base metals, which fluctuates a lot.' She was frowning now and speaking earnestly. 'The price has been down for some time now and I know that a lot of the miners have been thrown out of work. They are living in desperate conditions. It is a great shame.'

'Would they ever have taken part in wrecking, then?'

'Oh yes. The word would spread that a ship was in trouble, near, say, Bude and they would appear as if from nowhere. They certainly stripped clean Father's ship, when it was wrecked.'

'Ah, yes. The *Evershot*.'

The little donkey plodded into a rough, open space in front of the tall timber framework that was topped by the winding wheel, now still. Two women, sitting in the sunlight with their backs against the timber of the tower, sewing, looked up at them with interest. Their faces were black and the hair that hung scraggily from underneath turbans of old cloth looked as if it had not been washed for months.

'Good morning,' said Josh.

They both nodded but did not reply.

'Can you tell me how we can find Mr Robert Miller, the owner of this mine?'

One woman pointed to a brick-built building. 'That's 'is office there,' she said.

'Thank you.' Rowena pulled the donkey's head round, jumped down and tied the reins to a little hitching rail outside a door marked 'Manager'.

Then she reached up and helped Joshua to alight. Together they walked up four stone steps – every building except the winding tower seemed to be made from rough stone – and knocked on the door.

'Come in.'

Miller was sitting behind a table, one leg of which was broken and had been tied to a piece of wood. He was a man of middle age, with a jet-black beard and a battered top hat, which had long ago lost its sheen, pushed to the back of his head. He stood and offered a smile, which immediately lit up his face.

'Good morning. What can I do for you?'

Joshua extended his hand. 'My name is Joshua Weyland,' he said, 'and this is Miss Emma Acland. You must be Mr Miller.'

'I am indeed. Now,' his smile broadened, 'please do tell me you have come to offer to buy my mine.'

'I'm afraid not, sir. May we sit down and detain you for a moment or two?'

Miller pulled forward two battered cane chairs that stood against the wall. 'Of course. Sit down. You can detain me as long as you like for there is little work for me to do here now, alas.'

Rowena frowned. 'Why is that, sir?'

'Because my tin is almost worthless now, given the present market price for it, and it is an expensive waste of time me trying to bring it to the surface. But let me repeat, what can I do for you?'

Joshua squirmed for a moment on his chair. He realised that it would be crude and tasteless for him to confront this polite man with the question, 'Do your work people indulge in the wrecking of ships that run aground on the coast, and do they practise smuggling?' He coughed. He would have to dissemble.

'I write for the *Western Morning News*,' he said – Rowena shot him a startled look – 'and I am interested in researching the lifestyle of the tin miners of this part of Cornwall.'

Miller threw back his head and snorted. 'Lifestyle! My poor fellows hardly have one, for I can barely afford to pay them a few halfpennies to keep them turning up for work. In fact, they don't now.'

'Don't do what, sir?' enquired Rowena, with a puzzled frown.

'Turn up for work. At the moment, virtually all of my main workforce has set off to march to the north, in the hope that they can find some form of alternative employment. I am doing what I can to help them by offering their wives employment of sorts at vastly reduced wages, while their menfolk are away.' He gave a sad smile.

'Ah, I am so sorry, sir,' said Joshua. 'We have obviously chosen a bad time to call on you. What sort of work are they hoping to find in the north of the country?'

'Anything they can get their hands on. Some of the families are near starvation and I have been doing my best to provide them with basic food.

'As you are a journalist, Mr Weyland, you must know that this country is going through a period of great industrial depression.'

'Er . . . yes, of course.'

'In fact, the northern part of the United Kingdom remains locked in what can only be termed a General Strike. It started with what were called the Plug Plot Riots – so called because the workers removed a few bolts or plugs that enabled the steam boilers to operate – and seems to have spread from the mines of Staffordshire and affected the factories and textile mills of Lancashire and Yorkshire and coal mines from Dundee to South Wales and even here in Cornwall.'

Josh nodded. 'Is this unrest among the employees, then, the reason why your workforce is hoping for better pay in the north?'

'No. There is no real rift between employees and managers here in the tin mines. My people all know we just can't get a decent price for our tin and they don't blame me. No, it's the international market that is ruining our industry. But there is a huge division developing between management and workers elsewhere. The Preston strike in August this year resulted in a riot where four men were shot, and another six died in a riot at Halifax.

'As you will know,' he continued, 'this violence is getting worse, probably stoked by the politicians behind the Chartist Movement. In the north-west alone, more than 1500 strikers have been brought to trial so far this year.' He shook his head. 'We seem to be almost on the verge of revolution. So,' he smiled wearily, 'I suppose we can't really complain in our mines down here. At least the workforce is not about to hang all the owners of the workings. They understand the position we're in.'

'I must confess,' said Josh, 'that I have been abroad until recently and had not realised how bad things are here. There is obviously no alternative work for your people to do?'

'No. Many of them are well skilled and would be quite content to retrain to work on the land, or even as seamen. But there is nothing for them.'

Joshua coughed. 'Not even the occasional wrecking work on the beaches . . . ?' He let the words hang interrogatively.

'Good Lord, no. Yes, that can provide goods in lieu of wages but scraps from the ships that do go aground don't pay the rent. And, anyway, that all depends upon the weather.'

Josh looked up at the ceiling. 'I had heard that smuggling could be a profitable sideline for workers in this part of Cornwall and over the border in Devon, too.'

Miller removed his top hat and ran a hand through his thinning hair, before replacing it on the back of his head. 'There is a lot of nonsense talked about that.' He slapped one finger into the palm of his other hand. 'In the first place, it is true that there are some quite ruthless and profitable smuggling rings in operation. But not round here. They are much further north, round little places like Morwenstow and Hartland, for instance, where there is no industry, except some farming and a bit of fishing.'

Josh and Rowena exchanged glances covertly, as Miller continued.

'In the second place, these are quite sophisticated operations, which are organised to slip through anything the Preventers or the militia and the dragoons can do. My fellows are honest workpeople – and so are their wives – and they wouldn't get involved with anything so complicated as smuggling. And certainly not deliberate shipwrecking. Those days have long gone.'

He stood. 'So you will see, I am afraid I can't paint you a happy presentation of honest folk working in the tin mines of Cornwall. The lifestyle that you may be pursuing has gone with the wrecking. Now my poor folk have to march to the north to get bread. It is sad, very sad and, if you are to write about the lifestyle of Cornish tin miners, then you must paint a sombre picture indeed.' He extended his hand. It was clearly a dismissal.

Joshua was glad that he could drop his awkward impression of a daily newspaper writer and gladly accepted Miller's hand, as did Rowena. 'I will report accordingly, Mr Miller,' he said. 'But we can perhaps do more than that and follow the trail of your workmen and, even, perhaps, lend a hand to help them, if we possibly can. Either way, I wish you luck and sincerely hope that your mine can return to profitability soon.'

'Thank you. The men set off late yesterday afternoon. They took the inland road, due north. You should be able to overtake them easily.' He smiled sadly. 'They will not be moving fast. Good day to you both.'

Once they were on their way, Rowena turned to Joshua and frowned. 'Josh, I did not approve of you lying to that good man,' she said. 'Was it really necessary? He will probably now scan the *Western Morning News* for signs of your reporting for some days now.'

Josh wearily shook his head. 'I quite agree, but I had to think of some excuse for calling on him and virtually asking him outright if his workpeople were criminals. Let us see if we can catch them up.'

He lifted out a well-thumbed map from his bag. 'I got this from the hotel. Let's examine the way they might have gone. Yes, the coastal path would have been too arduous to take because it follows the line of the cliffs. Make the next turning to the right, Rowena.'

'Do we not return to our hotel for the night, then, Josh?'

'No. I will write and ask for our things to be sent on to us. We can manage for one night. I want to talk to the tinners. I have a feeling that they might well be running into trouble.'

Rowena prodded the donkey. 'Oh, how exciting,' she said, her eyes sparkling.

They did not overtake the emigrating workforce until dusk was falling and making it difficult to follow even the tracks of forty men who had trampled across the moorland turf. Then they saw the glow from campfires ahead of them – ten or twelve of them that could only come from the tinners bedding down for the night. Josh consulted the map and estimated that they were more or less level with Morwenstow on the coast, some two or three miles to the west. He pulled on the reins and reached behind them in the cart.

Rowena's grin virtually lit up the semi-darkness. 'Where do we sleep, then, Josh?' she asked.

'Off the road, right here. There is a ground sheet and a blanket in the back. Let us just hope it doesn't rain. I fear we will not be comfortable.'

'Oh yes we will. We can gather wood and light a fire and we still have the sandwiches we saved from the inn. If it gets cold, Josh, then we shall just have to cuddle. Do you know how to cuddle, Josh?'

Josh scowled. 'There will be none of that nonsense, Rowena. I promised your father, remember? And so did you, for that matter. Now behave yourself.'

He said all of this with as lofty a demeanour as he could summon but he could not deny to himself that his body was beginning to tingle at the thought of Rowena – slim, svelte, smooth-skinned Rowena – pressing her body to his to gain warmth. He coughed.

'See if you can find some wood,' he commanded. 'I will unload the cart and tether the donkey. If we lose him in the night it will be disastrous. It looks as though there is a stream here and I can gather water and boil it so that we can have tea.'

'Yes, Captain Weyland. Oh, Josh, what fun – and how romantic.'

'You won't think it quite so romantic, my girl, if a storm comes in from the west. There is little to cover us.'

'Then, we shall just have to cuddle. I am sure you can manage it, Josh. I will teach you.'

He swung himself awkwardly to the ground. His leg was improving day by day but he still moved with difficulty in alighting. 'I am sure you know how, my dear girl, but you really must behave yourself, otherwise I shall call back the donkey and we shall proceed onwards in the dark.' But he was secretly grinning.

Luckily, the night remained starlit, although, with October breathing its cool breath, the temperature fell with the disappearance of the sun. One blanket hardly covered them but Rowena insisted on tucking the edge underneath Josh's body to anchor it. He turned his back towards her but that did not deter her for one moment, for she folded her body to match the shape of his and put an arm around him to pull her own completely close to him.

'There, Captain Weyland,' she whispered into his ear. 'That is cuddlin'. Nice, isn't it?' and pulled him even closer.

They both awoke just after daybreak, tired and stiff from lying on the unrelenting ground. Rowena had fallen asleep almost immediately and Josh lay still for what seemed like hours, anxious not to disturb or, indeed, incite her. He fetched water from the stream, poked the dying fire into life and managed to make tea for them both.

'What do we do now, Josh?' asked Rowena, stretching her arms above her head.

'Go on and catch up with the tinners before they really get moving,' he said. 'I would like to talk to whoever is their leader.'

The miners' camp was astir early. Most of the men had brought with them single bivouac tents and it was clear that they were used to sleeping rough, for the tents were being packed away with quick efficiency. Josh was directed to a Mr Tom Clemence, who, he was told, was their foreman.

The man was in early middle age, dressed, like the others in old work clothes splashed with dried mud and wearing heavy boots. It was just as if they had all finished a shift in the mine and taken off as soon as they had reached the surface. Clemence had a worn, lined face and dark eyes that regarded Josh from within deep caverns. He looked ill, in fact, and Josh wondered if malnutrition had attacked him, for he was thin and bowed.

'What can I do for you, sur?' he said. 'We ain't doin' no 'arm in sleepin' out on the 'eath, now, are we?'

'Of course not, Mr Clemence. I have spoken with Mr Mitchell, your mine owner, and he has told me of your plight. I believe you are heading north in an attempt to find work?'

'That is true, sur. Do you know where we might find employment?'

'Alas, I fear not. But may I advise you to keep away from the coastal path, which is damned hard walking and will lead you only to a few hamlets and villages and there will be no work there for you. Keep on this inland road, heading towards the east – that is on the right – and it should take you, first to Bideford and then to Barnstaple and, if you continue north, to Ilfracombe. As I remember them, these are busy little towns where, if you break up, you could find some sort of work.'

'Thank you, sur. We will take your advice.'

'Now,' Josh fumbled beneath his waistcoat, 'I understand that you are short of money and of food.' He produced his little bag that had survived the rough surf of Morwenstow. Rowena's jaw dropped as she observed him open it. 'I have some savings here, Mr Clemence. Alas, I cannot spare you much, but I hope that these five guineas might provide a little sustenance for you.'

He pressed the gold coins into the other's hand.

Clemence looked down and raised his weary head. 'I am most touched by your kindness, sur, but I hope you won't be offended if I decline it. We all made up our minds not to accept charity on this journey. We seek work, not the kindness of strangers such as yourself.'

Josh nodded. 'I understand your feelings entirely but I insist you take the money. It just might make a little difference if one or two of you fall ill, which,' he looked around him, 'could well happen by the look of it. Some of your fellows seem to be all in.'

'Well that is so. Very well, sur. If you will give me your name and a place where you might be found, I will ensure that we shall repay you – although I fear it might take us some time to do that.'

'Very well.' Josh produced a scrap of paper and stub of pencil and scribbled his name and Dr Acland's address. 'I am in no hurry, Mr Clemence. Now . . . er . . . my companion and I must turn off this road towards the coast soon, but for a couple of miles, at least, we can offer transport for two of your men, those, perhaps, who are feeling the effects of this hard walking the most. Perhaps you will nominate them. I can walk and my . . . er . . . companion will be happy to find room in the donkey cart for them.'

'You are a kind man, indeed,' Clemence looked at the scrap of paper myopically and Josh realised that the foreman probably could not read. 'My name is Weyland,' he said, 'and I am lodging with a Doctor Acland in a little hamlet called Hartland Quay. They will know there where to find me but, let me repeat, I do not wish to have the money returned. Your need is much greater than mine. Now, I don't wish to hold up your march. We will accompany you for a little way before we have to turn off.'

Two men, quite old, judging by their grey hairs, were helped into the back of the donkey cart where they sprawled gratefully. Before stirring the donkey into motion, Rowena leant down and hissed at Josh: 'But that was the money you were saving for your wedding. Have you changed your mind about that?'

'No, lass. It will just have to be a quieter wedding, that's all.'

Rowena stayed looking down at him for a few moments more. Then she said quietly, 'You are a good man, Joshua Weyland,' blinking back tears. 'Come on, donkey. Giddy-up.'

The cavalcade, with the tinners stretching out on either side of the path onto the moorland and the donkey cart bringing up the rear, continued its passage until Clemence, who had been plodding along with Joshua, suddenly halted and pointed ahead.

'I smell trouble,' he said.

Stretching ahead of them and spreading out on either side of the path stood a thin line of men. Shielding his eyes from the early sun, Josh could see that there were about thirty of them, standing perfectly still, but clearly denying further progress to the miners. What's more, they all carried unsheathed cutlasses and one or two had muskets.

Instinctively, he looked to the left, to where the cliff rose to present a skyline. Yes, there he was. The figure on horseback, perfectly still, looking down on them from that familiar, hunched-back posture.

'It's the Preventers,' called Rowena. 'They are going to stop the tinners marching.'

'They can't do that,' muttered Josh, half to himself. 'These men are not the enemy of the Revenue.'

The men in the van of the tinners had now reached the Preventers. 'You go no further,' cried one of them. 'You are not allowed into these parishes. Turn and go back the way you came. You are not welcome here.' He emphasised his words by prodding a miner in the chest with the point of his sword.

Immediately, the tinner, a large man, swung his fist and caught the Preventer on the side of the jaw, sending him sprawling and the cutlass spinning away to land, point down, quivering in the turf. Most of the tinners had shaped sticks from fallen branches to help them walk and they now brandished these and moved towards the Revenue men.

Josh's jaw dropped as he witnessed these happenings. The sky above them was that soft, cloudless blue that often brightens the beginning of October. It contrasted sadly with the aggression that was developing beneath it. The tinners outnumbered the Preventers, but not by many, and the miners were clearly not fighting men. Their work-stained clothes contrasted with the blue and white garments, sun-bleached but still clearly uniforms, of the Revenue men. The tinners' sticks, cut to aid their walk along uneven paths, were clearly going to be no match for the steel of the cutlasses, gleaming now threateningly in the pale sunlight.

'My God,' breathed Josh, 'there's going to be a massacre, wooden staves against swords. Stop!' he cried loudly and began pushing his way through the ranks of the miners to where the fallen Preventer was now rubbing his jaw and picking himself up. He reached for his cutlass, its point still buried in the turf, but Joshua was there before him.

He grabbed the hilt of the weapon and wrenched it free. Raising the cutlass he cried out loudly, 'None of you Preventers should use your swords against these men. If you do, you will be breaking the law and I shall report you to a magistrate.'

'Oh yes.' A burly Preventer pushed his way through to face Joshua. 'So what 'appens if I cut your bloody 'ead off, then?' he sneered and he raised his cutlass menacingly.

Immediately, Josh leant forward, in approved fencing style, his left hand raised behind his back, as Cunningham had displayed, and he presented the point to the throat of the Preventer. 'If you bring your sword down, you will be a dead man,' he said, gently pricking the skin of his opponent.

The man sprang back, as though he had been stung, but then stamped forward, slashing with his cutlass fiercely, clearly determined to kill the stranger who now confronted him. A cheer rose from the rest of the Preventers, who closed round the two swordsmen to witness what they obviously presumed would be an execution.

In fact, the Preventer lacked the skill of his captain and, despite his injured leg, Josh was easily able to avoid the clumsy swings that threatened him. Coolly, he parried four of them, leaving his opponent panting for breath. He then engaged his cutlass by tapping the end of the other's steel, so provoking another swing, this time a horizontal swish that Josh ducked under.

'Oh, for God's sake stop,' cried Rowena. 'He will kill you, Josh.'

The cry of 'kill, kill' was taken up by the ring of Preventers. Josh was hampered by the pain that now shot up his injured leg as he tried to move away. Instead, he moved forwards. He slid his blade down the blade of the Preventer's cutlass until it reached the pommel, then, with a twist of the wrist – as demonstrated days before by Cunningham – he thrust the point of his weapon under the curve of the man's hand-protector and then flicked the sword out of his hand, so that it swung away, causing the nearest watchers to scatter.

The man, who did not lack courage, cursed and swung his fist at Joshua's head. It, however, was easily avoided and, picking his target with care, Josh thrust his cutlass forward, so that the point took the man in the shoulder, producing a spurt of blood and causing him to stumble and fall. Immediately, there was a massed intake of breath from the onlookers, who stepped back, as one man, from this stranger who demonstrated that he could, indeed, handle a sword with skill.

Then, there came a shout from the man on the ground. 'Go on, kill the bastard,' he called. "E's on 'is own. Kill the bugger.'

This seemed to give life to the Preventers, who now surged forward again towards Josh, their swords raised.

'STOP!' The shriek came from Rowena, who was now standing in the donkey cart, a huge, old-fashioned, double-barrelled, cavalry pistol, held in both hands and with its firing hammers cocked. She swung the muzzle slowly to cover the main protagonists. 'If you don't lay down those damned cutlasses now, I will shoot to kill,' she shouted. 'You too, Joshua. Put down those fuckin' swords.'

Joshua's jaw dropped – as much at Rowena's language as at the sight she presented, her jaw thrust forward, her eyes blazing and her hair flowing out behind her. She resembled some kind of avenging angel. He threw his cutlass to the ground. It was a gesture which, strangely, had the effect of encouraging the Preventers to do the same, and there was a clang as the steels were thrown down.

'Well, well, well, Emma. What a feisty little creature you are!'

The voice was modulated and the tone cool. Captain Cunningham urged his horse through the ranks of the Preventers and miners alike, the reins curled around the hook at the end of his left arm, his right hand holding his cutlass.

'Now really, Emma,' he went on, his teeth grinning whitely against the dark tan of his face, 'when I tell your father the kind of language you seem to have picked up from Mr Weyland, he will probably disown you. And, for God's sake, put that antique pistol down. If it was loaded, which I am sure it is not, it would probably blow your arm off if you tried to fire it. Now, put it down, there's a good girl.'

'Not until you throw that cutlass to the ground.' She swung the pistol round to aim it at Cunningham. 'And it is loaded and I will happily kill you if I have to, officer of the law or not.'

'He is not an officer of the law, Rowena,' interrupted Joshua. 'He is an officer of the Revenue and Customs, which is a distinctly different thing. Why, Cunningham, have you set up your men to stop these miners travelling to find work?'

Cunningham dismounted and, carefully, laid down his cutlass. 'Because, my dear fellow – oh, and congratulations on your swordsmanship, by the way, you must have been practising since we last met – I do not want this rabble marching through my territory, threatening to disturb the peace.'

Joshua took a deep breath to control himself. 'Firstly, this is not your territory. This is Her Majesty's highway, open to any of her subjects who wish to walk upon it. These men are not a threat to the peace of the parish here, for I – and . . . er . . . Emma – can vouch for the fact that they are law-abiding men. We have travelled with them from Bude and they wish to look for work in Devon, where they will stand a better chance of finding it. If you bring charges against them – and I am not sure you have the power to do that, anyway, because they are not attempting to avoid paying customs duty on contraband goods – but if you do, then Emma and I will give evidence on their behalf and I am sure that their employer in Bude, Mr Miller, will do the same. Now call off your hounds, Captain, before we lay charges against you and them for attacking defenceless men.'

A ragged cheer rose from the ranks of the miners. Cunningham slowly nodded.

'Ah,' he said, 'you add the skills of a barrack room lawyer to those of a qualified second mate.' He raised his voice. 'Very well, men. Let this rabble through. Pick up your cutlasses but sheathe them. Stand back and let the bloody miners march.' He lowered his voice. 'And for all our sakes, Emma, put down that ridiculous old pistol. It must have last been used by Oliver Cromwell.'

Josh walked back to where Rowena still stood, uncertainly holding the heavy pistol. 'Where on earth did you get that thing from,

Rowena?' he hissed. 'Why did you bring it with you?'

The girl lowered her lashes. 'I picked it off the wall in Papa's study,' she murmured. 'I put it in my bag in case it proved useful.' She looked up defiantly. 'And it did, didn't it?'

Cunningham strode towards them. 'Get that injured man into the cart, Brown,' he ordered one of his men. 'And put some sort of compress on to stop the bleeding, otherwise,' he shot a stern gaze at Josh, 'there will be a murder charge to be placed against Master Weyland. Now, Emma, pick up the reins, offload those tinners, they are not wounded so they can walk, and take the wounded man to your father for treatment. I have work to do so cannot accompany you. Good day.'

He touched the brim of his top hat, climbed back onto his horse and urged it forward so that he was able to wave the tinners through the gap that had now opened for them.

Clemence took Josh's hand. 'You have proved yourself to be a real friend of ours,' he said. 'And you are a most courageous man – and you, young lady,' he turned towards Rowena, 'have the sort of spirit that I remember from my late wife when we were first married. You remind me very much of her. Now we must be gone. But I am sure we shall meet again. Thank you both.'

He shook hands with each of them in turn, and then followed his men as they trudged up the hill ahead of them. At the top, he turned and waved.

Joshua and Rowena returned the gesture and then climbed back into the donkey cart. Josh looked down at the man he had wounded. 'Keep holding that compress to the wound,' he said. 'It is important that you don't lose more blood.'

147

'What the hell does it matter to you?' the wounded man growled. 'You caused it, anyway.'

'And I will stick that cutlass of yours through the other shoulder if you retain that truculent manner. Now keep the cloth pressing down hard and we should get you to the doctor before you bleed to death – which is no more than you deserve. Carry on, Rowena.'

The girl shook the reins and turned the donkey's head down a little lane that led, across the heath, towards what seemed to be the cliff edge, beyond which Cunningham had disappeared some moments before.

Joshua leant towards Rowena. 'I just wanted to say,' he said, keeping his voice low so that the Preventer could not hear, 'that I thought you were splendid back there. I was quite proud of you, in fact.' He gave her a slightly embarrassed grin.

Immediately, she turned and, taking advantage of his nearness, planted a quick kiss on his lips. 'If I was splendid, Joshua Weyland,' she said, 'you were magnificent. I didn't realise that you were such a good swordsman.'

He quickly leant away. 'As a matter of fact,' he said, 'neither did I.'

CHAPTER EIGHT

They jogged along without speaking for a little while, then Josh, keeping his voice low so that the wounded man could not hear, said, 'I noticed that most of the Preventers had their sleeves rolled up but I did not see one who bore any sign of wounds on the arm or, for that matter, a bruised cheek. Did you?'

'Ah, you were trying to identify the men who attacked you just above the village. But no, I did not. Perhaps they were not Preventers.'

'Perhaps not. But who were they?'

'I cannot imagine anyone from the village doing such a grievous thing, Josh. Maybe,' she jerked her head to the rear, 'he might know.'

'He might indeed.' Josh let the matter rest there for the moment. 'Can you stop for a minute?' He hauled himself clumsily over into the back and looked down at the wounded man. Bending, he removed the pad that protected the wound.

'Good,' he said. 'The bleeding has stopped. The wound looks reasonably clean. Are you still in pain?'

The Preventer looked puzzled by the attention and care being shown. 'It still bloody hurts, if that is what you mean.'

'Well, of course it does. We will see if the doctor can give you something to ease the pain when we arrive. Alas, we have nothing with us that can do so, but we don't have far to go now.'

He removed his jacket, rolled it into a pillow and pushed it behind the man's head. 'That might make you more comfortable.' He examined the man's forearm. 'It looks as though you were not one of the two men who attacked me a few days ago.'

The man looked genuinely puzzled. 'Attacked you? No. I never attacked you – and, as far as I know, none of our men did. Why should we?'

'Why should you, indeed? But two men, who kept their faces concealed, did so and I would like to know who they were, for I was able to wound one of them in the arm and the other on the face, and those wounds should betray them.'

'Well, it weren't one of our lads, that's for sure. I would know if it was.'

Josh nodded. He had a feeling that the man was telling the truth.

They turned down the steep path that led down to Hartland Quay. There was no sign of Cunningham and, as usual, the hamlet looked sleepily empty of human activity, although shouts could be heard above the sound of the waves breaking down by the harbour.

They stopped at the front door of the doctor's house. Rowena slung the reins over the brake handle and vaulted down, fumbling for her key. She opened the door and Joshua could hear her shouting inside. He carefully let himself down and then helped the wounded man to descend. Rowena reappeared, a puzzled frown upon her face.

'Father is not here,' she said. 'Mrs Brown, a neighbour, has been looking after the house. She says that Papa left for London two days ago and is expected to be away for a little longer. How strange.'

'Who is going to look after this fellow? That wound needs treatment.'

Rowena tossed her head. 'Oh, I can do that easily enough. Here.' She took the man's arm on his uninjured side and put it around her shoulders. 'Lean on me and keep the other arm still. We will go into the surgery. Josh, go on and open doors and start boiling some water.'

'Yes, Doctor.'

The Preventer turned a startled face towards Josh. 'She ain't a doctor, is she? I mean a proper doctor. I want a real doctor to see me.'

'Of course she is. There are two Doctor Aclands here. She is by far the better one. And the prettiest.'

Rowena shot Josh a grateful smile and before long she was gently bathing the wounded man's shoulder, carefully picking out the few threads of fibres from his coat that had been thrust into the wound, while Joshua held a bowl of warm water at her side.

The man gave a startled cry as iodine was trickled onto the wound. 'Oh, damn!' muttered Rowena, 'another shoulder dressing. Couldn't you have cut his arm off? Bandaging a shoulder is so awkward.'

'Well, you made a good enough job of mine, Doctor.'

Eventually the wound was dressed and the man's jacket was draped over his shoulders. 'Can you walk up to the barracks?' asked Josh.

'No,' interrupted Rowena. 'I don't think he should walk. He has had quite a shock. Can you take him up there in the cart? I have things to do here.'

'Of course.'

Josh walked the man into the street, helped him into the cart and climbed up beside him. They climbed the hill in silence until they reached the great front gate of the barracks.

Josh helped the man down. 'Bang on the door and I presume they will let you in. Come back in a couple of days to the doctor's house and we can change that dressing. The wound needs to be kept clean.'

The man looked at the ground for a moment, then switched his gaze to Joshua. He held out his hand. 'I am very grateful – not for the bloody wound – but for the care you and that doctor 'ave given me. I will ask about that attack on you and will let you know if I find anythin'. I honestly don't think it would 'ave been any of the Preventers who would 'ave gone at you like that. Not without provocation. I will let you know.'

He nodded, turned and banged on the door. Josh stifled a smile and turned the donkey's head down the hill. Mrs Brown came out to help him unharness the animal, before Josh rubbed him down and fed him oats in the little stable at the back. When he re-entered the house, Mrs Brown was bustling about and Rowena was carefully replacing the old pistol on the wall.

'Was it really loaded?'

'O' course not.' She gave him her great life-reaffirming smile. 'And I'm sorry about the bad language but I was worried no one was listening to me and believing that I wouldn't fire.'

Josh lifted an eyebrow. 'Where on earth did you get that sort of talk?'

She blushed. 'From Tom Pengelly. He has quite a vocabulary. I know a few other words if you would like to hear them.'

'No, thank you. Now, Doctor, if you could manage to make a mug of coffee I would like to sit and think for a moment or two.'

'Oh yes, Captain. Put your great mind to work.'

Josh settled in the drawing room and this time looked around him with care. There were decorative plates fixed to the walls, hand-painted by the look of them. Tentatively, he pulled open a large walnut sideboard and inspected the fine French Limoges dining service that was stacked inside. It would serve at least sixteen people, he estimated. On the other side of the sideboard, this time with a key inserted in the door, was a spirits cupboard. Josh removed a couple of bottles to examine them. In all, there were six bottles containing fine Jamaican rum and double that number labelled French Armagnac, obviously purchased in one consignment, for they were all marked with the same vintage, 1812. This sideboard contained no wine, but Joshua knew that the doctor had a wine cellar, the entrance to which was in the kitchen and was kept permanently locked. He shook his head. The doctor certainly lived in some style. How did he do this on the earnings he made from treating the poor people of Hartland Quay?

Rowena came in carrying a pot of coffee, which she put by the side of his chair. 'I will leave you,' she said, 'for I have work to do.' At the door she turned, a mischievous grin on her face. 'If Papa does not return tonight,' she said, 'we shall be in the house alone. You had better lock your bedroom door.'

Josh sighed and rested his head on the back of the chair. It was time to take stock. He moved his shoulder. No problem there, for the pain had gone. He lifted his injured leg off the floor. This, too, caused him no distress. He frowned. Surely, it was time now to hurry to Dover to see Mary? She would have received his letter posted from

Bude and in it he had promised he would be on his way to meet with her as soon as he was allowed to travel. He felt a huge twinge of conscience. She was his fiancée and yet, here he was, half flirting with an eighteen-year-old girl who, to say the least, was less than respectable, and he himself was seemingly brushing the edge of a gang or gangs engaged in law-breaking and violence. Why, he had even become a swordsman! Yes, it was time he moved on.

But . . . He closed his eyes. Could he leave behind him so many unanswered questions, here, on this iron coast – questions about the wrecking of *The Lucy*, about smuggling, about the violence that seemed to lurk just under the surface of these villages. And, of course, about the beguiling daughter of a gypsy. What to do about her?

He stirred in his chair and took a sip of coffee. It was excellent, of course. She made good coffee, naturally. Could he turn his back on her and leave her at the mercy of whatever villainy was being practised here? He reviewed the characters he had met so far. Cunningham, who professed designs on Rowena and had illusions of power here. The doctor, obviously a man of influence in this small community, who lived remarkably well. Then there was Tom Pengelly, the highly skilled sailor who allegedly knew this coastline like the back of his hand. However much Rowena shrugged him off, he was close enough to her to share language of the commonest nature. And what of the publican, who seemed to know everyone's business?

There was another player in this drama, however. Continually overlooked to the point where he could well be called 'the forgotten man' was the sailor who had helped Pengelly and who would, in all probability, have lifted him into the donkey cart. Why did Rowena seem to lie about seeing them there?

He shook his head. It was time he had a proper discussion with the girl. What was she hiding and why? His mind went back to what Miller, the owner of the tin mine, had said about smuggling. Without knowing from where they had come, he had specifically named Morwenstow and Hartland as centres of profitable and sophisticated smuggling operations. These two sleepy hamlets perched atop the cruel cliffs, with one tiny and hard-to-enter harbour between them. It was to think of them as nests of depravity.

But, there was no doubt about it. In his short stay here, Josh had stumbled upon some kind of criminal activity and had asked enough questions for him to be regarded as a threat to whoever was operating these rings.

He shook his head. Something was clear: he could not leave until he had unpicked some, at least, of the layers of secrecy that lay over the two villages. No. He could not set off for Dover just yet. But he must see Mary soon and shake off the silken threads that, like a spider's web, were beginning to bind him to Hartland.

Mary . . . he summoned up memories that he had cherished for so long. Mary, with her apple blossom, rounded cheeks, her full breasts and her soft, brown eyes; Mary, the woman he had promised to return to and marry. He sighed. She would have received his letter now and would write back to him immediately, of course. Then, he must, he really *must* make arrangements to make the long journey to the comparative sanity and tranquillity of the Dover parsonage and life with Mary Jackson.

Mrs Brown had prepared for them a rabbit and that evening Rowena converted it into a delicious stew for their dinner, swimming in vegetables and spiced with some sort of seasoning that was new to Josh. Damn it! The girl could cook like an angel, too!

'Have you any idea why your father has gone to London?' he asked her. 'Is it a journey he often makes?'

'No. He always says he hates going to cities, whether Exeter or London. As far as I know, he had no business in the capital.'

'Hmm. Do you remember, when he urged me to leave here for a couple of days, that he said he had some sort of enquiries to make – this was just after I had been attacked? Could it have been something to do with that, do you think?'

Rowena puckered her face into a frown. 'I just don't know, Josh. My father has always been a man who keeps himself to himself – even from me. He is deeply religious and, as far as I know, had no business interests at all. He is just a country doctor.'

'Of course.' Josh dipped a piece of bread into the excellent gravy. Looking into the grave face of the young girl opposite, he felt strangely reluctant to cross-examine her. But it must be done. 'Rowena, do you mind if I ask you a few questions about the night you drove me back here from Morwenstow, the night of the shipwreck?'

She cast her eyes down. 'All right.'

'Good. You remember that you told me that you did not know who had saved me from the rock at the foot of the cliff and carried me up what must have been a very slippery and dangerous path to where you waited at the top? You said that you thought they had been two of the Preventers?'

'Er . . . yes. The gale was blowin' real fierce and I could not see people properly, particularly as they was wearin' oilskins and the like.'

'But Mr Hawker and that man, who keeps the inn here, Jacob

Millbury, both told me that it was Tom Pengelly and a fellow seaman from the quay, who carried me up. They must have put me in your cart. You obviously knew both men quite well – Tom, very well – yet you say you did not see them or even exchange a word with them when they deposited my unconscious body with you?'

Rowena's head was still down but he could see that a tear was coursing its way down her cheek. He hardened his heart and remained silent.

Then she looked up. 'I don't know why you are questioning me in this way, Josh, have I done something wrong? Do you suspect me of bein' involved in all this law-breakin' here?'

'Now, Rowena, don't work your wiles on me. I am not accusing you of anything. But I am trying to get to the bottom of what seems to have been a whole litany of lies told to me about that night. Are you really telling me that you did not recognise at least Tom Pengelly that night?'

She put her head back and thrust her jaw forward truculently. 'Yes I am, Joshua Weyland. I was huddled on that donkey cart seat, tryin' to stop the rain from tricklin' down my neck. I didn't *care* who had put that man in the cart behind me, I just wanted to get on the road back to Hartland Quay and do my father's biddin' – which was to bring back anyone to the surgery needing help. There was lots of men millin' about that clifftop that night. Most of them I couldn't tell from the Queen of England because they were all huddled, as I said, in oilskins. So that's that. An' I'm not tellin' you no lies, so don't accuse me of anythin'.' She ended on a sob.

Compassion immediately consumed Josh. 'Oh, I am sorry, Rowena, I really am. Of course I believe you. I just had to ask you the questions. And, it so happens that there are so many to ask.'

'Well, don't expect me to know all the answers, because I don't.'

'No, of course not.' His mind raced. What she had said was perfectly believable. Why had he felt that she was lying? He must make amends.

'Of one thing, I am certain,' he said.

She looked up with that half-frightened, half-truculent look on her face with which he had grown so familiar. 'What's that, then?'

'This stew is delicious. There is no doubt about it. You are a better cook than Mary Jackson, I have to admit it.'

He knew she would be pleased and she was. The frown disappeared and her eyes lit up. 'Oh, Josh. You're just sayin' that to make up. I know.'

'No, I am not. Rowena, Emma Acland, you can frighten a milling crowd of Preventers, who were about to hack me to pieces, you can make delicious coffee, you can tend a wounded man as though you had passed through medical school and you can turn an old field animal into the best rabbit stew I have ever tasted. You are, without doubt, a marvel.'

'Oh, Josh,' her eyes were watering again. 'Do you mean it?'

'Of course I do.'

She took a deep breath. 'Will you sleep with me tonight, then?'

He could not prevent the grin from stealing across his face. The sheer cheek of her! The fundamental honesty that always seemed to motivate her. Why did he ever think that she could lie? If she had a thought, she had to express it. She could not, surely, dissemble to save her life.

He leant across and took her hand. She immediately grasped it tightly, as though to make sure that the answer she would get would be the one she wanted.

'No, my dear girl, I will not. And you know why. You may not believe it, but I am an honourable man. I gave my word to Mary, two years ago when I set off to the other side of the world, and I must keep it.' He sighed. 'Even though you are the best cook and the most desirable young woman in the world, I must be true to Mary.' He shook the hand that held his so tightly. 'You must understand that, Rowena.'

The tears were coursing down her cheeks again now. 'Of course I understand, Josh. Goodness knows, you've told me enough times.' She smiled through the tears. 'But Josh, I am a virgin, I promise you. No man has ever known me. I do feel . . . I don't know what the word is except that old-fashioned one: love. I do love you. And if I am to lose my maidenhood I want it to be to you. Even if you have to leave me afterwards for your Mary. Please, let me know you tonight. It will probably be our only chance. And I don't want to be deflowered by any other man than you. I promise you.'

Josh felt temptation rise within him like the high tide rushing round the harbour wall of Hartland Quay. She was so *desirable* and he had been chaste for so long. He gulped. The doctor need never know. And, for that matter, neither need Mary. *Just one night . . . !* Then he shook his head.

'No, Rowena. I could never do it. For one thing, after one night with you I could never just walk away. And, you must realise, that I must walk away. I know I must sound like a prudish prig, but I have given Mary my word. I am so, so sorry. In fact, more sorry than you could ever know. And you have given me the highest compliment a woman can pay a man.'

She took out her handkerchief and blew her nose noisily. 'You are indeed an honourable man, Josh. And I respect you for it. We will say no more on the matter.' She tried to smile through her tears. 'Would you like some more stew?'

He kissed her chastely on the cheek when they parted on the stairway and he climbed into bed wondering if he had done the right thing. He realised that he was now in love with Rowena Acland and just hoped he could control his emotions long enough not to break his word to Mary.

The next morning brought a letter addressed to him carrying a Dover postmark. He did not, however, recognise the handwriting. In fact, it was from Mrs Jackson, Mary's mother. She was so glad to hear from him, she said, and Mary would write soon. She was away for a few days and would respond on her return. It was a mercy and a blessing from God that he had survived the shipwreck. Mary would no doubt say more in her letter.

He folded it and put it inside his jacket, but he knew that Rowena would find it and read it. Ah well, that did not matter now. Yet he felt strangely depressed in absorbing the message. It was short and to the point – and, of course, it did not come from Mary. But it seemed strangely cold and compared sadly with Rowena's spoken passion of the previous evening. He took it out and read it again and then put his head in his hands. Oh God! Was he making a big mistake?

The wounded Preventer arrived later that morning and Rowena changed his dressing. The man briefly sought out Josh to say that none of his comrades in the barracks admitted to knowing anything about the attack on him. The Preventer spoke so earnestly that Josh believed him. If it was not the Preventers, then who the hell was it? He shook his head in bewilderment.

For the next couple of days, he and Rowena lived together amicably enough, but, of course, at what only could be termed arm's length. Josh felt that it was probably time to get rid of the irksome splints on his leg but Rowena insisted that he wait until the doctor's return. He conceded but decided that doing nothing while they waited for Doctor Acland to reappear was not an option for him. It was time, he decided, to talk to Tom Pengelly and also, if possible, the sailor who was his partner on the cliff path on the night of the wreck.

He decided not to tell Rowena of his intention and slipped out of the house one morning and made his way down to the harbour. Pengelly, however, was not to be seen and nor was anyone who might conceivably be the 'forgotten man'. He returned disgruntled to the house to find that he had a visitor.

'It's Jack Cunningham,' hissed Rowena at the door. 'He says he has come to see you and won't tell me what it is about. Be careful with him, Josh, I think he is honest enough but I have become nervous of everyone in this village now. He is waiting for you in the living room.'

'Thank you, Rowena.'

Cunningham rose as he entered and extended his hand.

They shook hands and Joshua gestured towards a chair. 'Do sit down, Captain. What can I do for you?'

'Ah, Joshua, you must call me Jack. I thought we were friends and that is why I have called on you, after that . . . what shall I call it . . . fracas on the heath with the tinners the other day.'

'Indeed, yes?'

'Yes,' Cunningham extended one long, elegantly booted leg. 'I felt I should explain to you my, ah, seeming resentment of the miners and of their marching through these parishes of Morwenstow and Hartland.'

Josh frowned. This was unexpected. 'Please do.'

'When we first met, I explained to you that most of the Preventers' work lay with preventing smuggling, although we have a responsibility for restricting the wrecking, that is the removal of cargoes from ships that founder on this damned coastline – you know?'

Josh nodded.

'Strictly speaking, wrecking is illegal. But everyone in Devon and Cornwall – and on the rest of the coastline of Britain for that matter – believes it to be their God-given right to take what the sea throws up to them. So we try and treat this matter with a reasonably light hand. Smuggling, however, is a different matter.'

He leant forward. 'When we first met, I tried to portray how seriously smuggling could affect the economy of these islands. Well, it's become a very serious matter and there is no doubt that a very sophisticated and successful smuggling ring operates on this particular border of the two counties.'

'So I have heard.'

Cunningham looked up sharply. 'Oh yes? What exactly have you heard, may I ask?'

'I called on the owner of a tin mine just outside Bude – the man, in fact, who employs those marching tinners. He told me that Morwenstow and Hartland housed just what you described: a ring of well-organised smugglers.'

'Hmm. Did he now? I don't like my territory having acquired such a reputation. But he was quite right. My sources tell me that there has been an increase in the importation of expensive contraband on this coast in the last few months. It has become worse and my employers in the Revenue are pressing me to put a stop to it.'

Josh nodded. 'Well, I can quite understand that.'

'It's all very well them telling me what to do, but how to do it is a very different matter.' He leant back and put his fingers together. 'Just like the wreckers, these smugglers believe that smuggling is their right and is a justifiable way of avoiding unfair taxes.' He leant forward again to make the point. 'And so many people of various levels in society are engaged in it that it is very difficult to bring anyone to court. Whatever my men and I do, we seem to be two or three steps behind the smugglers. They are damned well organised and they are getting better at what they do.'

Josh nodded. Where was all this leading?

'I have been at my wits' end in trying to put a dampener on their activities. I have even taken to riding the clifftop between Hartland and Morwenstow at various times of the day in an attempt to pick up clues. I think you may have seen me.'

'Yes, I did. I thought you were watching me.'

Cunningham's teeth flashed. 'Well, indeed, up to a point I was. I knew you had been cast ashore, but your arrival seemed to have stepped up several landings, which we were too late to prevent and I tried to keep an eye on you. But I soon realised that you were not involved.'

'What about the tinners?'

'Ah yes. I was coming to them. I heard that they were marching north. I doubted if they were involved in smuggling in any way, although God knows they could be driven to it by the fall in tin prices. But the last thing I wanted was to have them camped up on our heath, perhaps acting as a diversion to take up our time while contraband was landed.

As a result, I decided to stop them coming through this territory. And I would have done so, had you not intervened, Mr Mate.'

'Yes, well. It seemed rather high-handed of you to stop them using the Queen's highway on their way to find work.'

'I can see how a liberal-minded fellow like you, Josh, would have regarded the matter but, as I say, I was being pushed hard and trying to stop up all the holes I could find. Yes, perhaps I was a little heavy but you must remember that there is no police force here, Josh, no London Peelers, only the militia and us. And we never see the militia. I have a heavy responsibility.'

Josh nodded slowly. 'I can sympathise with you there.' He paused while he pondered how to raise his next point. 'You may have heard,' he said, 'that I was attacked here a few days ago, on the strip of land that juts out between the top of the street and your barracks.'

Cunningham nodded. 'Ah yes,' he said. 'The fellow that you wounded told me about this. I am sorry to hear it. If you have any idea who might have been responsible, do tell me and I will take action immediately.'

Josh looked at him quizzically. 'So your Preventers wouldn't have anything to do with it, Jack?' he asked. 'Maybe to warn me off making my own enquiries about the shipwreck and so on?'

'Good Lord, no. We only use violence on people who break the law, I assure you.'

'I believe you, but I would dearly love to know who it was. Two men. Quite young as far as I could tell. They were muffled to their eyebrows, but I fought them off and, in fact, one of them should have a nasty bruise on his cheekbone and the other marks of my knife on his arm.'

'In that case, definitely none of my people. I would know if anyone had been hurt in that way. But leave the matter with me. I will put my ear to the ground, so to speak. Not much goes on around here that I don't know about, except . . .' he smiled ruefully, 'the date and place of the next smuggling run.'

He rose, making a striking figure in that crowded and darkened sitting room. 'Now I must be off.' He thrust out his hand again. 'I hope we can remain friends. After all, we were both sailors. And I promise that your tinners can march back through my parishes without hindrance – as long as they don't linger.'

Josh gripped the hand offered. 'Very well, Jack. I suppose you could say – and we must say – that we are on the same side. If smuggling was involved in any way with the wreck of *The Lucy*, then I would certainly like to know. We should work together. If I pick up anything, I will pass it on to you, I promise.'

'Good man. Give my regards, of course, to the doctor when he returns.'

Josh raised his hand. 'Just one more moment before you go. Neither his daughter nor I have the remotest idea why Doctor Acland should make this sudden trip to London. I know that you and he are old friends. Did he confide in you why he was making this long journey to the capital?'

Cunningham shook his head. 'I fear not. Yes, we were and, indeed, are friends, but perhaps we are not as close as we used to be – and I know he does not consider me a suitable match for Emma, although I keep trying. He keeps himself very much to himself these days, which is a pity. Now I really must go. Goodbye, Mr Mate.'

'Goodbye, Cap'n Jack.'

As soon as the tall man had left the house, Rowena reappeared.

'What did he want, Josh?' she asked, her eyes wide.

Joshua related all that had passed between them.

'Ah,' she nodded her head. 'He has a difficult job tryin' to pin down all those that plan and carry out the landin's. I doubt if he will ever do it. Folk around here are much too close to let on. I sometimes feel sorry for him.'

Josh allowed himself to tease. 'But not enough to marry him, eh Rowena?'

She turned away quickly. 'Don't you play with me, Joshua Weyland,' she called out behind her, her voice breaking as she strode away.

Josh immediately felt ashamed of himself. But it was too late for remorse. He should not, he could not, play with Rowena's feelings. Instead, he strode after her into the kitchen.

He caught her arm. 'I am sorry, Rowena, it was a silly and unfair thing to say. I shan't tease you about him any more. But, I have had a thought and perhaps you could help me.' He explained his desire to find Pengelly and 'the forgotten man'.

'Ah, you will find Tom most days in the inn at about noon, having his lunch,' she said. 'But you mustn't keep them long. They only has the half-hour for their break now.'

'Thank you, I won't.'

He looked at the dial of the great-grandfather clock that stood against the wall. He had less than an hour before meeting them. But the inn was an ideal place for the meeting, as long as they could talk out of range of Jacob Millbury's wagging ears.

To fill in the hour and to exercise his increasingly stiff injured leg, he hobbled up to the level patch of ground on which he had been attacked. Instinctively, he looked up to the left to the clifftop. This time, however, there was no lone horseman, no Jack Cunningham patrolling his two parishes. He stayed for a while looking out to sea, breathing in deeply the fresh onshore breeze. He could see the outline of Lundy Island on the horizon and, to his right, the sharp, high promontory that was Hartland Point. From its head, the cliff plunged down almost vertically. The sea was a sharply blue colour and was studded with white sails. This coast, he mused, might be cruel and dangerous but it was strikingly beautiful. As a sailor, could he live here? He smiled and thought the answer might well be yes. Then he shook his head. What a ridiculous question! There was no possibility of that happening. More likely he would have to look to Dover as a base. He sighed.

He stayed a little while taking in the fresh clean air from the Atlantic and preparing himself for what he hoped would be a productive talk with the two sailors. At least, it would be men of the sea talking, men who followed more or less the same trade. There should be some sort of empathy between them.

He walked towards where the vertical piece of flat rock had given him some kind of protection from the attack. He hoped that perhaps there might be some previously undetected piece of detritus that might offer a clue as to who launched the attack on him. But there was nothing.

Taking his time, he walked towards the inn thinking. What did he hope to find from the meeting? Well, firstly, he would like an admission that it was they who had rescued him on the night of the shipwreck, so giving him the chance to thank them, for they must surely have risked their lives in scrambling out on that sea-swept rock at the height of the storm. Then, he would like some confirmation from them of seeing the burning beacon. They surely must have seen it and, if they had, could they throw some light on its purpose? Was it, indeed, a signal to the smugglers or was its role something far more sinister? And what were *they* doing on that rain-swept cliff? Finally, might they have a view on who it was who attacked him?

It was enough. He only hoped that they would be taking their break in the inn. They were.

Tom Pengelly, of course, he recognised immediately. Broad-shouldered, a face browned by sun and wind and wearing a seaman's striped jersey. There was one important addition, however, to Pengelly's appearance. He had a scar across his cheekbone. Ah! His companion, however, he had never seen before. He was slightly shorter than Pengelly by the look of him – they were both seated, of course – and slimmer in build. He seemed a little older, for grey had brushed the tangled curls on his brow. He looked up sharply as Josh entered and, immediately, a look of something – not fear, but perhaps apprehension – crossed his face.

Josh limped across and nodded to Pengelly. 'Hello, Tom,' he said. 'Let me fill up those glasses.' And he indicated the near empty tumblers that stood before their packages of bread and cheese.

'No need for that, Mr Mate,' said Pengelly. Josh could not help noting that that was the form of address used, jocularly, by Cunningham.

'No, let me buy you both a beer, because, according to Mr Millbury here,' he nodded to the publican standing behind the bar, 'and the Reverend Hawker, it was you and a fellow sailor who pulled me off that rock and carried me up the cliff. If that is so, the least I can do is to buy you a beer.'

He turned to Millbury. 'A pint for them both and one for me, please.'

He indicated the empty bench before them. 'May I?'

'Of course.' Pengelly indicated his companion. 'This is Jem Drake. He works with me on the dinghies at the harbour.'

Joshua reached out a hand. 'Have we met before, Jem?' he asked.

'I don't think so, sur.' The man spoke with a broad Cornish accent.

'Strange, I thought we had.' Josh nodded to Millbury, who put three brimming glasses on the table, and paid him. 'It's true that I was unconscious the first time, during the storm when *The Lucy* was lost. But I can't help wondering how you got that terrible bruise on your cheekbone and, you, Tom, picked up those nasty cuts on your own cheek and forearm. But let us not talk about those things just now. Did you, in fact, rescue me that night?'

The two men exchanged glances and Pengelly dropped his right forearm underneath the table to avoid the cut scars being seen further. 'Oh aye,' he said, 'we did. But it was only our duty. We were only sorry that we could not help the other poor fellows. I reckon you were right lucky to be cast up on that rock. You were all we could find.'

The man was happy enough to engage Josh in direct eye contact, but Drake seemed strangely averse to doing so. He held his head down and concentrated on munching his bread and cheese.

'The reason I asked – apart from wanting to thank you,' continued Josh, 'was that Rowena, I mean Emma, told me that she thought that it was two Preventers who had carried me up to the cart.'

'Ah no,' said Pengelly, 'she was wrong about that. It was us, all right.'

'Well, let me repeat that I am grateful to you. I suppose you must have saved my life that night. But tell me,' he leant across the table, 'did you see a brazier burning on a ledge just a bit below halfway up the cliff face?'

Drake appeared to be about to speak, but Pengelly forestalled him. 'No, I can't say that I did. I wouldn't know what it would be doin' there, anyway, on a night like that.'

'Ah, that's my thought too, Tom.' Josh took a deep draught of his beer. 'But, as *The Lucy* tried to weather the Point, I saw it from her deck. And then, more clearly as our idiot of a captain thought that it was a ship's riding light, indicating a safe anchorage, and turned the helm over so that we almost surfed onto the rocks.'

Pengelly spoke slowly, looking directly at Joshua, 'Well, I wouldn't know about that.'

Josh turned to Jem Drake. 'What about you, Jem? Did you see it?'

Drake shot a quick glance at Pengelly. 'Ah, no sur. I sor nothin' like that.'

'Hmm.' Josh realised he was playing a dangerous game, but the cut marks on Pengelly's arm and the bruise on Drake's cheekbone had, at first astonished him, and then filled him with anger. He pressed his point.

'But I went to that ledge shortly after my rescue and found a hole in the ground where, obviously, a firm stake had been thrust into it, and surrounding it, a ring of ash, that might well have been caused by the burning remains falling from a brazier.'

'Aye,' Pengelly held his gaze. 'That might well be so, but I wouldn't know about it, would you, Jem?'

'No, sur. I wouldn't know either.'

Josh nodded. 'Well, of course, I take your word on that. But, forgive me if I seem to be insistent, but I can't help wondering what you were doing out at Morwenstow on the clifftop on a night like that?'

Pengelly stepped in quickly. 'Well, I live there, o' course, and Jem here, who lives at Hartland, had come over to have a game of cribbage and a drop of ale or so. But the storm pressed in and stopped him from goin' home.'

'But the clifftop. Why be there?'

'We heard that a vessel, a brigantine, had been seen being blown by the gale towards the rocks at Morwenstow and, as sailors, we turned out to see if we could be of any help if the ship foundered. It's what anyone would have done.'

'I see. Well, you certainly helped me. Thank you.'

Pengelly stood. 'Well you must excuse us now, for we have to get back to the harbour. We just has the half-hour break, you see.'

'Of course.' Josh rose to his feet. 'Just one more thing. Two men attacked me on that ridge just above the street here a few days ago. I don't think they wanted to kill me and they didn't seem to be after money but they had cudgels and obviously intended to hurt me. Captain Cunningham has investigated and found that it was none of his men. Would either of you know who it might be? You must know everyone in these two small communities.'

Not a muscle in Pengelly's face moved. 'I have no idea. I am sorry. We must go now. Thank you for the beer.'

Josh stood and watched them go, then he sat down again and finished his beer. Millbury came bustling over. 'I 'eard that bit about you bein' attacked,' he said. 'Who on earth would do that, I wonder?'

'I wonder, too.' But Josh did not. He knew now – and felt strangely disappointed. Why should two sailors do that to a fellow seaman; particularly to someone they had risked their lives to save from the sea? He put down his empty glass, nodded to Millbury and left.

Rowena, of course, was waiting for him.

'Did you find anything out?' she asked, her face strained.

'Oh yes. I know now who attacked me. Tom Pengelly had recent scars on his forearm and cheek where my knife had cut him and his companion, Jem Drake, had the bruise on his cheekbone where I hit him. They didn't admit it, of course, but they were the men all right. Drake, in particular, looked most uncomfortable throughout our talk.'

Rowena put a hand to her mouth. 'Oh no, Josh. I know them both, o'course. They're pretty rough, I suppose, but they would never attack anybody like that, I'm sure.'

'Well, the evidence is there for all to see. I left those marks myself, but . . .' His voice trailed away for a moment. 'Looking back on it now, though, I realise that they called off the attack pretty quickly as soon as I showed fight. But if they were really serious, they could have knocked me down and given me a fair old beating, if they wanted – or even killed me. It was all so strange.'

Rowena stamped her foot. 'Well, I'm goin' to give that Tom Pengelly a good talkin' to. I will find out why they did it. You leave that to me.'

'No, thank you, Rowena. I would rather let things lie at this stage. They both know I know they did it. Let us see what happens next. I don't want to prompt another attack, but it will be interesting to see which way the cat jumps now. By the way, they both deny seeing a brazier burning on the cliff side.'

'But did they say that they were there on the night of the shipwreck?'

'Oh yes. Pengelly explained it by saying that they had come to help if anyone was washed ashore – as, indeed, they did with me. I was able to thank them for that.' He frowned. 'It's all so strange. One minute they save my life and the next they are beating me with cudgels. Why do you think that is, Rowena?'

'Oh I don't know, Josh. But look.' She seized his hand beseechingly. 'I promise I was tellin' you the truth when I said I didn't see them there that night. I was too miserable an' wet an' that.'

Josh squeezed her hand. 'Of course you were. I well understand that. I need to think about all this. There must be some explanation – and I think I might know what it is.'

'What would that be, then?'

'I am not sure. I need to think it through.' He sighed. 'I can't help wishing that your father was here. I am sure that he could help to unravel some of this mystery. No message from him, I suppose? Or, perhaps, another letter for me . . . ?'

'No. Nothing from Father and nothing from your Mary. Strange, that her mother would write instead of her, eh?'

Josh grinned inwardly. Of course, she had found Mrs Jackson's letter and read it. He decided to let the matter go. 'Well, she did explain that Mary was away . . . if you remember.'

Rowena had the grace to blush. 'I must prepare lunch,' she said and hurried into the kitchen.

Joshua limped into the sitting room and sat down and studied again the bric-a-brac that lined the walls. In addition to the fine pottery, there was the old cavalry pistol and, above the fireplace, two cutlasses crossed. On a crowded table in a dark corner stood an old telescope and a pair of navigator's dividers. All very nautical.

He sighed. The evidence seemed to be growing. The doctor was, at the very least, a good customer of the smugglers on this coast and, it seemed clear, Pengelly and Drake were active smugglers, present on the night of the shipwreck to help in a landing that was cancelled by the burning signal.

What next? Well, obviously, they must wait for the doctor's return. Josh knew he would be happier to leave for Dover if there was someone in the house to protect Rowena, should the strange pendulum of hate in this village swing towards her. He would also feel somehow more settled if, before setting out, he could receive a letter from Mary – and he would be so relieved if the doctor would agree to remove the surely now redundant damned splints on his injured leg. He sighed. Best to sit tight and see if that cat would jump within the next few days.

It did so in a way that was both tragic and shocking.

Two days after his meeting with the two sailors, Josh was awakened just before first light by a fierce hammering on the door of the house. Struggling into jacket and trousers he met Rowena hurrying down the stairway in her dressing gown.

He was close behind her when she opened the door to see Mrs Brown, her bonnet askew, standing there with a matronly woman new to him.

'Whatever is the matter?' asked Rowena. 'Mrs Brown, Mrs Drake, what is it?'

The second woman, Mrs Drake, was obviously too upset to speak but Mrs Brown blurted out, 'Jem, her son, didn't turn up for work at the harbour yesterday morning and he 'asn't been 'ome all night. We just wondered if he'd had an accident or somethin' an' he 'ad been brought 'ere . . . ?'

'Oh come in, come in, out of the cold.' Rowena gestured behind her and Josh moved aside so that the two women could enter. 'No, my dears, we haven't seen Jem. He is not here. But I am sure that there will be a simple explanation for what has happened. Now, come into the kitchen and I will make us all a pot of tea and we can decide what to do. Oh,' Rowena indicated Josh, 'Mrs Drake this is Mr Joshua Weyland, he is staying here for a while and, in fact, he met Jem only two days ago. Perhaps he might be able to shed some light on where he might be. Come on through now.'

As they sat and Rowena bustled around at the old stove, Josh leant towards the sobbing woman. 'Have you considered, Mrs Drake, that he might be with his mate, Tom Pengelly, perhaps staying overnight with him at Morwenstow? I gather he's done that before when the weather has been inclement.'

The old lady blew her nose. 'Oh no, sur, 'e's never done that. Never stayed out all night. 'E wouldn't do that because 'e knew I would worry. 'E's always been such a good son to me, y'see. He wouldn't want me worryin'. Where can 'e be?'

Josh frowned, recalling Pengelly's explanation of why Drake was with him the night of the storm. Another lie to add to the litany! He took the grieving old lady's hand. 'Never mind, Mrs Drake, it's getting light now, as soon as you've had your tea Rowena and I will go out in the donkey cart and make a search. There will be some innocent explanation for his absence. There always is.'

He made his excuses, climbed upstairs to complete his dressing and then went out to the stable to harness up the donkey and cart. By the time he had brought them round to the front door, Rowena was waiting for him fully dressed. She had the doctor's medical bag in her hand.

Josh nodded to it. 'Good idea,' he said.

First they rode down to the harbour. There was no body washed up onto the little beach by the stone workings. Then, they climbed the hill, past the Preventers' barracks and trotted a while on the road to Morwenstow. Nothing.

'I think we should look the other way, towards the Point,' said Rowena.

'Very well.' Josh pulled the donkey's head round. 'Why, though? What is up there?'

'Not much. Only the high clifftop and the heathland. I just think we should look, that's all. People have been known to thrown themselves off there, you know.'

'Very well. Giddy-up, giddy-up.'

Long before they reached the highest part of the Point they found Jem Drake. He was hanging from a branch of a tree at the side of the path, his hands hanging uselessly at his side. Gruesomely, his throat had been cut so severely that he was almost decapitated. He was swinging gently in the morning breeze and he was, of course, quite dead.

CHAPTER NINE

Rowena led out an involuntary scream but quickly stifled it. The donkey, sensing or perhaps smelling the evil above it, stood shivering. 'Can you cut him down, Josh, while I stop the donkey from bolting,' said Rowena, leaning over and taking the reins.

Josh stood up unsteadily and climbed onto the cart's bench, withdrawing his knife. He took Jem's weight off the noose so that the rope slackened and, reaching up, was just able to saw away at it with his knife. It parted suddenly and Josh would have tumbled over backwards as Jem's full weight descended upon him had not Rowena's steady hand at his back held him upright.

The corpse was lowered into the cart and Rowena touched the artery under the dead man's ear to ensure that no life remained. She shook her head and wrinkled her nose in disgust. 'Rigor mortis has set in. He must have been hanging for hours.'

They covered the corpse with the old blanket that had served them well that night on the moor. Rowena was about to flick the reins to galvanise the donkey when Josh held up his hand. 'Let me look about here for a minute,' he said, and lowered himself onto the ground.

Underneath the branch from which Jem had been suspended the grass was trampled. There were hoof marks mixed with impressions made by what seemed to be a riding boot. The boot marks, however, seemed to be those of only one man. The hoof marks were deep, showing, he mused, that the horse had been carrying a heavy burden; perhaps two men – or even one man and a corpse.

'I don't think he was killed here,' he called up to Rowena. 'I think his throat was cut and he was brought here to be strung up. But why?' He wrinkled his brow then struck his fist into the palm of his hand. 'Of course! As some sort of warning to others. This is what happens to you if you . . .' He did not complete the sentence.

'If you what?' called Rowena.

'I don't know, but I mean to find out. Look,' he pointed behind them, 'there are drops of blood on the track. They must have dripped from poor Drake as he was brought here.'

'If we follow them back it should tell us where he was attacked.'

'I doubt it. Whoever did this would be too clever to leave such a giveaway. But let's see. Turn the cart round.'

Rowena did so but the red trail soon ended and there were no hoof marks on the path. The horseman had obviously carefully picked his way through the bushes and tangled undergrowth on the moor itself, but there were no tracks to show from where he had come.

'Where do we take him?' asked Rowena.

'I suppose there is no alternative but to put him in the stable behind your house. Then, of course, we must inform the authorities.'

The 'authorities', however, proved to be difficult to find. The nearest militia post was in Bude, some fifteen miles away, and the nearest magistrate in Barnstaple far to the north. 'It will have to be Jack Cunningham,' said Rowena, after they had laid the body out on straw in the stable reserved for the doctor's horse, which was, of course, away with its owner.

'No, not just yet,' said Josh. 'Can you first of all go down to the quay and find Tom Pengelly and bring him here. Don't tell him the bad news. Just say that I would like to see him urgently.'

'Very well, Josh. But then we must tell poor Mrs Drake.'

'Of course. But Pengelly first. Go quickly.'

The two arrived within five minutes, Pengelly's sea boots still dripping.

'It's about Jem, isn't it?' demanded the sailor, his face white under its tan. 'You've found him, haven't you?'

Josh didn't reply but beckoned Pengelly to follow him into the stable.

'Oh, holy mother of God,' cried the sailor as Josh pulled back the blanket. Pengelly dropped to his knees, crossed himself and seized the cold hand of the dead man. 'Ah, Jem. Poor Jem.'

'He was murdered, Tom,' said Josh. 'We found him hanging from a tree up near the Point but he had been killed, I think, before that and taken there to be strung up. Now,' he paused, 'you were his friend. Can you tell me why?'

Pengelly hung his head and then shook it. 'No,' he said, 'I can't.'

'You realise, Tom, that you would be a prime suspect in this murder.'

The sailor turned his head quickly and looked up at Josh, his face flushed with anger.

'Me? I'm no suspect. Jem was my friend, my best friend. Anyone will tell you that. I wouldn't have harmed a hair on his head. Why,' the air of aggression deepened, 'you're a far more likely suspect than me, Second Mate. All kinds of strange things have happened since you came here.'

'Really? What sort of strange things would they be, then?'

'Well,' he paused for a moment. '*The Lucy* comin' in onto the Morwenstow rocks as though she was a fury, for one thing. Who's to say it was the drunken skipper who pushed the helm down and brought her in like that. P'raps it was you on the wheel that night.

'Then there was that cock 'n' bull story about you bein' attacked when only you saw those two men. Nobody else saw 'em. An' then suddenly we was invaded by tinners and there was a battle on the 'eath. All very strange.'

Suddenly, Rowena intervened. 'Now, don't you go accusing Joshua of bein' behind all that stuff.' Her voice rose indignantly. 'You say nobody saw those two men attacking Josh. Well, I saw 'em, admittedly they was runnin' away, the cowardly pair. But I saw 'em all right.'

She turned to Josh. 'Mind you, Josh, you shouldn't go accusin' Tom here of bein' involved in this terrible murder. He wouldn't do a thing like that, particularly to his old friend Jem.'

Josh threw up his hands. 'That may well be so, but I am plucking at straws here. I would like to feel that Tom here, whom you know well, was not involved. But who the hell was?' He turned back to Pengelly. 'Look, I know that it was you and Jem here who attacked me up the hill there. I know you will deny it but I've seen the scars I put on your face and arms and here, look,' he pointed, 'this discolouration on Jem's face. I did all that and remember clearly doing it. Those marks give you away. But it was you two who saved me at Morwenstow. Why then should you attack me? Someone put you forward for it, didn't they? If you can tell me who it was, and why he should do it, then perhaps we can begin to get to the bottom of Jem's murder.'

Just for one fleeting moment, Josh thought that Pengelly was going to reveal all. Then, his face assumed that sullen expression that he wore whenever he had been questioned. 'I know nothin' of these things,' he said, 'an' that's that. I'm goin' to answer no more questions.' He turned to Rowena. ''Ave you told Jem's mother . . . ?'

'No. Not yet.'

'Then I suppose I'd better do it. Where did you say you found 'im? I shall 'ave to tell 'er.'

'Up on the path towards the top of Hartland Point. A tree on the right.'

'I'll go to 'er now.'

Josh put a gentle hand on Rowena's arm. 'You had better go and make some tea,' he said. 'I'm afraid it will be very trying for everyone when Mrs Drake arrives, poor woman.'

'All right. But where are you going?'

'I will walk up to the Preventers' barracks and try and find Cunningham. He is the nearest thing we have around here representing law and order and I agree he should be told. Anyway, I shall ask him to send one of his men to Bude to inform the head of the militia there about the murder and another to Barnstaple to tell the magistrate. Then, it's up to them.'

He clasped a hand to his forehead. 'I wish to God your father would return. Perhaps some sanity might return to this place then.'

Rowena attempted to put her arm around his shoulder but he shook it off. 'I am really sorry you have landed in this mess, Josh,' she said. 'I really am. Perhaps,' she stifled a sob, 'you should go to your Mary now before things get worse.'

He smiled at her in apology at his roughness. 'I'm sorry, my dear, that I seem to be throwing accusations around, but I am determined to get to the bottom of this. Anyway,' he shrugged, 'there can be no question of me leaving Hartland Quay now until the coroner arrives.' He looked at her sharply. 'Who is the coroner around here?'

Rowena smiled wanly. 'Father, of course.'

Josh limped up to the barracks and banged on the huge door. The captain was out, he was told, so he left a message asking him to come to the doctor's house as soon as possible. There had been, he said, a brutal murder.

He heard the voice of Mrs Drake bewailing her loss long before he reached the bottom of the hill. He decided that he could not face a mother's grief and turned away from the stable and climbed the stairs to his room. There, he lay on the bed, his mind racing as he tried to tease some sort of thread of sanity out of the jumble of events that had happened. Pengelly was right. It had all seemed to happen around himself.

Then he sat upright. Would someone 'in authority' come to that conclusion, too? Would the trail culminating in Drake's murder point to this newcomer to the village? Well, of course, he knew he was innocent but this was a remote, even barbaric area. It would not be so very difficult to manufacture false evidence that could incriminate him. So who might do that? Who, in fact, was guilty? For one wild moment, he even considered if Rowena – wilful, jealous Rowena, with her Gypsy background and her head filled with romantic, even violent ideas perhaps – could be somehow involved. He shook his head. What nonsense! She might be a fantasist and a romantic but she could not be a murderer.

Captain Cunningham rode into the stable in a clatter of hooves and Rowena and Josh went to meet him. He studied the body in silence, bending down to turn Jem's head to study the wound.

'We need to inform the militia and a magistrate, I presume,' said Josh. 'I understand that Doctor Acland is the coroner around here and, hopefully, he should be back soon.'

'I have already sent gallopers to Bude and Barnstaple to do just that. I didn't say much: just that a murder had been committed and the Queen's peace had been broken.' He stroked his chin. 'For such a capital crime they won't delay, I am sure. And, as for the doctor, I understand he has been seen about two miles from here riding home. He will be here soon.'

'Thank God for that,' murmured Josh, and Rowena's troubled face melted into a smile.

'Where exactly did you find Drake?'

'About half a mile towards Hartland Point, hanging from a tree on the right of the track.'

'Hmm. I had better get up there right away, before people start tramping up there to look at the damned tree and removing whatever indications there might be of who strung him up there.'

Josh nodded. 'I noticed hoof marks and marks of a riding boot just under the branch from which he was hanging. That's about all.'

'Thank you. I must go and see for myself.' He nodded to them and swung onto his horse and, with a wave of his hook, galloped away.

A silence descended on the stable and Rowena and Joshua stood by the side of the body looking at each other. 'Oh, Josh.' Rowena moved towards Josh and put out her hands. He took them, as much to reassure her as to ward her off and gripped them tightly.

'We will find out who did this terrible thing, I promise you,' he said. Then he bent down and covered Jem Drake's head with a corner of the blanket. 'Come away from here now. Your father will know what we must do with the poor man.'

'Oh yes, Father!' Rowena put a hand to mouth. 'I've only prepared lunch for two. I must see what else I can do.'

The doctor rode into the stable yard behind the house half an hour later. He had ridden from the nearest rail station after an uneasy night's journey on the train and his eyes seemed sunken and his movements stiff as he dismounted.

Josh stood back as Rowena greeted him. 'Oh, Papa, we are both so glad to see you. A terrible thing has happened while you have been away.'

The murder was explained. 'Jem Drake!' exclaimed Acland. 'Jem Drake *murdered*! Who on earth would do such a thing? Everybody liked him. He wouldn't harm a fly!'

Josh briefly recalled how the second of his two assailants had seemed reluctant to attack and how easily he had been rendered virtually *hors de combat* by a blow on his cheek from a crutch. But the doctor was continuing.

'Where is the body?'

'I'm afraid it's in your stable, Father. We couldn't think of anywhere else to put him.'

'Very well. Fetch my bag. I must examine him right away.'

'But you must be tired, sir,' intervened Josh. 'Won't it do when you have had your dinner?'

'No it won't. As coroner I must be sure that the body is not interfered with before I have a chance of examining it.' He shot a keen glance at Josh, as though noticing him for the first time. 'Was it you who cut him down?'

'Yes, sir.'

'Well I shall want you to give evidence when I hold court. Which should be tomorrow. Has the militia been informed?'

'I believe that Captain Cunningham has done so.'

'Good. They must take care of the body and summon witnesses.' He sighed. 'I didn't think I would come back to something like this.'

'Quite so. Did you . . . er . . . have a successful visit to London?'

'What? Oh yes. I think so.' Rowena brought him his bag. 'Thank you, my dear. Now you must leave me to my work. Weyland, perhaps you would look after my horse, I confess to being tired. He had better go in with the donkey for the moment, I think.'

After Acland had completed his grisly examination, they ate luncheon in comparative silence, broken inevitably by Rowena. 'Father, why didn't you tell us you were going away? And what have you been doing?'

Acland, the lines on his face now accentuated by the flickering light – although it was not long after midday the sky was overcast and it was necessary to light candles to illuminate the gloomy dining room – touched his lips with his napkin. 'First,' he said, 'tell me about your journey to Bude. Did you find any evidence of the tinners' involvement in wrecking here?'

The question was addressed to Josh and he recounted their discussion with the mine owner and the clash with Cunningham and his men on the heath.

'Dammit,' the doctor seemed to speak to himself as much as to them. 'That man is getting ahead of himself. I have never thought that the miners were involved in smuggling, although they've all done a bit of wrecking in their time. They've gone up north, you say?'

'Yes, sir.'

'Well I'm not sure they will find employment up there. Things are no better in semi-industrial communities in this country than they are in rural areas.' He had been looking at his plate but now he looked up and regarded them both.

'Did you behave yourselves in Bude?'

Josh answered for both of them. 'Of course, sir. We had to sleep out of doors for just one night because I wanted to follow and talk to the tinners, but nothing untoward happened, I assure you. I gave you my word and I kept it.'

A half smile crept over the doctor's features. 'Yes, but,' he turned to Rowena, 'did you, my girl?'

His daughter blushed. 'Of course I did, Father. Really! What a question!'

'Very well, then. I think it time to tell you why I went to London and the result of the visit. I know it is only early afternoon, but I am extremely fatigued and I might be in need of refreshment to explain everything. So, Emma, my dear, fetch yourself some lemonade—'

'Oh, really, Father!'

'. . . and if, Weyland, you would be so kind as to find that bottle of cognac we tasted the other night, with two glasses, I can explain the action I have taken.'

'Very good, sir. Rowena, do as your father tells you.'

'This is ridiculous. How can I become an adult if I am continually being treated as a child?' But she rose and flounced to the kitchen to find her lemonade.

The doctor gave Josh the first full smile since his return. 'She is a good girl really, you know, Weyland. But she can be a little wayward, as you have probably found.'

Josh shifted uncomfortably in his chair. 'Oh, I don't think so, sir. Not really. Not really.'

Rowena returned, glass in hand and sat down. 'Now, Father. All kinds of strange things have been going on here, including you riding off to London while we were away. Now, tell us all about it.'

'Very well. Be so kind as to pour the cognac, Weyland. Yes, thank you.

'Now.' He leant forward. 'You say, my dear, that strange things have been happening while I have been away. Well, they were happening before I left and that's why I felt I had to go to London. You see,' he took a sip of the cognac, winced slightly at its strength, took another one and put the glass down. 'You see, I have been concerned for some time at the remarkably high number of ships that have foundered just along this ten mile stretch of coastline in the last year or so.'

He took another sip and nodded his head appreciatively before continuing. 'My old employers, the Blue Cross Line, have been particularly hard hit, losing four ships in that time. The loss of your ship, Weyland, brought things to a head for me, particularly with your accusations of seeing that light in the storm and then, as you say, finding the ashes at the place where you think it was placed. Then, the attack on you . . .' He shook his head. 'It seemed to be all getting out of hand.'

'I can well understand your thinking that, sir,' said Josh. 'And now, of course, there is this terrible murder.'

'Quite so. I suppose, as coroner and local doctor, I hold some sort of unofficial leadership position in this small community but I certainly felt it was beyond my capabilities to discover what was behind these shipwrecks – if, that is, there is anything, other than harsh weather and acts of God.'

'Oh, I don't know, Father.' Rowena seized her father's hand. 'If anyone can get to the bottom of all this then I am sure you can.'

Acland smiled and shook his head. 'Kind of you, my dear, but untrue, I fear. No. I felt that the insurers of these vessels must, at the very least, be uneasy about these claims on them, and that Lloyd's in London should have their attention drawn to them.'

'Ah!' Joshua nodded slowly. 'Yes. So you went to Lloyd's?'

'I did, indeed.'

'Who are they, Father?'

'It is, would you believe it, my dear, a very respectable institution founded in a coffee house in London about 150 years ago, where information could be exchanged about trade and shipping in particular. It grew into a place where insurance was taken out to protect shipowners and their cargoes in case of disaster and is now the world's leader in this. These insurers, as you will understand, have a vested interest in seeing that there is no foul play in trading on the high seas and no unfounded calls on their insurance policies. They are centred now, in a highly professional way, in the heart of the City of

London. Lloyd's publishes the Lloyd's List, giving details of sailings and so on, on a daily basis and, as you know, I have a collection of these publications in my workroom.'

'And what exactly did you ask Lloyd's to do, Doctor?'

'I outlined the facts as I knew them,' he puffed out his cheeks slightly now, 'and they listened to me, I believe with some attention, given that I am coroner here and, to boot, an ex-merchant seamen officer. I said that the number of shipwrecks along this coast seemed to me to be unusually high. I, of course, explained that the prevailing weather and absence of room to manoeuvre under sail would have much to do with this, but I also suggested that it was unusual for one shipowner, the Blue Cross Line, to lose so many vessels in this way. They listened, I am glad to say.'

'What was their decision, then, sir?'

'Well, they kept me waiting, dammit – with some damage to my wallet, for London is an expensive place – before giving me that. But it was worth it, I think, because they have agreed to mount an enquiry into these recent ship losses and they intend to do it – and to call witnesses – here at Hartland Quay, which will concentrate people's minds considerably, and the panel, or whatever we must call them, can look at the geography around here without having to rely on word descriptions painted in some London courtroom.'

'Well done, Doctor.' Josh rose and grasped Acland's hand and shook it warmly. 'I am sure you have rendered a great service to the Merchant Navy as a result of your visit. Was . . . er . . . there any mention of smuggling?'

Joshua watched closely the old man's reaction to the question. Another sip was taken from the glass and then he said, 'Not much, really. To investigate such a well-established custom in these parts, I fear,' he looked up with a sad smile, 'would probably take two or three more different enquiries, but the point was noted. The enquiry, I think, will be much more centred on the reasons why the ships foundered. If the need to land contraband on this coast was demonstrated as one of the reasons, well then, of course, any illegal act would be probed. That's all I can say on the matter.'

'When is the enquiry due to be held, Papa?'

'I made them promise that, in Shakespeare's words, "If it t'were done . . . t'were well it was done quickly." So, I would suggest, say, within two weeks. Witnesses would need to be called, some of whom, including the panel, no doubt, would need to travel down from London. But I gave them a few local names to be getting on with.'

'Can you mention names, sir?'

'I don't see why not. They will, I am sure, be contacted quickly anyway. Firstly, bearing in mind my own memories – and Cunningham's, too, as well as your more recent experience – I felt that a representative of the Blue Cross Line's management should be present. We shall definitely need you, my boy, to give evidence about the poor seaworthy state of the Line ships in the present, as I and probably Cunningham will concerning years ago.'

Rowena's eyes lit up. 'That means you will have to stay here for a while longer, Josh.'

'Yes, I am afraid so, Weyland. You are most welcome, of course, to continue to reside here. Which reminds me. I must look at that leg. But you look agile enough now, so I hope that those splints can come off. Much more comfortable for you.'

'Thank you, sir. I was hoping you would say that. But do tell me. What other witnesses did you suggest?'

'Well, Cunningham, of course. I presume that you will continue to tell your story about the burning brazier, so he must answer for that, as well as talking of the poor state of the Line's ships when we sailed in them. And the Reverend Hawker. He knows more about recent shipwrecks than most people around here, and I did put forward young Pengelly's name, as a practising seaman who knows this shoreline like the back of his hand. No doubt they might find others they wish to question. We shall see.'

'Hmm. We shall indeed. One last question to you, if I may.'

'Yes?'

'If I remember rightly, just before Row . . . Emma and I set off for Bude, which was just after the attack on me, you said that you had some enquiries to make?'

'What, oh yes. I was referring to Lloyd's, of course.'

'Ah, I see. Not in the village here or Morwenstow, then?'

The doctor took a rather deeper draught of the cognac this time. 'No. Not really.' He reached out his glass. 'My dear fellow, would you care to fill up my glass and, of course, do so for yourself, too.'

'Oh Father! You are falling back into bad habits. I expect you drank a lot in London too, didn't you?'

'Hardly a drop passed my lips, dear daughter.' He lifted his eyebrow to Josh and, for the first time, the young man felt a brief surge of liking for the old doctor, who had seemed momentarily to wrap him in a warm embrace of humorous and shared love with his daughter.

Josh lifted his glass, nodded to the doctor, turned to Rowena and said sternly, 'Now drink your lemonade, like a good girl, Emma.' Then he and Acland shared a grin and toasted each other.

The militia arrived the next morning, in the shape of a braided captain and a dragoon. After a consultation with Acland they took away the body to the Preventers' barracks.

'I shall have to hold the Coroner's Court there,' he said. 'I shall call witnesses but it looks as though it can be only you – I want to keep Emma out of this – and Cunningham. Oh, and Pengelly as the last person to see him alive. We will do it tomorrow.'

They did so and a few people from the hamlet attended in addition to the witnesses. Josh repeated the circumstances of finding the body and Cunningham added virtually nothing to it, except to confirm that he, too, had noticed foot and hoof prints in the mud and grass underneath the tree. Pengelly could only testify that he had said goodbye to Drake at completion of work on the day before, before he himself had set for Morwenstow on foot, as was his daily practice.

There was little that could be added and Dr Acland recorded that he had examined the body and that Jem Drake had died by a blow to the throat, which had torn it apart. The hanging had added nothing to the cause of death. 'My verdict,' he said at the end, 'is that the deceased was attacked by some person or persons unknown, sustaining a wound to the throat that caused his death and was therefore murdered. So I shall report to the magistrate. This hearing is now closed.'

Rowena and Josh walked away, as did Pengelly, who strode away quickly without a glance in their direction. The doctor and Cunningham stayed behind in close conversation.

Looking at them as they left, Rowena said, 'I suppose Papa is telling Captain Jack about the Lloyd's enquiry.'

'Hmm. I suppose so. Why, though, is Cunningham getting so heated with your father? Look, he is getting quite angry. It looks more like a quarrel than an explanation.'

'We'd better go. We shouldn't get involved.'

Back at the house, Josh realised that yet another day had dawned without a letter from Mary being delivered. She surely would have returned now from wherever she had been and would have had plenty of time to write. He shook his head. Things were getting *so* convoluted! He itched to see his fiancée now – if only to sort out his feelings for her – but it was clear that he would not be allowed to go until after the Lloyd's enquiry, at least.

Notification of the enquiry, however, came quickly. It was to be held in one month's time at the inn in Hartland Point. A judge of the High Court had been appointed chairman and the 'bench' would comprise a representative of the Blue Cross Line, and three underwriters from Lloyd's. The hearing would not have the force of law but witnesses would be expected to swear on the Bible before giving evidence. There would be no formal prosecution or defence for there was, of course, no plaintiff or defendant. A leading Queen's Counsel, however, had been appointed to conduct the examination of witnesses, although the Lloyd's members presiding could question them if they wished. The press would be allowed to report on the proceedings.

'This is all very unusual, of course,' said the doctor at the breakfast table, after he had finished reading from his letter. 'But it shows that Lloyd's is taking this matter seriously.'

'To whom will they submit the result of the enquiry?' asked Josh.

'I presume it will be to the management committee of Lloyd's, if there is such a thing. And, clearly, if wrongdoing is suspected the matter will then be passed over to the police.'

No one spoke for a moment. Then Josh said, 'I am rather puzzled by the fact that one of the presiding Lloyd's panel – one of the judges of the case, if you like – is a member of the Blue Cross Line company. If he is to be a key witness – and I hope he will have plenty to answer – then he should not be presiding, if you follow.'

Acland nodded. 'I take your point and this is probably my fault. But I was so anxious that this company should be investigated for its record on safety and, indeed, seamanship, that I feared they would not attend unless they were on the presiding panel. So I suggested it.' He looked sharply across at Joshua. 'On reflection, now, I wish that you had accompanied me to London, but we couldn't do everything at once.'

Rowena smiled at the compliment paid to Josh and he studied his plate in some embarrassment. 'I doubt, sir,' he said, 'that I could have made a significant difference. You got your enquiry, after all.'

'Ah well, it's done now. Right,' said the doctor, standing. 'It's time we looked at your leg. I think we can certainly remove those splints now, my boy. But I must examine the wound before we take that decision. Let us go to the surgery.'

'May I come, too, Father?' asked Rowena.

'I don't approve of non-medical persons being present at examinations, you know that, Emma. So I would rather you—'

Josh interrupted. 'If I may put in a word, as the patient, Doctor, I must say that while you have been away Emma has impressed me with her basic medical skills on several occasions. I don't mind at all if she is present.'

'Oh, please, Papa. You know I am interested.'

'Oh, very well. Come along.'

While Joshua lay on a couch in the surgery, the bandages securing the splints on either side of his leg were removed and the dressing underneath carefully unwound. To Josh, the wound appeared to be rather like an evil black crack below the knee, but Acland rubbed his hands with pleasure as he examined it.

'To be frank,' he said, 'I was afraid that the, er, obvious gallivanting that you have been doing since I first dressed the leg would have caused some friction and even produced an infection, but this looks clean enough.' He regarded Josh sternly. 'I should really have insisted that you stayed in bed for a week or more but I realised that you were young and healthy enough and that the frustration of keeping the leg still in bed would probably cause more harm than benefit.

'I know that, on the Continent, they have been experimenting for some time with a kind of starched bandage coated in plaster, which serves this type of injury well, but I lacked the skill and the materials to apply it, so it was a question of using the old-fashioned way by offering support with splints. But,' he adjusted his spectacles and looked closely, 'they seem to have served their purpose well. Yes, we can leave the splints off, but I insist you use a stick to help you walk. There are many in the kitchen. Choose one that suits you for length and so on. But,' he held up a warning finger, 'don't go galloping about. Treat the leg with care. I will just put a light dressing on it now, which should make you feel much more comfortable.'

He pushed his spectacles back up to the bridge of his nose. 'Would you like to apply the dressing, Nurse Acland? I shall observe how you do it.'

'Oh yes please, Father.'

For the next few days, Joshua followed a self-imposed regime of taking daily walks, sometimes alone, sometimes with Rowena, but always accompanied by a thick stick and his knife in its sheath at his back. He also wrote another letter to Mary, enclosing a note of thanks to her mother, explaining that he would need to stay a little longer than expected in Cornwall because he had to give evidence at the enquiry, but that, as soon as that was completed, he would set out for Dover. He gave a penny to a boy in the village to take the letter up to the post box situated in the village at the top. He no longer trusted Rowena to be postmistress.

The time passed pleasantly enough and the arrival of his and Rowena's overnight clothes from the hotel in Bude eased the problems presented by his sparse wardrobe, which had been supplemented after the shipwreck by old clothes from the doctor, few of which fitted him.

He attached no importance to the arrival back in Hartland Quay of the officer of militia accompanied by his dragoon. They were waiting for him at the doctor's house when he limped back after his walk and it was only the white face of Rowena, standing at their side by the doorway, that gave him pause.

The captain stepped forward. 'Joshua Weyland?'

'Yes.'

'I have a warrant here for your arrest on a charge of murdering Jem Drake. You may go to your room and pack an overnight bag – I will give you five minutes only – and then I must ask you to accompany me to Barnstaple.'

Joshua's jaw dropped. 'Murder? I have murdered no one. This is ridiculous.' He turned to Rowena. 'Where is your father?'

Rowena's lower lip was trembling. 'He is on his rounds. Oh, Josh. He will sort this out when he returns. I know he will. I will come with you to pack a bag now.'

The captain turned to his dragoon. 'Go with them,' then to Josh and Rowena. 'You have only five minutes. I have brought a horse for you, Weyland, and we must ride hard if we are to be at Barnstaple before dark, so be quick. I don't want to be caught out on the heath in a storm. So move yourself, man!'

CHAPTER TEN

The journey proved to be one of the most uncomfortable and depressing of Joshua's life. The horses were strong and the captain set a cracking pace, alternately walking, trotting and even, in short spurts, galloping them. Josh's attempts to question him about the details of the accusation against him proved completely unsuccessful, the officer grunting, 'I can give you no information, so it is no use asking me. For God's sake keep up the pace, man. We have a way to go yet.'

In fact, the light was fading as the trio arrived at the municipal jail in the centre of Barnstaple. It was a grey, forbidding place, built of moorland stone, with small windows criss-crossed with iron bars. Josh was handed over to a low-grade official at the desk, the captain was handed a receipt and he and his escort turned and left immediately.

''Ad anything to eat?' asked the jailer.

'Not since breakfast. I would be grateful to eat something.'

The man gave him a not altogether unpleasant smile, nodded, and called down a corridor. This was answered by the arrival of a huge, bearded man, who roughly pushed Josh against a wall, forced his legs apart and ran his hands over his body. He plucked out the knife and threw it into a corner, took the few coins that were in his pocket and then turned his attention to the bag that Rowena had insisted on packing for him. Everything within was thrown onto the floor, until the bag was held upside down and shaken to ensure that nothing was left hidden. His razor, brush, shaving soap and knife were confiscated and he gestured to Josh to pick up the contents and then pushed him down the corridor, which was lined by cell doors.

One was opened and a push in the back sent Josh flying into the interior, after which the door clanged shut and a bolt was pushed across. The only light filtered through a barred window high in the wall and, at first, Josh had difficulty in seeing anything within the cell. Then he made out a small iron bedstead with what appeared to be a straw mattress and two well-worn woollen blankets folded on top. A wooden chair, a cast-iron bucket and a bowl with a jug set within it completed the furnishings. The stone walls carried no decorations, of course, and they glistened with moisture. It was cold and the place smelt of urine and stale tobacco.

Josh sat on the bed and wrapped one of the blankets around him. Then, making sure he was unobserved, he took off his shoe and took out the golden guinea and a handful of shillings he had hidden there before setting out on the journey. They could prove vital, but how, he could not comprehend at this point. He had given up teasing his brain about who might have given evidence that had resulted in him being arraigned in this way. So he sat, his mind empty, his head in his hands, the money grasped in one of them.

He jerked himself upright as a bolt was slid back and a key turned in the lock of his door. The jailer who had 'received' him, backed in carrying a tray with some sort of sandwich set on it – no plate – and a mug full of what appeared to be cold milk. The stub of a candle burnt in a saucer, giving a flickering light.

'Bit of beef and bread to keep you goin' 'til the mornin',' he said. 'An' a drop of milk, which my wife 'as brought round for you.'

'Ah, that is kind,' said Josh. 'Please thank her for me.'

The jailer seemed surprised to find his prisoner speaking politely and in gentlemanly terms. 'What are you in for, then?' he asked.

'Er, murder. But I have no details of the charge and I have never killed anyone in my life.'

The jailer grinned, showing two broken teeth. 'Ah, that's what they all say.'

'Well, it's true in my case. I am an honest sailor. An accredited second mate and I don't take kindly to being locked up. When will I know the charge against me?'

'P'raps in the mornin', p'raps later. It depends 'pon 'ow busy the magistrate is. 'E 'as a big territory to cover, like, see.'

Josh took a grateful bite of the sandwich. The bread was stale but the meat seemed reasonably fresh and someone had spread a little mustard on the beef. 'What sort of man is the magistrate?' he asked.

'Oh, 'e's fair enough, is old Sir George. 'E won't stand no nonsense but 'e is an honest man. Good to the poor, for instance. I've gotta go now. Piss in that bucket and if you want a shit you'll 'ave to put it in the same place. You can empty it in the morning.'

'Thank you. And thank you for the mustard.'

The door clanged shut.

The milk was slightly sour but he drank it gratefully, for he was thirsty as well as hungry. On a thought, he emptied out his bag. It contained some undergarments, a second shirt, some woollen socks and his night attire as well as a face flannel and a piece of soap. But nothing else. He had half hoped that Rowena might have secreted away a knife of some sort or even a file, but there was nothing of the sort. He shrugged. It would have been discovered anyway.

By the light of what was left of the candle he washed in the cold water from the jug, shook the blankets hard and brushed his hand across the mattress. Tiny, speck-like creatures were crawling across his palm and he felt one bite him. That was the end of the mattress. He would have to sleep on the stone floor or be devoured by these savage little creatures. Oh, for the soft white mattress and clean sheets of the doctor's house!

The stub of the candle guttered and went out. Carefully he folded his topcoat and laid it as a pillow on the floor. He put one of the blankets on the floor and, fully clothed, lay down on it, tucking the other blanket around him.

So began the night, which proved to be acutely uncomfortable and very, very cold. He could find no succour in attempting to go through the list of people who might have accused him: Pengelly, Cunningham, the gossipy, all-seeing publican – even the doctor himself? He shook his head and managed to find a little sleep just before daybreak.

The clang of the door awoke him and the giant jailer brought in a board, which contained – again no plate – two rashers of bacon, the fat already congealing on them, a piece of bread and a mug of tea. At least the bacon and the tea were comparatively hot and he devoured both, before washing, again in cold water – he could not, of course, shave and this worried him, because Josh had meticulously shaved all his life, even when at sea in stormy weather. He did not fancy facing the good Sir George, looking like an unshaven ruffian.

But the magistrate did not put in an appearance that day and it was not until halfway through the following morning that his door was thrown open and the jailer cried out, 'Stand up for Sir George Lansbury.'

Josh rose immediately and regarded his visitor with interest. He looked liked the artist's caricature of the English landed gentleman, in fact, he reminded Josh of the cartoons depicting John Bull he had seen in Somerset during his boyhood and dating from the Napoleonic wars. Sir George was of medium height but wide in build and portly. His red face was dominated by a cherubic nose and fringed by luxuriant side whiskers. He wore a stunted top hat of the 'John Bull' variety and a white cravat tucked into a shirt poking out from the checked waistcoat, which tried its best to restrain a very large waistline. Riding breeches and boots completed the picture of rural prosperity.

'Sit down, boy,' he gestured. 'Sit down.' His nose wrinkled. 'Good gad, jailer. Don't you ever clean out these cells? See to it as soon as I have gone. D'hear?'

'Very well, Sir George.'

The magistrate took out a vivid red handkerchief and mopped his brow. 'Devilish hot,' he said, to no one in particular. Then to Joshua. 'But not in here. How many blankets have you got, boy?'

'Two, sir. But they are extremely thin.'

Sir George looked up immediately, in some surprise at Joshua's cultured tones, tinged with a West Country burr. 'Get him another blanket, jailer. He could freeze overnight and then I would have to sentence you to transportation, for what . . . ? Well, manslaughter in the least.

'Well, now. What have we got here?' He fumbled in his waistcoat pocket, adjusted a pair of reading glasses and pulled out a sheet of paper. 'Ah, he's the only one this morning. Thank God for that . . .' His voice trailed away as his lips formed one word: 'Murder'.

'By Gad, sir! Murder! Don't get many of those down here.' He looked at Joshua across the top of his spectacles. 'Did you do it?'

'Of course not, sir. I've never killed anyone in my life. I don't even know the details of the charge and who has brought it. I am a sailor, a qualified second mate, who was shipwrecked on Morwenstow, on the north coast of Cornwall, some weeks ago. I injured a leg on the rocks there.' He lifted up his leg. 'I am still trying to recover, sir.'

Lansbury stared at him for a moment, frowning. 'I don't care a damn about the state of your leg or where and why you landed here, sir. The point is that you have been accused of killing another human being unlawfully and you must be tried for it. As for your accusers,' he consulted his paper, 'they are, of course, the local militia. But someone obviously has given them information about the crime and you have been indicted. Who this person or persons are will come out at your trial.'

'When will that be, sir?'

'Oh, pretty damned quick, I would say. Just for once, we do not have a long list of miscreants waiting for trial in Barnstaple. I should explain that you will come before me in my magistrate's court. As this is a capital charge and beyond the jurisdiction of my court, my task will purely be to examine the evidence put before me and decide whether it is sufficiently strong to commit you for formal trial at the Assizes in Exeter. If you are found guilty there you will be hanged. Very few people are acquitted of this sort of crime.'

Sir George spoke without emotion. 'However, sir, you should know that just because the militia brings people before me, I certainly do not shirk my duty and simply pass 'em on to the higher court as a matter of form. No, sir, I have no desire to qualify as a wig-wearer. Certainly not.' He wheezed at his jest and blew his nose loudly on the red handkerchief.

'In these cases, I always – always, sir – make absolutely certain that the evidence presented to me is convincing enough to qualify it being presented properly at the Assizes. I believe I can say that I have that reputation, which is, I must confess, a tad unusual amongst magistrates in these parts.'

Joshua nodded. 'Well, I thank you for that, Sir George. What happens, pray, if you are not so convinced?'

'The case is dismissed. But do not take away the impression that this often happens. Indeed no, sir. The militia must have been impressed with the evidence against you before bringing the case. So do not build up your hopes.'

Josh felt his mouth go dry. Whoever was behind this charge was obviously determined to see him hang. 'Will I be able to see the evidence before I appear before you, sir?'

'Oh yes. But I will have no delayin' tactics in my court, sir. Be sure of that.'

'Delaying tactics?'

'Yes. Lawyer johnnies presentin' points of law to hold everythin' up.'

'Ah, so I will be able to appoint someone to defend me?'

Lansbury sniffed. 'If you can afford it. I am not here to give you advice – and damn it,' he pulled out a silver Hunter watch from his waistcoat, 'I have wasted enough time here as it is. But if your resources are limited, as I suspect is the case, then you will probably be best advised to save your pennies and spend them on getting the best man you can to represent you at the Assizes. Now I must go. Jailer!'

The jailer had left them during the conversation but Sir George's stentorian cry brought him back almost immediately.

'Right. I am off. See to cleaning this cell and getting another blanket.'

Josh stood. 'I am most grateful to you, sir, for taking the time to advise me. But I shall need help. May I have a visitor who can advise and help me?'

'Certainly. But we can't chase after 'em. If they arrive,' he nodded to the jailer, 'they must be admitted on proof of identity. No shilly-shallying. Understood?'

'O'course, sir.' The jailer knuckled his forehead.

With a brisk nod, Sir George Lansbury swept out, the jailer pausing only to lock the cell door before hurrying after him.

Joshua sat and thought quickly. He must get word at once to Doctor Acland and to Rowena. They were his only hope. He stood and banged on the door.

The jailer arrived, this time scowling. He had obviously not taken kindly to being criticised on the state of the cell. 'Don't you go bangin' the door. You're a murderer, not someone summonin' service in an inn. Now what the 'ell do you want?'

Joshua showed him a shilling. 'Can you bring me a pencil, paper and an envelope? I must get word to my, er, lawyer. Another shilling afterwards if you can have it posted today. It is urgent.'

The jailer's attitude immediately changed. 'Oh, of course.'

The writing implements appeared and Joshua sat and scribbled a note to Dr Acland:

I am being held in Barnstaple jail. I will be allowed visitors. Can you journey to see me, because I need legal help? I am to be formally charged in the magistrate's court soon and then almost certainly referred to the next Assizes in Exeter. My life is in danger. Please do come.

He tucked the message in the envelope and, this time, called through the grill on the door: 'Jailer.'

The man appeared quickly and unlocked the door. Joshua held up the two shillings. 'This is to be posted quickly,' he said. 'You have been kind to me and I am grateful and sorry if I have caused you problems with Sir George, but if this man does not visit me soon, I will realise that you have not posted the letter. Then there will be no more shillings from me. Understood?'

'Oh yes, sir.' The shillings were quickly pocketed and the door slammed shut and locked again.

Once more Joshua sat on the bed and put his head between his hands. Obviously, the so-called evidence that would be presented to the court would have to be challenged and proved to be fiction, but without knowing the details of the charge, he could not think constructively about it at this stage. He clenched his fist in anger.

Oh, why had he shipped on that coffin ship *Lucy*? His life had been equable until then. Afterwards he had been shipwrecked, surrounded by violence, suspicion, and – he had to admit it – suppressed lust for an eighteen-year-old girl. Now he faced the hangman's noose. What had he done to deserve all this?

The self-pity, however, soon disappeared when the giant jailer – Josh realised now that he was dumb – arrived with a blanket, a bucket of hot water, scrubbing brush and mop and set about cleaning the cell. He paid no attention at all to its occupant, apart from throwing the blanket at him, and the water was splashed everywhere. Josh made a virtue of necessity by giving the mattress a superficial wash. He felt that lying on the wet straw was preferable to being invaded by lice.

Dr Acland and, to his delight, Rowena, arrived the next day at midday. He realised that they must have set off before they received his letter and he shook the doctor's hand warmly before embracing his daughter.

'Take the chair, Doctor,' he said, 'and Rowena sit on the mattress. It's still a little damp but spread your raincoat upon it and it should be comfortable enough.' He sat cross-legged on the floor in front of them. 'I can't tell you how grateful I am that you have come.'

Rowena sat silently but with tears streaming down her cheeks. The doctor pulled a face. 'What foul conditions,' he said. 'I have never been in a jail before and this place gives me an added reason to stay on the right side of the law.'

Josh thought of the cognac and fine china and smiled inwardly. 'Doctor, can you tell me anything about the charges that have been brought against me? Who has done this?'

'Have they not told you?'

'No, sir.'

'Well, my boy, I can't help you there. The militia will not reveal details until your trial. Cunningham says he cannot help. And that's that. Now, listen. I am here to do two things. To try and get you out on bail – we have visited the magistrate's office this morning and there is no question of that. The charge of murder, it seems, is too, er, extreme to allow bail. But I have been able to secure the services of a lawyer to represent you at your committal trial. You will need one.'

'Oh, I am so grateful. But how will I pay him? I have only a few guineas left, saved for my, er,' he stole a quick glance at Rowena who was sitting staring at him with wide eyes, 'er, future and I doubt if it will be enough.'

The doctor held up his hand. 'Don't worry about that. I shall settle this. He is not exactly a Queen's Counsel but he is all I could get at short notice. I understand your committal trial is to be the day after tomorrow.'

'Good Lord! They are wasting no time. I shall find a way of repaying you, sir.'

'Think nothing of that. Now we will stay for the trial, of course, and I have arranged for this young lawyer – his name is Bright, and I distinctly hope he is – to come in this afternoon and you must tell him all you know. We will return with him. I have bribed the jailer fellow to allow this.'

The doctor leant forward. As his face moved into the light cast from the high window, Joshua noticed how much older he looked, with deep furrows running across his brow and from the corners of his mouth to his chin. 'Now, all is not lost, my boy. Obviously, it would be best if we could avoid committal to the Assizes but if we have to go to Exeter, then that gives us more time to arrange your defence.'

Rowena thrust something into his hand. 'I managed to find a hot-pie shop that was open this morning,' she said. She smiled wanly. 'It is not my cooking but this is still warm and will probably be better than anything they give you here. Eat it now, while it is hot.'

'Oh, thank you. Just what I need.' He broke open the pie and offered pieces to the doctor and Rowena but they both declined, so he began eating hungrily.

'It is not knowing what they are saying I did,' he said between mouthfuls, 'that is so frustrating. How can we construct a defence if we do not know this?'

'We will talk to young Mr Bright this afternoon about that.'

And so they did. Bright proved to be young, indeed, in fact hardly into his twenties, Joshua estimated, but already with a pronounced stoop and a receding hairline. He was tall, thin and bespectacled and he seemed to possess a nervous cough.

As the three of them filed into the cell the young man looked about him with distaste. Oh no, thought Josh, don't tell me that he has never seen the inside of a cell before!

The lawyer took the only chair as, it seemed, a matter of right, and Acland and Rowena sat on the mattress, while Josh squatted on the floor once again.

'Now Mr Wisland,' began Bright.

'No. It's Weyland,' said Josh.

'Ah yes, of course. Weyland.' He looked down at his notes. 'I understand that you discovered the body? Where and how was this?'

Joshua plodded through the events of that dramatic day while the lawyer made notes. In the end, he burst out: 'Can you tell me, Mr Bright, who has brought these charges against me?'

'Yes, of course.'

'Well thank goodness for that. Who are they?'

'It's the militia, of course. It usually is in cases like this.'

Josh sighed. 'Yes, yes, I know that. But who has fed them the evidence and accusation against me? They would not do that unless they had been given such information, surely?'

'Oh, quite so. Quite so. But we shall find that at the hearing, of course, and then I shall be able, er, to cross-examine the witnesses concerned.'

'But won't you need to prepare for that, in consultation, I presume, with me, beforehand?'

'Oh, I don't think there will be time. You see, Sir George has arranged the hearing rather quickly. But have no fear. I shall cross-examine with, er, great care. Now, Doctor, please tell me again when you think the murder was committed.'

'From my examination of the body, I think the man had been dead for about ten hours. Rigor mortis had set in.'

'I see. Now Mr, er, Weymouth . . .'

'Weyland.'

'Ah yes, of course. Weyland. Forgive me. Can you tell me where you were on the evening before you discovered the body?'

'Ah, yes. I believe I would have been having dinner at the doctor's house with Miss Acland here.'

'And was anyone else there; the doctor, for instance?'

Acland interrupted. 'No, as I have already explained, I did not arrive back home until the next morning.'

Bright nodded. 'Ah, yes. Of course. So there was just the two of you?'

'Yes.'

'Did you leave the house later that night?'

'No.'

'Very well.' The young man stood. 'That is good. We have a witness in Miss, er, Acland, which is good. That is all I need at the moment, I think. Now I must bid you good day. We will meet at the trial, of course. Be of good heart. Justice will prevail.'

'Won't we meet again before then, say tomorrow?'

The young man adjusted his spectacles. 'I fear not. I have another case to prepare and time is short. Good day to you all.'

Then he was gone.

The three regarded each other in consternation. 'I'm afraid that was not very impressive,' sighed the doctor. 'But I am assured by a senior partner in his practice that he is a young man of promise.'

'Will you give evidence, sir?'

'Oh yes. The coroner always must do so in this case. And I will endeavour to give evidence of your character and, indeed, of your medical condition. A man on crutches is not the obvious first choice for someone who has overpowered a young man in his prime.'

'I should think not, Papa!' Rowena's face was full of indignation. 'How could anyone think that Josh could do such a foul thing? Really!'

Bright made no appearance the next day and neither did the doctor. Rowena, of course, visited Josh but she explained that her father was not well and had taken to his bed in the inn where they were staying.

'Oh, don't say that he will not be able to support me at the hearing!' exclaimed Josh.

'Of course he will, my love.' They were sitting side by side on the mattress and she put her arm around him and pulled his head down onto her breast. 'I am sure he will be there. And so will I, of course.'

The warmth of her, coupled with his anxiety, was too much for Josh. He clung to her and found himself sobbing.

'Shush, shush, my love. You must be strong. You are not in this alone. We are with you.' She kissed away his tears. 'It will come out right. You will see.'

'Oh, Rowena.' He took out a tattered handkerchief and blew his nose, gently pushing her away. 'I am sorry to sound like a baby. But this is all too much. How did I get into this mess? Who hates me so much that they would see me hang?'

'Oh, Josh, I wish I knew. I just don't know.'

The day of the trial saw the sky hang over Barnstaple like a grey cloak, with soft rain falling. Josh had begged some hot water from the jailer and had been able to shave, giving him, he felt, some veneer of respectability, even though his clothing now had become creased and dishevelled.

He was escorted to the courtroom by a soldier from the Barnstable militia, his hands tied behind his back. Luckily it was a short walk and he arrived having avoided a complete drenching. His case was the first – perhaps the only one? he wondered – and his heart fell as he saw Rowena sitting alone in the gallery. Oh God! Was the doctor too ill to attend?

He was ushered into a box-like 'dock' as the soldier had called it, facing the magistrate's chair behind the high bench and he looked around the courtroom. Sitting before him was his counsel, looking young under his white wig and clutching a bundle of notes. A short distance to his right was another lawyer, considerably older. Prosecuting counsel, presumably. There were no witnesses that he could recognise. Perhaps they were not allowed in the courtroom until they were called to give evidence? The public gallery where Rowena sat, however, was crowded. Obviously, murder was a draw for the good people of Barnstaple who had nothing else to do that morning. He sighed.

'All stand.'

Sir George stumped into view from behind his chair, dressed exactly as before and Josh half expected him to be carrying a shotgun or fishing rod. He nodded to the court and everyone sat.

'Now, then.' The magistrate took out his red handkerchief and blew his nose. 'As usual I will explain that this hearing is merely to convince me that there is enough substantial evidence to retain the accused in custody and present him to the Assizes in Exeter on,' he consulted his notes, '15th December of this year for trial on this capital charge of murder. I will expect counsel to confine their presentations to this purpose.'

He nodded to the older lawyer. 'Mr Bowyer, please proceed.'

The prosecuting lawyer stood. 'Thank you, Your Honour. The defendant has already entered a not-guilty plea to the charge. I shall call witnesses to show that the accused,' he looked for the first time up at Josh, 'had the opportunity and the motive for murdering Mr James Drake and that there is indeed just cause why this case should be heard at the higher court.'

'Very well,' Sir George nodded. 'Get on with it, then.'

'Call Doctor Acland.'

Thank goodness, sighed Josh. The good man was well enough to attend.

The doctor came into the court and took the oath. He looked, indeed, drawn and haggard and Josh could not but help feeling distress on his behalf.

'Did you examine the corpse at Harland Quay on the morning of October 12th?'

'I did.'

'And what were your conclusions?'

'That the poor man had been killed by the cutting of his throat by a knife or some such weapon, which had caused severe bleeding and death. He had also been hanged and there were rope marks around his neck, but I am sure that these did not contribute to his death. He had died before being hanged.'

'Can you give us some indication of the time of death?'

'I should say some ten hours before my examination, which would put the murder taking place at, say, eleven or twelve of the clock the previous night. But I can't be precise on this point.'

'Thank you, Doctor.'

Sir George waved his handkerchief towards Bright. 'Any questions for this witness?'

'No, Your Honour.'

'You may stand down, Doctor Acland. Call your next witness, Mr Bowyer.'

Josh frowned. Did not the doctor promise to give evidence of his good character and of his injured leg? Perhaps there would be an opportunity later.

The appearance of the next witness, however, took him by surprise. It was Jacob Millbury, the landlord of the inn at Hartland. He scurried in, took a quick look at Josh and then stood importantly in the witness box, obviously enjoying every moment of the attention directed towards him. He was asked if he had been in the bar of the inn when Jem Drake and Tom Pengelly had been drinking with the defendant.

'Oh yes, sur. I wus there all right an' I 'eard most of what they were sayin', like.'

Counsel for the prosecution smiled coldly. 'And what were they saying?'

'Well, it was more of an argument, see. This young man 'ere,' he gestured towards Joshua, 'was particularly pressin' poor old Jem to tell 'im somethin' an' Jem wouldn't. I got the impression, sur, that 'e was bein' threatened by this fellow an' Jem was a bit frightened, like. 'Im an' Tom Pengelly scurried away as soon as they could.'

'Really? What was he trying to extract from the two sailors?'

'I couldn't 'ear that much. But this fellow 'ere,' he indicated Josh again, 'seemed particularly threatenin' to poor old Jem. I remember that very well.'

'Thank you, Mr Millbury.'

'Any questions for this witness?' Sir George's voice seemed to thunder through the courtroom.

'No, Your Honour.'

Joshua's jaw dropped. Was his counsel going to let Millbury get away with giving evidence that was all innuendo and certainly harmful? Yet he and Josh had not discussed the meeting with the two sailors so, presumably, he could not cross-examine. What to do? He shrugged his shoulders. No doubt his turn would come and he could then set the record straight.

The next witness was Tom Pengelly. Josh was now becoming apprehensive. Would he twist the facts?

Pengelly stood tall and straight in the witness box, not at all overwhelmed by his unfamiliar surroundings. He answered Bowyer's questions clearly and without hesitation. He said that the last time he had seen Jem Drake was the day before his disappearance when they parted as normal as he, Pengelly, began his long walk back home to Morwenstow. Yes, he remembered well the meeting in the inn. The defendant accused Jem of attacking him and grew angry when this was denied. Pengelly had to take Drake away to avoid possible violence. Then, he had been called in when the body was found and the defendant accused him of being a suspect in the killing, which was nonsense. Jem Drake was his best friend and shipmate and in no way could he ever hurt him.

Once again, Bright declined to question the witness. Josh shook his head in amazement. Where was this forensic cross-examination of witnesses that he had been promised? So far, all of the evidence that had been presented was incriminating towards him. When would he be allowed to answer these slurs?

The last witness was Captain Cunningham. The tall man presented a handsome figure in the box. He was wearing his best uniform of dark blue with a white stock at his throat and his boots were highly polished. His black hair had been pomaded and was brushed back so that it appeared almost burnished. He was authority and confidence personified.

Would Cap'n Jack, his self-declared friend, wondered Josh, tell the truth to the court at last? It soon became apparent that he would not.

He explained that, after seeing the body in the doctor's stable, he had immediately ridden to where the dead man had been found. At the base of the tree he found marks made by a heavily laden horse and, by their side, distinctive impressions in the mud left by a pair of riding boots, the right boot of which had some sort of attachment to it, as though a crutch was fixed to it.

A hush fell on the court as Bowyer looked up at the magistrate and then, meaningfully, at Josh. 'Captain, which person of any significance in this case was using a crutch to get about at that time?'

'The defendant, sir. He had damaged a leg on being shipwrecked at Morwenstow, but by that time was seen in the village and on the moorland walking comparatively easily. Indeed, some days before the murder, he had been involved in a fracas with some of my men on the moor and I observed him there swinging a sword very ably. He wounded one of my men in what seemed to be a fit of rage and I had to intervene to prevent further harm being done. He was obviously a man of high temper.'

Josh drew in his breath. The swine!

'There were no other footprints on the ground underneath the tree from which the victim had been hanging?'

'No, sir. These were very distinct and I took careful note of them. Sadly, people have been showing a maudlin interest in the scene of the crime and since my observation of the scene, many folk have walked up there to look at the tree, and the ground underneath it has been well trampled.'

'Ahem.' The magistrate leant forward. 'This is important evidence. Did you not think, Captain Cunningham, to ask the militia to cordon off the scene?'

Ah, thought Josh gratefully, someone was challenging Cunningham!

For a brief moment the captain looked nonplussed. 'I'm afraid not, Your Worship.' He cleared his throat. 'I have much to do and I fear the thought did not cross my mind.'

'Very well.' Sir George made a note.

Bowyer now returned to the fray. 'It is for His Honour to consider what you have said and apply to it whatever relevance he feels is appropriate.' He made a deferential half bow towards the magistrate, who scowled down at him. 'But it is clear that the defendant had the opportunity and the ability to carry out this crime. However, can you help His Honour as to the question of what motive he might have for committing such a dastardly deed?'

Cunningham flashed his teeth. 'I believe so, sir. For some reason, Weyland believed that Jem Drake had attacked him some time earlier, although there were no witnesses to that happening. I should add here, sir, that Drake was a simple soul, a sailor who was much liked in Hartland. He was of timid disposition and most certainly would not have launched an attack on anyone. Yet Weyland seemed to be full of revenge towards him, as you will have heard from a previous witness. This must have been a revenge killing. As a man of high temper, he must be the prime suspect in this case, I would suggest.'

'Well of course he is,' Sir George waved his handkerchief, 'otherwise he wouldn't be in the dock, damn it.' Then he blew his nose stentoriously.

'Indeed, sir.' Bowyer bowed to the bench. Then to Cunningham: 'Would you have perceived any weapon that he could have used in attacking Drake?'

'Oh yes. Weyland always wore a long knife hanging from his belt.'

Sir George leant forward. 'Where is it? Has it been found and examined?'

'I am afraid not, Your Honour.'

'Humph. Pray continue.'

'I have finished examining the witness, Your Honour.'

'Yes, well, I have not. You say, Captain, that the defendant wounded one of your men in an affray on the heath.'

'Er, yes, Your Honour.'

'Why, then, did you not arrest him?'

'Because, er, I do not have that power, unless the person concerned was contravening the law concerning Customs and the Revenue.'

'Why, then, did you not call in the militia and present a charge against him of unlawful wounding, eh?'

Cunningham was undoubtedly flustered. 'It just, er, did not occur to me to do so, Your Honour.'

'Yet you have done so to bring him to court today on a charge of murder.'

'Yes, Your Honour. It, er, seemed a much, er, graver matter that I could not overlook in this case.'

'Hmm. Very well. Please remain at the witness stand. Now, Mr . . .' Sir George looked down at his notes '. . . Mr Bright, you may now question the witness.'

'I have no questions for him, Your Honour.'

'Really? No questions?'

'No Your Honour. I do not think it necessary.'

'Well, well. Do you have any witnesses to call?'

'Only the defendant, Your Honour.'

'Then let us hear from him.'

Joshua, still trembling with a mixture of rage, indignation and fear from listening to Cunningham's evidence, stepped forward but remained in the prisoner's dock. He stated his name and his profession, 'Sailor, qualified second mate.' He looked up to the public gallery and

Rowena smiled down on him, clutching both her hands into fists and raised them above her head.

It had to be said that the defending counsel presented a much less imposing figure than the counsel for the prosecution. A titter ran round the public gallery as he stepped forward, carrying a bundle of notes – which he promptly dropped.

'Take your time, Mr Bright,' said the magistrate. 'We can wait.'

'Thank you, sir.'

'No, you must address me as "Your Honour". Now get on with it, er, as best you can.'

Bright coughed and put his notes onto the table before him. 'Mr Weyland,' he began, in a thin, reedy voice. 'Did you kill James Drake?'

'No, I did not. And I refute the evidence given that I bullied him. On the contrary, I owed him a debt of gratitude.'

'Why was that?'

'It was he and Thomas Pengelly who rescued me off the rocks of Morwenstow when my ship, the brig *Lucy*, foundered some six weeks ago. All of the crew were lost, except me, and I would surely have drowned had not Mr Pengelly and Mr Drake risked their lives to pull me off a rock that was continually being swept by the waves.'

Sir George's red handkerchief fluttered. 'Now, Mr Bright,' he said, 'this would have been better elicited from the witness Pengelly. Why did you not produce this information from him in examination?'

'Ah, er, I was not aware of that circumstance, Your Honour.'

'Well, you should have been. It has a bearing on the case. Now, Mr Bowyer, if your witness denies what I have just heard, you have my permission to bring him forward again. If he does not, then we do not wish to hear him a second time.'

'Very good, Your Honour.'

'Proceed, Mr Bright.'

'Ah, thank you, sir . . . Your Honour.' He looked down at his notes. 'You have heard two witnesses say that you bore a grudge against Mr Drake who, it seems, you said had assaulted you.'

Joshua took in a deep breath. He knew that this was a weak point in his case. Why had the two men who had rescued him attacked him later? He could give no rational explanation. He must tell the truth and hope that Sir George, who was maintaining a shrewd, common-sense control of the proceedings, would tolerate the seeming contradiction.

'Not a grudge. But I knew it was he and his great friend Thomas Pengelly who had, indeed, attacked me when I was alone about two weeks after my rescue.'

Bright's jaw dropped and it was clear that he did not know which way to go now. Sir George inevitably stepped into the breach.

'They attacked you,' he said, frowning down from the bench. 'Why was that?'

'That is what I was trying to ascertain when I confronted them in the inn at Hartland.'

'You recognised them, then, did you?'

'Yes, Your Honour. Not from their faces, though, because they were covered when they attempted to beat me with clubs. In defending myself – although I was handicapped by having to lean on a crutch – I drew my sailor's knife. I hit the smaller of the two, Mr Drake, across the cheek with my crutch, bruising his cheekbone, and I delivered a cut to the arm of Mr Pengelly and to his face before they both ran away. I recognised those wounds immediately when I saw them in the inn and therefore challenged them.'

Sir George ostentatiously made a note. 'Mr Bowyer, pray ensure that the witness Pengelly does not leave the courthouse. I shall wish to inspect his physical appearance.'

'It is a little unusual, Your Honour . . .'

'I don't care how unusual it is, sir. Make sure he stays here. D'yer understand?'

'Very good, Your Honour.'

'Now, continue, Mr Bright – preferably without my assistance.'

'I am grateful, for it, sir . . .'

'Oh get on with it, man.'

'Ah, yes sir. Now, Mr Westerly . . .'

'Weyland.' The correction came from the bench.

'Mr Weyland, yes. Were there any witnesses to this encounter?'

Damn your eyes! thought Josh. You are doing the prosecutor's job for him. You should have ascertained this before the hearing, so that we could have steered clear of it. 'No. As far as I know, none.'

'Very well. Now,' he bent down to pick up a fallen note. 'Can you tell the court where you were at about the time Mr Drake was murdered, that is about eleven or twelve o'clock on the night before you found the body?'

'Yes. I was in Doctor Acland's house and, I should think, soundly asleep in my bedroom there.'

'Can anyone confirm this?'

'Well, the doctor was not there, of course, because he was on his way back from London. But Miss Acland was in the house, although, of course, in her own bedroom. If I had left the house, however, she would undoubtedly have heard me. It is a very quiet house.'

'Indeed. When, the next morning, in answer to the deceased mother's anxiety, you volunteered to search for him with Miss Acland, why did you make for Hartland Point?'

'We did not, at first, but headed towards Morwenstow. Then, Miss Acland suggested we should climb to the top of the Point. I think that she felt this would be the obvious place for Jem Drake to make for, if, that is, he contemplated suicide.'

'Now, wait a minute.' The magistrate leant forward. 'Is there any evidence at all that the deceased did, in fact, contemplate suicide? Mr Bowyer? Mr Bright?'

Two wigs were shaken negatively. 'Very well, continue.'

Bright coughed again as he fumbled with his papers. 'What did you find underneath the tree when you reached it?'

'Well, of course, Jem was hanging and my first thought was to get him down in case there was still life in him. So, with Miss Acland's help, we cut him down and put him in the donkey cart. We were about to drive away when I stepped down from the cart to inspect the state of the ground, for it appeared to contain marks that could, perhaps, throw some light on the manner of his death.'

'And what did you find?'

'The marks of a horse's hooves that were quite deep, showing that the horse had perhaps been carrying a double burden. And there were clear footprints from a man who had been wearing riding boots, quite large boots, I would say. After that, of course, I climbed back into the cart, leaving behind my own footprints with those of the splints attached to my injured leg.'

'Now look here, Bright,' Sir George was clearly becoming annoyed.

'Did you say that the defendant was the only witness you were going to call?'

'Yes, My Lord, er, Your Worship.'

'Are you not calling Miss Acland to confirm or deny everything that the defendant has said?'

'I did not intend to do so, sir.'

'Well you damned well should. Is Miss Acland in court today, by any chance?' He looked around over the top of his glasses.

'Yes indeed, sir.' The cry came from high on the public benches at the rear of the courtroom. Rowena's voice rang loud and very clear. She stood and removed her bonnet. 'Very much present, Your Honour, and anxious to give evidence, although I was not asked to do so.'

The magistrate's irritation immediately disappeared as he looked up at the slim figure, holding her bonnet by its red ribbon. 'I certainly can't think why not, my dear,' he beamed. 'Pray, come down now. Let us hear what you have to say right away.'

Bowyer rose. 'I really must protest, Your Honour,' he began.

'Yes, yes, I know, Bowyer. Highly irregular, of course. But we are all in this courtroom anxious to see justice done, of course, and sometimes the rules have to be, if not broken, at least slightly bent to that end. By the way, is Pengelly still here?'

'Yes, Your Honour.'

'I shall wish to see him again later. Don't let him leave. Now where is this young lady? Ah, there you are, my dear. Please stand in the witness box. Yes, that's right. Now, you have heard what the defendant has to say. Do you agree with it?'

Joshua noticed that Rowena had applied a touch of lip rouge and a trace of face powder and looked exceedingly pretty and certainly older than eighteen. He looked around the courtroom and up to the gallery but could see no sign of Dr Acland, or of Pengelly or Cunningham.

Rowena nodded. 'Yes, Your Honour. We turned to go up to the Point at my suggestion, for it did occur to me that people do jump off that if they are in distress, it's a four hundred foot drop, you see.'

'Quite so, quite so.'

'We found poor Jem just as, Jo—Mr Weyland described it. I also concur that there were traces of a riding boot on the ground at the foot of the tree and that they were much bigger than those that he left. Oh, and there is one more thing, sir.'

'Pray continue.'

'It is not true to say that there were no witnesses to the attack on the . . . er . . . defendant earlier. I saw it – well, I saw the end of it. The two men were heavily cloaked so I could not see their faces but there was blood on the cloak of one of them and also on the ground where they had left poor Josh—the defendant, swaying on his bad leg. I took him down to our house and the doctor treated him.'

Sir George frowned. 'Is the doctor still in the courtroom?'

Bowyer shook his head. 'He has been forced to leave, Your Honour. It seems he is not well.'

The magistrate put his head in his hand in an exaggerated gesture. 'I well know how he feels, the way this case is being conducted,' he growled. 'Now, Miss Acland. You were in the same house as the defendant at the time when, it seems, the murder was committed?'

'Yes, Your Honour.'

'But it would have been possible, surely, would it not, for the defendant to steal out of the house while you were asleep and without you being aware of his absence?'

There was a pause before Rowena answered. 'Oh no, sir. Absolutely not. Because Mr Weyland lied about that, sir.'

An audible gasp ran through the courtroom.

'He lied, you say?'

'Yes, Your Honour.' Rowena cast down her eyes prettily. 'He lied to protect my honour, sir. You see, we were in bed together throughout that night. I can assure you he did not leave the house until we both rose to answer the door shortly after dawn. I would have known had he left.'

Sir George frowned to try and hide the smile that had begun to steal across his face. 'You slept together throughout the night? You are telling the truth – remember you have taken an oath on the Bible to do so?'

'Yes, Your Honour. We were together throughout the night. I remember it well.'

'Hmmm, I am sure you do. Is this true, Weyland?'

'Of course not. She is trying to protect me.'

'Well, damn it all,' Sir George blew his nose noisily, then continued.

'This case is complicated enough without people deliberately lying to protect their honour.' He adjusted his spectacles.

'Before we go any further, can I establish one thing? Is there anything known about the defendant, anything on record of past misdemeanour of any kind, any transgression of the law? Mr Bowyer, I presume you will have checked?'

'There is nothing that I could find, Your Honour.'

'Well, now.' Sir George settled back in his seat. 'There are quite a few factors about this case that I find unsettling and which give me no confidence in retaining the defendant to stand trial at the Assizes. For instance, you sir,' he glared at Mr Bright, 'took the unusual step of offering no independent witnesses in his defence and, further, you made no effort to cross-examine the prosecution's witnesses. Now why was this so? Would you care to tell us, Mr Bright?'

'Well, My Lord . . .'

'I am no one's lord, Mr Bright. I am merely Your Honour.'

'I am sorry, Your Honour. To be frank, sir, I felt that the defendant's answers to my questions would be sufficient to establish his innocence.'

'So you disregarded the evidence, produced by the prosecution's witnesses, about the defendant's alleged bad temper, his alleged antipathy towards the murdered man, the marks in the mud under the branch from which he hung, particularly those showing that someone had been there wearing a splint on his leg and, further, that the deceased's head had virtually been severed by a weapon, similar it seems, to that the defendant had carried? You chose not to pick back the layers of these allegations and show them to be exaggerations or false? Eh? Why not?'

Bright's sallow face was now coloured a bright red. 'I-I am sorry, Your Honour, but, I felt that . . . that . . . well, that this was, much, if not all of it, a matter of innuendo.'

'Did you now? Hmmm. Well, it may surprise you to hear that I rather agree with you.'

Joshua suddenly felt his heart lift and he exchanged a quick glance of surprise and hope with Rowena, still standing in the witness box.

'Innuendo is the word you used, Mr Bright and there was too much of that in the prosecution's case to make me happy about it. Which reminds me. Mr Bowyer?'

'Your Honour?'

'Is your witness, Mr Pengelly, still in the courtroom?'

'He is waiting outside, Your Honour.'

'Good. Have him come in, please.'

The silence that had hung over the courtroom following the recent exchanges now was broken and replaced by a buzz of conversation as Pengelly was brought to the witness box.

'Now, Mr Pengelly,' said the magistrate, 'you are still bound by your oath. D'yer understand?'

'Er, yes sir.'

'Roll up your sleeve of your right arm.'

'What . . . ?'

'I think you heard me. Roll up your sleeve.'

Reluctantly, Pengelly did so and there was an audible gasp in the courtroom when a still livid weal was displayed.

'How did you get that, young man and that mark across your cheek?'

'What? Oh, well, they are . . . they are . . . cable scorch marks picked up when a rope got entangled round me when I was bringin' a ship in.'

'Step forward and let me see.'

Pengelly offered up his arm to Sir George, who held it up high so that he could examine it closely. 'Hmm. I would say that those are marks resulting from a cut from a knife. Mr Bowyer, Mr Bright, I would like your opinions on this matter of the origin of these marks. Pray, examine the arm. They are wounds made by a knife, are they not?'

'Well,' began Bowyer, 'I can't be sure, Your Honour.'

'Er, neither can I,' said Bright.

Bloody fool, thought Josh. Incompetent to the end.

'Very well.' Sir George leant back in his chair and looked hard at Pengelly. 'So you deny they were caused by the defendant in defending himself when you and Drake attacked him?'

'Oh, I do that, sir.'

'Thank you. You may stand down.'

'Now, prisoner at the bar. As you will have heard, it is my duty to be quite sure that the evidence presented against you today is such as to give me no doubt that you should be retained in custody and then presented for trial on the charge of murder at the Assizes. I have to say that I do have doubts about it. This countercharge of the alleged attack on you is strange and you yourself could give no reason for it.

'This particular point could stand on its own as the subject of some future trial – the prosecution witnesses deny that it happened and say that no one saw the attack. But Miss Acland says she saw the end of it. Yet you could not explain it.'

The magistrate leant back and put the tips of his fingers together. 'I noted that as a mark in your favour. Everyone else, it seems, except this lady here,' he nodded and smiled at Rowena, 'seems quite happy to attribute motives to you for your actions. But you do not, when they do not exist, and, I also have to confess here that in your attitude and demeanour you do not give me reasons to attribute criminality to you – and I have seen enough criminals in my time to recognise such signs when I see them.

'I am also disturbed about the evidence given by Captain Cunningham, a no doubt distinguished officer in the Customs and Revenue Service. He said that your allegedly bad temper had resulted in a sword attack by you on one of his men, yet he took no action to bring you to task for it – and surely he could have done so. His evidence of the marks on the ground beneath the tree is contradicted by Miss Acland. He implies that the weapon that killed Mr Drake was a knife possessed by you. But the prosecution has made no effort to produce this alleged weapon and examine it forensically to detect signs of its use in this deadly way. Lastly, there is the evidence of Miss Acland – given, I may add, undoubtedly at some cost to her reputation – that you did not leave the doctor's house on the night of the murder. Now,' he spread his hands in a gesture of mock despair, 'who am I to believe? Eh, who am I to believe? Well, you see, I don't have to believe anyone. All I have to do is to convince myself that the case against you, prisoner at the bar, is strong enough to put you forward to the higher court.'

Sir George waited long enough to give maximum impact to his next words. 'And, most emphatically, I do not. Case dismissed. You may step down, Mr Weyland and leave this court without a stain on your character.

'Clear the courtroom.'

Chapter Eleven

Joshua closed his eyes and grimaced with relief. He looked down at Rowena, who, predictably, was crying. He rushed down to grasp her hand. She wanted an embrace but he felt that would be unsuitable, with both of them standing underneath the bench, so he held her at bay. He looked up to thank Sir George but the old man had gone. So, too, had the witnesses from Hartland and Morwenstow who had tried so hard to commit him for hanging. It was as though they had disappeared into the air.

'Rowena,' he said, keeping his voice low, 'I couldn't be more grateful for the evidence you gave. You may have saved my life. But, my dear, it was not the truth and I do hope it will not rebound on you to do you harm. Your reputation will be tarnished, you know.'

She smiled through her tears. 'I don't care, Josh. I would do or say anything to save your life. You know that. I love you, you see.'

He gulped. 'But you mustn't. I have nothing to offer you, my dear girl. You know the situation.'

Immediately, Rowena's air of adoration changed, her eyes flashed and the Gypsy girl reappeared. 'Yes, I do. And I know that your fat Mary has not replied to your letters. Oh, Josh. She doesn't love you, otherwise she would be here, offering to look after you and take you back to bloody Dover. But I do love you. I have proved it today. And,' she looked up at him provocatively. 'I am here.'

They were interrupted by a touch on Josh's arm from the court usher. 'If you have a moment, sir,' he said, 'the magistrate would be grateful if you could spare him a minute. In his chambers, behind the bench.'

'What? Oh yes, of course. I would like an opportunity to thank him, anyway. Excuse me Rowena while I go . . . oh, I am sorry. I forgot to enquire about your father. I am so sorry to hear that he is unwell.'

'Don't worry about that now, Josh. Go and see Sir George.'

'Yes, well. Don't move from here. I will not be long.'

Josh climbed the steps to the bench and tapped on the door behind. 'Come in,' a familiar voice growled. Sir George was sitting with his waistcoat unbuttoned with what looked like a glass of whisky in his hand.

'Sit down, boy.' He indicated a chair.

Josh did so and said, 'I am most grateful, Sir George, for two things. Firstly, for acquitting me and secondly,' he smiled, 'virtually acting as my defence lawyer. I really am most grateful.'

The magistrate waved the familiar red handkerchief. 'Well, we will say no more about that. That young man was a disgrace to the legal profession and I may well take the matter further. But I wanted to see you for a different reason.'

He blew his nose noisily and took a deep draught of the whisky. 'Excluding your remarkable female friend – was she lying by the way?'

'I have already answered that in court, sir.'

'So you have. So you have. Well, excluding her, you had three witnesses in court today, all giving evidence against you. The doctor I must regard as neutral, although, given his relationship to the lady who seems to be so in love with you, I would have thought he could and should have spoken up for you.'

'Yes. Well, I understand he is not well, sir.'

'Ah yes. I had forgotten that. Amazing, ain't it, how often physicians are not well. But enough of that.' He leant forward. 'Do you intend to return to Hartland?'

'Yes, sir. I must. I am due to give evidence soon at an enquiry, which is being conducted by Lloyd's of London in reference to the distressingly large number of ships that founder on the rocks on that coastline – as, indeed, did mine. It is to be held at Hartland.'

'Humph. Sounds strange. Should have been held in London. Well, never mind. I think you would be well advised to leave Hartland and – what's the name of the other place?'

'Morwenstow?'

'Yes, that's it. Get out as soon as you can. My dear Weyland, it seems to me that people in those two villages have something against you, they have a . . . a . . . what is that damned Italian word?'

'Vendetta?'

'Yes, that's it. They have a vendetta against you. Now, why do you think that is? Eh?'

Joshua paused. He had to be careful, for he was speaking to a man of the law. But better to speak the truth. 'I believe that in both Hartland and Morwenstow a smuggling ring is operating and, worse than that, they are sometimes luring ships onto that terrible coast there with false lights.'

'What? Smuggling I can understand. The practice goes on everywhere in this part of England, but wrecking . . . wrecking in the old sense of showing false lights is damned murder, there is nothing else to describe it. You have evidence, I suppose?'

'Ah, that is the problem, Sir George. It is only very circumstantial.' And he related his own experience of seeing the light at Morwenstow from out at sea and then finding the site of the brazier with the ashes at its base. 'I am hoping,' he concluded, 'that the Lloyd's enquiry will produce something harder.'

The magistrate's frown deepened and he took another draught of the whisky while he thought. 'I doubt it,' he growled. 'This will not be a proper court of law. One of the problems we face down here,' he went on, 'is the absence of a proper policing force. Peel has introduced one in London, which is beginning to do excellent work, I understand, but beyond the capital we have to rely on the militia, which is quick to put down rioting but useless, it seems to me, at detecting and doing general constabulary work. As in your case, for instance, which should never have been brought.'

The great red handkerchief was brought into play again. 'Yes, but, apart from being shipwrecked, what was your involvement in these nefarious activities? Why should you arouse antipathy, eh?'

'You may well ask, sir. The only reason I can think of is that my suspicions were alerted by that light, which drew us onto the rocks.

You see, I was the only man saved from the wreck. I lost all my shipmates – some good men. As a result, I have been asking a lot of questions. Perhaps too many.'

'Ah, that explains it. Well, now.' He thought for a moment, his brow corrugated. 'Trouble is, I can't do much to help you. In theory these places are within my jurisdiction as a magistrate but they are on the edge of my territory, so to speak. And, obviously, I cannot play a role unless someone is charged and brought before me. So . . .' He drew out the word.

'So, my advice stands. Get away from those two villages as soon as you can. And, while you are there, watch your back. It sounds as though you are handy with your sailor's knife. Don't go out without it.' He waved his hand in dismissal. 'Now off you go. If you insist on still asking questions and you get meaningful answers – I mean evidence – come straight to me, to no one else. Understand?'

'I do, indeed, sir. I must thank you again.'

'Away with you. If you are asked, this conversation never took place. Oh, one more thing.'

'Sir?'

'Marry that girl before someone else gets her. Good day to you.'

'Good day, Sir George.'

Rowena was still waiting. 'What did he want?'

'Oh, just to give me general advice. Come, we must go and find your father. I am worried about his health.'

They walked to the inn, via the jailhouse, where Joshua picked up his few belongings, relieved to find that everything, including his knife and his coins, were waiting for him. At the inn, however, Dr Acland was nowhere to be found. They were told that he was out walking.

'Well, that is good news,' said Joshua. 'It must mean that he is feeling better.'

Rowena said nothing but her face wore a worried frown. They sat by a window which gave a good view of the street and ordered tea while they waited for him.

'Ah, there he is,' cried Rowena, obviously relieved. 'Oh, but . . .' Her voice tailed away.

'Yes,' said Joshua slowly. 'He is talking to Cunningham, isn't he? I wonder what they are discussing?'

Indeed, the two men were standing in a doorway, some two hundred yards away, too far to see the expressions on their faces but not to observe their body language. Cunningham stood tall and erect and seemingly silent. Acland, however, was agitated, head thrust forward and gesturing with his hand.

'I want to see Cunningham, but not with your father present,' said Josh. 'I have a rather large bone to pick with him. But it looks as though your father is picking it already. He seems quite upset.'

Rowena put her hand to her mouth for a quick moment. Then she said: 'I expect he is remonstrating with the captain about the terrible things he said in the courtroom about you. That was disgraceful.'

'I quite agree, but I don't need your father to fight my battles for me. I will have it out with Cunningham when we get back to Hartland. I don't intend to let this matter lie.'

The anxious look returned to Rowena's features. 'No, Josh. I agree that the man has behaved disgracefully but I do think it would be dangerous to seek him out and cross him. Just let it lie for the moment. We shall be having that Lloyd's enquiry soon. Save yourself for that.'

'Well, I think that I have obviously crossed him already. But . . . Ah, your father is returning. I must say he is walking well and he has brought the stick I borrowed from him. That was thoughtful of him. Let's go and meet him.'

They hurried to the door and were greeted by a frown then a smile from the doctor. He seized Josh's hand. 'Congratulations, my boy, on what I suppose we must call your acquittal. I am sorry I was not there to hear it, but I felt rather unwell.'

'Well, your constitutional seems to have brought an improvement, sir. And I am glad of it.'

'So am I, Father.' But Rowena looked disturbed. 'But I am not sure you should be out and about. Why don't you go back to your room and rest before we set out for home?'

'Yes, I might well do that. But only for an hour at the most. Let us leave at, say, two of the clock. As it is we will have to break our journey, as we did coming here, Emma. I think you two should rest, too. You must drive the donkey cart, Joshua and I will ride my mare.'

'Very good, sir.'

They left promptly and Josh realised that none of them had referred to Acland's spirited conversation with Cunningham. He shrugged. Well maybe it had nothing to do with the hearing in court and the captain's evidence. He decided to let the matter rest there.

The weather was mild and it was not unpleasant riding through the moors on the way south. It occurred to Joshua that he should have enquired in Barnstable about the tinners, for he wondered if they had found employment. Perhaps Sir George would have known. But there had been little time to do anything other than worry about his own affairs. They found the inn where the doctor and Rowena had stayed on their journey north and arrived in Hartland the following day just as the wind was freshening from the north-west, threatening bad weather to come.

Joshua immediately asked Mrs Brown, who had house-kept during their absence, if there had been any mail delivered for him but she could only shake her head. What, he wondered, did this mean? Was Mary still away or could she simply not face writing to him? If the latter was the case, perhaps she felt she could not keep her engagement promise. What would that mean to him . . . ? He shook his head and refused to consider it. Mary was not like that. She would be writing soon.

Alone in his room, Joshua considered what he should do about the evidence given by Millbury, Pengelly and Cunningham. Of the three, Cunningham's had been the most venal and damning. He could not let that lie, particularly after he had been sought out by the officer and assured of his friendship. No. He would face him.

No time like the present. He swung himself down off the bed – his inactivity in the jail at least seemed to have served him well in terms of his injury, for it gave him little trouble now. Making sure that his knife was sitting snugly in its sheath at his back, he shrugged on his coat and picked up the doctor's stout stick from its position by the front door.

He closed the door gently behind him, for he did not wish to be delayed in arguing with Rowena, and set off up the hill. The forbidding gate at the barracks was guarded by a Preventer and Joshua demanded to see Captain Cunningham. The man eyed him dubiously – probably remembering him from the affray on the heath – and called out to another man, who disappeared indoors. Somewhat to his surprise,

Cunningham himself appeared, in his shirtsleeves but carrying a cutlass in its scabbard.

'I am not inviting you in, Weyland,' he said, leaning nonchalantly on the gate, 'in case you had thoughts of assassination in your mind. I wouldn't put anything past you in view of your bribing of that stupid old magistrate in Barnstaple. But I am here, if you want me, and, if it's swords you prefer, then I have mine and I can get you another one in an instant.'

'No, Cunningham. You tried to get me hanged but I don't wish you dead. But I do demand an explanation from you of the lies you told in that courtroom. Dammit man, it was only the other day that you visited me in the doctor's home and assured me of your friendship.'

The startlingly white teeth flashed in Cunningham's dark face. 'Did I? Well, I've changed my mind. I am convinced that you are a bad lot, Weyland, and have introduced violence to my parish. I am sure you killed poor old Jem.'

Without taking his eyes off those of the man before him, Josh slowly shook his head. 'You know that is untrue. I would have no motive or means of doing that. But I am here to give you a warning. I want you to listen carefully.'

'Oh, I shall do so, my dear Second Mate, I assure you.'

'Good. Now, I am convinced you are behind much of the illegal happenings here. I don't know yet exactly what they are but I am determined to find out and bring you to justice. I did not, of course, bribe the magistrate in Barnstaple. Men like that are unbribable, but he knows of my suspicions and will have his eye on you. And so will I. Good day to you.'

He turned on his heel and limped away – the hill had put a strain on the doctor's handiwork.

Cunningham called after him: 'I shall look forward to our final reckoning, Second Mate. But be careful of what you wish for. You could cause much hardship to the people here, for you do not know what you are blundering into. You are a fool, Weyland. Nothing but a fool . . .' The words faded away as Josh stumped down the hill, but he heard them all.

It set him worrying. What did Cunningham mean by his digging out the facts causing possible harm to the people of Hartland and, presumably, Morwenstow? He shrugged his shoulders. What was planned would come to pass, whatever he did.

The atmosphere at the dinner table that evening, Josh felt, was a little strained and he wondered if the doctor and his daughter had exchanged words. It was a feeling that continued during the next few days. Josh studied the hill now every morning to see if he could stop the postman and make sure that no letter had come while he had been away. Or perhaps one that had been intercepted by Rowena. He shook his head. He was still unsure now how much he could trust her in the role of postmistress.

He avoided going down to the harbour, for he knew that if he saw Pengally the temptation to demand an explanation for his evidence would be too strong to resist. For the same reason, he forsook the dubious comfort of visiting the inn. Then at last a letter arrived for the doctor. It informed him that the date for the Lloyd's enquiry would be in just one week's time. A day later another arrived for Joshua, summoning him to appear as a witness.

He sighed with relief. At last something was happening! Whatever the result of the enquiry, he resolved to leave for Dover immediately afterwards, although he did not inform the doctor or Rowena of his decision. He tried now to thrust the image of the doctor's daughter from his mind and replace it with Mary's buxom face and figure. But he found this difficult, not least when Rowena approached him and jerked him out of his melancholy.

'Come now, Josh,' she said, her eyes sparkling. 'We have a few days remaining before this enquiry. Let us get out in the donkey cart and enjoy this wonderful scenery. Mrs Brown, who knows these things by the reaction of her arthritic joints, tells me that the weather is due to be fair tomorrow. Shall we go up on the moor for a ride?'

He looked into her bright face and couldn't think of saying no. 'What a good idea. And let us walk a little on the moor. I could do with some exercise.'

'Good. We shall set off immediately after breakfast.'

True to Mrs Brown's forecast, the day dawned brightly and Rowena hummed a tune as she prepared a luncheon picnic for them. Even so, Josh was careful to sharpen his knife on the doorstep before they set out and to borrow the doctor's stick, although he had taken to leaving it behind on his usual walks along the high street.

They set off and Josh drew in deep breaths of the air that came in from the sea. Was there any finer air, he found himself musing, than that which blew off the ocean along these frightening but impressive cliffs? He found himself saying as much to Rowena – and immediately regretted it, for, of course, she used the question to turn on him.

'Will you really leave me and all of this, then, when you hear from Mary?' she asked, a tear not far away in her eye.

'I think I must, Rowena. I know I shall hate having to do so but my staying here, after the enquiry, will, I think, just provoke my enemies and make everyone upset – both in your father's house and in the village.'

She tossed her head. 'Well it won't make me upset and I don't care a toss what the people of the village think.' She paused for a moment. 'I have to say, though, that I think Papa is a little restive. I am not sure whether that is because of your presence or the promise of the enquiry. I have a feeling that he is regretting opening that can of worms. But, look,' she turned to him, giving him that familiar smile that lit up her face, 'let us not waste this lovely day talking about things like that. We are young and we must enjoy ourselves.'

She gave his knee a squeeze and flicked the whip at the donkey. 'Where do you want to go?'

'Oh, I don't mind. You know the country better than me.'

'Well, the view from the Point is wonderful. We never did get there that awful day.' He frowned and she hurried on. 'But we won't go on the path with the tree. I know another way.'

'Fine.'

They had long since passed the Preventers' barracks and Josh took a casual look down and back at the grim building. He was surprised to see about a dozen men trot out through the entrance, line up outside and then march up the hill towards them. He shrugged his shoulders. A patrol, he assumed, and turned his attention back to the path they were following, away from the cliff edge now and onto the moor itself.

Larks were rising from the low bushes and singing their way upwards, and patches of blue sky were showing between the ever-present clouds that hung over the cliff. Josh felt his spirits lifting by the minute. For the first time since the loss of *The Lucy* he felt a desire to go back to sea, to the life he had chosen as a career, and he found himself thinking of applying for his first mate's ticket, which would demand new studying. Where would he do that – at Dover or, he frowned, here on these windswept cliffs?

His musing was interrupted by Rowena. 'Nearly there, Josh. Nearly on the Point. Just as well,' she nodded at the donkey, 'poor old Edward is getting old for this sort of climb. In a few moments I'll show you one of the finest sights in old England. If the clouds don't close in we should be able to see across to Wales.'

And, indeed they could. They were high – some four hundred feet above sea level – and the wind plucked at their clothing as they climbed down from the cart and warily approached the edge. It was terrifying to look down almost vertically to where the sea below them crashed onto the rocks that seemed to have been scattered there by a giant hand, causing white spray to rise in a curtain like a bride's veil.

'It's a bit windy to picnic here, don't you think, Josh? Shall we go back a bit further onto the moor?'

'No. Let's stay here. I love to feel the wind coming straight off the sea.'

'Oh, so do I. Put the waterproof down and put this blanket on top. I'll bring the food.'

Josh staked Edward out much further from the edge and left him contentedly grazing, while Rowena laid out plates and bottles of cider and then cold chicken and ham slices and began cutting into a loaf.

'Oh, Josh,' she said, 'we should do more of this. It really is . . .'

She didn't finish her sentence for Joshua was staring over her shoulder. 'I wonder what the hell they want,' he murmured.

Rowena turned and saw the Preventers breasting the crest of the hill leading to the village and were now spreading out in a half-moon crescent, making to stretch out around them from the cliff edge on either side of them and steadily advancing. They all carried cudgels but cutlasses hung from their belts.

'Damn!' hissed Joshua. 'I might have realised. They're coming to do Cunningham's dirty work for him.' He reached back and drew out his knife. 'Get behind me, Rowena, and whatever you do, don't go near the edge. They're going to push us over the edge and claim that it was suicide. Two tragic lovers and all that.'

'Oh no, Josh. They surely wouldn't do that.'

He turned and kissed her soundly on the lips. 'I'm so sorry that I've got you into this, Rowena. It's me they really want but they can't afford to leave witnesses. Now, I suggest you lie down behind me. The very act of having to pick you up might deter them.'

'No. I am not lying down, thank you very much.' Rowena had once more reverted to being a Gypsy. 'I shall stand with you and fight them.' She brandished the sharp kitchen knife she had been using to slice the loaf. 'I have a knife, too, now. Let them come.' She tossed her hair back but Josh could see that she was trembling.

'You are a remarkable girl, Rowena. But wait, let me talk to them first.'

He stepped forward and ran his eye along the line that was gradually closing in on them, hoping to find the man whom he had wounded on the heath and who had been tended by Rowena. He, at least, might have proven to be a restraining influence. But every face was grimly set and bent on violence. Of Cunningham, of course, there was no sign: no distant horseman watching events this time.

'What do you want?' Josh shouted.

No one replied but they all kept moving onwards, closing the half circle around the pair. Then one of them jeered: ''Ope you left a note.'

'What does he mean?' asked Rowena.

'Never mind.' Josh lifted his voice. 'If you want to throw us over the edge, then by all means come forward.' He held up his knife. 'We both have knives and know how to use them. We promise to take at least two of you with us. Oh, and you should know that Sir George Lansbury, the magistrate at Barnstaple, knows your game and, if we disappear, then you and Cunningham will be behind bars in an instant.'

The mention of the magistrate by name seemed to give them pause for a moment, then the man who had jeered threw down his stick and drew his cutlass. 'I'm not afraid of a boy and a gal,' he called out. 'I'll show you how to deal with these two.'

He broke into a run, cutlass raised, and Josh prepared to parry the downward swing of the weapon, but Rowena was quicker. She moved quickly away to the right of Josh and, as the Preventer's downward blow was taken on the crosspiece of Josh's knife, she leapt in, thrusting her own knife into the man's side. The blade did not penetrate far but it drew blood and made him swing round, enabling Josh to plunge his own blade deeply into the shoulder of his sword arm, twisting to withdraw it, so causing blood to gush from the wound and the man to fall to the ground.

A perceptible hiss – of admiration or hatred, it could have been either – rose from the men and they paused again. The men in the middle exchanged glances, nodded and then three of them ran forward, cudgels raised.

For a split second, Joshua hesitated. What to do? The answer came quickly into his brain. Do the unexpected.

He flung Rowena behind him, so strongly that she fell to the ground, and then, knife held out before him like a short sword, he ran directly at the man who was in the middle of the trio. This was unexpected and the Preventer halted and swung his cutlass horizontally at Josh's head. It was a mistake, for it was easy to duck underneath the blade – he even had time to remember Cunningham's cry of 'use the point, use the point, don't swing' – and, bending low, he thrust the knife into the man's thigh. Without stopping to measure the effect he turned to the man on his left and thrust his bloodstained blade into the exposed armpit as the man raised his cutlass. The man screamed and fell onto Josh's shoulder, causing him to fall backwards, so missing the sword thrust of the last of the trio.

Mindful of Rowena being left exposed, Josh scrambled on all fours towards her to find her standing, alone, and with a grin that seemed to split her face, pointing with her knife out onto the heath. He turned and then he saw them: about forty of the tinners running as fast as they could towards the Preventers, cudgels and sticks of their own raised and led by a panting Tom Clemence. Immediately, the Preventers turned and ran, back down the hill, along the path that led to the hanging tree.

Ignoring the three bleeding Preventers, lying moaning on the turf, Josh ran towards Clemence and, taking his hand, shook it vigorously.

'My God, Mr Clemence,' he said, 'I am so glad to see you.'

'Sorry, can't talk. Out of breath.' And the old man put his hands on his knees and took in deep draughts of air. Immediately, they were surrounded by the other tinners and joined by an almost equally breathless Rowena.

'We zaw what was 'appenin' from up there, on that 'ill,' said Clemence. 'We couldn't believe our eyes. These bastards were carryin' on where we left 'em a couple of weeks ago. Only this time, it looked as though they was tryin' to kill you an' all.'

Rowena nodded. 'Josh thinks they were goin' to toss us over the edge there so that, when we were found, people would think we'd jumped of our own accord. Suicide, you see.'

One of tinners turned and nodded to the three men on the ground. 'What d'yer want to do with these bastards, then, Tom?' he asked.

Josh intervened. 'Oh, throw them over the edge,' he said loudly. 'They deserve it. It was what they were going to do to us, after all.'

Immediately, the three Preventers set up a howl.

'Oh, put them in the donkey cart over there,' said Josh. 'We can dump them outside the barracks. They are not hurt so badly that they're going to die on the way.' He turned back to Clemence. 'I'm afraid things have gone from bad to worse here. But tell me, it's a miracle you turned up here as you did. What has happened to you? Did you find work in Barnstaple?'

'A few of us did,' said Clemence, pushing back a lock of grey hair, 'and we've left 'em in Barnstaple, with the women and kids. We had a message from Bude to say that the mine had reopened. Price of tin has gone up, y'see, an' there was work for us. So we are 'urryin' back 'ome, thank God. But we decided it was only right an' proper for us to deviate a bit an' call on you – I've got your address 'ere, somewhere – to say thank you properly for what you did for us against this lot. Looks as though we did the right thing.'

'You certainly did and we are most grateful.'

'What's been 'appenin' 'ere, then?'

While the wounded men were loaded into the donkey cart and Rowena was grudgingly doing her best to prevent them losing any more blood, Joshua briefly related to Clemence the events of the days since they had parted out on the moor.

The old man nodded. 'That Cunningham sounds a bad lot. Can't you report him to the militia?'

'Wouldn't do any good. The man has friends in the militia in high places, high enough to throw me into jail. I only have circumstantial evidence against him. I want to collect hard facts and find out exactly what he is doing here. That will be the time to accuse him, when I have proof.'

'Would you like us to wait around 'ere, to make sure he doesn't make another attempt on you an' the maid?'

'That's kind of you, Tom, but we mustn't detain you. You mustn't do anything to threaten your jobs.' He nodded to where the three men were groaning in the donkey cart. 'I think we've shown Cunningham that we can defend ourselves. But we must be extra careful in the future. Now, be on your way, with our blessing.'

There was much shaking of hands and clumsy bows to Rowena and then the tinners set off to the south, while Rowena turned the donkey's head out onto the moor to avoid having to return in the footsteps of the Preventers and so risk being ambushed in the patches of woodland that fringed the top coastal path.

When they reached the barracks the large gate was unguarded for once. Josh helped the wounded men to descend. 'Tell Cunningham,' he said, 'that next time he should not send boys to do men's work.'

The few days leading up to the opening of the Lloyd's enquiry dragged, not least because Josh felt it would be too dangerous to go walking on the heathland. He and Rowena had both decided not to tell the doctor about the attack on them, for it would be bound, said Rowena, to prompt the old man to face the captain and so incur possible danger to himself.

This decision caused Josh to wonder anew about the relationship that bound the two former shipmates. There seemed to be no love lost between them and yet, somehow, they seemed to remain close. He shrugged his shoulders. Perhaps the enquiry would throw some light onto it.

CHAPTER TWELVE

The little hamlet of Hartland seemed to assume a new lease of life when, on the day before the enquiry was due to open, a coach arrived from London carrying a complement of elegant gentlemen wearing frock coats and top hats, plus two who looked out of place: a diffident, bespectacled man wearing plain worsted – obviously a clerk – and a weather-beaten, middle-aged man in rustic tweed, whom the doctor felt was probably the Blue Cross Line representative. They all moved into the inn, watched by wondering eyes peering from windows in the high street.

Joshua was half expecting that some, at least, of the visitors would pay a courtesy call on Doctor Acland but none did so. Perhaps, as the doctor was a witness, it was felt that no contact should be made with him outside 'the court'.

The large dining room of the inn had been converted into a

temporary courtroom, with a high table providing a kind of magisterial bench and some degree of authority for the High Court judge, the three underwriters and the director of the Blue Cross Line. A side table had been set for the examining QC, another for the succession of witnesses, and a third for the clerk. Three chairs had been set for the press and a small roped-off standing area for members of the public. The dining room had never been so well patronised.

The witnesses were all asked to group in uncomfortable close proximity to each other – Cunningham and the doctor staring stolidly ahead in a corner of the room, none of the others talking to each other except the Reverend Hawker, who was jocularity personified – while the judge who was to chair the enquiry made his introductory remarks.

This was, he said, not a court of law, although he expected everyone concerned to behave, in terms of adherence to the truth and respect for the distinguished people involved, as though it was. It was an enquiry, set up by Lloyd's of London, to investigate the reasons why so many ships had foundered on the coastline stretching from Bude in the south to Hartland Point in the north during the last decade or so. The results of the enquiry would be submitted to the 'names' of Lloyd's who, if it was felt that criminality of any kind was involved, would submit the findings to the appropriate legal authorities. The judge, of suitably solemn bearing and appearance, was grateful for the witnesses who had given up their time to assist as well as, of course, the distinguished commercial figures who were sitting to hear the evidence. The examining of the witnesses would be conducted by barrister-at-law Mr Kenneth Knight, QC. It was not expected that the enquiry would last longer than two days. Members of the public were welcome to attend in the public enclosure but would be expected to remain silent throughout.

'Well,' whispered Josh into Rowena's ear, 'that seems fair enough. I wonder if everyone will abide by the rules.'

The judge then formally opened the proceedings by explaining that the enquiry had been prompted by the local coroner, Dr Acland. He then called on the doctor to explain his reasons for doing so.

The room was hushed as Acland – a rather pitiful-looking sight now, thought Josh: bespectacled, stooped and limping – made his way to stand behind the witness's table and was faced by the much younger figure of Mr Knight.

The doctor explained that the most recent shipwreck in the area, that of *The Lucy*, on the rocks of Morwenstow, had resulted in the death of all but one of its crew, and had been, by his calculations, the fifth vessel of the Blue Cross Line to founder on this coastline in the last few years.

'How many years, Doctor?' asked the barrister.

'I can't be quite sure but less than a decade.'

'And would you say that was unusually high – I believe you are a former merchant sailor yourself?'

'Yes, I would and yes I am. I know from my own days as an officer sailing in that line, that its ships often dock at Bristol or Gloucester, at the end of the Bristol Channel. The captains and crews of those ships will all have known of the dangers presented by the weather and sea conditions of the Channel.'

'Please tell us about those dangers.'

Acland did so, telling of the prevailing north-westerly winds, which could turn into virtual hurricanes within minutes, the narrowness of the shipping channel and of the necklace of deadly, half-sunken rocks that fringed the northern coasts of Cornwall and Devon, capable of tearing a ship's keel to pieces once she was lodged onto them.

'And, why, then, do you think that ships of the Blue Cross Line would be particularly vulnerable to those conditions?'

Acland took a deep breath, looking up at the little man in Scottish tweeds who was busily making notes. 'Because,' he said, 'it was my experience in the days when I was sailing under the Blue Cross pennant that the ships were comparatively undermanned, poorly maintained and not well mastered.'

Under questioning, he went on to say that the ships were not responsive to the rudder in rough weather, their bottoms were often fouled and not scraped, and the rigging was old and liable to tear and break in storms.

At this point, the Blue Cross Line director on the bench raised a finger and asked, in a strong Scottish brogue, 'When did you last sail in one of our ships, Doctor?'

'It was in 1822, some twenty years ago, when, incidentally, I narrowly escaped drowning when my ship was wrecked on the rocks at Bude. My leg was broken that day and has never satisfactorily been healed. That is why I walk with a limp.'

The little Scotsman sucked his pencil. 'You say it was twenty years ago. Have you had a chance of sailing in or inspecting any other Blue Cross ships since that time?'

'No. But I have spoken to seamen who have and they tell me that there has been no improvement. Your vessels, sir, I understand, are known in the Merchant Service today as "coffin ships". I think that speaks for itself.'

'Hmmm. Well, Doctor, I think if you had an opportunity to sail in one nowadays, you would see a vast improvement.'

'I rather doubt it, sir, as you will hear from other witnesses.'

Joshua whispered again into Rowena's ear: 'Your father hasn't mentioned the brazier. I thought he was going to do that.' Rowena shrugged her shoulders.

The QC then asked of the bench, 'Any other questions or comments for the doctor, gentlemen? None? Thank you, Doctor. You may step down.'

He looked at his notes. 'I now call Captain John Cunningham of Her Majesty's Customs and Revenue Service.'

There was an undoubted stir in the room as Cunningham made his way to the witness's table. He cut, of course, an imposing figure, with his shapely, waisted uniform, polished riding boots and black hair, brushed back like a gleaming helmet.

Mr Knight went straight to the point. 'You have heard Doctor Acland's description of the dangers of sailing up the Bristol Channel. I understand you sailed with him before you joined the Revenue Service. Do you concur with his views?'

'Most certainly. But I would go further than him concerning the vessels of the Blue Cross Line. Like him, I was on board one of the Line's ships when it was wrecked off the rocks at Bude. In my view, it was bad seamanship and poor conditions on board that were the main reasons she went aground.'

'Really?'

'Absolutely. It would have been quite possible for her to have weathered the headland there had the ship been conned properly, with enough crew on board to have trimmed the sails promptly and had the general condition of the ship's hull and sails been kept up to the mark. I had sailed with the Line for some years in a variety of their ships and they all seemed to exhibit these failings.'

Cunningham's opinions were expressed with a conviction that seemed to border on venom and the barrister frowned. 'But, of course, Captain,' he said, 'I presume that you are not saying that the numerous other ships that foundered on this coast were similarly badly handled and maintained?'

'No, of course not. The waters off this coast are notoriously dangerous because of the weather and narrow shipping lanes, but the way in which this shipping line was managed – penny-pinching and so on – made its ships particularly vulnerable.'

'Hmm. Were there any other factors, in your view, which could lead to such a high level of shipwreck here?'

Cunningham frowned. 'I am not sure I get your meaning, sir.'

'Could any land-born factors have added to the dangers faced by ships making passage up the Channel?'

'If you are raising, sir, that age-old myth that lights were deliberately stationed on the cliffs to lure ships onto the rocks in the hope of finding safe anchorages during a storm, I would deny that completely. There were rare instances of that happening in the last century and before but certainly not now. My men and I patrol these cliffs regularly and we would know if that foul practice is being followed still. It is not, I assure you.'

'Damned liar,' whispered Josh.

'Very well. Your main occupation presumably is the stamping out of smuggling along this coast?'

'It is.'

'And is smuggling rife here?'

Cunningham flashed his teeth in a rueful smile. 'I am afraid that is true, sir. We do our best, but the nature of the terrain here – distance from the capital city, the absence of any real law enforcement, apart from my own few men, plus the nature of this long and, er twisted coastline with its little hidden bays – all make it difficult to stamp out this practice.'

Mr Knight let his head fall back and studied the ceiling for a moment before asking: 'Could it be, Captain, that some of these shipwrecks were caused by ships attempting to land contraband, sailing too close to the rocks?'

Cunningham considered the question, frowning, for a moment before answering. 'I doubt it, sir. There are very few safe anchorages on this coast for ships of the size that foundered. In my experience, the ships carrying illicit cargo stand off the shore, while small craft ferry the contraband to isolated beaches and such like.'

The Blue Cross director then repeated his questions, aimed at depicting Cunningham as a man out of touch with modern, much improved conditions on his ships, which the captain denied, saying, as had Acland, that he was still very much in touch with men of the sea, who all confirmed that conditions had not improved since he, Cunningham, and the doctor had sailed in them. Then he was allowed to stand down.

Next to be called was the Reverend Hawker, who described how he had made it his business wherever possible to help in saving men who were shipwrecked at Morwenstow and in giving the dead seamen Christian burials in his churchyard. He painted a grim and tragic picture of *The Lucy* trying to round Sharpnose Point, just to the south of his village, but failing and crashing onto the rocks. Only one man, he said, had survived the shipwreck. His churchyard, he declared, was filling with the battered bodies of sailors torn to pieces by the black rocks of Morwenstow, just below his vicarage. He was not questioned about the possibility of *The Lucy*, or any other vessel for that matter, being lured onto the rocks by a false light.

'Damn,' mouthed Joshua into Rowena's ear. 'The vicar's honesty would undoubtedly have led him to mention the brazier, if he had been asked.'

'Shush!' she whispered back.

Thomas Pengelly was the next to be called to give evidence. He gave a detailed account of his work in Hartland Harbour, so giving credence to his abilities as a seaman and his knowledge of the sea and the coast of north Cornwall and Devon. He claimed to be unaware of conditions on Blue Cross ships but described vividly watching as *The Lucy* had got into trouble in the 'worst storm on this coast for years'. Such was the force of the wind and the height of the waves, he said, that he could not see how the ship could possibly have avoided being thrown onto the rocks. He, of course, had seen no sign of any deliberate intention by people on the shoreline to lure the ship so dangerously inshore. There certainly were many men of the Revenue Service there, but they, like himself and his friend Jem Drake, were there hoping to give help to whoever survived the vessel being driven onto the rocks. He and Drake had been fortunate enough to rescue just one seaman, whom they had pulled off a rock and carried up the cliff to safety. The rest of the crew had all perished. He blamed the terrible storm of that night and the consequent state of the sea for their loss, nothing else.

At this point, the judge, who had been making careful notes throughout the day, called the proceedings to a halt and adjourned the enquiry until nine o'clock the next morning. Immediately, Josh intercepted the Reverend Hawker as he made for the door.

'Can you spare a moment, Vicar?' he asked.

'Of course, my boy. Goodness, you are walking well now. Speaks wonders for the skill of the good doctor, does it not?'

'Er, yes sir. Indeed it does. But can I ask you, Reverend, why, in giving evidence today, you did not mention your opinion that there might well have been a burning brazier low down on the cliff that night and that it would have been a signal to smugglers?'

'Well, firstly, my boy, I was not asked about it. Secondly, what I told you, if you remember, when you visited my cabin, was that that would be my explanation for the brazier that you, er, said that you saw. But that it was only supposition on my part. I doubt if this enquiry would have any truck with supposition. It wants facts.'

'And, presumably, sir, you would not wish to imply that smuggling was a common practice in Morwenstow?'

The vicar laid a large hand on Josh's shoulders. 'Now you mustn't attribute such cowardly motives to me, young man. I always try and speak the truth, as the good Lord would wish me to do. And that is what I have done today. And I do hope, Joshua, that you will follow the same precept when you deliver your evidence tomorrow.'

'Oh, I most certainly will, Reverend, I most certainly will.'

'Very good, my son, I shall hear what you say with great interest. Now good day to you, Joshua. Look after the doctor. He doesn't look well to me.'

Josh watched with a growing sense of frustration as the vicar walked away. Would no one in this strange community help him to reveal the truth about these shipwrecks? And why, throughout the day, was the word 'wreckers' not once mentioned?

Accordingly, when he was called to give evidence immediately after lunch the following day, he decided firmly that he would, in the words of his father, 'set the cat among the pigeons' and provoke some reaction, at least, from the underwriters, who, so far, seemed only to have shown interest in the criticism of the Blue Cross Line. It was, however, on this subject that Mr Knight began his questioning. As a watchkeeper, what had been Josh's experience of sailing on *The Lucy*?

'Very poor, sir. I concur with everything that has been said about the standard of seamanship on board her. We were undermanned, meaning we had to work unduly hard, the anchor chains were rusty, the rigging frayed and, I have to say, the master was often drunk and kept to his cabin most of the day.'

'These are very robust views. Were these factors, do you think, which led to the foundering of the ship on the rocks of Morwenstow?'

'Well, they certainly contributed to it, in my view. In my spells of steering her across the Atlantic, I had noticed how unresponsive she was to the helm. I attributed this to the fact that her bottom was foul. However, there was one more factor – even more serious – that led to her going onto the rocks.'

'What was that?'

Josh held his breath and looked around the room, which was now completely silent. Cunningham was scowling and regarding him with a look of complete hatred. The doctor was frowning and looking up at the ceiling. Rowena had her hand to her mouth and Hawker was smiling faintly, as though he was trying to recall a phrase from the Bible to lighten his next sermon. Only Pengelly seemed almost disinterested, his eyes half closed.

Mr Knight lifted an eyebrow. 'Well, tell us. What was that?'

'I was in the rigging when we were trying to claw our way round Hartland Point at the height of the storm. Looking towards the black line of cliffs abreast of Morwenstow – I am familiar with this coastline, for I sailed past it many times as a boy, so I knew roughly where we were – I saw a light, low down on the cliff face. It was stationary but burning brightly, even in the wind and rain.'

A hiss, as of breath being drawn in, came from the public enclosure. 'Go on.'

'Looking down, to where Captain Lucas was standing by the wheel, I saw him point to the light and direct the helmsman to put the helm down and steer towards the shore. I shouted down, but could not make myself heard above the roar of the elements.'

'So what did you do?'

'I immediately slipped down to the deck and ran to the wheel and told the captain that there was no safe anchorage there. He told me that he had seen the riding light of a vessel so that there must be a harbour there. I told him there were only terrible rocks and begged him to put the helm over, but he said that I was being insubordinate. The wind was now dead astern and we were almost surfing towards the cliff face and the rocks and it was too late to turn the ship. We struck the rocks almost immediately afterwards.'

Joshua looked past Knight to the judge and the underwriters. All – including the Blue Cross director – were scribbling hard. Not a sound could be heard in the room until the barrister spoke.

'Who else saw that light, then?'

'The seaman I was with, trying to double-reef the topsail, undoubtedly saw it but, like everyone else, he was drowned. I was the only survivor.'

'So you are the only witness of that strange light.'

'I am afraid so, sir. But I definitely saw it.'

'What did you think it was? Presumably, there was no ship anchored there, taking refuge from the storm?'

'Oh no. There is no anchorage at Morwenstow, only a small shingle beach, which it would have been impossible for a ship larger than a dinghy to reach by threading through the rocks that stretch out from the cliffs. I had no idea what the light could have been, for there is no dwelling facing out to sea from those cliffs. I had no idea, that is, until later . . .'

'What do you mean by that?'

'Shortly after the shipwreck, I was curious to see where *The Lucy* had struck. I could hardly walk because my leg was badly hurt when I was thrown onto the rocks, so I persuaded Miss Acland, the doctor's daughter, to drive me to the scene in a donkey cart. We ventured down the cliff face via a pathway that exists there . . .'

'You could make your way down what almost sounds like a precipitous path on the cliff with a wounded leg? Surely not?'

'Doctor Acland, sir, had fixed splints to the leg. This enabled me, with the help of Miss Acland, to reach perhaps two-thirds of the way down, to where there is a small plateau – a large ledge, if you like – putting out from the cliff face. I judged it to be roughly in the position on the cliff where I saw the light.'

'Yes, yes, go on.'

'There was no light there then, of course. What there was, however, was a square hole in the ground, perhaps something like six or seven inches square, as though a stake had been hammered into the ground. Around the hole there still remained – despite the ravages of the storm – a ring of ash, such as would have fallen from an open brazier mounted on top of the pole or stake. In that position, it would have been visible from the sea.'

'Even in the wind and rain?'

'Oh yes, sir. If it had been continually fed with something combustible.'

The barrister turned to face the bench and put both his hands onto the lapels of his gown. He paused for a second and then asked loudly, 'And what do you think would have been the purpose of that light? Why was it being fed?'

'It was a signal light, sir.'

'A signal to whom?'

'To lure a ship out in the channel to turn towards Morwenstow, pretending to be the riding light of a ship safely at anchor but really to pull her onto the rocks for the purpose of salvaging her cargo.'

A murmur rose from the public enclosure, including one cry of 'No!'.

Mr Knight turned back to Josh. 'Let me understand you correctly. You are saying, Mr Weyland, are you not, that this was a deliberate act of, what shall I say, land-bound piracy, of the sort that allegedly used to be practised on this coast many years ago and for which a penalty of death still remains for those who perpetrate it?'

'I am indeed, sir.'

'Do you know who was responsible for mounting this brazier and lighting its contents?'

The judge leant forward. 'One moment, Mr Knight, please. Mr Weyland,' he spoke slowly with a well-modulated voice that carried with it the experience of a hundred courtrooms. 'I must point out to you that this is not a court of law, as I stressed yesterday at the beginning of these proceedings. This means that you do not speak here under the protection of the law, so to speak, which, in turn, means that if you challenge here some person or persons with a crime of this magnitude and if you have no proof of their culpability in the matter, then you lay yourself open to a charge of criminal slander. If, on the other hand, you have such proof, then you must, in all conscience, submit it to us here so that we can take appropriate action. Do you understand?'

'I do, Your Honour.'

'Very well. Then you may answer Mr Knight's question.'

Joshua gulped. He had to be careful here. 'I am fairly certain of the identity of such a person. The evidence I have is circumstantial, however, and I lack positive proof. I intend to establish the truth and submit the evidence to the law. However, I must confess that there is one other possible reason for the presence of the light, which I must put forward for your consideration.'

'Really?' A tone of faint sarcasm now tinged the barrister's voice. 'Then do share it with us.'

'It has been suggested to me that the light could have been put there by smugglers as a warning to their accomplices out at sea who were due to carry out a landing of contraband – a warning that Preventers were present and that the landing would have to be aborted.'

'Ah. We have heard already from Captain Cunningham that smuggling is rife in this part of the world. Would he have been the source of this suggestion, which I must say has the ring of probability about it?'

'No, sir. He has denied to me that such a signal existed on the night of the wreck of *The Lucy*.'

'But you think it is a rational explanation for its existence?'

'No, I do not. I mention it only as a possibility. There are several reasons why it is unlikely. Firstly, there would be no question of smugglers attempting to carry out a landing with such a storm raging. The state of the weather, in my view, would be enough to abort the landing. No captain of a ship would contemplate attempting to guide her through the rocks at Morwenstow to effect a landing, nor would he launch a dinghy in those seas to carry the goods ashore. So a burning light as a signal, which would in itself attract the attention of the Preventers, would not be necessary.'

Mr Knight nodded slowly and Joshua saw that the Reverend Hawker himself was nodding in agreement. 'You said that there were several reasons,' the barrister continued. 'What would the others be?'

'Let us presume that, given some warning that the storm was imminent, the smugglers on land had lit the brazier well before the storm broke, it would have been extinguished by the wind and rain as soon as the heavens opened. But I am sure that, to keep it blazing during the storm, when I and Captain Lucas saw it, it would have had to be fed. There would have been no need for smugglers to have done that. There is one last point, sir.'

'Pray continue.'

'It is most unlikely, anyway, that Morwenstow would have been selected for a landing of contraband at night. The rocks there run out in razor-sharp fingers, making it dangerous even for a dinghy to effect a landing. There are other, far more suitable, little bays and inlets along this coast that can be used for such a purpose.

'As a result, then, I strongly believe that the light was set up for the purpose I have described: to draw in a ship to founder on the rocks for the purpose of stripping her of her cargo. In a word, wrecking in the old sense.'

A murmur rose from the public enclosure, one conveying assent or disagreement. It could have been either, or a mixture of both, but Josh, looking back, noted that most of the faces in the enclosure were scowling at him.

'One last question, Mr Weyland. You were thrown into the sea when the mast broke on the vessel after it hit the rocks. Is that correct?'

'Yes, sir.'

'How did you – the only member of the crew – survive?'

'My leg was smashed against one of the rocks but I somehow managed to claw my way up onto the top of one of them. This was swept by the sea but I managed to cling on, although in great pain and only partially conscious, until I was rescued by Mr Pengelly and his companion. I glimpsed men on the shingle and I was told later that they were Preventers. But I lost consciousness at some point then. The two men carried me to safety and then up the path to the clifftop, from which I was taken to the house of Dr Acland.'

'Hmm. On your passage up the cliff path, you must have passed this shelf or plateau you have described as being the site of the alleged brazier. Did you see it?'

'No, I was unconscious by that time.'

'Thank you, Mr Weyland.' Knight turned to the bench. 'If you and your colleagues have no questions for this witness, Your Honour, I would like to call Miss Acland to the witness stand and also recall Captain Cunningham and Mr Pengelly.'

'I would expect you to do so, Mr Knight. Pray proceed.'

Rowena was questioned, firstly about the reason for her presence on the clifftop on such a night. She explained that it was at the request of her father, who felt that any survivors would need his attention but who felt unwell and unable himself to travel to the site. Then she confirmed that Josh seemed to be quite unconscious when he was laid onto the straw in the cart and, lastly, she confirmed, in a loud, clear voice, all that Josh had said about finding the hole in the ground and the ring of ash.

The recall of Cunningham and Pengelly brought the questioning of them on one point only: did they see any light, such as had been described by Josh, or any sign that there had been such a burning brazier during the storm. They both answered in the negative.

The judge, however, had one question for the captain. 'Mr Weyland said that there were men on the shingle, who, he was told later, were Preventers, presumably your men, Captain Cunningham. Were they, in fact, Preventers?'

'Yes, Your Honour.'

'What were they doing there? Did you suspect that there might be . . . what is the word, ah yes, there might be a *landing*?'

'No, Your Honour. I had turned them out because I thought we might be able to help the survivors from the stricken ship. Unfortunately, however, there was only one.'

'And why, do you suppose, that Mr Pengelly and his friend were there?'

'I expect for the very same reason, sir. All of us living along this stretch of the coast are used to turning out to offer help when a ship is in distress.'

'Indeed. It does all of you credit.'

'Thank you, sir.'

'Bloody hypocrite!' hissed Josh into Rowena's ear.

'Now,' the judge rapped with his gavel to gain order, for another murmur had risen from the public enclosure. 'This completes our questioning of witnesses and, as this is not a court of law, with prosecuting and defending counsels, there will be no summing up from Mr Knight, or from myself or anyone on the bench here. We will now, therefore, close these proceedings and retire to London, where we shall meet and give what we have heard our keen attention, before submitting our findings to the authorities at Lloyd's.

'I thank everyone for attending and bid you all good day.'

A hum of conversation immediately broke out in the crowded room and everyone stood back while the judge and his colleagues made their way into the bar of the inn and then up the stairs to their rooms. Joshua and Rowena immediately made for the doctor, who was engaged in earnest conversation with the vicar.

'Ah, Joshua,' said the Reverend Hawker, 'I thought you pursued your theory of the illicit light admirably, but I wished you hadn't done so. I still can't believe that there is anyone in my parish who could be guilty of such a thing and I fear that your intimation that there is could have upset the people, both in Morwenstow and Hartland.'

'Well, I am sorry, Mr Hawker, if you think that I have done so, but I felt I had to answer the question honestly.'

The doctor intervened. 'I think we should go now, Joshua. I think the people who were in the public enclosure could be getting angry and we have had enough violence here recently. I don't wish to prompt more. Come along, Emma. Good day, Reverend.'

The trio made their way to the door but outside they had to run the gauntlet of the crowd, who now hissed at Joshua as the three pushed their way through. Joshua was about to attempt to reason with them, but Acland took his elbow and they took sanctuary in the doctor's house.

'Let us go into the living room at the back of the house,' said the doctor. 'If we sat near a window fronting onto the street, I fear we might stimulate further physical expressions of disagreement, such as the smashing of my windows.'

They sat together in the half gloom of the room and Acland nodded to his daughter. 'The cognac, I think my dear – and, of course, the lemonade.'

'Oh really, Papa.' But Rowena hurried out and returned with the Armagnac, two glasses and a third containing her lemonade.

The glasses were filled and raised to the lips, without any faux toasting, for there really was nothing to celebrate.

'I am afraid that you have trailed your coat, Joshua,' said Acland, 'and people are liable to jump on it now.'

'I am sorry if you feel that I have stirred a hornet's nest here, sir, but I can't help feeling that the holding of the enquiry – particularly sitting it here – has been partly, if not completely, responsible for that.'

The doctor frowned. 'Certainly not *completely* responsible, for your own actions have played their part.'

'That maybe so, Doctor, but I have always been rather puzzled as to why you travelled to London to prompt this enquiry. It has undoubtedly drawn attention to the happenings here.'

A silence fell on the room for a moment and Rowena anxiously switched her gaze from Joshua to her father and then back again.

'Well,' Acland, began, rubbing a hand over his jaw. 'I have to confess that I wish I had never done it. There was one real reason and that was to draw attention to the conditions under which the Blue Cross Line is still putting its ships out to sea. I wished to have an enquiry made into the Line's record and its cheapskate practices. However, the damned thing got rather out of hand and Lloyd's mentioned they might broaden the enquiry into the many shipwrecks we have experienced on this coast. I was, of course, powerless to stop them. Cunningham particularly felt that what I had done was unwise, although, as you heard from his evidence he had no love for the Line either.'

Joshua nodded and his mind's eye recalled the two men arguing in the street after Drake's inquest.

'Well, my purpose may have been served,' the doctor continued. 'But between us – you with your unfounded allegations about that damned light and me with my complaints about the Line – we have thrown Hartland and Morwenstow into a most unpleasant light. You have made many enemies here now, Weyland, and endangered my daughter. I fear that I must ask you to leave this house.'

'Oh no, Papa.' Rowena bit her lip but her face was set grimly. 'I know you think I say that because I am fond of Joshua,' her face coloured, 'and it is true, I am. But there are other reasons why I think he should stay, at least for a while longer.'

The doctor sighed. 'Very well. Let me hear them.'

Rowena took a gulp of her lemonade, the bubbles of which tickled her nose and made her sneeze, very much to her annoyance. She blew her nose fiercely.

'Firstly,' she said, 'for Joshua to set out alone on leaving this house – even at dead of night – would put him in danger. There are people out there, Father, and I do not just mean the silly mob who spat at us, I mean criminals who wish him dead. If you insist on him going, I will accompany him.'

Josh squirmed in his chair. 'Of course, I shall go, sir,' he said, 'and alone. I can look after myself and I wouldn't think of putting Emma into danger.'

Acland sighed. 'You have other reasons, Daughter?'

'Oh yes. There is something terrible happening here and it is not of Joshua's making. The people who are engaged with these strange happenings are trying to imply that this recent violence is all his fault. He is, after all, a foreigner to these parts and people don't like strangers anyway . . .'

'Particularly,' the doctor intervened, 'when this violence has occurred only since his arrival. It would be wrong to overlook this.'

Josh leant forward. 'But, Doctor, I am not – I repeat not – responsible for it. As Row—er, Emma has said, I am very much the innocent party. But in view of all that has happened, of course I must leave your house. I will do so immediately.'

'And I will go with him.'

'No, Rowena.' Joshua stood and put a hand on her shoulder. 'You will do nothing of the kind. I do not wish you to come with me. It will be a long journey and I cannot be impeded. You must understand that.'

Tears were now trickling down the girl's cheeks and she buried her face in her handkerchief.

'Joshua is right, Emma.' Acland struggled to his feet. 'I will not have

270

you put in danger. Now, listen. I am persuaded that, indeed, it would be unwise and, inhospitable to say the least, to throw you out of this house, Joshua, at this time, where, I have to agree, danger seems to stalk the land. So, if you wish, you may stay, but on one condition.'

'What is that?'

'That you spend as much time as possible indoors and don't go poking your nose into the activities of the villagers here. Then, when things have quietened down, I must ask you to leave. In any case, I believe you have a fiancée waiting for you in Kent, do you not? A fact, which, it seems, Emma happily overlooks.'

'Yes, it is true, sir, that I have a fiancée in Dover. But, although I have sent her several letters, she has not responded. I am, indeed, anxious to see her again,' he stole a glance at a white-faced Rowena, 'but I am concerned about the safety of both of you. There is undoubtedly something evil based here, Doctor, and I feel I must reveal it and, indeed, play a role in protecting both of you.'

'Then you also must ignore that feeling, sir. I insist. Those are the terms on which you will either stay here or leave. Let me have your decision now.'

Joshua took a deep breath. 'Very well, sir. Then I must leave. I will go immediately, while it is still light.'

'Oh no!' Rowena put her hand to her mouth. 'Where will you go?'

'I don't know. I will aim for Dover, but once I have sorted out my own affairs, I shall return. I promise. I will go and get my things now. Thank you for your hospitality, Doctor, and for your splendid work on my leg, which I think is virtually healed now.'

A tearful Rowena murmured, 'I will help you pack.'

Bowing their heads to the doctor, the two of them left the room and climbed up to Josh's bedroom. There, Rowena put her arms around his neck and said, 'Don't go. If they kill you, I die too.'

'No one is going to murder me, my dear, be sure of that.' He untangled her arms from his neck. 'But you will appreciate that I must leave here, but I shall not leave the district. Now, listen to me. If my plan succeeds, I will remain in the vicinity, but I want you to tell your father – and indeed, I would like you to spread the word – that I have left to ride to Dover to meet Mary.'

Her eyes widened. 'But you won't really go there, will you?'

'No. And I shall find a way of getting in touch with you. You remember the hanging tree, of course?'

She pulled a face. 'Of course.'

'When I looked at the ground near the tree, I noticed that there was a hole in its trunk, away from the path. I will leave messages for you there, every third day after I have found somewhere to hide. It will be an ideal place for communicating, because the villagers, I would think, would be too superstitious to linger there. Will you look for them, because I shall need your help?'

'Oh, of course I will, Josh.' She forced a smile. 'I am so glad that you are not really leaving, but am worried now that you will get into more trouble.'

'Well, I think that Cunningham and his thugs will roam the countryside looking for me, but if my idea bears fruit, he will not find me. Now, there is one more thing, Rowena.'

'Yes, yes?'

'I feel that something is brewing here in this village, maybe another landing. I don't suppose you would know anything about that, would you?'

She immediately looked at the floor. 'Of course not. Why ask me?'

'Never mind that. But I would like you to put your ear to the ground here, so to speak, to see what you can discover. If there is to be a landing, then I feel Tom Pengelly will be involved so, my dear,' he forced a smile, 'be nice to him and see if you can get any idea when it might happen. But be very discreet.'

'Of course I will.'

Joshua began throwing garments into a soft bag that they had given him when he was taken into the house. 'Oh, Rowena.'

'Yes?'

'Do you think you could make me a sandwich and give me a flagon of water. I have a feeling that I am going to be hungry.'

'Yes, of course. And there is something else. It could be difficult for you to go on foot everywhere. You are so recognisable here, now, Josh, and, as you say, the Preventers will be looking for you, so . . .'

'Yes?'

'You may remember me telling you that I have a little pony that Father gave me. It is kept in a small stable behind Father's mare, but I have hardly used it since you came here. You will find a saddle and harness hanging in the stall. Take it. He will graze on grassland. And I have an old hat of Father's and a cloak of his that I have been meaning to give to the poor. You must take them also to give you some sort of disguise. Now, I will make your sandwich, but don't be long. The light goes quickly at this time of year.'

'Oh, Rowena. You are a splendid young woman – and damned resourceful.'

Within fifteen minutes he had left, Rowena waving sadly to him from the doorway. Tied from the saddle pommel was a bag containing what seemed like a huge number of sandwiches, half a meat pie and some cheese, plus Josh's treasured waterproof bag containing his savings, now sadly depleted. The pony was skittish, after his long stretch of inactivity, and Joshua was not the best horseman in the land, but he guided him successfully up what seemed to be a little-used track that wound up back from the hamlet, so that he would not have to pass the barracks. At the top, crouched under the doctor's old cloak and with his hat pulled well over his face, he altered direction and headed for Morwenstow.

He did not want to attract attention by galloping but he urged the pony into an occasional canter and it was not long before he had reached the cluster of dwellings set above the Reverend Hawker's house. He had passed no one on the way and he turned into the little track that led down to the vicarage and there, under the cover of some trees, he halted and sat thinking.

He did not want to attract attention to himself by calling at the door of the big house, so how to find the vicar without making a fuss? His question was answered when he heard Hawker's voice, humming a hymn, as he climbed up the steep path astride his horse.

'Good gracious, Weyland. You startled me.'

'Oh, I am sorry, Reverend, but I am so glad to have met you here. Sir, I am in urgent need of your help.'

'Really? Well, of course, I will be happy to help if I can. Won't you come into the house? My wife has made some tea and I was just getting a little exercise. What can I do for you?'

'Well, sir, I suppose you could say that I am appealing for sanctuary.' With a rueful smile, Joshua explained the doctor's decision to ask him to leave and his own determination to stay for a while longer in the area between the two villages to observe the happenings there.

'What happenings, my boy?'

'I don't know. But my instincts tell me that something is going to happen shortly – most likely a smugglers' landing – and, if I can, I want to observe what happens and who is involved.'

Hawker frowned. 'You are playing a dangerous game, young man. I could not describe spying on folk as the most Christian of pastimes. And it could be dangerous. Don't you think you should leave?'

'I am sorry, Reverend, but I don't. Apart from anything else, I am concerned about the safety of Emma and even, perhaps, the doctor, for they have been linked to me recently. I want to be here to protect them if anything happens.'

'I see. But I fail to understand how I come into this. Pray explain.'

'Of course, yes. I am most concerned about Captain Cunningham, for I know he has told deliberate lies recently. He sees me as an enemy and his men will be combing the coast and the moor looking for me. So I must remain under cover, stealing out probably at night.'

'Under cover? Where?'

'Mr Hawker, the last place they would look for me would be in your little hut-cave, whatever you call it, here on the cliff. Would you allow me to hide in there, for, say, the next two weeks? I have some food for the next few days but would appreciate it if I could buy some sustenance from you after that. But Mrs Hawker and your servants should not know I am there.'

The frown on the vicar's face gradually merged into a slow smile.

'What a shame,' he said, 'that we don't have a pond or river with bulrushes. You could emulate Moses there and we could replay what I have always considered to be one of the most exciting stories in the Bible.'

Joshua grinned. 'I fear I might catch cold, with winter coming on. But do you think you could help me in the way I have described?'

The vicar thought for a moment. 'You mentioned sanctuary and I suppose I must regard your request as seeking that. In that case, I certainly cannot turn you away. But, my dear fellow, do be careful in whatever it is you are planning. You must not bring disgrace or harm to this little community.'

'I fear that evil already exists here, sir. But the last thing I would want is to extend it. I will be most careful, I promise.'

'Very well. There is precious little room in my outdoor study and you might find the smell of opium to offend your nostrils – ah no, you told me that you had inhaled in the East, so that should be no problem. But it can be frightfully cold in there at night, I would think . . .'

'Emma has given me two good blankets, sir.'

'Very well. You may take over my little cave, but not for ever. It would be unfair to deny its use to me for longer than, say, three weeks. Would that be fair?'

'Very fair, sir. I promise to leave it at the end of three weeks, if not before.'

'Now you wish me to conceal your presence there from my servants and even my wife?'

'I am afraid so, sir. If the word got out, the Preventers would be swarming down here within minutes. I promise you that.'

Hawker ran his hand through his thinning hair. 'Well, I have to confess that I don't like the underhandedness of it all. I cannot be asked to lie on your behalf. That would be going against my principles – you understand?'

'Of course, sir. All I would ask is that if you have to tell anyone, you let me know to give me time to get away. Oh, by the way, may I graze this pony – it is Emma's – with yours? I am told he will graze on grassland.'

'Not necessary. He can be stabled with mine. There is room and only I go there.'

'Thank you very much, sir. I am truly grateful.'

'I shall pray for you, Joshua. And you, of course, must say your prayers every night. I hope you do.'

'Of course, sir. Every night.'

CHAPTER THIRTEEN

The Reverend Hawker was right, the hut-cave was damned cold, confining and, all in all extremely uncomfortable for anyone who was not a hardened opium smoker. Joshua shivered and squirmed inside it, trying to find a position that didn't induce cramp. As he lay contemplating his future, he could not but come to the conclusion that he was a fool for staying on in this Cornish–Devon corner, hanging like some seabird on this precipitous cliff face. Why hadn't he taken to his heels immediately after the enquiry to find his fiancée in distant Dover and demand to know why she hadn't written to him?

He knew the answer, of course. He was in love with this young woman, half-Romany, half-respectable doctor's daughter, who taunted him with her sexuality and stirred his admiration for her courage. He had undoubtedly kicked a hornet's nest in these two villages, Hartland Quay and Morwenstow, and she had become linked to him. He could not walk away and leave her to the mercy of Cunningham and his Preventers – and whoever else was involved in the criminal acts that he was convinced lay under the seeming rural domesticity of both places. There would be time to confront Mary when all this had been brought to an end.

In the meantime, as he pulled both blankets up to his chin, he was cold. Hadn't he been impetuously foolish to hide away and hope to unravel some of the mysteries of this bleak coast by springing out from his eyrie and catching the wrongdoers in the act? Which posed the question: what act? Presumably smuggling, for both villages had been under too much public scrutiny recently to allow a landing to take place. But the smugglers earned their real living by slipping in contraband. They must be needing a landing about now, he pondered.

He stayed in the reverend's 'outdoor study' for three days, only leaving it to scramble up and down the cliff at Morwenstow as the light faded each day. Just as what was left of *The Lucy* was fast disappearing, he hoped that if there was a hue and cry for him, it would have abated by the fourth day. In any case, he was too bored and uncomfortable to stay in the hut any longer.

As dusk was falling, then, on that fourth day, he saddled up the little pony and set him out on the clifftop path to Hartland, taking a detour inland for a while to avoid meeting anyone on the path.

By circuitous route and in semi-darkness he found his way to the hanging tree. Cautiously, tying the reins to a sturdy bush, he approached the tree – and was startled almost out of his life when Rowena suddenly materialised from behind it.

She threw herself into his arms. 'I've been so worried,' she said, her face white in the moonlight, 'because you said you would leave a message every third night and this is the fourth night since you left – and nothing. Are you all right?'

Josh nodded and disentangled her arms from around his neck – and it fleetingly occurred to him that he seemed to have spent much of the last month doing just that.

'No, I am fine, thank you. Did anyone see you come this way?'

'I am sure not. I was very careful and walked here, looking behind me all the way. Where are you hiding, then?'

He told her. She grinned. 'Very clever. No one would look for you there.'

'Well, it is damnably uncomfortable. But do you have any news for me?'

She nodded, looked around her and then drew him into the bushes that fringed the path. 'Yes, well, I think so. You seem to have an instinct for knowing something is going to happen. How do you do it?'

'I don't know, just an intimation. But for goodness' sake tell me. What is afoot?'

'Well, I can't be sure, but I think there is going to be a landing.'

'How do you know?'

She hesitated, looking at the ground, then lifted her eyes to look into his. 'I am sorry, Josh, but I don't think I can tell you that and I can't be sure, but I think it will be tomorrow night at about midnight. And at the quay.'

'Ah! Splendid.'

She seized his arm. 'What do you propose to do? It would be terribly dangerous to try and interfere with it – and you mustn't tell the Preventers, for there could be violence if you do.'

He grinned. 'They would be the last people I would tell. No. Don't worry. I just want to observe what goes on and, particularly, note who is in charge of the landing – who is leading the smugglers, if you like.'

A silence fell between them for a moment and Josh resisted the desire to take her in his arms and cover her frowning face with kisses.

'And then what will you do?' she asked.

'To be honest, I don't really know. I just know that I have to find out who is behind this smuggling ring – and, well, see what ramifications there could be . . .' He finished lamely and felt distinctly uncomfortable to confess that he had not the faintest idea what he would do next.

'I want to be with you, then.'

'Oh no. I am sorry, Rowena, but I couldn't allow that.'

'Why not? It is I who gave you the information. And, anyway, you can't stop me creeping up to look at what is going on.'

Josh frowned. He remembered he had prompted her to 'be nice' to Tom Pengelly. Presumably he was her source – and he felt, ashamedly and ridiculously, jealous. He cleared his throat gruffly. 'Very well, then. Is there a place we can perhaps look down on the quay without being seen?'

'Oh yes. There is a little path that winds up the cliff face above the harbour.'

'Oh yes. I think I used it when leaving your house four nights ago. But won't it be used by the smugglers?'

'Perhaps, but just off the path there is a large bush where . . . where,' it was now her turn to clear her throat, 'where Tom Pengelly and I used to play as children. It hangs low over the edge of the cliff about a hundred feet above the harbour and lime kilns. We could crawl inside and look down without being seen from below or from the path.' She looked up at him and grinned. 'It's really quite cosy in there.'

'I'm sure it is.' He had to make an effort not to sound disapproving, for he knew that Pengelly must be all of five or six years older than Rowena. It was most unlikely that they had played there as children – but perhaps as adults? 'Very well, then. Let us meet here at – what shall we say – ten o'clock?'

'No. Make it a little later, for it will be difficult for me to leave with Father still up. Say a little before eleven, say quarter to.'

'Very well. Quarter to eleven. Meet here.'

'Yes – oh, I almost forgot.' She turned and, thrusting aside the bushes she made her way to the tree and put her hand into the hole in its trunk. 'I left you sandwiches and a piece of cherry pie yesterday,' she said, thrusting the bundle into his arms. 'And there is chocolate cake in there, too. I hope they haven't become too stale. I didn't want you to go hungry.' She put a hand to his cheek.

'Oh, Rowena.' He grasped the hand and kissed it. 'You are so thoughtful.'

She stared at him unsmilingly for a moment. 'It's because I love you, Josh.' She said the words simply, as though reiterating a well-accepted fact.

'Oh, er, well yes.' He released her hand quickly. 'Now, we both must go. Won't your father have missed you?'

'No. I told him I was visiting Mrs Drake, the mother of poor Jem.'

'Good.'

'Oh Josh.' She looked up beseechingly into his eyes. 'Won't you at least kiss me goodnight. Kiss me properly, that is.'

Joshua's thoughts raced, a jumble of desire, conscience and fear – fear of what might ensue. 'I don't think so, Rowena. I mean it could . . . oh very well, then.'

He seized her roughly and, once again, she wrapped her arms around his neck. They kissed, Rowena's tongue questing into his mouth and his responding, until he pushed her away.

'Rowena! Where on earth did you learn to kiss like that?'

She grinned provocatively and then mocked him. 'Joshua, where on earth did *you* learn to kiss like that?'

'Well . . .' he stumbled. 'I am considerably older than you.'

'Yes, well I am eighteen, which is quite old enough. Let's do it again.'

'No. We must go. Thank you again, my dear. Be careful on your way home. And I will see you here tomorrow night.'

She put her tongue out at him in mock dismay, then touched his cheek with her hand. 'Yes, tomorrow night. You be careful, too, my love. Goodnight.' She turned and disappeared into the darkness.

Josh stood and fingered his cheek, looking after her, his brain still in a whirl. Then he unwrapped the package and bit into the pie. It was only just a little too crusty from staying overnight in the tree. Ah, the girl could cook as well as kiss! What a terrifying combination! He sighed as he chewed.

He spent the next day holed up in the hut, not daring to go out in case news of the projected landing had leaked to the Preventers, causing them to patrol the coast. He did, however, study the cloud formation out at sea to the north-west to pick up signs of an adverse change in the weather, which might well cause the landing to be cancelled. All seemed tranquil, however, with the sea looking like smooth glass.

Josh found Rowena waiting for him, in the bushes by the tree at the appointed hour. Predictably, she had brought some tea in a jug, once hot but now only warm, together with a welcome pile of ham sandwiches. As he ate he couldn't help wondering if Doctor Acland had noticed the remarkable increase in Rowena's appetite.

Still chewing, they hurried to find Rowena's bush, where she and Tom Pengelly had 'played'. It was, indeed, the perfect hiding place, the foliage sweeping down to the earth in a green curtain around the trunk of the bush and seemingly impenetrable. Once inside, however, there was plenty of room for two – ah, what sort of games had she and Pengelly played there? – and, by parting the curtain where the ground steeply fell away, they could easily look down onto the quay and the little harbour.

What's more, by the poor light from the half-obscured moon, Josh could just make out the distant, but unmistakable outline of a lugger, her sails backed, lying out at sea about halfway to the horizon.

'Look,' he whispered, 'can you see her? I am told that luggers are almost always used by smugglers. They are roomy but quite fast sailers so they can give the Revenue boats a run for their money.'

Rowena nodded. 'I know,' she said.

Josh shot her a sharp glance, then put his fingers to his lips. Men, heavy-footed, were hurrying down the path, tramping past the bush on their way, presumably, to the harbour below.

Putting her lips to his ear, Rowena whispered, 'They're coming this way, rather than using the main path, to avoid passing the Preventers' barracks.'

'So they would have come from Hartland village, up on the top?'

'Yes. Not from where we live.'

'Hmm. Interesting.'

He peered through the hanging branches to look at the quay below and at the lime kilns and huts that fringed the edge of the water, facing where the harbour wall curled around to afford protection to small vessels. There was no sign of activity of any sort. The wall, the slipway and the buildings were deserted.

'I have brought something that might help,' whispered Rowena. She unbuttoned her coat and produced a telescope, which she slid to its full, open length and handed to him.

'Oh, Rowena. You think of everything.'

'I must take it back, though, before Father misses it.'

'Was he in bed when you left?'

'I think so. At least, he had retired for the night and there was no sound from his room.'

'Good. Let me look.'

He gestured for Rowena to turn round and then rested the telescope on her shoulder, gently thrusting the end through the hanging foliage and focusing it on the lugger, now just a dark shadow out at sea. The ship slid into sight but he could see little detail, except . . . yes . . . he could just about make out figures moving on the deck.

More men were now coming down the path and Rowena huddled closer to him, for once more in fear, he realised, than desire, for one of the men lightly brushed the foliage hanging down onto the edge of the path, as though about to part it to look inside. But he did not do so and trod on, until silence descended onto the hiding place once more.

Crouched there in the darkness and hidden by the curtain of branches and what was left of their leaves, Joshua felt a stab of anxiety as he realised how close they were sailing to danger. If they were

285

discovered it was likely that they would be killed, for smuggling was an offence now punished by banishment to the Australian colonies, which usually meant no return to the homeland for the guilty. And these men were from the village on the heath above, not from the quay, and would have no compunction in removing any trace of evidence of their wrongdoing, for they were unlikely to have any regard for this stranger and his seeming lover from the hamlet below.

That is how they would be regarded and, crouched in the cold and dark of their hideaway, he instinctively put his arm around Rowena and pulled her closer. She was trembling but her fear could not subdue her sense of humour.

'I knew you would like to cuddle, Josh.'

With a sigh of exasperation, he pushed her away and turned to look down on the harbour below once again. The first of the men were now debouching onto the slipway and, then, the later arrivals climbing up to the sheds that surrounded the lime kilns.

Two of the men on the slipway moved to untie a rope securing one of the dinghies to a ring set in the stonework.

'Ah, look Rowena. They are taking one of the dinghies out to ship some of the contraband from the lugger.' He raised the telescope to his eye. 'Oh, yes. As I feared. It is Pengelly who is climbing into the dinghy. Here, look.'

She focused the glass and nodded glumly. 'Yes, it is Tom. He is one of the smugglers without a doubt.' She bit her lip and handed back the telescope.

Josh sighed. 'Did you always know that, Rowena, or just suspect it?'

She matched his sigh. 'Oh, I think I always knew it, Josh, but it was never talked of. You see,' her voice took on a lower, more intense, tone, 'smuggling is just not considered a crime here. In some way or another, everyone around here seems to be involved, either by running the contraband ashore, as, it seems, Tom is about to do, or distributing the goods or,' he could feel her shrug, 'buying the smuggled goods, if they can afford them.'

Joshua was about to say, 'Like your father,' but bit off the retort. 'Yes, I think I understand,' he said quietly. 'The problem is that it is regarded as a serious crime by the government, earning heavy penalties. And doing this, virtually next door to Cunningham and his Preventers, surely is asking for trouble.'

'Ah, I think that's partly why they do it. Cunningham is not loved around here, Josh. That is clear. They are, what is the phrase? Yes, "cocking a snook" at him and the authorities by landing the goods under his nose. The boys around here will love doing that.'

Joshua levelled the telescope through the curtain again. 'Ah. Another dinghy is about to be launched. Do you know the men who are manning them, apart from Tom?' He handed back the glass.

She squinted one-eyed. 'Oh, I know their faces, I think, but I don't know their names.' She handed back the telescope and smiled ruefully. 'Father didn't like me mixing with the boys from Hartland on the top. He said that they were a rough people.'

Joshua tightened his lips. 'But Tom, coming from Morwenstow, was acceptable, was he?'

He felt her hot breath on his ear. 'Now, now, Mr Weyland, don't tell me that we are getting jealous, are we? Oh good. Splendid!'

'Certainly not. Of course not. Now, be quiet for a moment and let me concentrate.'

He watched as the two dinghies were pulled round the harbour wall and out to sea. 'Of course,' he breathed, 'the slipway makes an ideal landing place for unloading the goods, although it is not exactly hidden away. I wonder . . .' He stopped as a handful of the men walked up to one of the huts. One of them fumbled in his pocket, produced a key and opened the door. 'Yes,' continued Josh, 'and the contraband is hidden there temporarily, among the workings from the kilns, before being taken away and distributed to the customers. It is all very well organised. The manager of the kilns must be in on the whole thing.'

'How many men are doing all this?' asked a now more relaxed Rowena, sitting back and extracting another sandwich from her bundle.

'Not many. Only about eight or nine in all, including the four men in the dinghies. Not all that many to unload . . .' He stiffened and fell silent. Then:

'Oh my God! The Preventers have arrived. Now there is going to be violence . . . No. They are shaking hands with the smugglers. What on earth is going on?' He handed the telescope to Rowena. 'You tell me. They *are* Preventers, aren't they?'

She seized the glass. 'Oh yes, they're Preventers all right. They are wearing the uniforms.'

'Perhaps they stole them?'

'No. I recognise three or four of them and . . . one is hobbling. He must be one of the ones you hurt when the tinners came down to save us, up on the top. Look.' She handed back the telescope.

He focused. 'Yes. Preventers all right. Good Lord! They must be in on it too. No wonder they can unload here in the quay, just down from their barracks. They must be doing it behind Cunningham's back.'

He stayed looking through the glass for a moment. 'No.' He said quietly. 'They are not. Cunningham has joined them and has given a key to one of his men to open another storeroom.'

He lowered the telescope and turned to Rowena. 'Why didn't I think of it before? The bloody man is a smuggler, probably the leader of the whole gang. His Preventers are part of the ring. No wonder he has been complaining sadly about the rise in smuggling in the area. He and his men are causing it – and doing so without fear of being caught, because they are the catchers, so to speak. Damn it, Rowena, it is a devilishly clever arrangement. I suspected Cunningham of doing much worse things – the light luring the sailors to their destruction, but I never contemplated that he would be running the smuggling operation, too. And villagers from the top, at least, are in on it too. The whole area is corrupt.'

He looked at her steadily. 'You must tell me, Rowena, did you know about any of this?'

She returned his gaze equally steadily. 'Of course I knew that there was smuggling going on, because . . .' She stopped, then went on. 'I knew it was happening, although I have never seen a landing. I managed to get Tom Pengelly to hint that something was going to happen tonight, but apart from him I never knew who was involved. And certainly not Cunningham and his Preventers.'

Josh sighed. 'Well, I suppose, strictly speaking, nothing has happened yet, so we could not accuse anyone at this stage even if we wanted to. Nothing has been landed.' He focused the telescope out to sea. 'Yes, I can just see the two dinghies approaching the lugger, although the light is virtually dying now and they have almost disappeared.' He sighed. 'We will wait and see the landing.'

A silence fell between them, now rather uncomfortable. Then Rowena broke it. 'What will you do about it, then, Josh? I don't like the thought of Tom going to prison and then even being shipped abroad, because of what he told me.'

Joshua put his head in his hands. 'I just don't know. I can't let Cunningham get away with this. But how to prove it?' He looked up, appearing incongruously like a vagrant in the doctor's old, now rather tattered cloak. 'It would be just our word against his.'

'Unless we could inform the militia and they suddenly searched the barracks and found contraband hidden away there.'

He shook his head. 'Cunningham is a clever man. He would not be so foolish as to let his barracks be used for storing smuggled goods. It will all be put overnight in those huts and then distributed quickly under cover of his men going out on patrol. On patrol to catch smugglers.' He grinned weakly.

'Oh, Josh. What are we to do? I don't like the idea of . . . of . . . some of the villagers of the quay being suspected and even being charged.'

Josh regarded her sadly. 'And I think I know why. But let us wait and see exactly what they do with the contraband once it's ashore.' He levelled the telescope out to sea. 'It won't be long now. I think I can see the dinghies pulling for the shore.'

He reached out his hand and took one of hers in it. For once, however, she did not respond, merely letting it rest there while she hung her head. Joshua felt a great wave of pity sweep over him. She would be distraught, of course, if her beloved father was accused of buying contraband goods, which seemed now to be surely the case.

They sat quietly, hand in hand, for some time. Joshua, peering down, could now see the dinghies coming into normal vision and a jackbooted Cunningham giving orders to his men and pointing to the various huts.

Then he stiffened. 'My God,' he whispered.

'What's the matter?'

He raised the telescope and trained it onto the face of a man who was now in earnest conversation with Cunningham, pointing with him to the huts, as though suggesting ways they could be used. 'Yes,' he said, an air of sadness creeping into his voice. 'Rowena, it's your father. He is talking to Cunningham. It looks as though he is helping him in some way.'

'What! It can't be. I am sure he was in his room when I left.'

'I think not, my dear. Here, take the glass and look at the face of the man who is discussing things with Cunningham.'

She did so, holding it there for at least thirty seconds. Then, slowly, she handed the telescope back to him. 'Oh Josh,' she said eventually, 'I long suspected that he was buying contraband cognac and fine pieces. He just couldn't resist good brandy and that fine china and so on . . .' Her voice fell to a whisper. 'That is why I tried to stop you investigating this whole smuggling business here. But I never thought he would be one of the smugglers himself.'

'More than that, I fear, my dear.' Joshua was training the glass on the two figures below. 'He is undoubtedly discussing where the contraband should be stored, once it is landed. He is clearly jointly in charge.'

Rowena was now softly weeping. 'Oh Josh. You won't give him up to the militia, will you? He is too old to go to prison. He would die there. Please, oh please, say you won't.'

Josh bit his lip. 'No, no. Of course not. We will find a way of getting him out of this,' but his brain added, *God knows how.*

He held her close for a moment longer, then pushed her away. 'Look, you should get back to the house, in case your father decides to return early.'

'No. I can't go just yet. I want to see what they do with the contraband.' She looked at him tearfully. 'And make sure you get away safely.'

'Oh, please don't worry about me. I shall stay here until I am sure the last man has gone. But I insist you go now, before they start returning up the path. You should be quite safe while they are waiting for the goods to arrive. Go on, please, Rowena. The last thing I want is for you to be caught spying on the gang. Anything could happen. Please . . . go now. I shall stay hidden for some time yet.'

'When will I see you again, then?'

'Oh, I am not quite sure, Rowena. I have some thinking to do.' And then, half aloud: 'I wonder if I should ask Hawker's advice?'

She seized his arm. 'No. No. He would have to follow his conscience and hand Father – and Cunningham, of course – over to the militia. You must tell no one, Joshua. No one, please.'

'Very well. But go now, my dear, while it is still safe. I will communicate with you via the hole in the tree.' He held her tear-stained face for a moment between his hands, looking into her eyes. 'Don't worry. We will find a way out of this, I promise you.'

Slowly, she nodded. 'I trust you,' she whispered. She kissed him quickly on the lips and then was gone.

Joshua parted the curtain and looked down. The two dinghies were now rounding the end of the harbour wall, very heavily laden, for the gunnels were virtually lapping the water. He blew out his cheeks. What on earth was he to do?

Well, the first thing was to see what was unloaded and where exactly the contraband was stored. He had retained the telescope and he trained it now on the dinghies as they were hauled a little way up the slipway. They were laden with small barrels and sturdy boxes, so that he couldn't see the contents, although it seemed clear that the barrels contained wine or spirits, almost certainly French.

Cunningham seemed to have disappeared for the moment and the doctor now appeared to take charge. He put one of the smaller kegs to one side on the slipway – his perquisite? – and directed that the others should go to one of the two huts that had been opened. The boxes were now being levered open and Acland peered inside each one, obviously checking their contents. Satisfied, he gestured for them to go to the second of the unlocked huts.

'All present and correct, would you say, Weyland?'

He wheeled round, still on his knees, and met the sardonic smile of Captain Jack Cunningham, who had quietly parted the curtain of foliage and was looking down on him. Two of the Preventers quickly appeared on either side of him.

'You should never use a telescope when you are spying, my boy. Even in the semi-darkness there was enough moonlight to glint off the glass. Foolish of you.' He turned to the man on his right. 'Take him to the barracks and lock him in the punishment room. Don't treat him gently.'

The two men sprang forward and roughly pulled Joshua to his feet. He had just time to kick the telescope into the undergrowth before they dragged him through the hanging branches onto the path, where a length of cord was produced and his wrists were bound tightly behind him. Prodded by cutlasses, he was marched quickly down the track and then up to the barracks. There, he was bundled into a dark room, completely bare of furniture and lit only by a barred window through which pale moonlight filtered. He was thrown down onto the earthen floor, kicked several times and left to lie, without cover of any kind, as the door was locked.

His cheek lying on the beaten earth, Josh lay, cursing. Then, he grimaced. Had Rowena left in time to evade Cunningham and his two men? He tried to concentrate. Yes, she would surely have seen the three leave the quayside and so be able to reach the doctor's house before she was discovered.

That, however, was small comfort. He was now completely at the mercy of Cunningham. It was a desperate situation. There was no point in worrying about the doctor now. There were more immediate problems to face.

CHAPTER FOURTEEN

Rowena had reached the door of the house when she suddenly remembered that she had left her father's telescope with Joshua. It was something he used every day and he would undoubtedly miss it if it was not returned to its place on the table in the hall. She turned to retrace her steps but stopped when she heard Cunningham's voice as he walked up from the harbour. She slipped inside the door, leaving it slightly ajar so that she could see through the gap.

As he came abreast of the doorway, she heard him say '. . . yes, in a bush which hangs over the little path . . . watching us . . .'

Horrified, Rowena put her hand to her mouth. Could she overtake them and warn Josh? No. There was now only one way to the bush and Cunningham and his Preventers were ahead of her. To call out would alert not only Cunningham but her father at the quayside.

What to do? Quickly, she made up her mind. Wrapping her shawl tightly around her shoulders, she pushed the door open a little wider and watched as the two men walked up the hill to where the little trail that clung to the cliff face branched off from the main path. Gently, she pushed the door fully open, slipped through it and closed it behind her. Then, keeping close to the wall, she followed the three men and watched them turn off onto the track.

Damn! There was no way she could warn Josh, all that she could do would be to see where they took him. Keeping a healthy distance, she followed them, slipping into the undergrowth and watching them as they stopped at the bush and pushed into its interior.

Josh almost immediately reappeared, his hands tied behind him and being prodded by cutlasses down the track towards her. She resisted the temptation to run at the two men, screaming and throwing her fists at them, and shrank even further into the long grass that fringed the path, watching as they passed. She waited until Cunningham strode by. No one was carrying the telescope, so she ran up the track, ducked into the hiding place and quickly seized the long glass from where Josh had kicked it into the grass.

Checking to make sure that there was no more human traffic on the track, she ran down the hill to where it met the path that climbed up to the barracks. She easily made out the tall figure of Cunningham striding down to the harbour and then, with more difficulty by the light of the now waning moon, the two Preventers pushing Joshua through the big door leading into the barracks.

Ah, the obvious place to keep him! But she knew that the interior was labyrinthine. In which of the many rooms would they incarcerate him? She could not possibly tell, and so, with great reluctance, she turned and made for the house, once more flitting from doorway to doorway in case the smugglers, having stored the contraband, came back up the street.

Carefully replacing the telescope on its stand, Rowena climbed the stairs to her room and sat by the slightly ajar window waiting for the men to return.

Within the hour, they did so, led by her father and Cunningham speaking in low voices. The two men paused under her window and Rowena gently pulled aside the curtain so that she could hear them. They were talking, of course, about Joshua and she strained to pick up the words that Cunningham was saying.

'. . . Off the Point, it's the only way . . .'

She drew in her breath in horror. But her father was disagreeing.

'No, no. There has been enough violence, Jack. Let me have him. If he gives us his word to say nothing, I will make sure he leaves for this fiancée of his in Dover. And even if he did betray us to the militia, who is going to believe the word of an itinerant sailor, who has already made one appearance in court, against that of the local coroner and of the Captain of the Preventers, eh?'

'I would rather be sure. There won't be any talking at all if we fling him from the Point.'

'No. I won't have that, Jack. I can handle him. Deliver him here in the morning.'

'Very well, have it your way. But he is an interfering, cocksure little swine and if it goes wrong, I shall blame you and I shall make sure that the truth about Emma gets out.'

'No, you mustn't do that, Jack. You promised.'

'You're too damned soft, Acland, that's your trouble. Make sure that Weyland says nothing, or I will make sure for myself.

Now I'm off to bed. At least we had a good run tonight.'

'Aye, I suppose so.' The doctor's voice had taken on a tone of great sadness, but Rowena gave it no heed. She rested her head against the soft curtaining and looked unseeingly out into the dark street. What on earth did Cunningham mean by 'the truth about Emma'? And why was he using it as a threat against her father?

Hearing Acland mount the stairs, she hurriedly closed the window and slipped into bed fully clothed. She heard him softly open the door and, through half-closed eyes, she saw him look down on her, before closing the door and retiring to his own room.

CHAPTER FIFTEEN

Joshua had been too cold and uncomfortable to sleep on the cold earth and it was, then, a relief when he heard the key grate in the lock and his jailer cry, 'Get up, you lazy sod. It's another day and probably your last.'

He had tried, during the course of the long night, to rub the cords that bound his wrists against the bone handle of the knife that still rested in its sheath hanging from his belt at his back, but they resisted all his efforts. He felt quite sure that Cunningham would kill him now. After all, who – apart from Rowena – would miss him? Mary seemed to have given him up and the doctor was clearly in league with the Devil. He would make one last bid for freedom somehow, but how?

They took him, blinking, into the courtyard and he realised that it was shortly after dawn. The sun must have risen, for the sky was that dirty grey that often accompanied the low cloud and light drizzle of an autumn morning in the west of England. So how was he to go?

He realised that it would be by cold steel when he saw Cunningham emerge from the main building. He tensed. A head butt and a kick would perhaps delay the inevitable for a moment, but not for long. Nevertheless, he would administer some sort of pain before he died. The man deserved that, at least.

'Hah, good morning, Weyland.' Cunningham sauntered over, scratching his unshaven chin. 'You will never know how lucky you are, my snivelling Second Mate. You are not going to die, at least, not yet. The doctor, old fool that he is, has spoken for you. But let me tell you this.'

The large man, usually so elegant, but now dishevelled, clad in a dirty shirt and with his breath smelling of alcohol – French brandy? – pulled Joshua close to his face and spoke slowly and very quietly. 'If you try and tell anyone what you saw last night,' he said, 'you won't be believed, for it will be only your word against that of the doctor and myself. But if you try, I will tear out your throat as I did Drake's.' He held up his hook. 'And I will hang you from the same tree where I strung up young Drake. So get out of here and find your whore in Kent, or wherever she is. And stay there.'

He flung Josh away from him so that the young man staggered and nearly fell. 'Take him to the doctor's house,' Cunningham snarled, 'but don't let anyone see you doing it.' Then he strode away.

Joshua realised that he had been holding his breath and he exhaled now and shook his head. So he was not to die! And he owed his life to Doctor Acland – or, more likely, Rowena.

It was too early for anyone to be about in the little hamlet and no one saw the two Preventers throw him against the door of the doctor's house, knee him in the groin and then raise the knocker and let it fall. It was a wide-eyed Rowena who opened the door almost instantaneously and put her arms around Joshua and then helped him inside.

She turned to the Preventers. 'Get away from here and, if you value your lives, never let me see you again.' Her face was white but her eyes, cold black, were flashing. They turned and made off, walking quickly.

'Bring him into the surgery, Emma, and please don't make such a noise, so early in the morning.' The doctor's voice was cool and balanced, almost mellifluous. Josh, still bent over from the blow to his genitals, staggered into the surgery and sat on the edge of a chair, turning his back and mutely offering up his wrists so that his bindings could be cut.

'Did those swines hurt you, Josh?' Rowena was full of concern.

Josh shook his head. 'I think not,' he muttered. 'Nothing serious. I will live.' He looked up at Rowena beseechingly. 'Would it be possible to have a cup of tea, do you think? I have had nothing to eat or drink for some time now.' He realised that he sounded pathetic but he did not care.

He looked up at the doctor as Rowena scuttled off to the kitchen. 'So, Doctor,' he said. 'What do you propose to do with me now? I know everything, as, of course, you are aware.'

The doctor nodded and, rather unexpectedly, asked, 'How is your leg now?'

'What? Oh, much better I think, thank you. I can walk and even run.'

'Good. Now we should talk. Thanks to you and your interference here, young man, Emma knows everything. Which is not what I intended, but it can't be helped now. Actually, she does not quite know . . .' The doctor's voice broke for a moment before he resumed '. . . everything. She overheard a conversation I had with Cunningham last night and she has demanded to know the meaning of it. I told her I would tell her after your arrival this morning, for, thanks to your activities here, Weyland, I feel I must now make a clean breast of . . . as I said . . . everything. In fact, it will be almost a relief.'

He looked up and gave Rowena a weary smile as she bustled back into the room. 'Ah, tea and scones for us all. Well done, dear. I realise I am quite hungry too. Please pour and let us be comfortable before I make my, er, confession.'

Joshua looked frowningly from father to daughter. He thought that he knew what would be coming but not, perhaps, 'everything', whatever that was. He sipped the tea gratefully and took a huge bite from the scone. He could hardly refrain from smiling as he savoured the rapid transformation from near execution in a cold courtyard at dawn to taking tea in the comfort of an English country cottage. But the doctor was beginning.

'I must first of all confess,' he said, his face quite grey in the bleak light that came through the windows, 'that I have shamelessly been a customer of the smugglers that have always operated, it seems, on this coast.' He waved his hand. 'You can see that I have a liking for fine china and other foreign *objets d'art* and you yourself, Weyland, have sampled my, ah, imported French cognac.'

'Yes, Father,' Rowena nodded her head, 'and you may not have realised but I always felt that you were a good customer of the smugglers.' She quickly added, 'And I thought none the less of you for that, for smuggling has always been practised here, I knew.'

The doctor nodded his head gravely. 'Yes, well, thank you for that, my dear. Now, however, there is more. I never wanted to know who was behind the smuggling ring here and I never enquired. It was young Pengelly who would supply me with what I needed, but I knew he was not the leader. I did not, however, ever suspect the commander of the Preventers himself of organising and running the ring.'

'How did you find out?' asked Joshua.

'Yes, well, I am coming to the point of my story. But, pray, do drink your tea, both of you.'

Obediently, they lifted cups to lips.

'One day,' the doctor continued, 'Cunningham came to see me. You will both know that we served together many years ago on a ship of the Blue Cross Line and after our shipwreck he had come to live here where I practised, he commanding the Preventers. His arrival, I may add, was a pure coincidence. So we knew each other well.'

The doctor bit into his scone and brushed the crumbs into his cupped hand fastidiously, depositing them onto his plate. 'I enjoyed very much living in Hartland Quay, becoming good friends with the Reverend Hawker. He looked after the spiritual well-being of his flock and I their physical health. The problem was that being a country doctor here brought me very little income to fund my, ah, indulgence in good wine and fine art. Inevitably, I ran into debt.

'News of my position reached Cunningham and, as I say, he came to see me. He revealed that he had established a thriving business by employing people, mainly from the village up above here, in smuggling, aided and abetted by Pengelly and his friend Jem Drake, who led the seafaring side of the smuggling ring, using their local knowledge and fine sailing skills. Do you follow?'

Joshua and Rowena nodded, now completely intrigued by the story being unfolded to them.

'Cunningham, however, wanted someone who could help him with the . . . what shall I call it . . . the administration of this business. Someone who could help with the forensic side of things, the distribution and so on. Would I assume this responsibility? Well, frankly, I had no desire to become so involved, but it offered me a way of paying off my debts, which were now growing, for Cunningham could pay well. So reluctantly, I agreed.'

Rowena was now leaning forward and frowning. 'But, Papa, how could I possibly become involved?'

Acland's face now seemed quite drawn. 'Yes, my dear, I am coming to that and I warn you that you will not welcome what I have to tell you.'

'What is it, Father? What is it?'

'Be patient, child, I must tell this story in my own way.'

'I am sorry, Papa. Please continue.'

'Very well. I was able in this way to pay off my debts and continue to indulge in my purchasing – at very affordable prices, of course – of contraband goods. But I became more and more uneasy at being directly involved in what was – is – a criminal activity. It was all very well being a customer, but very much a different matter being part of the management, so to speak. So I told Cunningham that I wished to discontinue working with him in this matter.'

Joshua leant forward. 'Which he did not like, presumably?'

The doctor shot him a keen glance. 'Indeed so. It seems, you see, that I had become invaluable to the running of this disreputable business. So he became threatening.' Acland turned wearily to his daughter. 'And this is where you come in, my dear.'

'What? What? How could I?'

Joshua realised that he knew now what was coming and he bent his head and rested it in his hand.

The old man took a deep breath. 'If I did not continue helping him, Cunningham swore to tell all world and, indeed, to tell you in particular, that the woman who was my late wife and whom you thought to be your mother, was not, in fact, so.'

Rowena's jaw dropped. 'What do you mean? My mother was not my mother.'

'She never was your mother, my dear. You see,' the doctor sighed, 'just as my wife became pregnant with our first and only child, I fell in love with a . . . a . . .' his voiced faded for a moment . . . 'a most beautiful Gypsy girl who was passing through the village and I lay with her. So the two women whom I loved desperately became pregnant at roughly the same time. Both, alas, died in childbirth and I was unable to save my wife or our child. But I was able to save you, my dear, although your Gypsy mother died.'

Now it was the turn of Acland to put his head in his hand. 'I did my best to keep this a secret in the village, although I sensed it had leaked out. Nevertheless, I did not wish you to realise that you were . . . were, well a bastard child, of ignoble birth and born of my sin.' The old man looked up, now with a solitary tear trickling down his cheek. 'I pretended that I had adopted you to replace my other child, who was also a daughter by the way. I could not face you 'knowing the truth, so I did what Cunningham bade me to do and carried on smuggling.'

'So you mean,' Rowena spoke slowly, as though trying to grasp the truth, 'that the grave where I have been laying flowers for so long does not contain the remains of my mother?'

'That is so, my dear. You see the Reverend Hawker, such a broad-minded man, so truly a Christian, who baptised you, knew the truth and offered to have your mother interred quietly in his churchyard in Morwenstow, where she lies now. When I can, I lay flowers on her grave.'

He heaved a great sigh. 'There, now you have the truth. I was always going to tell you but wanted to wait until you were older. But,' he smiled, 'you are very much your mother's daughter, my love; full of her fire and warmth of heart. Cunningham always wanted to marry you but I told him that if he persisted in his suit, I would tell the militia of his activities and damn the consequences. So in the end,' he smiled sadly, 'we each seemed to be blackmailing the other. Comic if it were not so tragic.'

Rowena sat for a while, her face a mixture of emotions. Joshua wanted to enfold her in his arms to comfort her, but what could he say? He realised that he had to stay merely an observer of one of life's tragedies, although he had been responsible for revealing it.

Eventually, Rowena reached out and took her father's hand. 'Nothing you have told me, Papa, diminishes my love for you. I now will put flowers on the graves of both of my mothers, and yes' – she looked across at Joshua – 'I think I know where my real mother's grave is.' She tightened her grip on her father's hand. 'Well now you can tell Cunningham to do what he likes, for I now know the truth. You must stop smuggling, Father. You can do so now.'

Slowly a smile spread across the seamed face of the doctor. 'Thank you, my child. You can never know how much those words mean to me.'

Joshua cleared his throat. 'I am loath to interrupt your story, sir.'

'Oh, I have finished it now.'

'Not quite, sir. This morning, in threatening to have me killed if I stayed here, Cunningham admitted that he had killed Jem Drake.'

'What?' The doctor looked genuinely astonished.

'Yes. If I remember his words – and they were spoken only a short time ago, in fact – he said that if I did not leave this area soon he would cut my throat and string me up to the same tree where he had hoisted Jem Drake.'

The doctor sat in silence for a moment. 'I am astonished,' he said eventually. 'I knew that he was a strong, evil man but I never believed he was capable of cold-blooded murder.'

'Oh, Father, you don't really know him, even after all these years.' Rowena spoke quickly, her face now flushed. 'It was he who ordered Tom Pengelly and Drake to attack Joshua, and, despite all that he has always said about wanting to marry me, he set his Preventers onto Josh and me when we were picnicking on the Point. I am sure we would have been tossed over its edge, if it had not been for the arrival of the tinners.'

Josh now spoke again, in a quiet, firm voice. 'You examined Jem's body, Doctor. Who did you think had killed him?'

'Well, at first, I thought it was you and, indeed, Cunningham virtually convinced me. Then, later, I thought it unlikely that a man still hobbling on crutches with an injured leg could have overpowered such a strong young man as Drake.'

'But you testified against me when I was accused of murder.'

'Yes, but, if you remember, I gave no hard evidence of any kind connecting you with the murder. It was all very circumstantial—'

Josh interrupted: 'And you hired and paid for the lawyer acting in my defence, for which I thank you.'

Acland grimaced and looked up at the ceiling. 'Well, that is certainly true, but . . .' He paused and looked shamefacedly at them both in turn. 'I have to confess that I have always been ambivalent about you, my boy. I felt that you should be defended professionally and no one else could arrange that but me.'

'Yes.' Joshua nodded. 'And, again, I thank you for that.'

'But what you don't know is that I deliberately chose a young, half-trained solicitor who appeared to me to have not the faintest idea of how to conduct a defence. And that proved to be true.'

Rowena threw back her head. 'Oh, Father. How could you?'

The old man moved his head from side to side. 'It's that ambivalence again, you see. I wasn't sure if you were guilty or not, so I chose a ridiculous halfway house sort of compromise, hiring an idiot to defend you and leaving the verdict in the hands of God and the magistrate. I knew Sir George as a good man and rather left it to him to identify the undoubted prejudice that existed in that courtroom. There was another fact, however, of which I am ashamed.'

'What was that, Father?'

'I was jealous of this young man, cast up from the sea and into our lives. I knew that you cared for him and I was afeared that he would take you away from me. Again, I took the route of compromise and, if you remember, did not attend the court again, after giving my evidence. I pretended to be ill, but was not. I just wanted no

308

part of the decision for or against you. That was quite wrong and I apologise.'

Joshua nodded slowly. 'You have answered several questions that remained in my mind, Doctor,' he said. 'But I must return to one more point.'

Acland regarded him intently, his face ashen. 'Yes?'

'The light that showed during the storm—' The doctor began to interrupt, but Josh held up his hand. 'You don't believe it existed but I was there and you were not. *I saw it, Doctor*. I want to know why Cunningham would do such a thing.'

'Ah, I wish I knew. I can't imagine why he should kill Drake nor why he, a former sailor, should lure fellow seamen to their deaths. It just doesn't make sense.'

Rowena was switching her gaze between the two men and opened her mouth to speak, but Josh held up his hand.

'I have been thinking about all of this intently,' he said. 'Indeed I pondered it all night long as I lay in that cell at the barracks and I think I have come up with a motive for both acts.'

'Pray proceed, I shall listen closely.'

'I think that, if we check the records, we shall find that the ships that were lost *with all hands* at Morwenstow over, say, the last decade, were Blue Cross vessels. Just as with *The Lucy*, they were driven hard onto the black rocks below the vicarage in a fierce storm. When they realised where they were heading, it was too late, for they were sailing expecting to find a safe anchorage, lured in by the false light. Other ships, sailing under different pennants, were often able to make a passage around the Point and escape the rocks, because there was no light enticing them in.'

The doctor lifted his eyebrows. 'So?'

'I remember well Cunningham's evidence at the hearing at the inn here. He was almost incandescent with rage at the Blue Cross's record of poor maintenance of their vessels and even poorer seamanship.'

'Yes, he feels even more strongly than I on this point.'

'Quite so. I believe that Cunningham makes careful note of when a Blue Cross vessel comes up the Channel. He has all the recent Lloyd's Registers in his room, so he is able to check. Those who make the passage in fine weather, of course, he can do nothing about. But the ships in some distress in foul weather are his prey and he lures them onto the rocks. In other words, he is conducting a deadly vendetta against the owners of the Line, for what they did to him when you lost most of your shipmates at Bude years ago. The man, of course, is quite unbalanced.'

A silence leaden with horror fell on the room. It was Rowena who broke it. 'But Josh,' she said, 'how does the death of Jem Drake fit into all this?'

'That has been puzzling me, too. I believe, though, that the answer lies in my reaction when I first saw his body hanging. Do you remember?'

'Well, no. I can't quite recall . . .'

'I said that the body was left swinging there as a warning. A warning perhaps to others in his band of smugglers or even among the Preventers, who threaten to give him away to the militia. A terrible warning that he would kill – murder – if he had to.'

The doctor nodded. 'Can you prove any of this, Joshua? I agree that your reasoning has credibility, but we will need proof.'

'Only circumstantial evidence, Doctor. You see, what set me

thinking was the fact that Pengelly and Drake saved me. They virtually entered the sea at the height of the storm to pull me off that rock and carry me up the cliff to safety with Row—Emma. I could not understand why, after saving my life – and Cunningham would have undoubtedly had me killed, if they had not done so, for he wanted no witnesses of the light – they should attack me later, almost certainly at Cunningham's bidding. And attack me they did, because I saw the marks made on them by my knife, but they attacked without any real menace. I was able to frighten them away, merely with my seaman's knife, so to speak. And particularly, Drake whose heart was certainly not in it.'

'Yes, but you have not yet explained why Cunningham should kill that young man.'

'The key lies in the fact that Pengelly and Drake were smugglers, yes, but they were also true sailors, seafaring men, not Preventers. My theory is that they had never been part of the luring-light disgrace. True seamen would never lure other seafarers and their ships to destruction and death. I am a seaman and I can sense that.'

Rowena frowned. 'But they were there that night, as part of the gang.'

'They were not part of the gang. They were there for the reason that they gave: to help rescue any men saved from the sea and the rocks. What they saw that night, with the brazier burning away and being fed to keep it going as a lure to *The Lucy*, I think disgusted them. It weighed most heavily on young Drake, as I sensed when I met them both later at the inn at the quay. I believe that he decided to confront Cunningham with the truth and threaten him with giving evidence against him to the militia. So Cunningham killed him and strung him up as a warning to Pengelly and any of the smugglers or the Preventers tempted to be disloyal to him. The man, of course, is a despot as well as an unhinged criminal. Then he threatened to turn Pengelly in as a smuggler, captured by the Preventers, if he opposed him, or even tried to leave the gang. It all fits, you see.'

The doctor nodded slowly. 'I see that. But we still need proof. How can we get it?'

'I don't know, but I sense that Pengelly is the key to it. If I can persuade him to give evidence against Cunningham, it might be enough, together with what we ourselves have seen, to turn the scales against him.'

Rowena leant across and seized his arm. 'But Josh, how can we do all this without incriminating Father in the smuggling – and Tom Pengelly, for that matter?'

Acland raised his hand. 'Oh, I am quite prepared to take my medicine, if we can put this beast of a man up on the gallows.'

'No, Father. They could still send you away to the Colonies and I couldn't bear that.'

Silence again fell on the room, only broken by a distant whinny from Acland's mare in the stables.

'No.' Joshua shook his head. 'I agree with Emma. We don't want that. But let me talk to Pengelly, anyway. We might be able to come up with a solution. Will he be at the harbour now, Doctor?'

'Yes.' The old man nodded sadly. 'There will be much work to do in taking the proceeds of last night's landing to our customers spread around the county.'

'Very well. I shall go now.'

Rowena leapt to her feet. 'I will come with you, Josh.'

Joshua shook his head. 'I would rather you stayed here, Rowena. Let me deal with this alone.'

'But what if the Preventers see you? You are supposed to have left for Kent, don't forget.'

'That doesn't matter. I must see Pengelly.'

The doctor now joined the other two standing. 'All of this,' he said, 'poses the question of what your intentions are regarding your, er, young lady in Dover. It would, of course, be much safer if you set off there at once. What do you intend?'

Joshua hesitated, for he was not sure now what he *did* intend to do. But Rowena answered for him. 'You must understand, Father,' she said coldly, 'that Joshua is a man of principle and honour. He has given his word to this lady and he will keep it. I understand and accept that. So go now, Josh, and speak to Tom Pengelly. Then come back here and say goodbye.'

Josh didn't know what to say, so he merely nodded mutely. Then he made his way into the street and strode down towards the quay, exuding a confidence he did not feel.

The men at the kilns were busying themselves and he had no idea if they were among the gang but he could see Pengelly working his dinghy around the head of the wall to meet one of the smacks about to enter the harbour. Josh wasn't sure how he was going to approach him, so he was glad of the opportunity to sit on a bollard for a moment to collect his thoughts.

Once again, he admired the skill of the young man as he took his hobbler towards the smack, throwing the line adroitly on board at just the right moment, so that the slack could be taken up and the smack swung round the curve of the wall. A good sailor, then, but a smuggler!

As Pengelly rowed his hobbler back to the slipway, Josh called down to him. 'Tom, I must talk to you. It is urgent.'

He saw the surprise on the man's face and realised that the news of his capture by Cunningham must have spread, so that his reappearance had clearly taken Pengelly aback. But he nodded. 'Let me make fast and I will talk to you behind the shed over there,' he indicated the building.

'Now, what do you want with me, then?' They were standing behind the shed, in a small space between the wall of the building and the sheer face of the cliff, out of sight of any onlookers.

'I want to talk about Jem.'

Pengelly turned his sun-browned face to look away, up towards the clifftop.

'What's there to say about him? He's dead and that's all there is to it.'

'No it's not. Cunningham has told me – less than an hour ago – that it was he who killed him. But I expect you know that, don't you?'

'What if I do?'

'Jem was your friend, wasn't he?'

'Course he was. Best friend I ever 'ad.'

'Don't you want to bring his murderer to justice?'

Pengelly shifted his weight from one foot to the other and stared at his sea boot. 'I don't know what you're after and I don't see 'ow anything can be done about the poor lad's passing.'

Josh sighed. 'Look, I know you are in the smugglers' ring and I know that you are a vital part of the whole business. But as a seaman myself, I am surprised that you are involved in luring vessels onto the Morwenstow rocks and the killing of fellow seamen.'

'What?' For the first time, Pengelly's surliness disappeared and was replaced by a look of anger. 'I never was involved in anythin' of the kind. I would never kill a fellow sailor. You ought to know that, for it was Jem an' me who pulled you off that rock an' took you to the top an' safety.'

'Yes, and I'm grateful for that. But to carry me up, you must have passed the brazier that was kept burning through the storm to bring in *The Lucy* onto the rocks. You must have seen it.'

Pengelly's expression changed, his anger replaced by a look of contrition. 'Yes, well, we hadn't seen it at first because we'd come down to the shingle by the side o' the stream that comes down to the beach. We couldn't carry you back that way because it was too wet an' slippery. So we went up the path. That's when we saw the light a'blazin' away, despite the wind an' rain.'

'Good, so you did see it.'

'Course we saw it. That's why we 'ad the blazin' row with the captain, after we'd loaded you onto Rowena's cart.'

'What row was that, then?'

'We told him that what he was doin' was wrong an' if he didn't dowse the light, we'd report him to the militia.'

'How did he react to that?'

'He told us to mind our own business. But the light was out by this time, anyway. So there wasn't much we could do about it.'

'Did Cunningham threaten you?'

The young man nodded slowly. 'Oh yes, he said that if we told anyone about the light he would turn us into the militia as smugglers, caught by his gallant band of Preventers.' His tone had lapsed into sarcasm. 'An' that would mean deportation, for it would be our word against his – and probably the doctor's, too.'

'But why would he kill Jem, then?'

'Because dear old Jem, although he was quite a meek-mannered chap, also had backbone.' Pengelly looked at the ground. 'More than I 'ad, as it turned out. Later on, he told me that he was gettin' out of smuggling and was goin' to tell Cunningham. I warned him not to an' I thought he had taken my advice, but then he disappeared and I knew that Cunningham 'ad seen to 'im.'

'Look. The doctor has decided to get out of all of this and accuse Cunningham and, if necessary, to confess to smuggling. If you would tell the militia and a court of law what you have just told me, between all of us, we could get this man hanged.'

Pengelly threw back his head. 'Oh yes. An' the doctor an' me will end up in – where is it? Australia, wherever that is, for smugglin'. I can't do that an' you know it.'

'That's not necessarily true. If I could negotiate an agreement with Sir George Lansbury, the magistrate up in Barnstaple, guaranteeing the freedom of yourself and the doctor in return for giving evidence against Cunningham and his Preventers, would you do it?'

The sailor frowned. 'An' what would 'is word be worth? I'm just a humble seafarin' man, with no influence. The doctor might get off, but not me. Look, I can't stand an' talk here any longer. There are two smacks to be brought in yet and I can smell that bad weather is on its way. Why don't you take Rowena with you and bugger off to where you first started from. Hartland Quay, at least, will be glad to see the back of you.'

He turned on his heel and strode away.

Joshua shook his head in frustration. Was no one else going to stand up against Jack Cunningham? He walked to the quayside.

Pengelly was right, black clouds – *very black clouds* – were forming low on the horizon to the north-west. It looked as though a very severe storm was brewing.

Reluctantly, he made his way back to the doctor's house and was met by an anxious Rowena.

'What did he say?'

'He will not give evidence against Cunningham. He is frightened of deportation.'

'So, what will you do now?'

'Oh, I don't know, Rowena. I just don't know. I am not sure that just your father's evidence, backed up by us, would be sufficient to persuade the militia to make an arrest. Frankly, I just don't know what else we can do.'

Rowena drew herself to her full height. 'Then, my dear, you must get on with your life. Leave us here and go to your Mary. We will be all right. I shall look after Father, Cunningham knows that. If he touches a hair on his head I shall kill him myself.'

Josh couldn't resist a smile. 'I am sure you would, because you are the bravest, strongest and most beautiful girl in the whole world.'

Rowena grimaced and Josh could see that tears were not far away and wished he hadn't been so fulsome.

'So brave and beautiful that you will leave me for your fat fiancée in Dover? No. Don't answer that, I know you must go. When will you leave?'

'Will you and your father allow me to stay for one more night, anyway, while I think things through? At the moment, I am very tired and a bit confused.'

Immediately, Rowena's haughty air disappeared. 'Oh, my dear,' she said, putting her hand on his arm. 'I forgot that you spent a terrible night in the barracks. Now, go this minute to your room and take a rest. You don't need to leave until you are good and ready. Please . . .'

He nodded and climbed the stairs and threw himself onto his bed. He was tired but knew he had to face up to the choice he had to make. He lay quietly and summoned up the face of Rowena, black-eyed, always near to tears, impetuous and, it had become clear, probably Pengelly's lover. Then Mary, apple-cheeked, loyal, balanced and faithful, appeared. She had done nothing wrong, how could he betray her? Put like that, he knew what his decision must be. Almost relieved, he slipped into sleep.

A thunderclap that seemed to shake the house woke him and he realised that he must have slept through much of the daylight hours. Rain was now pounding the roof and windows and he decided that there was little left to do but to shed his clothes and slip between the sheets. At least his mind was made up.

He was awoken rudely by Rowena shaking him by the shoulder.

'Oh, Josh, Josh,' she cried. 'Get dressed please. It is after midnight and we are in the middle of a terrible storm. I heard Father going down the stairs and tried to stop him going out in this weather. But he tells me that he has seen with his telescope that there is a ship in great distress out in the Channel. He has consulted the Register and he believes it to be one of the Blue Cross vessels. He is sure that Cunningham will know this and try and lure it onto the rocks at Morwenstow. So Papa has rushed out, saddled his mare and ridden off to stop him. What's more, he has taken a cutlass with him. We must stop him.'

'Of course. Get dressed. Do you have oilskins?'

She nodded, wide-eyed.

'Good. Is your pony still up on the heath where I left him?'

'Yes, I meant to go and get him but I forgot.'

'Never mind. We will hitch up the donkey cart. I doubt if we can overtake your father but we might be able to get there before he gets himself into trouble. Go now.'

She nodded. Joshua threw on his clothing, pulled on his boots and ran down the stairs. On impulse, he ducked into the living room and took down the one remaining cutlass that hung over the mantelpiece, then, head lowered, he ran through the rain to the stables, where Rowena was already pushing the reluctant donkey between the shafts.

He nodded to her, feeling ridiculously relieved that he was being called upon to take some form of action, at least. 'Wrap up,' he called. 'I think it's going to be a long night.'

CHAPTER SIXTEEN

They pulled out onto the street, where the brown rain had turned the gutter into a millstream. Rowena had taken the reins, Josh acknowledging her to be the better driver, and she forced the poor donkey to head uphill into the wind and rain. The noise of the sea crashing against the harbour wall behind and below them demonstrated that this storm had developed into one of the worst of the nor'westerlies. Crouching beside Rowena, clutching the cutlass under his oilskin, Josh could not stop the words of the old cliché 'God help sailors on a night like this' running through his brain.

They were even more exposed, of course, once they had turned into the clifftop road to Morwenstow. Sleet was now mixed with the rain and stung their faces and eyes. 'Are you all right?' he mouthed to Rowena. She nodded her head and he could not help but marvel at the skill this young girl demonstrated now, as the donkey slipped and slithered in the mud, she holding him firmly, flicking the whip into the wind and onto his rump to keep him pulling forward.

Josh prayed that the doctor had been able to keep in the saddle on this exposed road in such conditions and, at every turn of the path, he half expected to see a riderless horse standing, shivering, at the clifftop edge. The old man, he reflected, must be as good a horseman as his daughter was a cart driver.

In such conditions, the journey that would normally have taken them just over an hour, lasted for nearly ninety minutes. As they crested the hill, leading down onto the plateau above the vicarage at Morwenstow, Joshua stood, clutching at Rowena's shoulder to steady himself and peered out to sea, which in all its foam-topped majesty, was sporadically lit by flashes of lightning.

Great billows of white-tipped waves were surging toward the shore from the north-west and yes, there she was! – a brigantine, running with only scraps of sail hoisted now, but still pressing, her starboard rail well underwater, to round Hartland Point. Certainly, there seemed to be no pushing the helm over to change her course towards Morwenstow. Had, then, their journey been in vain? Perhaps there was no brazier lit halfway down the cliff face? Certainly, there was no sign of Preventers here on the clifftop.

Motioning Rowena to halt and tie up the donkey, he slid down the side of the cart – wincing a little as the old wound twinged – and hurried down, past the vicarage, huddling safely against the storm in its niche in the hillside, and began the perilous descent down to the rocks and the little shingled beach. He stopped for a moment and sniffed the air. Yes, he thought so. Smoke – smoke from a brazier was being borne inland on the wind. It must be down ahead, where

321

it was before, on the little shelf that was partly sheltered.

Suddenly, as the wind dropped momentarily, he heard a sound behind him on the path. Whirling, he saw Tom Pengelly, slipping and sliding towards him, cutlass in hand.

So this was to be the moment of truth, here on the cliff face!

He pulled his own cutlass from under his waterproof and prepared to defend himself. But Pengelly, hardly pausing in his run down the path, waved him to stand away and rushed by him, pushing him against the mossy cliff face to make room for his passage. He disappeared, still descending in great leaps, as sure-footed as a mountain goat.

And then, inevitably, Rowena came into view, doing her best to hurry downwards but hampered by her long oilskin and the slippery surface. He gestured to her to go back but, her face hidden by the hood of the waterproof, she shook her head violently.

Torn between following Pengelly in the hope of preventing whatever mischief he might create and waiting for Rowena to help her down the path, he decided to wait. She could so easily slip and be pitched down onto the rocks below. He held out his hand and, with a gasp, she took it.

'Did you see Pengelly?' he shouted.

'Yes,' she was sucking in rain and air desperately to fill her lungs.

'What the hell was he going to do with that cutlass?'

'Going to rescue Father. He had seen him from his cottage window going down the path and ran after him.'

'Good Lord! Let me go on, too. You wait here.'

He knew she would not and, sure enough, as soon as he turned and continued his descent she followed him down, one hand on the cliff face to steady her descent.

Sparks from the brazier were now being borne on the wind and flashing past his head as he grew nearer to the little plateau. Then, as he rounded a bend in the path, he saw the fiery light, in exactly the position that had been betrayed by the ring of ash he and Rowena had found. This time, however, the shelf was lit by the glow from the brazier and further illuminated by sporadic flashes of lightning, as though some heavenly stage manager was turning up the spot lamps to dramatise the scene being played out below.

There was no need to dramatise it, however, as Joshua stopped in his tracks and held out his hand to warn Rowena, close behind him.

Doctor Acland lay on the turf, clutching at his shoulder where blood was oozing between his fingers from a savage cut from, obviously, a cutlass. Cunningham, painted a fiendish figure now by the brazier, was stacking the fire with brushwood and what looked like faggots, a bloodstained cutlass thrust into the ground at his feet.

Then Josh saw Pengelly, crouched by the side of the doctor and partly hidden by a projection of rock. The young man was desperately trying to fix a neckerchief around Acland's shoulder to stem the bleeding. He tied a knot at last and slowly rose to his feet, cutlass in hand. He shouted something at Cunningham who, probably seeing him for the first time, laughed at him, his teeth flashing in the brazier's light, picked up his cutlass and beckoned Pengelly forward with a derisive, wagging finger.

Pengelly shouted again and then bounded forward, his sword blade high above his shoulder.

'No,' cried Josh, but his voice was lost in the howl of the wind.

The young sailor had obviously never taken a fencing lesson in his life, but the anger and hatred he expressed now in his wild swinging of the cutlass had the effect of making Cunningham duck and dance around that firelit arena as though the Devil himself was bearing down on him.

Josh dropped to one knee to look out to sea beneath the glare of the brazier to see if the brig had altered course. At first, he could not make out her direction, but then he could see the foreshortening of the hull as the wheel was turned. Damn! She had taken the bait and was heading now straight for the rocks. It was enough, and with the despairing cry of Rowena in his ears, he bounded down the last few feet of the path and, ignoring the two combatants, he made for the brazier, hooked the blade of his cutlass between the iron bars of the cradle and wrenched it around, so that, with a crackling hiss, its burning contents fell to the ground, sending a shower of sparks to be borne away by the wind. The light of the fire was still there, but it was defused immediately by the burning brands being scattered around on the sodden turf.

Still ignoring Cunningham and Pengelly, Josh stamped around the shelf, kicking away the embers so that they sizzled and died. Rowena's scream made him turn. Cunningham had brought Pengelly to the ground and had thrust the point of the cutlass into his breast. Then, in one terrifying movement, he swung his hook back and down and slashed open the young sailor's throat so that blood gushed from it in a crimson torrent.

But Rowena's scream had alerted Cunningham as well and he looked up and saw Joshua. He had stripped off his uniform jacket and his sodden, white shirt was clinging to his body as though bonded to it, his hair was plastered to his forehead and he now advanced on Joshua with the light tread of a fencing master, his bloodstained blade pointed directly at him.

He shouted above the raging of the wind and rain. 'Second Mate.

You seem to have completely ruined my life here. It is time, therefore, to cut out your heart and throw it into the surf. But first, I shall make you bleed and give you pain. Look out!'

He feinted to Josh's face and then bent low and thrust forward to the midriff. Clumsily, Joshua parried the move.

He tore off his heavy oilskins to free his arms and then threw them to one side. 'You're mad, Cunningham,' he shouted. 'Look, the ship has put about and is making out to sea again. She sees no light now, you deranged swine. Your work here is done. Even your Preventers have disappeared.'

Cunningham replied, his white teeth gleaming in his dark face, by stamping forward and attempting to repeat the move that had disarmed Josh on their previous encounter – sliding his blade down that of Josh's, engaging the point in the hand protector and, flicking the wrist to throw the weapon away. Josh, however, remembered the move and countered by forcing his opponent's blade downwards. Cunningham immediately swung his blade upwards in a circular motion and tried to then bring it down vertically. But the move was telegraphed and Josh skipped away.

For a moment, the two men stood, breasts heaving, regarding each other. 'You won't win here, Weyland,' shouted Cunningham. 'You are an amateur, facing a professional. This will be the death of a thousand cuts for you, Mr Mate. *En garde!*'

And he advanced, flickering his blade point, forcing Josh to move backward. Then he made a lightning thrust and his point brought blood from the upper part of Josh's left arm.

'Just a touch, you see,' shouted Cunningham. 'But it hurts, doesn't it? There are plenty more to come.'

Once more he stamped forward, always using the point of the clumsy weapon, thrusting with it as though it was a rapier or foil. Somehow, Josh survived this latest onslaught, holding his blade high and parrying each thrust.

Round and round they circled, with Cunningham usually attacking and Joshua somehow defending, blocking, ducking and occasionally rallying, albeit clumsily. The end almost came when, retreating again before the thrusts of the big man, Joshua stumbled on the slippery turf, just where Rowena was tending her father. Josh went down on one knee and his cutlass slipped from his fingers.

Immediately, Cunningham stamped on the blade preventing Josh from retrieving it. He stood for a moment, looking down and grinning at his helpless opponent, savouring the moment. Then, he drew back his cutlass to deliver the *coup de grâce*.

It was then that Rowena threw into his face the handful of gravel that she had been nursing and waiting for an opportunity to deliver since the duel began. The tiny stones caught Cunningham in the eye and, as he cursed and tried to clear his vision, this gave Josh just time to regain his sword and his footing, parrying the two vicious swings that were now directed at his head.

It was becoming clear, however, that although Cunningham had the superior skill, he was facing a much younger man, who, unlike the Preventers' captain, had spent his whole life at sea, climbing rigging, hauling on heavy sheets and struggling while holding helms against strong currents. He lacked Joshua's fitness and his constant attacks were making him gasp for breath now and, frantically, to look around for some new form of attack.

It was now Josh's turn to move forward and, feinting to the right, he thrust to the left, his blade cutting through the other's shirt and grazing his skin. The cut, though superficial, caused Cunningham to wince and, for the first time, Josh saw fear come into the captain's eyes. Perspiration was mingling with the rain that coursed down the man's cheeks and, sensing Cunningham's tiredness, Josh decided to use brute force. Forsaking any attempts at finesse, and ignoring the pain from the flesh wound in his arm, he swung his heavy blade down, beating aside Cunningham's listless parry and then looping it round horizontally, cutting into the man's neck and producing a gush of blood.

Cunningham uttered an oath and, dropping his cutlass, he put his good hand to his neck to stem the bleeding. At the same time, he staggered backwards and, then, on the edge of the ridge, he slipped on a wet rock. There was nothing to save him and, with a scream, he fell backwards down onto the jumbled, foam-covered rocks some forty feet below.

A breathless Joshua fell to his knees and crawled to the edge. He just had time to see Cunningham's body being tossed on the crest of a wave and thrown down onto the very rock that had held his own body. The man desperately clawed at the rock's slippery surface to gain some purchase but to no avail. Back he slipped into the surfing water, a trace of blood now just discernible on the white foam. He raised one despairing hand, as though in supplication, before being pulled beneath the surface. Josh stayed watching, but the captain's body did not surface again.

He suddenly realised that Rowena was by his side. 'Oh, Josh,' she cried. 'Has he gone? Is he really dead at last?'

'I think so.' Josh breathed heavily to regain his breath. 'Nothing could live in that sea. He will be ground like chaff against the rocks, becoming . . . what is that awful word? Yes, a gobbet.' He shuddered. 'Thank you for doing what you did back there. You undoubtedly saved my life. Oh, but sorry, I had forgotten. What about Pengelly and your father?'

He could see the tears on her cheeks. 'Oh, Josh. Tom is dead, brutally killed by that terrible man. But Father, I think, will be all right.' She tried to smile. 'He is tough as old leather and he now has a good nurse to look after him.'

They both turned and looked back at where the doctor was painfully crawling on his hands and knees towards Pengelly. He reached the body of the young man and examined the dreadful cut to the throat. Then he looked across at the couple and shook his head negatively.

Josh nodded. 'Yes, the poor boy's gone, Rowena. He obviously had had enough of Cunningham and was trying to avenge his friend Jem.' He looked round. 'But where are the Preventers? I thought I would have to fight them all to get near Cunningham.'

'Yes, Father was able to tell me while I was tending his wound. He came down here, of course, on his own. When he arrived, Cunningham was stacking the brazier and the Preventers were unloading the wood. Papa said that there weren't many of them so perhaps some had already deserted the captain. Papa turned on them and told them that he had written to the magistrate accusing them all of murder, with Cunningham as the ringleader. He said that the militia was on its way and urged them to flee before it arrived and not to be seen here or at the barracks again.'

She smiled. 'It was all lies, of course. Father can be very dominating and strong when he tries. They fled immediately, going down to the path by the stream because they expected the militia to come down the way we came. That's why we didn't see them as we scrambled down.' Then she gave a sob. 'It was then that Cunningham, his old shipmate, tried to kill Papa.

'Father fended him off with his own cutlass for a while, but eventually he was wounded in the shoulder. Cunningham would certainly have killed Papa, but he knew he had to keep the brazier burning, so he turned back to it. As a result, Tom was able to pull Father away and somehow bandage his wound before launching himself against Cunningham.'

She paused a moment to regain her composure. 'Josh,' she said, 'I am so glad it's all over . . . ah, my goodness, you've been hurt. I had forgotten. Here let me see.'

'Oh, it's only a pinprick. But I am not quite sure that it *is* all over, Rowena. Look, we must go back to your father. At his age, a wound like that will be very serious.'

'Yes, of course. But I have been able to stop the bleeding so I think he will be all right. Yes, but, oh Josh. What are we going to do about Tom? We can't leave him here.'

Joshua nodded. 'Of course not. Now, do you think your father is strong enough to climb the path to the top if you help him?'

'Yes, I think so, if we take it slowly.'

'Good. I think I have just about enough puff left to carry up Tom's body. Let's try, anyway. We can't stop here all night.' He looked up at the sky and then out to sea. 'Thank God it looks as though the storm has mainly passed over and the brig must have turned the Point, for there is no sign of her.'

He walked to where the bloodstained corpse of Tom Pengelly lay, crumpled on the ground. He turned to Rowena. 'He lived here in Morwenstow, did he not?'

'Yes, he lived alone after his mother died and, apart from his friendship with Jem, kept himself very much to himself.'

'Hmm.' Joshua pondered for a moment. 'Go and see to your father. I will be over in a minute.'

Puzzled, Rowena nodded and then ran to where her father was attempting to struggle to his feet.

Josh knelt over the body of the young sailor and, with his thumb, pulled down the eyelids. He bent his head and murmured: 'I'm not sure that what I'm proposing to do, Tom, would be approved of by the good Lord or the Reverend Hawker, for that matter, but it's the only way I can see out of this mess. I hope you will forgive me, for the sea was your home, anyway.'

He stood and walked to where Rowena was pulling her father's good arm over her shoulder. 'Doctor,' he said to the old man, who regarded him with a weary smile. 'You did a very brave thing tonight and I salute you. Now, let your splendid daughter help you up this damned path and I will follow on carrying poor old Pengelly. Please start now, if you will.'

Rowena frowned. 'All right, Josh, but be very careful climbing the path carrying . . . carrying such a weight. It's still very slippery.'

'I will be careful. I need to get my breath back before beginning the climb. Off you go.'

Father and daughter, arms around each other, slowly began their climb and disappeared around a bend in the path. Joshua wrinkled his face in disgust and stood by Pengelly's body for a moment, before picking it up in his arms and staggering to the edge of the ledge. Then, closing his eyes he tipped it over the edge. He stood long enough to see the body bounce off the rocks and then slide into the still-agitated sea, disappearing beneath the surface almost at once.

'Goodbye, Tom,' he called. 'Forgive me.'

He turned and collected the three cutlasses and hurled them away, one by one, as far out to sea as he could. They bounced off the rocks into the water, sinking immediately. Then turned and began his climb.

At the top, he found Rowena carefully laying her father down on the straw, which had been scattered on the floor of the cart for just such a purpose, and covered him with her cloak. The old man now seemed unconscious. Josh climbed up and sat beside Rowena.

'Josh, where . . . where is Tom? What have you done with him?'

He put his hand to her cheek. 'He was a sailor and spent much of his life at sea, love,' he said. 'So I returned him to his spiritual home.'

She pushed away his hand and, her eyes wide in shock, put her own to her mouth in horror.

He clutched her other hand, squeezed it and began speaking quickly in a low voice: 'It was the best – the only – thing to do. There would have been all sorts of questions asked about his death and, indeed, that of Cunningham if we had brought Tom's body back. What is left of them both won't be found, if at all, for weeks yet and then they will be unrecognisable.'

Josh held her gaze. 'It was the only way out of this mess,' he continued. 'Of course they will both be missed, but who will suspect your father, me or you, for that matter, of being involved? The Preventers, what is left of them, will have scattered – although we must check on that. It will just be presumed that the storm and the sea had claimed Cunningham and Tom somehow. Men are disappearing all the time on this cruel coast, particularly in weather like this. Please, Rowena, don't be upset. What I did was for the best, don't you see that?'

She did not reply, remaining staring at him, as though still puzzled by the explanation. He shook out the oilskin that he had jettisoned when the duel began and retrieved for his climb up the path and carefully draped it over her shoulders. Then he took the reins from her fingers, shaking the pony into life.

They passed through the hamlet at the top of the cliff, seeing no one, for the ship had been too far out at sea for the news of its possible distress to have had time to be spread. Now she had escaped anyway, there was nothing to attract folk either to offer help or by the thought of salvage. So on they trotted, back to the quay, with no one to question their presence on the clifftop in the middle of such a dreadful night.

On reaching the house, Rowena helped her father, now conscious but appearing to be dazed, up the stairs to his room, Josh unhitched the cart, pushed the donkey back into his stall and rubbed him down.

Now thoroughly exhausted, he crept into the silent house. Noticing the door to the drawing room open and with one candle burning low, he entered and realised that, blessedly, the key to the drinks cupboard was still in place. He carefully selected the best vintage cognac and poured three fingerfuls into a glass. Then, sighing, he sprawled into a cushioned chair, sipped the brandy and thought of the journey ahead of him.

CHAPTER SEVENTEEN

He slept late the next day and rose when he heard Rowena moving around in the next bedroom. He slipped into his clothes and, knocking on the door, entered the doctor's room.

'Ah,' said Rowena, giving him a warm smile, 'I need your help. Father's wound must be stitched. I can do it, for I have always been a good needlewoman, but I must bathe the wound first. Can you please heat some water and bring it in in that little bowl? Thank you.'

Josh was amazed at the change in the girl. It seemed as though, now there was something positive to be done, all her dazed despair at the death of Tom Pengelly and the brutal disposal of his body had dissolved and been replaced by her usual down-to-earth positiveness. He breathed a sigh of relief, lifted an eyebrow interrogatively and nodded at her father, who was sitting up in bed surrounded by pillows but seemed still asleep.

'Laudanum,' she whispered. 'It's the only anaesthetic I could find. It seems to be working. Now, come along, Nurse. Hot water, please.'

Relieved at what seemed to be the removal of blame on him for his despatch of Pengelly's body, Josh rushed down to the kitchen, lit the fire under the stove and filled a kettle. Rowena was threading what seemed like catgut through a needle when he returned to the bedroom.

'Good,' she said. 'Was the water boiling?'

'Yes, Doctor.'

'Splendid.' With the help of a pair of tweezers, she began extracting threads of clothing from the ugly wound in Acland's shoulder. The old man only stirred once as she went about her task. 'Good,' she murmured, 'the laudanum seems to be working.' She dipped a freshly laundered facecloth into the hot water and began gently swabbing the wound. She looked up. 'Can you boil some more water, Josh? I need to cauterise this needle and thread properly before I begin sewing. Oh, and bring up some iodine, please. It's in the cabinet in the surgery.'

'Yes, ma'am.'

Within an hour the cleaning and stitching of the wound had been completed, with only the odd twitch of the doctor's eyelids conveying any discomfort. Joshua had sat patiently, holding the hot-water bowl and handing Rowena the various instruments she needed, throughout the whole operation.

'Rowena,' he said at the end, 'I am full of admiration for you. To my untrained eye that seemed to be carried out completely professionally. Well done.'

She smiled, although a half frown still lingered on her forehead. 'You see, Mr Weyland,' she said, 'that I am no longer a silly little girl, falling in love quickly and wanting, er, sexual gratification all the time.'

He coughed, in some embarrassment. 'Certainly not, Doctor.'

Rowena tested her father's temperature by putting a hand on his forehead, nodded with satisfaction and tucked up the bedclothes beneath his chin. Then she sat back and regarded Josh unsmilingly. 'You know,' she said, 'we need to talk. But not here. Down in the drawing room.'

'Of course.'

They sat together on the sofa and Josh resisted the temptation to clutch her hand.

'Now,' she said, 'what needs to be done, Josh? I mean about Cunningham, the Preventers, the smugglers and so on. Can we really leave things as they are now? Shouldn't someone in authority be told?'

He heaved a sigh. 'I honestly don't think so, Rowena. We have left no evidence, except perhaps a few bloodstains on that ledge and I can deal with both. In addition, I think that there are only two things to be done.'

'Yes, what are they?'

'I am not sure that the Preventers will have fled the barracks. I must go there to find out and, perhaps, give them your father's warning again. The other task is for me to visit the Reverend Hawker, to thank him for harbouring me and to explain what has happened. He will miss his friend, your father, and sooner or later will come calling and see his wound. We must take him into our confidence.'

'Very well. But it will be too dangerous to go to the barracks alone. I will come with you.'

'No thank you, my dear. I will borrow your father's mare, if I may, for I may need to beat a quick retreat. But we will not need a doctor for that visit, Rowena. Please stay here and look after your father.'

She nodded glumly. 'Very well.' Then, she regarded him from under her eyelashes. 'And then, Josh, and then . . . will you go to Dover?'

He put his hand to his head. 'Oh, my dear, I have agonised about it, but I fear I must. You know, Rowena, that I would much rather stay here with you. But there is something wrong about things in Dover. Mary has not replied to my letters and I suppose she will not now. So I must confront her and offer to keep my word and marry her. Then I shall have done my duty.'

'What if she says no?'

'Then I shall return here. It would be unfair to make you promises of this conditional nature, so I will not. We must leave it there. Once I have settled the whereabouts of the Preventers and visited the vicar and once we are sure your father will recover, then I shall leave for Dover.'

Rowena's features did not move and, for once, there was no promise of a tear. She merely nodded her head. 'Very well,' she said.

Joshua saddled the mare and, after searching the house for a suitable weapon, was forced to take down the doctor's antique cavalry pistol. It might perhaps serve as a deterrent once more. Then, apprehensively, he rode up the hill to the barracks.

For the first time in his experience there was no guard outside the big gate and the huge doors were ajar. Cautiously, he edged the mare inside. The courtyard was empty except for two small boys who had found two rusty old cutlasses from somewhere and with a clash of steel were fencing. He recognised one of them as a boy from the high street who had posted his letters.

'Good morning, George,' he called. 'Be careful with those old swords. They can both still cause harm.' His stomach rolled as his brain recalled the flash of steel by the light of the storm. He thrust the image away. 'Now, boy, come here.'

Reluctantly, the urchin did so.

'This place seems empty. Have the Preventers all gone?'

'Yes, sir. They all buggered off, like, this morning.'

'Now, don't swear. Where did they go to?'

'I saw 'em all go to the quayside and take stuff from the huts there. Then they all rode off. Everythin' seems to 'ave gone from inside 'ere like, as well. Everythin' stripped out, see. All we could find to play with was these old things.'

'Hmm. Thank you. As I said, do be careful. Even rusty swords can kill.' He pulled on the reins and rode out of the barracks. No need to check inside. He realised what had happened.

Down at the quay, the doors of the sheds that had housed the contraband had been left open and seemed to be empty. A handful of smelters were going about their business, but a young seafaring man looked up as he pushed one of the dinghies into the water. 'D'yer know where young Tom is, sur? We've got two smacks comin' in from Wales in an hour an' we need 'im.'

Joshua gulped. 'No, sorry. I have no idea. But give me a minute or two and I will come down and give you a hand with the dinghy. I am used to dinghies.'

The man knuckled his forehead. 'Well, that's kind of you. Can't pay you, though. That will be Tom's money.'

'Don't worry about that. Give me ten minutes.'

Back at the house, Rowena was waiting. 'Were they there?' she asked anxiously.

'No. They have stripped the barracks bare, it seems, then gone and taken the contraband from where it was stored and vanished with their ill-gotten goods, presumably to sell them and pocket the money. I don't think we shall see them again.'

'Thank goodness for that.'

'How is your father?'

'Grumpy, I expect because of the wearing-off effects of the laudanum. He said that he would like to see you on your return.'

'Sorry, but he will have to wait. I have promised to take Tom's place on the dinghies. Two boats are coming in.'

A slow smile crept across Rowena's face. 'You won't be as good as Tom. He was the best in the business.'

He gave her a mock salute and a half bow. 'Well, I shall just have to try, won't I? Do you have an old pair of dungarees I could wear?'

For the next six hours, Josh worked as hard as he could remember, taking it in turns with Tom's mate to row out the dinghies and then secure the smacks behind the shelter of the wall.

On his return, Josh slipped off the dungarees and wearily climbed the stairs to see the doctor. The old man was sitting upright, propped up by pillows. He reached out a hand and Josh took it.

'I was in pain last night when you arrived on that ledge, but I saw you kill Cunningham.' Acland's face was frowning in concentration. 'Emma has also told me how you, er, disposed of young Pengelly's body.'

Joshua bit his lip. 'I want you to know,' the doctor went on, 'that you did the right thing in each case and I don't want you to blame yourself for it. In fact, you were very brave to duel with Cunningham and you held your own magnificently and removed him from all our lives. You have been blamed because your presence here seems to have prompted all of this violence. That may have been true but it was not specifically your fault. There was evil here and it would have outed itself sooner or later. You were just the catalyst.'

He lay back, replaced his head on the pillow and gave a wan smile.

'Thank you, sir,' said Josh. 'I feel I must tell one man about the happenings last night. Do you think that the Reverend Hawker would feel compromised in any way if he is told the truth? Would he keep it to himself?'

The smile broadened. 'Hearing that I am ill, he will surely visit me. If I told him that I had accidentally fallen on a cutlass blade I don't think he would believe me for a minute. So yes, tell him the truth but ask him to keep his mouth shut. That will be difficult for him because he loves a good story, and I venture to say that this is a good one. Perhaps he will write it one day. But if he does, his flock will just think that this is one of his opium dreams that he has put down on paper.

'Now,' he held up a hand. 'Would you be so kind as to reach into that little drawer in the bedside table? Yes, that one. Please hand me the little bag you find in there.'

Puzzled, Joshua did so. The bag was heavy.

The doctor pulled back the drawer string and then peered inside. 'Emma tells me,' he said, 'that you had thirty guineas with you when you survived the wreck of *The Lucy*. She also tells me that, one way or another, that sum has been severely eroded during your stay here. So . . .' he reached out and handed the bag to Josh. 'This is fifty guineas. It is given to you as a wedding present,' he smiled, 'whichever way your heart goes and whichever lady walks with you up the aisle – and for all I know there might be more than two for you to choose from.'

Joshua shook his head and made to hand the bag back, but the doctor refused to take it. 'Joshua,' he said, 'you fight like a tiger and no doubt you are a splendid sailor, but you must learn to accept kindness with grace when you meet it – and God knows that we meet little enough of it in this life. Now, please leave me, for all this talking and giving away of badly earned money has exhausted me.'

He smiled and waved Josh away.

Rowena met him at the foot of the stairs. 'What did Papa want?' she asked.

Embarrassed, Josh held the bag behind his back. 'He advised me about the reverend,' he said, 'and feels that I can tell him everything safely. I am tired now, but I will ride to see him tomorrow.'

'And then will you set off for Dover?'

'Er . . . perhaps the next day. I can walk to the stagecoach. I shan't impose on you.'

'Very well.' She showed no emotion and made no attempt to dissuade him, merely turning and retiring to the kitchen.

The next day, Josh rose early and harnessed the donkey cart, putting a pail of water, with soap and a scrubbing brush into the back. This time the journey to Morwenstow was far easier than when poor Edward had been forced to head into the storm. On arrival at the vicarage the maid informed him that the reverend was 'composing a sermon in his study on the cliff'.

The familiar smell of the East met Josh's nostrils as he navigated the narrow path on the clifftop, down to the little hut. Hawker was, indeed, wreathed in sweet smoke, but also scratching away with his pen on a notebook. He looked up with a smile as Josh coughed to alert him.

'My dear Joshua,' he said. 'Come and sit down. I have two of your blankets here. Would you care to share a pipe with me?'

'No thank you, Reverend. I have come to tell you something.'

'Oh, I do hope it is an uplifting tale that I can weave into my sermon. Pray tell me, do.'

'I rather doubt it, sir. But let me begin.'

The vicar listened quietly, puffing at his pipe and rarely revealing emotion until Joshua recounted the violent scene just below where they now sat. He put his hand to his mouth and shook his head in dismay as he heard of the doctor's wound and the death of Pengelly. Cunningham's death evoked only a sigh.

'As a matter of fact, Joshua,' he said, 'I never liked the fellow. Too overbearing and I rarely saw him in church. But there . . .'

After due reflection, and much puffing of the pipe, Hawker finally agreed to keep the details of the smuggling, the light in the storm and the activities of the Preventers a secret, although he protested that he disliked secrets, for when revealed they usually did the Devil's work. He promised to visit the doctor soon and it was only then that Joshua produced ten guineas from his newly acquired bag and asked the reverend to spend it how he thought best on the poor of the parish. Then he left the clergyman to his labours, took the bucket from the cart to the scene of the deaths on the ledge and scrubbed away the bloodstains that had defied the rains of that terrible storm.

Before he left, Hawker had asked him if there was any news about the result of the enquiry. Joshua had to confess that he had completely forgotten about that great event in Hartland Quay, but that no, nothing had been heard.

In fact, on his return, he was summoned to the doctor's room by Rowena, leaning over the balustrade eagerly.

The doctor was reading a letter that had come by the midday post and was specially sealed.

'Listen to this, Josh,' he said, adjusting his spectacles.

The members of the Enquiry have come to the conclusion that there was ample evidence to indict the management of the Blue Cross Line for negligent maintenance of its vessels, the undermanning of the same and poor seamanship displayed by its masters. These findings have been passed on to Her Majesty's Board of Trade for it to respond appropriately.

'Now listen to this bit,' cried Acland, waving his spectacles. 'It will make you smile':

However, the Enquiry found no evidence of the existence of smuggling and the like and certainly none of the practice of 'false lights' luring ships onto inhospitable shores in this part of the north Cornish–Devon coast and proposes no further action to be taken in this regard.

Joshua did smile but only faintly. 'Bloody fools,' he said. 'Stupid, bloody fools. But it's what you would expect of Londoners still wearing wigs.'

The result of the enquiry lifted Acland's spirits. 'I began to worry that I had stirred things up too much,' he said at dinner for which he had left his bed. 'But it is just the result I wished for. After eating, let us take a little of that Armagnac, Emma, although I am sorry but you must celebrate with lemonade, I fear. But celebrate we must.'

In fact, the high spirits of the little trio were now confined to the doctor, for both Rowena and Josh were thinking miserably of the long journey Josh would have to begin the next day.

It dawned with low, pewter-coloured skies and a thin drizzle. Josh threw his few belongings into a bag and went downstairs to have his last breakfast in the doctor's house. Rowena served him bacon and eggs without speaking and, all in all, it was a melancholy meal. Josh, with his mind agonising about whether he was doing the right thing, did not hear the knock on the door.

He was finishing his tea when Rowena, tears now streaming down her cheeks, flung open the dining room door and announced, 'Miss Jackson for you, Mr Weyland.'

'What!' Josh looked up in astonishment as Mary Jackson walked through the door, which, with a last despairing look, Rowena shut firmly behind her.

'Joshua.' Mary advanced, her hand extended.

'Mary! What on earth are you doing here?'

'I have come to see you, Josh. I had to.'

'What? Er, yes.'

He took her hand and, decorously, she offered him a cheek to kiss. He did so, awkwardly, and looked around. 'Mary, do sit down. Would you like, er, tea or something? I am sorry, I was not expecting . . . Do sit down, please.'

He cleared an armchair of clutter and Mary lowered herself into it. Josh looked at her intently. There was no doubt about it, Mary was *fat*, now quite broad in the beam and her once beguiling breasts had spread to produce an imposing front. Her face, however, although set above two rippling chins, remained smoothly pretty.

'You look well, dear,' said Josh, hopelessly.

'Oh, Josh. I should have asked – how is your leg? Any better?'

'Thank you. Virtually healed now, in fact, my bag is packed upstairs and this very day I was due to set off for Dover. You see, I never had any response to my letters and I wondered . . .' He tailed off.

Mary produced a delicate, rose-embroidered handkerchief and dabbed at her eyes. 'Yes, I know, Josh. That is why I am here. I felt that I simply could not put in a letter what I had to say to you. It would have been, well, cowardly. So I decided to come here to meet you face-to-face again and . . . it has been such a long time, Josh.'

'Yes, it has. Of course.' His mind raced. Cowardly . . . what did she mean?

'Yes, such a long time. I'm afraid that what I have to tell you will hurt you. That is why I could not put it into a letter.' She gave a small smile that did not reach her eyes. 'I was never a very good letter writer, anyway, was I, dear?'

'No. I mean, yes. No, I always looked forward to your letters and I have them now.'

'Do you? That is sweet of you. But, Josh . . .'

'Yes?' A small glimmer of hope, no, of delight, was beginning to creep into Josh's brain as he groped to see where this strange, halting conversation was heading.

'I have changed. People do change, you know, in, what has it been – two and a half years.'

'What? Yes, I suppose they do.' Inconsequentially, his brain asked the question: how on earth did Rowena know that she had become fat?

'Yes. I suppose it was inevitable.' Mary opened a small purse and produced a small ring. It glowed dully, because the gold was obviously of the cheapest variety and the jewel it contained also laced pretension. She handed it to him. 'I must give you back your ring and ask you to release me from my promise to you.'

He took it slowly and put it on the table, beside his plate containing bacon remnants. He cleared his throat, unsure of what to say. 'Yes, of course. Thank you.'

'You may remember that I wrote to you about the young clergyman who came to lodge with us?'

Josh nodded dumbly.

'We are due to be married shortly. In fact, he has come with me from Dover and we have stayed at the inn at, I think it's called Stoke, on the top there. Although, of course,' she looked demurely at the floor, 'we stayed in separate rooms.' She lifted her eyes and looked beseechingly into his. 'Oh I promise I have not betrayed you, er, physically, Josh. But Mother – who sends her regards to you, by the way,' he nodded again – 'Mother felt that he was a better match for me than a sailor who was away so much.' She leant forward now to give emphasis to her words. 'You see, Charles is truly a man of the Church, a real Christian. In fact, it was he who persuaded me to come here in person to beg your forgiveness.' She held out her hand. 'Oh, Josh. Do tell me that you forgive me and give me your blessing for our match. Please do.'

Josh felt as though his heart would burst with happiness but he forced his countenance to remain set in earnest misery. 'Oh I do,

Mary. I wish you both much happiness. Er, are you sure you won't have a cup of tea?'

Mary rose. 'No, thank you. Charles is waiting for me. Oh, Josh.' She took his hand. 'You have made me feel so happy and lifted the guilt from me.' She kissed his cheek. 'What will you do? We still have some of your clothing and possessions. Shall we send them here?'

'Yes, please do. Now, I know you must get on. Give my regards to your mother. Goodbye, Mary.'

'Goodbye, Josh. God bless you.'

She swept through the door and imperiously summoned the brougham that was waiting for her. Then she was gone.

Josh closed the door and leant against it, his heart dancing. He suddenly became aware that Rowena, her cheeks wet, was sitting on the stairs.

'Are you going . . . going with her, Josh?'

'Now, Rowena, have you been listening at the door?'

'I tried to but you were both speaking so quietly I couldn't hear.'

'Oh, I am sorry about that. Will you do me a favour, dear?'

'What? Oh, I suppose so.' She blew her nose noisily and slowly came down the stairs.

'Is your father up?'

'No, he is sleeping peacefully, so I didn't disturb him.'

'Good. I will wish to speak with him a little later. But first, would you go to his drinks cupboard and bring out the vintage cognac and two glasses.'

'Two glasses!' The tears came back into her eyes. 'Ah, she is coming back, of course, to fetch you.'

'Don't worry about that for the moment. Please take them into the sitting room.'

Attempting to stem her snivelling, Rowena brought in the bottle and the glasses. Slowly, Josh poured the amber liquid into each glass. 'Now,' he handed one glass to her and took the other himself. 'If you are going to be my wife, you will have to learn to do two things: stop crying all the time, for goodness' sake, and to drink cognac – particularly if you are to go to medical school, as you will. I shall see to that. Now, take a sip.' He toasted her. 'Cheers, my dear love.'

Her jaw had dropped, so Josh gently lifted her glass to her lips. She sipped and then grimaced. 'Lord, it is awful,' she said. And then flung herself into his arms.

Author's Note

Unlike my other novels, *Black Rocks* is only remotely based on fact. It is almost completely a work of fiction. The only real life character in the story is the Reverend Hawker, whose elegant vicarage still sits snugly in a cleft in the clifftop at Morwenstow and is now arguably the best value for money B & B in southern England. It is kept by Jill Wellby who has become a sturdy guardian of Hawker's reputation, instantly refuting any hint that he might have been involved in wrecking in any of its interpretations.

In fact, I should point out that the 'luring light' practice, as described in the book, almost certainly had died out by 1842, and had only existed on a very minor scale in the eighteenth century. The Reverend Hawker was certainly an opium-smoking eccentric, but he was a good man, a fulsome recorder of life in his parish, who would never have been involved in wrecking.

But smuggling certainly was prevalent along this brutal coastline, although it was not as active as on the more hospitable shores of the south of the Cornish–Devon peninsula. In fact, cases are still being reported today.

The Preventers, of course, existed but in my research I never encountered any intimation that they might have been involved in smuggling themselves. The nefarious activities of Captain Cunningham's men are, therefore, figments of my imagination.

What is not is the beauty of the north coast of the peninsula. Perhaps in the novel, to suit the plot, I have painted it as being rather more sombre than it deserves. If so, then let me hasten to say that the views are breathtakingly spectacular, the air is like champagne and the people of modern-day Morwenstow and Hartland Quay warmly welcoming.

ACKNOWLEDGEMENTS

I had an unusually large collection of helpers in researching and writing this novel. Let me thank them in chronological order from my use of their help in the story.

Firstly, Bostonian lawyers Herb Holtz and his ex-judge wife Nancy, who have one of their homes in Key West, were invaluable in helping me to describe the town of 1842. And it was Nancy who pointed out the origin of the name. Then all my inaccuracies in describing life at sea in a brig and its shipwreck were corrected by old friend and neighbour, Neil Pattenden, ex-naval lieutenant commander, translator of Russian and modern-day sailor.

The aforementioned Jill Wellby was most helpful, not only in giving us a roof over our heads while my daughter and I went about exploring the coast, but also in feeding us with much information about the Rev. Hawker.

As usual, I must thank my agent, Jane Conway-Gordon, and Susie Dunlop, my publisher, for their unfailing support, and the staff of London Library for letting me raid their bookshelves for literary guidance.

My wife, Betty, my long-serving and loving research assistant and proofreader, became ill just before the book was conceived and she died in October 2015. But her role was filled by our daughter, Alison Ledgerwood, who brought to the task new energy, competence and skills of which I was previously unaware. I owe her a great debt.

Thanks perhaps to Daphne du Maurier (I did toy with the idea of calling my book 'Jamaica Out' but wise minds advised against it); there is a considerable bibliography about wrecking and smuggling. The books I found most helpful were:

Bathurst, Bella, *The Wreckers* (London, 2006)

Hawker, Reverend R. S., *Footprints of Former Men in Far Cornwall* (Self-published, 1870)

Myers, Mark R. and Nix, Michael, *Hartland Quay, The Story of a Vanished Port* (Hartland Quay Museum, 1982)

Pearce, Cathryn, *Cornish Wrecking* (Woodbridge, 2010)

Seal, Jeremy, *The Wreck at Sharpnose Point* (London, 2002)

Trounson, J. H., *Mining in Cornwall, Vol. 1* (Cornwall, 1980)

Viele, John, *The Florida Keys, Vol. 3, The Wreckers* (Florida, 2001)